Relative Secrets

Relative Secrets

a novel by

Collen Dixon

This book is a work of fiction. Names, characters, and places are the product of the author's imagination or to be used fictitiously. Any references to actual events, locations, organizations or persons, living or deceased, are for the purpose of lending a sense of reality. Any other references or resemblences are purely coincidental.

Library of Congress Cataloging in Publication Data
Dixon, Collen

Relative Secrets/Collen Dixon

ISBN 0-97-10566-0-9 Paperback

Library of Congress Control Number: 2004098503

Printed in the United States of America
by
the FIN group, inc.

First Edition

<u>How to Order:</u>
www.collendixon.com or
The FIN Group Publishers
12138 Central Avenue, Suite 293
Mitchellville, MD 20721
301.758.8700

Book Design by:
Candace K. Cottrell

Author Photo by:
Valerie N. Phillips

Author's Hair Design by:
Pat Sugick

Shhh!! The Secret's Out...

dedication

This book is dedicated to all of us who are
fearless enough to pursue our dreams...
Despite the negative energy we may encounter...
Or the harsh realities we face...
Motivation, talent & desire are the only tools we are equipped with...
But we acquire humility, gratefulness and endurance...
As we continue doing what we do...
Journeying on the ultra difficult quest to satisfy
our overwhelming inner desire to make ourselves happy...
At our own expense...
And it comes at a heavy price.

One Love,
Collen

RELATIVE SECRETS

Prologue

Secrets. Sometimes they're good, sometimes they're bad. Sometimes we keep them for the right reasons. Sometimes we keep them to protect others.

And sometimes we keep them to protect ourselves.

Secrets.

The mere word invokes suspicion, questions and misgivings. Add the term relative to secrets, and it makes the meaning even more dubious.

Relative means familiar. Close. Related. Connected.

And they are normally worse than your basic secret.

And when the Cavanaughs keep them, they are exponentially worse than our normal secrets. They are deeper, deadlier and costlier to the soul.

Relative Secrets.

Do you have any?

You may want to keep them to yourself. Especially after you read what happens when the Cavanaughs finally tell theirs.

Relative Secrets... There's a reason why we have them...
And a better reason to keep them.

RELATIVE SECRETS

Chapter 1

Sylvia Cavanaugh frowned, and then pulled down the shade on the airplane's portal-style window. The glare from the sun was overwhelming, and it prevented her from seeing the pages of the August 1992 *Ladies Home Journal*. Not that she was all that interested in the periodical; she just wanted something to take her mind off of what consumed it. She cracked the shade, but the sun was still too bright. She pulled her jet black Chanel sunglasses from their resting place atop her scarved head, but once they were placed on her nose, she still wasn't satisfied. Now, it was too dark. She slammed the shade shut and dropped the sun shades in her lap.

Sylvia was uncharacteristically agitated and flustered. She felt like a child on a see saw, her life teetering between exhaustion and frustration, with each side becoming more forceful. And like a child, each time the momentum increased, she thought that she would be thrown off at any moment, and end up in a bloody, crumpled heap on the concrete playground.

She tilted her head backward and sighed, her platinum and diamond Bulgari cross sparkled as it lifted and fell as her chest expanded and contracted. She tried to find something of interest in her magazine, but her mind refused to stay focused on the articles. Gone were the buoyant thoughts of planning her annual holiday soiree and getting some much needed rest and relaxation for she and her beloved husband, Harry. Try as she had, all of her efforts to help Harry recuperate from a recent, near fatal heart attack had been for naught. Peace was a fleeting concept as she, Harry, her brother Joseph "Jolly" Russell and his wife Penny braced themselves as their tiny chartered jet ascended from the runway, and headed for home.

Sylvia had been elated with the progress Harry had made during their month-plus sabbatical on their favorite island. His radiant, café au lait glow was returning, and he seemed to be getting the rest that he required. That was until earlier that morning.

The few weeks of tranquility had come to a screeching halt. Serenity and solitude at their Bermudan Estate, *Il Mare*, had been summarily interrupted when Harry received an ominous phone call from Robeson, a high-ranking DEA official, and one of the more trusted family moles. He reported that a murderous debacle had occurred at the Baltimore Harbor, involving their son Conrad and Harry's estranged brother, Edgar. Connie and Edgy, as they were better known, had somehow crossed paths, and the encounter had been extremely devastating.

At least that was what Sylvia overheard from Harry's side of the conversation, and what he later confirmed. Though the call was brief, Robeson conveyed enough information to compel them from their tropical paradise, and on to the first thing smoking out of Hamilton, Bermuda. Robeson just advised the returning Cavanaughs to keep a low profile, and act like nothing was amiss. Once they arrived back in the States, the plan was for the family to meet at Grand's, Harry's father's house, at which time Robeson would provide the specific details.

Sylvia shuddered and tugged on the linen jacket draped over her shoulders. She scolded herself for not listening to her intuition that had tapped her on the shoulder right before Robeson called. She should have known that difficulties were on the horizon when during breakfast, Harry's sunny disposition suddenly darkened.

"Something's not quite right, Syl," Harry said, and stroked his chin. He was wearing a Riccardo Tubbs, Miami Vice style five-o'clock shadow, and Sylvia thought that it really looked handsome on him. Harry was reading the imported Washington Post Newspaper that morning, and had honed in on an article.

Sylvia glanced up from her notepad where she was jotting down ideas for the annual Cavanaugh Holiday Extravaganza that she and Penny could discuss later. "What is it, dear?" She figured that it was something in the business or Metro section that had Harry riled up, so she didn't pay too much attention to the trepidation in his voice.

"There's a small article in here about a drug deal that went awry last night. And, it involved a renegade FBI agent named Brian Hunter," Harry said, and kept reading and re-reading the item, peering into his half reading glasses. "That just doesn't sound right. Normally those 'just say no' folks broadcast this kind of fodder on the front page. Hmmm, I wonder why Robeson didn't contact me about this. Syl, I've got a funny feeling about this."

Sylvia shrugged it off, and wondered why Harry even mentioned it to her. Perhaps it was because Jolly hadn't yet gotten up, and Harry was trying to make small talk. She was never involved in the more sordid areas of the family business, but maybe Harry wanted to share more with her. "Umm, hmmm," she mumbled, and went back to her brainstorming.

Harry was still looking at the paper when Robeson phoned. It was a very eerily timed call, and Harry looked confused when he hung up the phone. *"Questo non può succedere."*

"Excuse me? What did you say, dear?" she asked, more out of reflex than concern, and continued eating her poached eggs and English muffin.

"I said, 'This can't be happening." Harry shook his head, and removed his glasses. "I told you something was amiss. This article is about a situation that our family's involved with. We have to get back home immediately." Harry shoved himself back from the table, and mumbled something about needing a good shave and one of his suits.

"What? Are the children okay?" Sylvia asked, with her fork stuck in midair, and her voice was fraught with anxiety.

"Now, don't you get upset. I'm assuming that Robeson would've told me if any of our children weren't okay. But something he said confused me. He said that the agent who was involved was named Justin. That's not who the paper named."

Sylvia cleared her throat. "Who did Robeson say it was again? Justin who?"

"Pasqual. Justin Pasqual."

Sylvia dropped her fork and nearly choked on her meal.

The name made Sylvia feel faint. Justin was the young man their daughter Madison was involved with. A few weeks ago, Madison had giddily phoned Sylvia to tell her all about him, and Sylvia's motherly instincts instantly flared up. There was something that didn't set well with Sylvia about Madison's new paramour, and while Sylvia knew that trying to tell a woman in love that her man might not be good for her was a hapless idea, she tried to tell her only daughter so without dashing her feelings. And now this confirmed it. Sylvia had mentioned Justin to Harry, but he normally didn't retain information such as who his daughter was dating. Yet Sylvia wondered if he remembered who Justin was.

Harry didn't appear to recall him, so Sylvia just decided to remain silent about that little detail until later. She wasn't about to give her darling Harry another heart attack.

Shortly after Robeson called, their son Joey had also phoned, but he and Harry's conversation was quite one sided. Harry never once responded to anything Joey might have said, but just fired off a list of orders. The most important one was for Joey to corral his siblings, and for all of them to be at their grandfather's house by six o'clock that evening. Grand's house was far more inconspicuous than she and Harry's estate, and the gathering place to discuss the more delicate family issues.

On the quaint eight-passenger Cessna Jet, a cleaned shaven, business attired Harry was practically inconsolable. Sylvia spoke slowly and softly to him, imploring him to just stay calm. But, he was livid, and kept muttering in broken Italian, which was the language he spoke when he was most upset. He kept repeating, under his breath, "*Quel figlio di una femmina. Quel figlio di una femmina.* That son of a bitch. That son of a bitch." It was a direct reference to the bad seed Edgar, one that Sylvia easily interpreted.

Sylvia could hardly blame her husband for referring to his brother as such. Harry's rift with Edgar was long and deep, and caused by a vicious rivalry for control of their family. Ultimately, it was their father, Grand, who sat Edgar down, after he stubbornly refused to end his torrid affair with well-known socialite, Marjorie Newton Blake, who happened to be married to Simon Blake. Their affair became more detestable when Marjorie became pregnant, and Sylvia, Harry and Grand suspected that Edgar might be the father. Needless to say, Grand silenced Edgar, and Edgar, unwilling to accept his reprimand, fled to whereabouts unknown. And no one had spoken to him since then, and that was over twenty years ago.

Knowing that Edgy was involved in a mishap with their sons was just appalling to Sylvia. She was nearly as disturbed as Harry, and her blood pressure elevated, but she steeled herself. She had to, for her family's sake. She took her sunglasses from her lap, and placed them on her nose, and then raised the window shade. She stared out into the clear sky, and watched her beloved little island disappear from sight. She exhaled, and tried to envision just how this unexpected episode would impact her family, and prayed that it wouldn't be as bad as when Harry and Edgar first parted ways years ago. Instinctively, Sylvia knew that something would happen when they left their children in charge while she had taken Harry. But, as Harry had said, they were all grown.

"They're adults. *Gli adulti*," he said repeatedly. Sylvia just sighed. History was truly repeating itself in a devastating manner, and it was her greatest fear realized. That her children would perpetuate the same destructive legacy that nearly destroyed their family years before. And now the nightmare was becoming a reality.

Sylvia's underlying dread that her children would fall victim to the sins of their heritage had always been offset by the stability of her marriage to Harry, and the active manner in which she involved herself in their lives. A mother's love had been absent in Harry and Edgy's lives, and Sylvia always felt that their lack of motherly cultivation had contributed to their lack of compassion in handling certain matters. Sylvia was determined not to let that happen to her children, and she was a constant force in her their lives. And she was a force to be reckoned with.

Consistency and hands on involvement were essential tools in how Sylvia ran her family. Her family meant the world to her, and outside of them, there were only two other constants that held precedence in her life. The first was the famed family jewel, *Il Rosso*, which was the cornerstone of the Cavanaugh Empire. It was the blood red, three-carat ruby that Harry's mother Pia had escaped with when she and Grand ran away from New York and started their family in D.C.

Il Rosso belonged to Pia's old Italian Family, the Sallones, who had banished her when she became involved with Grand, because he was a Negro. Its value represented the ultimate cost of being a Cavanaugh. And, as it was passed down, it was the most vivid reminder of what being a Cavanaugh meant. Passion. Danger. Contentiousness. Sometimes even murder. Those attributes were the foundation on which this family was built, and as time had proven, they would never change. All Sylvia could do was to minimize those deadly components as much as possible, and try to instill in her children other ways to handle their issues.

"It's too chilly in here. Is anyone else cold?" Sylvia asked, and before she could press the call button, Jolly sprang to his feet.

"Don't worry, sis. I'll check with the attendant," Jolly said, and he lumbered off to the front of the jet.

Sylvia smiled. Jolly was the other constant in her life. He and Penny were unwavering in their support, and just as concerned about the well being of their family. They were essential vertebrae in the family backbone. Sylvia knew that no matter how dark the hour became, Jolly and Penny would always stand in her corner.

And that's where she needed them to be. In her corner, where she felt like she was about to collapse. She wondered if she was aging rapidly, and pulled her silver Tiffany compact from her bag and checked her face for any new wrinkles. Thank God, she didn't notice any. But she did notice the floral scarf wrapped around her head and cringed. Perhaps it wasn't so bad that Robeson had pre-empted their trip. Bermuda was great, but there was no one on the island that could give her a good touch up or tame those errant gray strands like Mozell, her hairstylist at home. Whenever they vacationed in Bermuda, Sylvia normally flew Mozell down to do her hair at least once during her stay. Unfortunately, she didn't have time for a personal consultation.

The flight from the little island was less than three hours from D.C., but it seemed to take forever. Sylvia wrung her jeweled hands until they ached, while Harry continued mumbling in Italian, and Penny and Jolly made small talk, and tossed down Bloody Marys.

They flew into National Airport, where a long, black limo was waiting to jettison them home. In the limo, as they cruised up the tree-lined Rock Creek Parkway toward their massive estates on the Gold Coast, Harry spoke his first coherent sentences in hours.

"Jolly, I want you to get all of your people together, and detail exactly what occurred over the past month. I want to know everything. The who's, the where's, and the why's. You need to make sure that they've been doing their jobs. You got that?"

"No problem, Harry. What else do you want me to do?" Jolly asked.

"*Lasci il mandato.* Just stand down. I'll contact you as soon as I've met with Robeson and my children. Then I'll be able to tell you exactly what I need. Immediately."

"Are you sure, Harry? You know I'm here for you. I've got your back-- just like always," Jolly said, and reached out for his brother in law's shoulder. "I'm sorry about this, Harry. But, I'm not surprised."

Jolly had actually travelled to Bermuda to warn Harry that Connie was up to no good, but it was Harry's decision to let the chips fall where they may. Jolly had reluctantly accepted Harry's decision.

Harry shook his head. "I'm sorry, too. But right now, we don't have time for sorrow. We have to circle the wagons, and do what we do best. *Proteggere ciò che è il nostro.* Protect what's ours."

Jolly nodded. "Understood."

After the driver dropped Jolly and Penny off at their house, he drove directly to Grand's home. Grand's mansion was a short distance from Harry and Sylvia's estate, but it was where Harry felt most secure.

If any of the Cavanaugh's security had been compromised, it would never happen there. Grand's estate was like a vault. Or a crypt.

After a curt greeting to Trudy, Grand's tall, thin, dark-skinned Trinidadian caregiver, Harry and Sylvia headed toward the drawing room. To Sylvia's pleasant surprise, there was soft, soothing, classical music emanating from their destination, and flowing down the hallway. Sylvia knew that it had to be her fastidious son Christian.

They entered the room filled with authentic Italian and French antiques, and the entire hardwood floor was nearly covered by a gigantic Persian rug. Framed family pictures and etchings from the masters adorned the walls, and thick, drapes framed the windows. They were drawn, and the late evening sun cast an orange-ish hue. Christian was seated behind the grand piano, tinkering on a few notes, and sipping on a steaming cup of tea. He glanced up at his parents, with a puzzled expression plastered on his wide face.

"M'Dear. Father," he said, and stood to greet his parents. He gave the customary hand kiss to his mother, and for his father, a firm handshake. Christian was a thick, stocky man, who wore round, Ben Franklin style glasses. But, he was handsome, and always impeccably dressed. Today he wore a pair of crisp, blue gabardine trousers, and a plaid, button down, Polo dress shirt.

"Welcome back. I hope that you had a good flight." He smiled politely at his parents. "Now, what's going on? Joey called me and told me to be here by six." He glanced at his gold Patek Philippe timepiece. "I know Madison's normally late, but where's everyone else?"

"They're on the way, I'm sure," Harry said, as he sat down on a wing-backed chairs.

Sylvia sat down on the sofa and fanned herself. It was warm in Grand's house, and although it was August, the air conditioning was barely on. "Christian, please see about adjusting the air, please. And pour me a sherry."

"Yes, M'Dear," Christian said as he marched over to the thermostat like a tin soldier and turned the dial. He then headed toward the bar, an authentic, marble-topped, 18th century walnut enfilade.

"And I'd like something to drink, too," Harry said, and rested his chin on his fist. "Except you can add a little scotch to that, and just nix the sherry."

Christian cut his eye at his mother, who normally would intercept any of Harry's attempts to imbibe alcohol. But today, she just waved her hand, with a blank look. She had choose her battles carefully, and at this moment, she had entirely too much on her mind to wage this battle with her husband.

"Okay, Father," Christian said, his voice reluctant and drawn. He poured the drinks, handed them to his parents, and slowly took a seat on one of the Italian Provincial chairs that set around a large, ornate, claw-footed coffee table.

Madison flounced in, fashionably late. She was bubbly and gorgeous, and seemed oblivious to the somber mood that engulfed the room.

"Hello, everyone. Father. Mother. Welcome back," she greeted them with warm embraces and kisses. Madison was sharply dressed, in crisp linen shorts, and a pink, sleeveless blouse. Her hair was pulled back in a fluffy ponytail, and enormous diamond studs sparkled in her ears. They immediately caught Sylvia's eye.

"Beautiful earrings, dear," Sylvia said, as Madison slid down beside her on the sofa. Sylvia drew her daughter nearer, for closer inspection. "They are quite exquisite. Colorless, excellent polish and symmetry, a substantial size and excellent in clarity. Very nice."

"Thanks, M'Dear," Madison said, and fingered her ears. The stones caught the subtle rays of sunlight in the room, and twinkled brilliantly. "They were a gift. My friend has exceptional taste." She winked and smiled broadly.

Sylvia gently patted the side of her daughter's face. "I'm sure he does, Madison. I'm sure he's a man of many talents." Each word was spoken with painstaking deliberation.

Madison's brows furrowed, but then she shrugged. "You're absolutely right, M'Dear," she said with a girlish giggle. "I can't wait to—"

Sylvia placed a tender, yet firm, hand on her daughter's arm. "Not now, dear heart. Let's refrain from speaking about this at the moment. We have more pressing business to discuss."

Her words sent a sobering message to Madison, and she calmed down for an instant. But within a few moments, she resumed her idle chatter until Joey nearly stumbled in.

"Hello? What on earth is the matter with you?" Madison said, her voice nearly screeched. "Excuse me, but you look like hell. Really. Maybe we need to enact some sort of dress code for these meetings. Don't you think so, mother?"

Sylvia glanced at her handsome son, and was immediately alarmed. Joey had dark rings under his eyes, and his clothes were wrinkled and disheveled. His normally striking face was ashen and lackluster, and he was growing a stubbly beard.

"Hello everyone," Joey said, his voice raspy and uneven. Underneath his thick, long eyelashes, his eyes were red and downcast. He turned toward his sister, trying to summon up enough courage to sound better and stronger than he felt. "I'm okay, Maddie." He tried to sound confident, but his words were so vilely incorrect, that they resisted leaving his mouth.

"Son," Harry said, and extended his hand. Joey grasped it, and leaned down to hug his father.

"Father, I, uh," Joey said, his voice stammering.

Harry removed his hand from Joey's grip, and patted him on the back. "Not now, Son. *Non ora.*"

Joey stood back up, and reached for his mother's hand. He kissed it, then, headed directly toward the bar. He poured a glass half full of scotch and downed it. The dread in his soul rose with the potent beverage, but he gallantly held them both down. His hands shook nervously. He had no idea how the revelation about or the post mortem of last night's events were going to play out.

Joey was the only one left standing who really knew the deal about what had happened last evening. The only other person with firsthand knowledge was Connie, and he had been rushed to the hospital after being shot. By none other than Joey.

It was a long, devious and extremely complicated story that began when Connie found his long-suffering wife Beverly and his best friend Stewart in bed, and he killed Stewart, and permanently maimed Beverly. A gravely injured, grief stricken Beverly had confided in Joey, and gave him specific details of Connie's corrupt scheme, and Joey managed to construct a plan to thwart Connie's efforts. Joey's D.C. police officer friend Kelly intercepted Connie and Justin on the way to the rendezvous point, and absconded with the money that Connie had planned to use as his half of the required funds. The deal fell apart when Edgy met with Connie, and he had insisted that Connie was being dishonorable by conspiring behind his father's back, and without obtaining Harry's consent. Edgy's intentions were to close the deal, and claim the leadership of the Cavanaugh family, using Connie's betrayal as his justification.

Things went from bad to worse when Edgy and Vincent discovered that there was no money, and thought that Connie was trying to pull a double cross on them. The deal ended in a hail of gunfire, and even when he was outgunned and outnumbered, Connie refused Joey's help. Justin had tried to kill them, but Joey pushed Connie aside, and Connie blasted Justin to kingdom come. Before Justin's body hit the ground, Lauren, Joey's quasi-girlfriend and covert FBI agent approached them, with her gun drawn. When she shouted at them to drop their weapons and put their hands up, Connie turned his gun on Joey. After a heated, yet brief struggle, Joey shot his brother in the chest. The last thing Joey saw was Connie convulsing on a stretcher. Lauren was about to handcuff Joey, and cart him off for questioning, until Kelly again came to his rescue. Dressed up as an FBI agent, Kelly pulled rank, and took Joey into his custody, and drove him away from the crime scene. They drove to Harrisburg, Pennsylvania, and hid out during the night, until Joey could figure out his next move. The whole incident just shredded Joey's nerves, and he shook from the memory.

Madison spun her head around, and stared at each of her family members. "What's wrong with you? Why does everyone have such dire expressions on their faces?" She held her palms up. "Hello? Have I missed something? What's going on? Can I get a clue, please?"

The drawing room door swung open, and everyone turned their attention toward it.

Chapter 2

"Indeed you have missed quite a bit," Robeson said, as he casually entered the drawing room. The heavy wooden door closed behind him with a loud thud, and he quickly riveted his eyes on benefactor Harry.

Stylishly dressed in an olive green, double-breasted Armani suit with matching beige tie, and walnut brown Bally shoes, Robeson projected an air of confidence and calm control. With his mixed grey hair and chiseled good looks, Robeson was the perfect compliment to the Cavanaughs. Refined and authoritative, he was excellent at accomplishing all of the tasks his employers required. With discretion and precise execution.

After grasping and shaking Harry's hand, Robeson formally greeted the rest of the family, and then crossed the room and stood by the heavily draped windows.

"Before I begin, let me reassure you that everyone and everything's been taken care of," Robeson said.

Christian raised his hand. "Don't you think that we should wait for Connie? After all, we'll just have to sit through your repeating everything." Christian, a stickler for time, tapped the face of his watch.

"Not to worry, Christian. Connie won't be joining us this evening," Robeson said as he turned his attention toward the scholarly son. "I'm sure that you all are quite perplexed about the events of last evening, but, as I said, I have personally taken care of everything."

"How did Connie get out of coming to the meeting? I want to know how he got let off the hook," Madison said, and shoved a hand on her hip.

"Madison and Christian— please stop interrupting." Harry said, as he held his nearly empty glass up. "Go on, Robeson."

Robeson cleared his throat. "Connie hasn't been let off the hook. In fact, your brother was seriously injured last night."

Sylvia gasped, and sprang to her feet. "What? Oh no. Robeson, why didn't you tell us before? Harry, did you know? Where is he? I must go see my child. You all can talk business without me. Who's with him? Is Beverly with him? Oh, my God."

Harry downed his drink, and set the glass on the cocktail table. He motioned for his wife to sit back down. "Sylvia, Connie's stable. And he's getting the best care possible. I didn't tell you he was hospitalized because I didn't want to upset you even further," Harry said.

"Now, Beverly's not with him, but Connie's safe and being attended to by the best physicians. And you'll get to see him, as soon as we hear exactly what *all* of the facts are from Robeson." Harry glanced at Joey, who seemed preoccupied with staring at an innate object on the rug. "Please, go on," Harry said to Robeson. Sylvia sat back down, and closed her eyes, and clutched her chest. Madison placed a comforting arm around her mother, who was on the verge of an emotional meltdown.

"Well, as we all know, there was an intensified investigation of the drug activity in the D.C. area. It was common knowledge that the kingpin was an unidentified figure named Moses, and the DEA's objective was to take Moses's organization down. Anyone that had been arrested on a drug-related charge, we were trying to get to roll over. But, none did. We had observed their activities, and during the investigation, a picture of Connie was somehow taken, while he was in the company of one of the felons being tailed."

"Now, I thought that things had quieted down after Simon's death, and I personally saw to it that we reported that his minion Blinky was identified as Moses. That publicity alone should've ended the investigation. But, my understanding is that several operatives had already been placed in the area, and that someone in the agency was trying to earn his stripes by keeping the investigation going." Robeson paused, allowing his remarks to sink in.

"This was unbeknownst to me, and unfortunately occurred while I was on vacation. Evidently, your family was somehow targeted. All of you were susceptible, but it appears that Joey and Connie were the specific marks. But, it was the one agent assigned to Connie who caused the most trouble."

Sylvia gasped again, but Robeson continued. "An agent was able to deeply infiltrate your ranks. An agent by the name of Brian Hunter. And his alias was—"

When Robeson spoke Justin's name, Madison's mouth dropped. "*Whaaat? What* are you talking about, Robeson? That can't be true. That's a lie. A flat out lie. You obviously don't know what you're talking about. You should be fired, Robeson."

Sylvia opened her eyes and grabbed Madison by the arm. "That's enough from you, young lady. And it is true, Madison. And you will not utter another word, do you hear me? Not another word."

Madison's body shook, and she practically hyperventilated. "You don't understand, M'Dear. You just don't understand." She kept repeating the same statement, her voice fading in and out.

Christian glanced around the room with a dumbfounded expression on his face. When he met Joey's gaze, Joey looked away. Joey glanced at his little sister, and then dropped his chin. He bit his lip, and shook his head slowly.

"Who was the other agent?" Harry asked.

"Her name was Lauren Malloy. But, she was using the alias Lauren Murray," Robeson said. "Isn't that right, Joey?"

Joey didn't respond. He had dated Lauren for a number of months, and was completely floored when he discovered that she was an undercover agent. And, he hadn't realized that until she was pointing a gun at him last night on the docks.

Harry shook his head and sighed. "So, they put the female agent on Joseph, huh? Well, they knew exactly what to do. They had everyone covered. We were under seige at every turn." Harry paused and stared at Robeson with an intense glare. "I just want to know how all of this happened? I want to know exactly how they were able to infiltrate our midst so thoroughly, in such an abbreviated length of time."

Robeson proceeded to explain how both Lauren's and Justin's dossiers had been expertly fabricated, six or seven layers deep. There was no way that anyone would have known that they weren't legitimate, unless they spent months investigating them.

Lauren had befriended Joey, but she was working the periphery. She was a by the books type agent, who was basically observing and fact-finding. None of her reports included any damaging evidence. Justin was the real renegade. He had targeted and romanced Madison, just to get next to Connie. But, the kicker was that the drug deal on the docks wasn't even authorized or approved by the agency. Justin was being just as devious, working both ends against the middle, and taking advantage of whichever side would put him further ahead of the game. And who knows how far he would have taken it. If the deal had gone through,

Justin probably would have worked Connie and his connections until he got what he wanted. And then he would have turned Connie in. And gotten a major commendation for it.

But despite the company he was keeping, Connie was the ultimate villian in this fiasco. He had been in secret contact with his estranged Uncle Edgar and his son Vincent, and they had entered into a surreptitious arrangement that would blow the crack market wide open in the Baltimore-Washington area. Their plan was to come up with a half-million dollars to purchase product that would have a street value of over four million dollars. But, when the deal went down, there was a major double-cross and everyone turned on each other. Therefore, the body count rose.

"So, Edgar was trying to form some back door alliance with my son, and it got dirty, huh?" Harry wiped his brow, and tapped the rim of his now empty glass. "Now that the smoke's cleared, who's still standing?" Harry asked, and then folded his arms across his chest.

"We've identified two of Connie's men, Stevie and Ellis, and three of Edgar's men. They were dead at the scene. And Hunter died en route to the hospital," Robeson said.

Madison shrieked and burst into tears, and Sylvia promptly escorted her out of the room. They were gone for a few moments, but Harry motioned for Robeson to continue over Madison's elevated sobs. "Connie's in intensive care, suffering from a critical gunshot wound to the chest. Edgar and Vincent have minor gunshot wounds in the upper and lower extremities. Edgar was hit in the shoulder, and Vincent's leg was grazed. Nothing serious. They are all at Johns Hopkins, registered under assumed names, and under 24-hour armed guard."

Sylvia and Madison returned, and Joey was certain that his mother had given her the patented speech on Cavanaugh decorum and how to properly conduct yourself in front of strangers. Madison appeared dazed, and her eyes were dark red, puffy and teary.

Harry barely acknowledged their return. *"Chi il colpo mio figlio?"* Harry asked, and palmed his fist in his hand. When Robeson didn't immediately respond, Harry restated the question, this time in English. "I said, 'who shot my son?'"

Robeson shrugged. "That, I'm unclear about. When I questioned Agent Malloy about it, she wasn't quite sure either. We're assuming that it was Agent Hunter that fired his gun at Conrad, but ballistics will be the only way to determine that. Not unless," Robeson paused and then turned to Joey. "Would you happen to know?"

"You were there?" Harry and Sylvia both asked, in startled unison.

Everyone zeroed in on Joey, who was still nursing his drink. Joey was surprised that Lauren didn't say that he was the one who had shot Connie. It made him wonder why she hadn't disclosed that information, but now was the time for him to hold his cut card.

"Yes, I was there. I told you, I tried to stop it, but everything happened too fast. The last thing I recall is that Justin fired at us, and Connie and I both dived for a gun. With all of the gunfire, I'm not sure how Connie got shot."

"Well, as I said, only ballistics will determine that. But that's contingent upon them being able to remove the bullet from Conrad. And my understanding is that might be highly unlikely." Robeson shrugged. "Perhaps it's better if you don't know. I mean, we can pull some ballistics, but unless we can piece together the chain of events that led to the actual shooting, then the evidence isn't really going to buy you anything. All we know is that it was someone present who did it; and none of them should've been there. None of them."

Joey felt like a coward, but he couldn't let on. His immediate purpose was accomplished. He diffused a volatile situation, and it bought him some time. It was the right thing to do at the moment, and he had left himself an out, just in case the real story ever was revealed.

Harry exhaled heavily, and leaned over in his seat. "I understand." He paused and then cupped his chin in his hand. "Now, I just need to know how you've made this all go away. As you can see, we have a lot vested here. And I need to be reassured that from this point going forward, this is a non issue, Robeson." Harry's voice was calm, yet tight, and he stared at his mole with an unwavering glare.

"Understood, Harry. The spin is that *Justin* was the mastermind behind the whole illegal operation. He was the leader of a major New York Drug Cartel, who was trying to infiltrate and take over D.C. You know what they say, dead men tell no lies. Since he was technically working outside of the agency's authorization, it was the perfect ending. The agency looks good, because we actually copped several million dollars worth of uncut cocaine, a substantial amount of cash, and arrested some minor drug runners. We've eliminated what we've *finessed* as yet another major drug lord. The Drug Czar and the other 'just say no' folks are happy, and the public feels safer that we're being aggressive and doing our jobs. The only one that stands to suffer is Brian Hunter. And who cares about that common criminal? We're not even sure what happened to the seed money he'd been given, which was in excess of

$200k. But, at least we recouped Edgar's end. Yes, I tell you, that Hunter fellow was a greedy opportunist who needed to be handled. And he has been."

"We appreciate you not mentioning his alias in the newspaper, Robeson," Sylvia said. "I couldn't bear the thought that someone might be able to connect the likes of him to my child." Madison moaned and groaned softly, and murmured incoherently in Sylvia's grasp.

"I agree, Sylvia. I made sure that there weren't any references to Justin Pasqual in print," Robeson said. "Absolutely."

"And to further ensure that your family's privacy is intact, Connie, Edgar and Vincent are being treated as anonymous, key informants and material witnesses, and will not be subject to prosecution." He paused. "I figured that you may want to deal with them on your own," Robeson said, and flashed the "all's fair" sign.

The room was silent, except for Madison's now nearly muted sobs.

"Umm, Robeson. What's going to happen to Lauren?" Joey finally asked.

"I'm not quite sure, yet, Joey. I believe in having the punishment fit the crime, but I'm not sure what she's guilty of. From what I debriefed from her, she really didn't know a whole lot about you. She was able to successfully bug your home, but that was about it. Nothing else of any relevance turned up in her investigation." Robeson stared at Joey. "But, if you're concerned about her welfare, she'll certainly be transferred out of the area, so she won't be a problem."

Joey acknowledged the statement, and finally took a seat on a chaise lounge that was near the sofa.

"I want Edgy and his son brought here tomorrow, okay? I don't care if they're on life support or if you have to cut a landing pad on the lawn and Medivac them here. And, whatever you do, make sure that they think that they're still in the Feds custody. *Faccialo accadere*, Robeson. Make it happen," Harry said. Finally, he stood, a clear indication that the meeting was over. "Is that it?"

Robeson nodded, and took the cue. "I'll be in touch, Harry. Rest assured."

Christian rose to his feet. "I'll show Robeson to the door, Father."

Madison broke down hysterically, as soon as Robeson departed, her body collapsed so hard that her shoulders nearly touched. Sylvia cradled her daughter, and gently stroked her hair.

"There, there, Madison. Try to calm yourself, darling. You'll be okay." Sylvia rocked Madison in her arms, and her warm words of consolation turned to a frosty tone when she spoke to Harry. "And why on earth are you bringing your brother and his son here? Don't you think that they've done enough already? Now is not the time for a family reunion." Sylvia rolled her eyes, in a dramatic, fluttering fashion. "Well, we'll speak on that matter later." She patted Madison's back and whispered in her ear. "Madison, Dear Heart. I'm going to have to go now. But I will be back to be with you, okay? But try to pull yourself together. Remember, you are a Cavanaugh." Then she turned to Harry again. "I tell you what, Harrison. If you're done, I'm going to see our son now. And, I suggest that you join me," she said, as she rocked with Madison in her arms.

Harry grunted and took a deep breath. "Joseph? It goes without saying that I am morbidly disappointed with you. *Morbosamente.* Morbidly. I cannot believe that in less than a month's time, you allowed this to happen. I am deeply ashamed and disgusted."

He peered at his son, his eyes piercing and exact. "You failed to mention *how* you knew to be at the docks at the time of this little fiasco. Care to share?"

Joey cleared his throat. His mind had drained of any appropriate response, and as his father glared at him, words hung in his throat.

He didn't know what to say, but when he opened his mouth, a credible lie escaped. "I, uh, I kind of got a sense that something was going on. So, I was following Connie."

Harry twisted his mouth, and squinted at Joey. "So, you were tailing your brother. Because you *sensed* something. Hmmph. Somehow, I find that difficult to believe. And you were all by yourself? Not knowing what you might encounter?"

"Yes, Father."

Harry shook his head. "Interesting. Since your senses were so acute, did you *sense* anything about that young lady you were seeing?"

Joey tried to speak, but Harry cut him off. "Frankly, I don't want to hear anything more from you, Joseph. Not unless there's something else I need to know about what transpired while I was away. Otherwise, that's it. *Fini.*"

Joey rubbed his aching eyes, and watched a poker-faced Christian as he reentered the room. Joey sought to carefully select his words, for he knew that they would be forever etched in the stones of his father's memory. Telling lies and fabricating stories was taking its toll on him, and with the suffocating air of devastation dominating the room, Joey couldn't fathom saying anything else to his father. Especially, not the whole truth. And there was plenty more to be said about that.

He didn't want to say that Connie's wife Beverly had told him everything after Connie had beaten, violated, and then performed a crude female castration on her. And this was after Connie had killed Stewart, who was also one of their top security personnel. It was all so extremely convoluted and overwhelming.

Despite the neck-high, boiling hot water he was in, Joey still cared about Beverly's welfare. Connie had become Beverly's world, for she was an only child to elderly parents that had both died less than five years ago. She didn't have a lot of friends or outlets, and Joey was concerned that she wouldn't be able to survive on her own. He just wanted to make sure that she was as far removed from this situation as possible, and although he and Kelly had arranged for her to leave the city, headed for parts unknown, Joey still wasn't confident that she was safe.

And, Joey couldn't say *how* he knew that Justin was an agent, because Kelly had told him. And then he'd have to explain who Kelly was, and it would bring too much scrutiny on their closeted relationship. That was a very long story, and included too much information about his personal life. Information he wouldn't share. Not today, and probably never.

Though he had contemplated this moment endlessly for the last twenty-four hours, now that the time had come to finally tell his parents what a rotten son Connie was, Joey just couldn't further break their hearts. Nor did he think that Madison would've taken Justin's death so badly. So, instead of letting the truth set everyone free, Joey decided to let it imprison him for a while longer. He swallowed deeply, and decided to keep what he knew to himself, and shoulder whatever blame came his way. He wasn't trying to be a hero, but he wasn't game for showing his cowardice either. The outcome was a lose-lose, any way he cut.

"Father, I just can't apologize enough. I know that I had a responsibility to the family, but my hands were kind of full. I was trying to keep up with Howard and Royce, too, and I guess I dropped the ball with Connie."

Howard and Royce were two other moles in the Cavanaugh employ, whose activities Joey was supposed to have been monitoring. But Harry wasn't buying it.

"I don't care, Joey. There's no way you should've been too busy to prevent this debacle from occurring," Harry said. "Part of being a good leader is being responsible for your actions. And providing direction and support for the people working with you. And accountability. You have to be able to do more than one thing at at time. Now, I don't know what you could've been doing that kept you so busy that you couldn't do what you were supposed to do, but I hope it didn't have to do with that female agent."

Joey struggled to find a way to address his father without being flippant. "When I heard about what was happening, I tried to stop Connie, but I couldn't. See, I didn't know every detail of his deal, but what I knew, I tried to act accordingly on. To protect him and our family." Joey's hands fell to his side. "I'm just ever so sorry that it happened."

"You're sorry? Well, *spiacente* isn't quite good enough, Joseph," Harry said.

"Especially with your brother laid up in the hospital, fighting for his life," Sylvia said, her voice cracking. "I'm sure that there was *something* you could've done."

"I've had my fill of you and Connie's childish rivalry, and I warned you before not to let this situation get out of hand. You, Joseph, know better. Yet, you forget your place and what's important to this family, and let something asinine like this happen. I am just hurt and appalled by your actions. Or lack thereof." Harry's cheeks became flushed, and his voice elevated.

Joey cast his eyes downward. He knew that his mother would take Connie's side, regardless of it all being Connie's fault. "Yes, M'Dear," he said. In a warped way, his mother was on point. What Joey could've done was let Edgy, Vincent or Justin kill Connie. But, Joey knew that his parents would never understand that despite the fact that he was trying to help Connie, Connie had actually tried to kill him.

Harry shook his head. "They're both at fault, Sylvia. In fact, they are all at fault. I can't believe that all of this is a result of Conrad being pictured with some common criminal. I've told each one of you about the company that you keep. We are Cavanaughs, damnit. And with that comes a certain level of expectation *and* accountability." Harry shook his head. "It's not like you haven't heard this since the day you were born. But, your mother and I go away for a few weeks, and everything goes straight to hell. Tell me, did any of you ever listen to me? Did you ever try to benefit from my experience or words of wisdom?"

Harry sucked his teeth. "*Non ho pensato di sì.* I didn't think so. You're all very spoiled and selfish, and your behavior has done irrepairable harm to this family. Through your inability to act as siblings, you've allowed interlopers and law enforcement to do what has *never* been done before. Which is to undermine my business. The business I've worked all my life to nurture and thrive. The business that's kept all of you in the best of everything. And how do you thank me? By being so self-absorbed that you forget about family for your own selfish, immoral gain."

"Christian!" Harry shouted, and Christian flinched and averted his eyes. "Look at me when I talk to you. Exactly where did Connie get the share of his money? Surely, you knew something about this. And you should've known something about it. But, whether you did or didn't is a sad commentary in and of itself for you are supposed to be responsible for our family's financials. You should be able to tell me where he got every bloody cent of that money." Christian hung his head and tugged on his collar as his father continued his tirade.

"And Madison, how could you allow some wanton lothario to infiltrate our family like this? You can't get so enraptured that you lose track of your senses and better judgment. Jesus Christ. No, Sylvia, they're all accountable. And what a fine mess they've made of this family in as many days as it took years to build it. A fine mess. *Il bel disordine.*"

"Christian, call your Uncle Jolly and tell him to dismiss everyone that works in that security department of his. And I do mean everyone. I want to clean house. Immediately. And tell him that I want at least four guards here tomorrow. And Joey, you get in touch with Howard. And Royce. I want you to find out if they know anything about this. And if they know anything, find out what they know, and how they know it."

Harry sighed, his anger finally dissipating. He took a few thoughtful moments before speaking. "Madison," he said, and he knelt down in front of his only daughter. He lifted her tear-streaked face, and lightly touched his lips on her warm forehead. "I know that your heart is broken, but, you've learned a very valuable lesson today. Very *di valore.* Love is an extremely dangerous commodity, especially for us Cavanaughs. I know that you've heard this before, but now you've experienced it firsthand. But you have to understand that your first love has to be your family, because when it's all said and done, we're the only ones that will always be there for you. Understand? *Capisca*?"

Chapter 3

"Oh shit!" Joey cussed, and slammed on his brakes. He instinctively reached back to brace Madison from the sudden movement, but she remained motionless. The rear of his Range Rover tilted forward as the front end dug in, and the rotors grinded the vehicle to a halt. He narrowly missed clipping the lanky teenager in the crosswalk, and when the young brother flipped him the bird, Joey could only shrug. And thank God that his windows were tinted. He was dead wrong, because he hadn't seen the guy or anyone else. His mind was elsewhere. It was on a spaceship, cruising along in a galaxy far away, in search of Planet Sanity. It was a place he had been exiled from months ago. And he longed to return.

Being consumed with treacherous thoughts was quite dangerous, considering the fact that Joey was driving a sizeable SUV through Washington's congested streets. The evening's earlier events ravaged Joey's mind, relentlessly interrupting his thoughts and preventing him from focusing on any other matter that required his immediate attention, including the lives and safety of the pedestrians and other drivers. And there were a number of important things his father had insisted that he do. And in addition to his father's provisos, his mother had stepped into the fray with her own demands. Namely, that he check on Connie's house and belongings. Joey reluctantly agreed, despite the fact that he was already feeling overwhelmed and unable to figure out what he really needed to do to get himself out of this jam.

Joey felt a momentary relief when his parents went to the hospital to see Connie. But when Christian insisted on going, Joey wondered why his younger brother felt so compelled to go. Then it dawned on him. Christian was probably just trying to clean up his own dirty work.

He was petrified that Connie would awaken, and tell the real deal about Christian's culpability in his deadly little game. *What a coward*, Joey thought. But then again, Christian's behavior was so damned typical.

Joey instead opted to stay with Madison at their Grandfather's house until she regained her composure. Once their mother was gone, Madison cried to the point that she started gagging, and Joey led her to the bathroom, and found himself holding her head as she vomited in the commode. It was so ironic. The beautiful porcelain throne was symbolic of the depth of depravity that the lives of the Cavanaugh Collective had plunged to, and the contents of Madison's stomach were symbolic of the rancid mess all of their actions had created. Intentionally or otherwise.

After she had finished purging herself, Joey carried Madison's listless body out to his Range Rover, where he laid her across the spacious back seat, and then drove her home. While she lay there, almost in a catatonic state, Joey drove his enormous SUV in silence, only his thoughts raging. Everything was just so screwed up. The whole world was out of order. Joey was also dismayed that this was the first time he had visited his grandfather's house, and didn't even get an opportunity to say hello to his beloved Grand.

But the reality was that today wasn't the day for a social call. He felt bad about not even asking Trudy about Grand, but there hadn't been time. Too many critical issues were vying for his attention, but Joey made a mental note to return early tomorrow, so he could spend a few moments with Grand.

Joey clicked on the stereo, and Soul II Soul's *Back to Life* was on. It was almost too ironic. Joey had to get back to life and back to reality. And he didn't even know where to begin. And with Madison so out of it, he didn't know what to say to her to help her.

He constantly checked on her with his rear view mirror, but she seemed worse. Every so often, she'd moan or mumble, and he was torn about how to respond. So he kept saying, "Things are going to get better, Maddie," nodded a lot and kept driving, while his heart ached for her. It was evident that she really cared for Justin, more than Joey had ever thought possible. Madison had never as much as given a second thought to a dude, but this time she was truly broken-hearted. But Joey couldn't figure out if she was in such dire straits because of Justin's deception or because she was mourning his loss. Maybe it was both.

"I really loved him, Joey," Madison said. She was sobbing, and repeated herself over and over. "Why didn't you tell me what was going on?" Her mascara was running, and snot dripped from her nostrils, but for the first time, Madison didn't care about her appearance. "And that damned Connie. How could he do something like this to me?"

Stopping at an ill-timed traffic light, Joey sighed, and then reached around and patted his sister's hand. "I'm sorry about everything, Maddie. I swear, I didn't really know for sure what was up, and when I did find out, things moved too fast. The last thing I wanted was for you to get hurt, and I'm so sorry you did."

Madison wheezed, and curled herself into the fetal position. "I'm more than hurt. I'm devastated. He's the first man I was ever in love with. And I know he loved me too. I just know he did." Madison's voice trailed off.

"I'm sure he did," Joey said. "I could tell he cared a lot for you."

"I just can't believe he's gone. You should've told me. I would've expected Connie's selfish ass to do somthing like this, but not you."

Joey was rendered speechless by the pain currying in his sister's voice. He was relieved when his cell phone rang, because he had no reply for his sister. But, he wasn't thrilled that it was Christian, calling from the hospital.

"What's up, Chris?"

"I was calling about Conrad. He's still unconscious, but stable. The bullet ripped through his chest, piercing his right lung and his intestines before becoming lodged near his spine. The doctors had to remove part of his lung, but couldn't remove the bullet. Given the amount of blood he's lost, they're unsure how long he'll remain unconscious," Christian said, his tone flat and emotionless.

Joey battled his inner conflict, a very formidable opponent. But he tried to keep the pitch in his voice from betraying his true feelings. If they couldn't remove the bullet, then they'd never know who's really shot Connie. His relief was tempered by the reality of his brother's injuries. If his intestines were pierced, there was a real possibility that Connie might need a colostomy bag. Joey couldn't imagine his playboy big brother trying to mack a woman with that contraption on. The thought actually made Joey feel remorseful. "Damn. Really, Chris?"

Christian paused before replying. Finally, he spoke. "Yes. They're also concerned that when he does awake, if he would ever walk again." This time, his voice had a little feeling in it.

Joey rubbed his eyes. He was toeing a fine line between further disrupting Madison and dealing with the reality of Connie's condition. He found his voice, and was able to quietly speak. "Well, I'm sorry to hear that. Is there anything I can do? How's M'Dear?"

"She's doing as well as we could expect. She's vowed to keep a vigil at Connie's bedside until he gets better. But she's demanding to know where Beverly is. Are you sure you don't know?"

Everyone wanted to know the same thing, but Joey honestly didn't know where Beverly had fled. He just hoped that she'd never return. After his mother kept pressing him about Beverly's whereabouts after the family meeting, Joey had lied and told his family that Beverly had gone on vacation. Inwardly, he was torn about being more specific. Sylvia made no secret that she did not appreciate the fact that Beverly was in absentia during Connie's crisis, which Joey had difficulty digesting. Connie had treated Beverly like a Stepford Wife since they married, and besides heaping the shame of having children outside of his marriage on Beverly, his mother thought that her son still deserved a loving, caring wife. And Sylvia's anger, misguided as it was, was being veered in Beverly's direction. Before Sylvia left for the hospital, she shoved a set of keys into Joey's hands and insisted that he go take care of Connie's menagerie of vicious pets, since Beverly clearly wasn't living up to her responsibilities.

Now, Joey wasn't easily shook, but he didn't relish the thought of tending to deadly animals and reptiles such as pythons, vipers, piranhas, and least of all, those two killer beasts of his, who were aptly named Caligula and Diablo. They were two of the fiercest animals Joey had ever seen that weren't caged in and at the zoo. They were massive black-brindle Presa Canarios, and they were so ferocious that the city required that Connie maintain a $500,000 liability insurance policy on each of them.

Joey thought quickly, and to appease his mother, he agreed to check on Connie's premises first. But then he insisted that the best course of actions was to hire someone to maintain both the animals and the property. Joey suggested that they contract employees from Madison's best friend Ashley's staffing agency. Though his mother was initially reluctant and extremely insistent that Joey not shirk the responsibility, she eventually relented. For Joey, it was a small victory, but a victory nonetheless.

Now that his mother had one less concern, Joey hoped that she would concentrate on Connie's recovery, and get over talking about Beverly. Again, Joey prayed that his sister-in-law would never set foot in D.C. again.

And Joey even extended his prayers to include Connie, whose prognosis was quite disturbing. In fact, it was mind numbing, and the guilt nearly doubled him over. He couldn't imagine the virile, brash, gun-toting, club-hopping Connie paralyzed and unable to walk. It was unthinkable. Joey couldn't imagine how his brazen big brother would deal with something so humbling and life-altering.

"Christian, I really don't know where Beverly is. But, I'm sure she'll be back. Until then, I'll go over to their house and check things out, but I'm going to make sure that Ashley gets someone over there as soon as possible." Joey clicked off the phone, and turned toward a still morose Madison. He was tempted to ask if she needed anything, but he knew that there was nothing he could do for her except be there.

After they arrived at Madison's Watergate condo, Joey removed her shoes, and then helped her into the bed. He covered her limp body with a heavy down comforter, and then laid down across the foot of her bed until she finally drifted off to sleep. Unable to rest, Joey glanced around her room,and saw various personal belongings of Justin's; some of acid-washed jeans, a pale red silk shirt, a ribbed wife beater, and a pair of burnt brown leather sandals. It gave him the creeps. While Madison slept, he quickly stowed the items in her hall closet. He was attempting to remove any signs of her painful liaison, but then he thought about the memories that lurked at his house. Thankfully, he hadn't allowed Lauren to nest there. Although she hadn't left any of her belongings, he was still certain that he'd feel her presence.

Joey silently acknowledged that it was going to be a long time before any of them fully recovered from this melee, but despite that, life had to press on. And in the interim, he had a lot of challenging work to do to get his life back on the right track.

Joey spent an uneasy night on the living room sofa at his Capital Hill row house. BET's *Video Soul* rocked him into a brief sleep, but when he awakened to mind-numbing infomercials, Joey turned off the TV and allowed the silence to keep him company. Though his neighborhood was still and quiet during the wee hours of the morning, restful sleep still evaded him. The issues on his mind wrestled with his lethargy and consciousness, and both were fighting for domination. His father's called meeting worried him. It was a genuine family council, one he nor his siblings had never really participated in. The last formal one was held when Edgy was silenced. Edgy. As an adult, Joey had never been face-to-face with his uncle, and he wasn't relishing the meeting. But he had to get over it. Right now, the only thing Joey needed to concentrate on was carrying out his father's instructions.

It was late evening when he left Madison, and Joey was going to stop by Connie's house, but decided to wait until morning. He was exhausted, his bones ached and his eyes felt gritty and heavy, and he just wanted to go home, crawl into his bed, and shut the world out. But, then he thought of another task he could complete quickly, which was calling Howard. Joey called Howard from his cell phone, but he didn't answer, so Joey left a message on his voicemail, asking him to return the call. Then Joey called Royce, who answered, but seemed a bit jumpy. Royce assured him that all things were quiet, and that Howard had left word that he was going on an extended vacation. A major sabbatical where he couldn't even be reached on his mobile phone. Joey thought that was odd, especially given all that was occurring that Howard should be aware of. But, Royce maintained his ignorance regarding the specifics of Howard's whereabouts, even after Joey grilled him. Satisfied that Royce was telling the truth, Joey grudgedly let it ride. After all, it was still summertime, and Howard did have a right to get away. He just had really bad timing.

Howard's primary function for the family was to keep an eye on Simon, and now that Simon was missing and presumed dead, Howard really didn't have a job. But Harry had given Howard specific instructions to keep the Cavanaughs apprised of any public relations interests, and yet Howard had left without a word. Joey shrugged. He didn't particularly care for Howard anyway, because he always presented himself as a slick opportunist. But, Royce wasn't much better than Howard either. He was like a mini Howard; with a little less panache, but just as smarmy.

But, Joey discounted Royce, too. If the only thing Royce had to do was keep an eye on Howard, then he was pretty worthless in Joey's estimation. But, Joey had to bear in mind that worthless wasn't always synonymous with harmless. Especially for the Cavanaughs. And Royce did seem a little shady.

After his terse, uninformative conversation with Royce, Joey immediately phoned his father with the update. His father was still cool toward him, and expressed his displeasure at Howard's unavailability, and by Royce's lack of information. His father grumbled a few acerbic words, and then slammed the phone down in his ear. Again, Joey felt like a failure. But, at least his father couldn't accuse him of being irresponsible by not bringing forth pertinent information.

Joey was still restless as he stewed in the darkened silence in his wife beater and silk boxers, and unstuck himself from his leather sofa.

He was hot and sweaty because the air conditioner wasn't on; he left it off for fear that someone would think that he was at home.

Then Joey's cell phone rang, and the annoying sound shattered his sullen thoughts. He glanced at his wristwatch, and it wasn't even five a.m. yet. Who on earth would be calling him at this ungodly hour? He checked the caller ID screen, and it read "anonymous." He decided to let the caller leave a voice mail message, but after the caller hung up, the phone rang again, with the same "anonymous" indentifier. Vexed, Joey answered it, and after saying hello, there was no response. He held the phone for a few moments, and then turned it off. Whoever it was, he didn't have time for the nonsense.

But then he thought that perhaps it was Kelly. He had called a couple of times on Joey's home phone, and when Joey saw his name on the caller ID, he didn't even answer the phone. Maybe Kelly had gotten slick, and figured out a way to call him without his number or information showing up. Since they had returned from Harrisburg, Joey hadn't spoken to him, and Kelly was probably concerned. But since Kelly didn't leave a message, Joey didn't feel compelled to return the call. Kelly wanted to catch up with Joey personally, and not speak to some machine. But Joey wasn't sure if he wanted to be caught. At least, not now.

Kelly was a good man, but he had his own issues. He was a D.C. cop, and had gone way out on a brittle limb to help Joey deal with the trouble Connie had caused. And although Kelly had been privy to some highly sensitive information, Joey hadn't told him everything about the innerworkings of his family. He felt ashamed that he had put his friend at risk, while he hadn't been completely honest. But, his concealment had a two-fold purpose. He wanted to protect Kelly from being in a clear conflict of interest as a policeman, and he wanted to protect himself from exposing too much family information.

There was no telling what kind of trouble Kelly might be in because of his aiding and abetting Joey, and though he would forever be indebted to Kelly for it, unfortunately, Joey really had no way of helping him now. He couldn't barely help himself, and he certainly couldn't ask his family or Robeson for help, for that would reveal his connection to Kelly. Joey's only option was to wait for directions from his father, who now resumed the helm of the family. Joey was relieved by the return of his father's control, but also saddened that his father, who was still not 100%, had to resume his position because of their unnecessary and thoughtless actions.

Joey dozed off for a moment, but was awakened by a loud bang on his front door. It was still well before dawn Sunday morning, and he figured that it was the paperboy hurling the overstuffed Post onto his porch. Then, Joey thought about the bundles of papers that were probably strewn across his porch, and he decided he'd better go gather them before the wind scattered it across his lawn.

He opened the door, and bent down to gather the newspapers, when he heard a rustling sound, and Kelly stepped out of the shadows. He was wearing his uniform, and his black and white squad car was parked in Joey's driveway. Joey's stomach dropped to his ankles, and his gut retreated to the soles of his feet.

"Wha-what are you doing here, Kelly?" Joey asked, and gripped the storm door. There was no way he was letting him in.

"I figured you wouldn't open your door," Kelly said, and grabbed the storm door frame. "We need to talk." Kelly was a tall, well-built man, with rich, dark brown skin and piercing eyes. Clean-shaven, and sporting a military style fade, Kelly was subtly scented with Calvin Klein cologne, and Joey felt dirty and disheveled in his presence. And rightly so, since he hadn't showered since Friday, and had covered a lot of ground since then.

"Now's not a good time, Kelly. It's the damned break of dawn, and as you can see, I'm not quite presentable for company."

Kelly snatched the door open, and charged past Joey. "I think we're past the point of me being company," he said in his deep, rich, baritone voice.

Joey collected his newspapers, and a small blank envelope fell out of the pile. Joey figured it was just a payment notice, so he tossed it on his desk as he reluctantly followed Kelly inside. He didn't want to create a scene, and the sight of the patrol car sitting in his driveway made him cringe. Even though he and Kelly had been through a lot, Joey wasn't quite sure where Kelly was coming from. Was he hostile? Angry? Joey couldn't tell. And after his parent's earlier lecture about keeping family issues close to the collective vest, the last thing Joey wanted to do was to air some of his dirty laundry. He switched on a small desk lamp that was under the living room window, and stared at Kelly, who was standing near the fireplace mantel.

"What's going on, Joe? You're all holed up in here, with no lights on, not answering your phone. What's up? You know I was concerned about you." In the dim light, Joey caught Kelly's eyes, and felt warmed by the genuine expression on his face.

"I appreciate your concern, Kelly, but I've got a lot to deal with right now. Personal things. No disrespect, okay?"

"None taken. But, you know I'm here for you, right? And I still have that bag with your cash," Kelly said. "I didn't bring it with me, but, let's just say, I'm not feeling too comfortable with it in my possession. I'm a working stiff, and we aren't known to carry around bankrolls like that. I.A. would have a field day with me if they found out I was holdin' that much loot."

The cash. Joey had somehow forgotten that on the night of the drug deal, Kelly had intercepted Justin and Connie, and switched their cash-filled duffel bag with a decoy bag stuffed with newspapers and gym clothes. How could it have slipped his mind? If his father found out, this would surely be the last straw. Joey was truly grateful for Kelly's honesty. It wasn't everyday that someone hands you $250G's, and you have to remind him that you even have it. With that much loot, a less scrupulous man would've vanished, and been on his way to starting another life.

"Thanks so much for that, Kelly. I mean, I can't thank you enough for being honest." Joey didn't know what he was going to do with that money, but that wasn't really an issue now. "Seriously, Kelly. I really appreciate what you've done for me. I tell you what. Let's try to hook up this week, and I'll get it from you then, okay? But, like I said, I can't deal with anything but my family right now," Joey said. "Everything's just in an uproar with them these days."

"That's cool. So, how are your folks doing? And Connie. How's he doing?" Kelly said, and he crossed the room to stand near Joey.

Joey stepped sideways. "He's barely hanging in there. He's unconscious, and we're not even sure if he's going to be able to walk when he does wake up."

"That's messed up, Joey. And I'm sorry to hear that. Hopefully, he'll recover, but remember, he didn't get in this predicament by accident, you know. Connie had a major hand in why he's in the jam he's in. If he hadn't been tryin' to do his dirt, he would've never been there in the first place."

Joey glared at Kelly, and tried not to bite his head completely off. "Thanks for the advice, Kelly. Trust me, I know all of that and more. But, it doesn't make me feel any better that he's laid up in the hospital. And that I'm the reason why he's there."

Kelly shook his head. "You're taking too much blame, Joey. You tried to stop him, and he refused to listen, remember? And you said he fired at you first."

"Whatever," Joey said. "But, like I said, I've got to deal with my family right now. And, for your sake, you probably don't need to concern yourself with what happened that night anymore. You have your own well-being to worry about."

Kelly had gotten Joey an impounded car and a few untraceable guns from the precinct's confiscated property department so that Joey would be armed and prepared once he got to the docks to try to stop Connie's madness. Joey didn't ask how, but he knew that Kelly pulled some major strings and stuck his neck way out to do so.

"That's not what friends do, Joey. You don't turn your back on somebody. Now, I'm dealing with my bosses, and I'm gonna be okay. I got a little heat for fudging the paperwork so that I could get you that vehicle and those weapons, but they'll get over it. I've seen some of the other officers do a whole lot worse that that. Shoot, they'll reprimand me for a minute or two, and probably make me pull some ugly shifts and walk some beats again or something, but nothing too serious. I'm not sweatin' it."

Joey was relieved that Kelly's career wasn't in shambles, and that Kelly hadn't ratted him out to save his own ass. But, Joey didn't want him further involved in the fallout. Joey would have to handle it himself.

"Now, about us," Kelly said, but Joey raised his hand and cut him off. He was not about to talk about their sexual dalliance, or about their simmering mutual attraction. Kelly was comfortable being gay, and Joey hadn't even come to terms with being quasi bi-sexual.

"That's not a conversation for now, Kelly. And no time soon, either." That statement was really becoming his mantra.

Kelly stared a hole through Joey before he responded. Kelly stepped in front of him, and stood so close that Joey could smell the Juicy Fruit gum he was chewing. "Well, I just want to let you know that I'm not going anywhere, you understand?"

Joey tried to side step him again, but Kelly blocked his path. "That's your choice, Kelly. But, I'm not making any promises, nor am I abiding by some imaginary timeframe you've manifested in your mind."

"I got that part. You just understand where I'm coming from."

"And you just understand where we're not going," Joey said, and pushed his way past Kelly, and swung the front door open. Joey hoped that Kelly would leave, and take Joey's painful, un-reconciled, and unwanted feelings with him.

Chapter 4

The library in Grand's house was dark and closed, just like the drawing room was the day before. With it's rich, masculine, mahogany bookcase lined walls, and matching conference table and heavy leather captain's chairs, the room had an air of authority and intimidation. But, it hadn't been used in quite a while, and was a bit stuffy. Joey had forewarned Trudy to air it out, and she had tried to brighten it up by placing some fresh cut flowers on the large conference table.

The day had started off on a downbeat note. After his encounter with Kelly, Joey had received yet another pre-dawn phone call, by the anonymous caller. He was beginning to wonder if it was Kelly tripping out. Or maybe it was Lauren. Whoever it was never responded, and after being awakened before four, Joey just got up and decided to go jogging. When he returned home, he showered, and forced down two huge bowls of Froot Loops, before laying down on his sofa, and waiting for the sun to rise.

His stomach gurgled, the mixture of milk and sugar churned as he tried to calm his unsettled nerves. He was antsy and anxious, either from lack of sleep or by the pangs of guilt that punctured his lie-ladened life. He hated lying, but he had to, at least until he had a better perspective on what his uncle and cousin were going to disclose during the family meeting. He had to wait, and either remain silent or feign ignorance. Joey's options were few, and each had outcomes that teetered between bad and worse. Lies beget more lies, and playing dumb now meant that he couldn't know anything later. And that later might be when Connie was back on his feet. And likely to sell Joey out the moment he regained consciousness.

Connie. Thinking of Connie reminded Joey that he still had to go over to his house. He mulled it over, and tried to rationalize any reason not to go. But there was no getting around it, so he decided to just get it over with.

Connie's house was just as Joey had expected: a mess. Inside, it was evident that Beverly wasn't around. Mail from the door slot and Connie's shoes were strewn in the foyer, and in the kitchen, dirty dishes were in the sink, and left on the kitchen table.

Joey stepped back over the scattered items in the foyer and called out, but didn't expect a response from anyone. He ventured down into Connie's basement, and even in the brightness of daylight and the illumination from the florescent lights, the basement was still dark and foreboding. Joey looked around the room, his imagination prompted him to think that the animals had freed themselves, and were slithering and roaming about. Thankfully, that wasn't the case, and his nerves settled down. As he surveyed the room, his eyes focused on the cocktail table and the items that laid on it.

The sight of Connie's backgammon board made Joey extremely uneasy. Connie almost always kept that game within his reach, and it was odd to see it there without him. The moment caught Joey off guard, but he quickly regrouped and went about completing the business at hand. The reptiles were in their cages, and the piranhas in Connie's wall-size aquarium. After locating their food supply, Joey forced himself to feed the slimy creatures, and tried not to gag while watching them devour dehydrated mice and other rodents.

In the utility room, Joey checked the refrigerator, removed four pounds of raw meat, and then made his way out to the chain-link fenced dog run, which was clearly in need of a good cleaning. The beasts growled and snorted, and barked as he approached, and sniffed the air, their keen senses honing in on the white-wrapped package Joey held. Spotting a garden hose, Joey picked it up and washed away the waste and feces, and then sprayed the snarling animals as they angrily bit at the forceful streams of water. He wished he had some disinfectant to pour on them too, but he figured that the professional could bathe them.

After the hounds were fed and re-caged, Joey was about to leave, when he thought that he'd better put Connie and Beverly's mail away from the hired help. He started picking up the letters and evelopes, and neatly stacked them in the drawer of the foyer desk. He wasn't even remotely curious about the contents of Connie's mail, even though he knew that if Connie had access to his mail, he would have read it all by now. But, Joey tried to stay above the pettiness, and do the right thing. Now he was content that he had completed his daily tasks, so he decided to go back home and rest before tackling the remainder of the day and the even greater priorities that lay smoldering ahead.

Just as Harry had stipulated, Edgy and Vincent were transported to Grand's house early that morning, under heavily armed security guard. The Cavanaugh's personal security men were holding them upstairs in one of the guest bedrooms, until the emergency family counsel was convened that afternoon at four.

Forcing himself out of his self-induced funk, and attempting to cleanse himself of the sickening feeling from being around Connie's creatures, Joey took a scalding hot shower and found something fresh from the dry cleaners to wear. Fresh shaven and meticulously dressed, in a crisp white shirt and dark chocolate slacks, Joey looked like he stepped off the pages of *GQ*. He was following one of the Cavanaugh's codes of conduct. Always dress and look your best. Never let the world see what was really going on behind closed doors.

Joey had arrived a half hour early, because he hoped to see Grand, but he was taking his afternoon nap. While restlessly waiting for his family to arrive, Joey absent-mindedly ran his fingers over the numerous bindings of the books on the shelves. He was extremely ill at ease. Joey had never met his cousin Vincent, and this would be the first time Joey had even been in the same room with his uncle since he was a young boy. And the first time was when he was staring at him through the sight of his rifle. Just before Joey shot him. And then Joey shot Vincent. What an introduction.

It was quite incongruous, this whole situation. The vestiges of Connie's lies and deception had inadvertently reunited the Cavanaugh men for the first time in nearly a lifetime. Life was coming full circle, for Harry and Edgy had parted ways under nearly the same circumstances of lies and deception.

The door to the library opened, and Christian strolled in, holding a leather valise under his arm. "Hello, Joey. How are you doing?" he asked, and laid the case on the table. He extended his hand for his brother to shake.

Though close in age, Joey wasn't really close to Christian. But he sensed that today would require them to tighten the fabric of their brotherly bond. Joey grabbed his brother's hand, drew Christian close to him, and hugged him around the shoulders. "I'm doing, Christian," he said, his voice full of dread.

Christian, ever fastidious, brushed down the front of his hunter green Izod sweater, and straightened his tie. "Looks like things have really hit the fan, huh?" Christian said, as he reached for and slid out a chair that was located near the door, and then stopped. He pushed it back in, returning it to its original place, and then Christian moved further down to the opposite end of the table.

Joey nodded and observed his brother without commenting. Christian was always the most non-confrontational Cavanaugh, yet by far the most intelligent. And today, Joey could appreciate that quality about him. Joey figured that the D.C. based Cavanaughs needed every advantage, not knowing what level of hostility his New York relatives would bring to bear.

Joey overheard voices in the hallway, and then his father and Uncle Jolly walked into the room. Similarly outfitted in their dark gabardine suits, they made a spiffy looking pair. Harry was dwarfed by the larger Jolly, but his presence was far more commanding. They closed the door behind them and lowered their voices to a whisper, when they realized that the room was occupied.

Named after his Uncle Joseph, Joey had a close relationship with his uncle. He was even the one who nicknamed his uncle Jolly, because his enormous belly always jiggled when he laughed. Jolly was a large, rotund, bald-headed man, who had an overall pleasant disposition, but would exterminate you in between chuckles. Jolly was in charge of the family's security, which included protection and enforcement. He was a humorous man, but Jolly was no joke.

Joey knew things were serious when Jolly and his men were involved. Jolly and Harry were just like brothers, a position he assumed when Edgar had left. They were so close; they could almost complete each other's sentences. The dynamic of Edgar's arrival would only serve to make matters worse for everyone.

"Good afternoon, boys," Jolly said, and gave Joey and Christian big bear hugs, nearly swallowing them into his mushy midsection.

Clinching an unlit cigar between his teeth, the room suddenly filled with Jolly's familiar scent, a warm blend of Aramis cologne and cigar smoke.

Joey and Christian greeted their father, and Harry took a seat at the far end of the table. Like Malcolm X, Harry never sat with his back to the door. It was the classic power move that Joey recalled Connie often mimicked.

Christian and Joey took their seats, each anchoring Harry's elbows, and Jolly sat down in the corner behind Harry. As always, he was covering his brother-in-law's back.

"Sons, I wanted to speak to you briefly before your uncle and cousin join us. You need to understand what you are about to witness."

Join us, Joey thought. His father actually sounded gracious. Joey found it amazing that his father made it sound like Edgy and Vincent were really welcomed guests or like they had a choice in the matter. But Joey also knew that his father was formal and diplomatic to a fault. Even in matters of deciding whether someone would live or die, Harry was keen on proper protocol.

"You've sat in on councils before, but this is different. This is family. *Familia.* And we handle matters a lot differently than when we are involving outsiders, you understand?"

Joey and Christian nodded, and their father continued. "Now, no matter what, Edgar is your uncle, and he is to be treated with that much respect and regard. No matter what the outcome of this tribunal, you should always be cognizant of that. This goes without saying."

"We'll listen to what is said, and then we'll figure out how to proceed from there. Do you understand? *Capisce*?" Harry asked, and then scanned his son's faces.

Harry signaled for Jolly to collect Edgy and Vincent, and Joey swallowed deeply, and was barely able to pass the lump in his throat. Nervous energy assailed him but Joey stayed solid because he had to. Jolly spoke briefly into his cell phone, and nodded. "They're on their way," Jolly said.

Harry leaned back in his seat, and folded his hands across his lap. Jolly cracked his knuckles, Christian fiddled with his briefcase, and Joey tried to remain calm.

After a few moments, the door finally opened. Joey started to stand, but Harry motioned for him to remain seated. Everyone stared at the doorway, as one of the Cavanaugh's gargantuan security men stepped in, leading a less than enthusiastic Edgy and Vincent.

Edgy was a brown skinned version of Harry, with a distinct New York flair. He was wearing an open necked silk shirt, and the same wrinkled trousers and shoes that he had on at the shootout. He was about Harry's size, but where Harry's hair was black, straight and slick, Edgar's was mixed gray and slightly curlier.

His fingers were adorned with numerous oversized gold rings, and on his wrists were heavy herringbone bracelets that clinked as he walked. His arm was in a sling, and he was wearing Ray Charles style, black, Gucci glasses.

Joey nearly gasped when he saw Vincent. Seeing him up close, Vincent was almost a carbon copy of Connie, except he was much more buffed. Now, Joey was no slouch in the area of working out, and had the body to show for it, but Vincent looked like he pumped up on steroids. He had the same sleepy-eyed expression as Connie, and his skin was dark and glossy, like the color of the wood in the library. His hair was cut in a curly fade, with a long, thin tail at the nape of his neck. He had on a tight, black muscle shirt, black slacks, and thick gold rope chains around his neck.

"Harry," Edgy said, and reached for the seat at the opposite end of the table. Harry shook his head no, and signaled for the guard to seat Edgy in the chair next to the end.

Joey absorbed the scene with ardent interest. This episode was an intriguing faction, masterfully choreographed, where every move was calculated and purposeful. Harry wasn't about to give Edgar that much respect, from not having his sons stand to greet him, to not having him sit at the end of the table. That was a position obviously reserved for someone more worthy.

Edgy shrugged as he acknowledged the repositioning of his seat, while Vincent scowled. Edgy sat, and then gestured for Vincent to do the same.

"I'll stand, Father," Vincent said, and folded his bulky arms across his cut chest.

"Sit," Edgy said, his voice stern.

Vincent rolled his eyes and sat down next to his father with a huff. Jolly gave his man the signal to leave, and then Harry gazed at his brother.

"Edgar," Harry finally said.

"It's good to see you, *mio fratello.* My brother." Edgy said, his voice slightly strained. "I just wish I was better dressed for the occasion, but as you can see, I'm not quite at my best today." Edgy pointed at his wrinkled garb and sling. It was evident where Connie inherited his glib personality.

"I wish this could be under better circumstances, Edgar," Harry said. "But, that's beside the point. You know why you're here, and it's not for a social call. So, let's not mince words, shall we. It's been too long, but some things don't change. I was never partial to your sense of humor, and I'm not now."

Harry cleared his throat. "Based on your treason and treachery, I only want to hear *why* I should let you live."

"What?" Vincent shouted, and postured like he was getting ready to wail on someone. "What are you talking about? What do you mean, *'let him live.'* You aren't going to *let* him do anything. What kind of shit is this? We don't have to answer to you."

Jolly slipped his hand under his jacket, and rustled in his seat. Harry nodded and placed a calm hand on the tabletop. "Edgar, I'm sure that you've had this conversation with your son, but you better check him. Remind him that he has not been recognized in this matter, and is not to speak unless first spoken to. Especially, not to me."

Edgy shook his head at his defiant son. "Harry, you know how this new generation is, so *caldo moderato.* So hot headed. So quick to respond without ample thought. Kind of reminds you of how I used to be, huh?" Edgy placed his good hand next to his son. "*Lei ha ogni destra.* You have every right to ask me that question, Harry."

"So, hopefully you have an adequate answer. But, from where I sit, you have far exceeded the level of betrayal you demonstrated in your younger years. And I don't see how this can possibly be explained, not to my satisfaction. Especially now that my son is fighting for his life because of you and your disrespectful actions."

Edgy scratched his face, and stared thoughtfully at Harry. "I understand how you feel, Harry, but you must know the truth. Word had gotten out that your son was seeking a partner for a major score. At first, I refused to believe it, but then Connie contacted me. That's how we got connected. And the only reason I became involved."

Harry grunted, and re-folded his arms. "And I should believe that? *Perchè?* Why?"

"Because I did it to protect you. To preserve our family's honor."

Harry snorted, and let out a stream of Italian expletives. "Good Lord, Edgy. You'll never change. You must think I'm a fool. Only you could twist this to try to make it seem like you were concerned for me. *Quello è irragionevole.* That's absurd."

"Not at all, Harry. I did try to protect you from the actions of your wayward child. Conrad basically made our entire family vulnerable to outsiders. I never intended to go into business with him behind your back, but I planned to teach him a valuable lesson about honor and respect, that only his elder could teach. I'm assuming that he was unaware that he was dishonoring and disrespecting you by his actions," Edgy said, with a smug expression on his face.

His uncle's greasy lies stank up the room, and Joey couldn't resist interrupting. "Is that why you tried to kill him?" Joey asked, but Harry waved a disapproving hand in his direction.

Edgar leaned back in his seat and shrugged. "Well, I see that honor and respect seem to be a lesson another one of your sons needs to learn."

"If they do, you're certainly not the one to teach it, Edgar," Harry said. "Now, continue. *Continuare.*"

"Well, things got a little out of hand on the docks, and unfortunately, when you put yourself in volatile situations, you can't really predict the outcome. I'm sorry that Connie got injured, but it was not my intention to bring harm to him," Edgy said with a shrug. "How is he, by the way?" Edgy's tone was hollow, and he almost looked like he was smirking.

Vincent snickered and toyed with his jewelry. Joey caught his eye, and Vincent winked at him. Joey recalled how Vincent was the one that had wanted to do Connie. Vincent was the one who had drawn first. Joey felt flush with anger, but the words clogged his throat. There was nothing that he could say that wouldn't reveal his own culpability.

There was a lull in the discussion, and a slight commotion was heard coming from the hallway. Jolly and his men reached for their weapons as the door creaked open, and the entrant surprised everyone. It was Grand, hobbling on his crystal-topped cane. Weapons were returned to their holsters, and the whole room automatically stood at attention, except Vincent. Edgy nudged him until he lumbered to his feet.

"Papa? Why are you here?" Harry said, as he walked toward his father.

Grand, dressed in a burgundy paisley-designed smoking jacket, ascot and lounge pants, shooed his oldest son away. "Harrison," Grand said, as he slowly crept toward the table. "I'm here because I live here, or did you forget that? My goodness— I thought I was the one with the memory problem." He pointed the crystal top of his cane at Edgar and squinted. "Is that you, Edgar?" Grand asked, and peered at his younger son.

Edgar's eyes misted and he reached for his father's hand, and grasped it firmly. "Yes, Papa. It's me— Edgar."

"*Che cosa state facendo qui?* What are you doing here?" Grand asked, and he patted his prodigal son's cheek.

Joey was floored. Grand was suffering from severe dementia, but had rare moments of clarity. Perhaps Grand sensed that his prodigal son had returned, or maybe he had overheard something, but nevertheless, he was on point today. Grand's voice was strong and assured, probably like it was the last time he and his two sons spoke.

"I, uh, Harry and I had some urgent business to discuss," Edgy said, and glanced at his brother, who nodded in agreement.

Grand didn't miss a beat. "I am so glad that I am able to lay eyes on you once again, my son." Grand leaned forward and embraced Edgy, and then stepped beside him. "You have returned home, which is all that matters. I want this to be settled between you two. It's been far too long and too many things have happened for our family to be fractured and split apart like this. And before I close my eyes for the final time, I want to know that my sons are brothers again."

"But, Papa," Harry said. "Things aren't that simple."

Grand brought his feeble fist down on the table, while Edgy held fast to his other hand. "Things are just that simple. As long as I live, I have the final say-so. My word is all that matters. And I want to call a truce to this, *una volta per tutte.* Once and for all."

Edgy shook his father's hand, seemingly relieved that Grand had come to his rescue. He then turned to face Harry. "We've both lost a lot in this whole thing. Blood has been shed, lives lost and injuries sustained." Edgy turned back toward his father. "I agree, Papa." He then extended his free hand to his brother. "Don't you, Harry?"

Harry sighed and glared at his younger brother. "You both need to understand that it will be difficult to let bygones be bygones, especially given the severity of this situation. I'm not sure if I can, or if it will be in the best interest of the family."

"I insist that you do," Grand said again, and finally sat down at the head of the table. "*Insisto*. I insist."

An uncomfortable silence filled the room. Harry shifted his stance, and shook his head. "Very well, Papa. Very well. As you wish." Harry clasped Edgy's hand, and cupped his other hand over it. "But, let me say for the record, that this is against my better judgment, and only at the Consigliore request. I still run this family, and will not ever, I repeat, ever, be placed in this position again. There will not be a next time, do you hear me, Edgar? *Lo sentite*?"

Edgar gripped Harry's hand firmly. "Oh, yes. I hear you loud and clear." He shot Harry a strained smile, and cleared his throat. "Now, perhaps we can clear up another little ditty. Like, where's my money? I'm sure that since your folks made this little incident go away so nicely, I can recuperate my funds. You know, a quarter of a million dollars is nothing to sneeze at."

Harry laughed, and slowly removed his hand from Edgy's. "A quarter mil, huh? That's a small price to pay for your life and your freedom, wouldn't you say? From where I sit, you're getting off cheap. *Realmente economico.*"

At that exact moment, Sylvia waltzed in, her face registering surprise at Grand's presence. She looked stunning, with her hair freshly coiffed, and wearing a long embroidered denim dress. She greeted Grand by kissing both of his sunken cheeks, and whispered in his ear. She and Grand cackled at Sylvia's sly ear play, and then she went and stood beside her husband, who was still holding Edgar's hand.

Edgar lit up when he saw Sylvia, and dropped Harry's hand, and reached to embrace his sister-in-law.

"Syl," he said, but before he could finish, Sylvia turned her rings around, and then took her jeweled hand, and promptly smacked Edgar across his cheek. Then she spit in his face.

"Edgar," Sylvia said, her voice teeming with emotion. "That's for what you've done to my son. And, I want you to know, that if he dies, I will personally see that you never enjoy another day on this earth."

Edgar wiped Sylvia's saliva from his reddened face, and slowly licked his fingers. "You're still as sweet as ever, Sylvia." He cast her a lustful look. "It's nice to see you again, too, darling," he said with a lingering leer.

Chapter 5

Sprawled out on her ice white leather sofa, Madison's swollen, bloodshot eyes were stuck on the timepiece on her stark white living room wall. The hands hadn't moved for the past hour, and seemed to be stuck on eleven-forty five. Madison finally understood the definition of time standing still.

As a medley of Phyllis Hyman and Sade ballards radiated from her Bose speakers, the melancholy music only anchored her to the furniture, and made it difficult for her to even raise her head. Although it was morning, Madison had forgotten what day it was. Ever since the family meeting, she just couldn't get a firm grip on her life, or on the other matters that ravaged her mind. She just couldn't fathom the fact that Justin was dead. Or that he was actually a federal agent. Or that she now had to live with the shock, and the shame, of it.

It made her sick to her stomach, and she had thrown up several times as literal proof. She couldn't hold anything down, and now her throat, stomach and chest felt sore and strained from the strain of dry heaves. Madison had taken to her bed ever since Joey had brought her home, but she was through with him. She had absolutely nothing to say to him. To know that he and Connie were involved with the death of her beloved made her angry beyond explanation. She felt betrayed. And though she was always closest to Joey, when he said that he was sorry for her loss, his words were nothing but a bitter reminder of the tragedy that now governed her life.

Joey had called several times, but she turned away from the phone. After the third call, she kicked the phone off the hook, and even turned off her cell phone. She realized that Joey was probably hurting too, with his friend Lauren being involved, but Madison didn't have the wherewithal to really care. She was too consumed with her own pain.

The one person Madison thought would call, but hadn't, was her mother. Madison hadn't spoken to or seen her since the family's fateful meeting. Although everyone knew that Connie was Sylvia's favorite, Madison thought that her mother would have some sympathy for her during this traumatic time. But, apparently not. "She's far too wrapped up with Connie now to even think about me or what I'm going through," Madison said aloud, and set another pretty place setting at her pity party.

With her drapes drawn and phone off the hook, Madison had shut out the world, including her best friend, Ashley Vickers. Ashley was someone Madison could depend on to support her, no matter what. But for the moment, Madison just wanted to ensconce herself in the comforting surroundings that brought her the most joy. Her home, her condo. Where she and Justin spent many intimate moments, sharing their deepest thoughts, dreams, and desires.

She felt in her heart that Justin loved her. No, he never said that he did, but she knew it. A woman always knows. And what she shared with Justin, she had never shared with any of her other boyfriends. In Madison's heart and mind, it didn't matter what any person or agency said. No man had ever made her feel like he had, ever. What she and Justin had found was special. It was real. It was no con.

And she had been with enough men to know the difference between having sex and making love, and Justin had always made sweet, tender love to her. He always made sure that she was completely satisfied. No one had ever curled her toes like he had. That was simply no act. He passionately sang to her. He cooked for her. He had seen her without her makeup, several times, and hadn't run screaming from the building. He sometimes just held her until she fell asleep in the crook of his manly arms, her face pressed against his solid chest. Justin spent quality and quantity time with her. That was no job. No damned assignment. She'd never believe that.

Sylvia's caustic words burned in Madison's ears. She was a Cavanaugh, and was expected to act as such. And she would. She would do exactly what was important to her, but in an uncustomary discreet manner. She'd find out everything she could about the real Justin Pasqual or Brian Hunter. Had he lied about everything? She had to know if he was anything like he had presented himself to be.

She also couldn't bear the thought of not knowing where his final resting place was, or what the F.B.I. would do to a disgraced agent. She wouldn't be able to rest unless she knew that the man she loved wasn't buried in shame. And she didn't care what her family's thoughts were on the subject.

Madison sat up, and felt dizzy. It was an odd feeling, and although the thought of eating made her feel worse, she still felt ravenous. She decided to contact Beatty, one of her family's former security people, and have him gather all of Justin's information. Beatty had the hots for her, and Madison figured that she'd use what she had to get what she needed. A few soft spoken words, and then he'd get her what she needed swiftly. And then she'd get cleaned up and call Ashley to bring her something to eat. It was high time for Madison to pull herself together, in the appropriate Cavanaugh fashion.

"Oh, Maddie. I can't tell you how sorry I am to hear about Justin's heart attack," Ashley said, and reached for Madison's hand.

Madison had showered and was sitting upright in her bed, with a thick red terry cloth robe and matching slippers, as Ashley brought in her tray, which was laden with a take out seafood platter from The Market Inn, one of she and Justin's favorite haunts. After Madison had gathered up enough strength to phone her, Ashley had dashed over within the hour, just like Madison expected her to do.

Madison sighed as Ashley set the tray down on her lap. She hadn't told Ashley the truth about Justin, and wouldn't ever. Though Ashley was her number one fan, Madison didn't want her to think any less of her man. It was best that Justin be remembered as he was. But Madison was thankful that Robeson had kept Justin's name out of the paper. Although people like Ashley and others in their social circle rarely read the Post's crime ridden Metro section, you never knew who might run across the information and use it against her.

Despite her emotional issues, other things were working in Madison's favor. Beatty responded positively as Madison assumed he would, and he had promised to fax the background information to her before tomorrow morning. Because he wasn't familiar with the name or person Brian Hunter, Madison passed off Brian Hunter as an old college acquaintance of hers who had recently expired. She urgently needed specifics of his funeral arrangements, and she was okay if the other details came later. But not too much later.

Usually one to pass on bread, Madison slathered butter onto every crevice of the warm roll, and wolfed down it and her crab imperial in the most unladylike manner. She hadn't eaten for a few days, and it showed. Her gurgling stomach welcomed the tasty meal.

"Gee whiz, Maddie. You must've been starved," Ashley said, as she picked at her scallops sautéed in garlic sauce. She pushed her thick glasses up on the bridge of her thin, pointy nose.

"I guess I was, Ash. I didn't realize how grief-stricken or famished I was."

"I understand, Madison. So much is going on with you and your family, and I know it must be taking a toll on you. Joey contacted me earlier, and he told me that Connie had been hospitalized. And that he needed me to get some help over to Connie's house. I've gotten someone lined up already, so I don't want you or your family to worry about that. I'm sure your mother must be wrecked by all of this tragedy."

Madison groaned and kept eating.

"And how are you holding up? Ashley asked. "I can't imagine how you must be feeling. I was absolutely shocked when you phoned me about Justin's death. I know you really loved him. And, he was quite charming. And so fine," she said with a blush. "You two made a perfect couple. I can't believe that someone his age could have a heart attack."

"Yes, well, it was an undiagnosed congenital condition that caused it." Madison looked at her friend and sighed. She hated lying to her friend, but Madison knew that Ashley's soothing nature and sincere face would comfort her. Ashley was a very kind woman, but a bit dense. By contrast, she was quite adept at handling business matters, and in fact, had her own temp agency. Madison sometimes marveled at how diametrically opposed Ashley's personal attributes were to her business acumen. And, on top of that, Ashley was frumpy too. Not that she was poor or didn't shop at high-post stores like Neiman-Marcus or Saks, but her taste leaned towards the traditional plaids and tweed styling of Laura Ashley, and not chic fashion designers, or Madison's favorites, like Fendi.

Ashley's hair was long, thick, and bushy hair, that she insisted on getting old fashioned wet-set. And when her heavy locks dragged the curls out, she'd part her hair, and wear it braided down the back. Ashley also wore thick glasses that always seemed to dangle on the tip of her nose. Though it never really occurred to Madison that Ashley could use a total makeover, for some reason today, Madison actually felt a little sorry for her. Perhaps it was the sorrow gene that had kicked in and was working overtime, but Madison suddenly wanted to help her. But, then Madison thought better. Ashley was going to be her pet project when she returned from Justin's funeral. Right now, she had to focus on getting herself together, which was ultimately more important.

Madison decided to see Graham, her hairstylist, and also get a manicure and pedicure. She was going to put Ashley's administrative skills to good use, and had Ashley schedule all of Madison's appointments. Ashley was quite adept at doing Madison's bidding. She also encouraged Ashley to make an appointment for herself, after Madison's was already confirmed. Then Madison would corral Ashley along to get her nails and draconian feet done when Madison did. Her salon of choice was an elegant Asian-owned nail salon on Connecticut Avenue that had multiple operators. They could do Ashley at the same time, and not inconvenience Madison.

While Ashley was on the phone making the arrangements, Madison's fax machine clicked on, and Madison leaped out of the bed. She nearly flipped over her tray in her efforts to grab the documents.

Just as Beatty had promised, he faxed the information on Brian, née Justin's, funeral arrangements. Even though Madison was pleased with the quick turnaround, the reality of the specific details saddened her. Justin's funeral was going to be held in two days, on Wednesday, in Van Nuys, California.

It didn't matter. Madison would be there, even if it was going to be held on the moon. She'd charter a rocket if she had to.

She ruminated briefly about taking Ashley with her for support, but then she thought better of it. She'd never have enough time to make Ashley presentable, and then again, she might have to tell Ashley the truth. And that would be too much information for her to have. Madison didn't know what she'd be facing once she landed in Cali, but the beautiful swan didn't need the ugly duckling tagging along. Fuddy-duddy Ashley and her dead weight would only bring her down. And Madison had to ensure that she was fleet of foot. And fly as hell.

"Ashley?" Madison said as she reentered her bedroom, her strides a bit steadier. "Please call United Airlines. And book me a flight for tomorrow morning out of National to Los Angeles. First class, of course."

Holding a wedge of parmesan cheese, Joey breathed deeply, and took the grater and shaved a mound on top of his bowl of spaghetti. After applying a thick layer, Joey laid the grater down and stirred up the steaming entree. The twisted noodles reminded him of the tangled entrails of his life. He was sitting in the sunroom of his parent's home, attempting to enjoy the warmth of the August evening. Eating a serving of their housekeeper Genevieve's famous pasta, Joey twirled the noodles around his fork, and shoved in a massive mouthful.

Christian had retreated to the family's corporate offices, while Sylvia had returned home to pick up a few items for Connie, and then planned to hastily return to Connie's bedside. His condition remained stable, but Sylvia's disappointment with the missing Beverly was escalating. Joey kept his mouth shut, though his mother's venom was spewing.

"I just can't believe that girl still isn't anywhere to be found," Sylvia had said, as she thrust her overnight bag into her driver's arms. She balled her hands up and slowly forced them down by her sides. "The absolute nerve of her. After all my darling Conrad and this family has done for her. How dare Beverly not be here when her husband needs her the most."

Up to this crucial moment in time, Beverly had been Sylvia's favorite daughter-in-law. But Beverly had unceremoniously forfeited that coveted crown, and there wasn't any other contenders vying for the abandoned position.

Joey maintained a rigid expression, and kept eating despite his mother's continued diatribe. In the scheme of things, Beverly's whereabouts were inconsequential. The less said, the better. And despite his mother's great guilting skills, she'd never bait Joey into giving up any information on Beverly. Never.

Sylvia was so enraged that she threatened to allow Jade, Connie's other significant other and the mother of his son Seth, to come to the hospital. When she said that, Joey realized that Connie's illness and Beverly's disappearance were really devastating his mother. Although Connie's visitors were restricted to his immediate family, Sylvia had further instructed the guards to notify her if anyone even tried to visit Connie. Joey had thought that this was his mother's way of keeping tabs on the undesirables, and making sure they stayed away from her son. And Jade topped the list of his mother's undesirables. Normally, his mother would've almost stroked out at the mentioning of Jade's name. Now, she was actually bringing up Connie's mistress.

"At least she's called several times. She acts like she cares about Conrad's welfare," she said. "Even that other girl bothered to call."

The other 'girl' his mother offhandedly referred to was Lynne, the mother of Connie's other child, Forrest. And Lynne had quickly gotten on Sylvia's bad side because she wasn't caught up in kissing Connie's ass. They had become involved, but when she realized he was married, Lynne refused to play his fool. Even after she found out she was pregnant. As long as Connie made his child support payments, Lynne never made any waves. Joey had to give her credit for that.

"I'm sure they both care, M'Dear," Joey said with a pause. "I went by Connie's and took care of his mail and what not. Ashley's promised to send her best caretaker over there this afternoon, who'll also tend to the animals. I dropped Connie's key by her office this morning."

"Very good, Joseph. I'm glad to see that you've taken an earnest interest in your brother's well being. And I hope that Ashley will ensure that Conrad's household is well taken care of. I want someone trustworthy, not somebody's who's going to be rummaging through his belongings. We have to make sure that everything is perfect for when my son goes home. And I certainly can't rely on Beverly to do it."

Harry walked in on the tail end of Sylvia's diatribe, with an exasperated expression on his face. Harry had changed from his buttoned up business attire into an almond colored warm up suit, yet he didn't appear relaxed.

"Sylvia, dear. I realize that you're concerned about our son, but if you don't calm down, you'll be in the hospital too. Now, I'm sure that if Beverly knew Conrad was injured, she'd be here," Harry said, and then wrapped his arm around her shoulder. "Now, what time do you plan on returning?"

"Why? I'm not sure," Sylvia said. Her voice was slightly defensive, like she thought that Harry was trying to rush her.

"Well, why don't you call our massage therapist and see if she can come over this evening and give both of us a massage?" Harry asked.

Sylvia nearly squealed. "Oh my, that is a wonderful suggestion. I have missed Mena's services. And my poor bones could use a really good deep tissue massage."

Harry smiled. "Great. And since you're going to Baltimore, why don't you see if Penny can accompany you, and you two have a nice meal down at the Inner Harbor before you go to the hospital. You could go to O'Bryckie's or Mo's for crab cakes or something."

Sylvia tilted her cheek for her husband to kiss. "That sounds like a simply delicious idea. You always know what's best for me. And you always know the right thing to say, too, Harry."

"And when to say it," Harry said, with a wicked little laugh.

"I'll give Mena and Penny a call right now." Sylvia turned to go, but then paused. "Now, this doesn't mean that I won't see you at the hospital, does it?" she asked Harry, without even turning back around.

"Yes, dear," Harry said, and Sylvia's heels clicked across the floor.

"Hospitals. I hate those damned places," Harry said, and then took a seat opposite Joey, who still hadn't stopped eating. Joey was relieved that his father had such great timing, and had expertly diverted his ornery mother. It was almost second nature for his father, since he had spent over thirty years perfecting that craft.

"That smells good, Joey," Harry said as he took a fork from his place setting and pointed at his son's bowl. "Let me have a little bit."

On cue, a diminutive Genevieve appeared with Harry's meal. It was a healthy serving of lemon broiled salmon filet, with herbed rice and a mixed green salad. Harry's face contorted. "All this 'good for me stuff' is going to kill me. I'd rather have some of that pasta, Gen," he said. "And some garlic bread, heavy on the butter. And the garlic. I heard that garlic's good for your cholesterol. Isn't that right, son?"

"We're just following doctor's orders, Father," Joey said, and kept digging in his bowl.

Harry snatched his linen napkin and laid it on his lap. After saying grace, he picked at his fish. "I'm just about tired of this low fat, no taste diet. What's the point in living, if you can't enjoy your life? Not even a decent meal," Harry grumbled. "Well, at least I can put some of that fresh cheese on my salad," he said, and reached for the wedge.

Joey took a breather from his feast and pulled the cheese from his father's reach. As Genevieve brought in a gigantic iced mug of beer for him, and a glass of diet soda for his father, he handed the wedge to her. She smirked and headed back into the kitchen.

Harry scowled and pointed to his glass. "See what I mean?" he said. "*Vede che significo?* I can't even get a decent drink around here."

"We just want you to be around for a while, Father," Joey said with a hint of humor, but then his tone turned serious. "After all, there's a lot about our family that I want to know, but I just don't comprehend. I've got a lot to learn. Like the family council this afternoon. I just don't get it. I mean, how can you ever trust Uncle Edgy again?"

Harry sighed and picked at his food. "I know, son. Sometimes things happen unexpectedly. But, you try to make the best of them. Regarding your uncle, well, because your grandfather is the Consigliore, it was well within his power to request that your uncle's deeds be forgiven. Out of respect for him, I did. Certain things you do, you agree to, but don't necessarily like."

"But, don't think for one second that I've forgotten what he did, or that I don't still question why he did what he did. But, I have to honor the truce. We all do."

Joey swallowed a big gulp of his cold brew, and it chilled his searing pipes. "I understand, Father. I'm truly sorry about what happened, and I realize that neither Connie nor I are without fault in all of this. We're both to blame."

"I concur. In fact, I'm sure that all of my sires have had a hand in this fiasco. Including Christian and Madison. If your brother wasn't so gravely injured, I'd have all of you called on the carpet for your actions." Harry rested his fork, and folded his arms across his chest. "Let me tell you something. I may be old, but I haven't lost my marbles yet. You all are being quite closed about what occurred in my absence, and I know there's a lot more to this little debacle then what's being said."

Harry squinted at Joey, and Joey felt like he was a little boy again, who had gotten caught riding his dirt bike through his mother's prized lilies. "I want to know exactly where Connie got his stake from, and I'll call for an audit if I have to. So, if you have anything else you think you should share with me, now would be the time."

Joey looked his father in the eye, with an unwavering glare. "I don't have anything else to say about me or Christian or Connie, Father. Not at this moment."

Harry paused and searched Joey's face. "*Molto bene.* Very well. Hopefully, the moment you *want* to further discuss things will come quickly. And in the interim, I trust that you're trying to do the right thing. But, unlike before, you'll know when to ask for help, before it gets too late."

Joey nodded. His father was giving him the benefit of the doubt, and he jumped at the reprieve. "Thanks, Father. I appreciate the vote of confidence and advice. But, could I ask you a question?"

"Certainly."

"I know a lot of questionable things have transpired, and we all want to put this behind us. But, you'll have to forgive me if I have my doubts about Uncle Edgar's sincerity. And Vincent, well, he goes without saying. He appears to be worse than, well, worse than Connie. And, neither he nor his father seems really contrite."

Harry nodded, and used his fork to separate the grains of his rice. "Indeed. But, just because we have to adhere to your grandfather's edict doesn't mean that we turn a blind eye and deaf ear to what my brother or his son does going forward. Especially since they plan on staying in the area for a while. We have to protect what we've worked hard to build, and I'm not just speaking about monetary things. It's our reputation, our heritage, our standing in the community. It's who we are. It's our family's future, and no one is going to destroy that. No one. *Il sangue o altrimenti.* Blood or otherwise."

After Sylvia haughtily interrupted and abruptly left yesterday's meeting, Edgar had expressed his sincere desire to reconnect with his family, and take care of some loose ends. He decided that he and Vincent were going to stay with Grand, so that they could catch up on all of the missing years. Harry promptly nixed that idea, saying that it would not be in Grand's best interest to have his household disrupted for an extended period of time. Instead of offering them rooms at his home, Harry strongly suggested that they check into a hotel. Edgar downplayed his brother's strict recommendation, and said that they would check into the Grand Hyatt. Vincent seemed simply thrilled by his father's power play, and Harry was infuriated.

"I think that it would be in all of our best interest to know what my dear brother is up to. Especially, those loose ends he casually mentioned. Jolly has some of his best men watching them, but I'm still concerned. Let's just say that based on what I've heard about how Edgar's been handling his business in New York, I'm none too pleased," Harry said.

Joey figured that his father had been keeping tabs on Edgy, even though he never discussed it. Harry went on to say that Edgy's operation in the Big Apple had been involved in a number of sordid activities, including drugs. He was a major player in prostitution, extortion, heists, racketeering, illegal gambling and fencing. With Vincent flexing more and more power in his father's organization, those Cavanaughs were known for being exceptionally bloody and ruthless. They demonstrated little or no interest in cultivating any legitimate businesses, or being discreet in their actions. They were buck wild and didn't give a damn.

"They don't seem like the type of relatives we need to be associated with, Father," Joey said, as he pushed his bowl to the side. Suddenly, he had lost his appetite.

"Indeed," Harry said. "But, as you can see, it is quite complicated. As long as Edgar remains true to his word and doesn't deviate from our established practices, there's nothing that I can do. He is part of our family, and my brother will be treated as such. By all of us."

Harry grasped the back of his head and leaned backward in his seat. "Unless—"

"Unless, what?" Joey asked, his eyes narrowed and focused on his father.

The corners of Harry's mouth dropped, and he raised his brows. "Unless there's something that I'm missing. You know, there is one thing that has always bothered me, son. When Edgy left, he left in such a huff, that he took very little money with him. Not to say that he had a lot, anyway. Edgar was always quite free with his money. Quite flashy. But anyway, I know Papa didn't help him in any manner. But to his credit, your uncle is quite resourceful, and downright cunning. But, I've always wondered how he was able to get so far so fast in New York. Especially, given our history with the old families there. I would've thought New York would've been the last place he'd go."

Joey wasn't the least bit surprised by his father's revelations. Grand had shared with him the true history of the Cavanaughs, and it ran long, deep and bloody in New York. In short, Grand was the illegitimate son of an old school mobster named Vincenzo Cavanista and a Harlem showgirl named Maybelle Shaw. The Cavanaugh family name was a derivation of the Cavanista and Shaw surnames, and the false beginning of their lineage. It probably foreshadowed the unseemly events that followed their legacy, generation after generation.

Because the mulatto Grand impregnated and then married the daughter of another mobster named Salvatore Sallone, much blood and havoc were waged on the Cavanaugh sires. New York was the last place that Harry and Grand thought he would go. But it was the first, and only, place that he went.

Joey scratched his chin. Things didn't quite add up. "So, you're also wondering how Uncle Edgy got his stake?" His father nodded.

Anxious to redeem himself, Joey volunteered to find out. He knew it wasn't going to be easy, dredging up the past, but he had to find out. He had endured enough dealing with Connie all of his life. There was no way he was going to sign up to deal with the likes of Edgy and Vincent now that he was a grown assed man.

His father was reticent. "Just be discreet, Joseph. I can't outwardly condone what you're doing, because then I would be breaking the bond. And risk our position. And I don't want this to blow up in our collective faces, understand? *Capisca*?"

Joey stood and firmly shook his father's hand. "*Capisca*, Papa," Joey said, and mustered up a look of confidence. He knew that he would never let his father down again. Even if it meant that he'd have to give his life in the process.

Chapter 6

Madison's hand shook visibly as she sat in her first class seat on the Boeing 767 flight from Van Nuys to Washington, holding her complimentary barf bag and glass of fizzy ginger ale. She watched the tiny golden colored bubbles ascend from the bottom of the tumbler, and pop once they reached the surface. Even the minor sound of the fizzle was getting on her nerves, and she was thankful that she didn't have to be bothered with someone sitting next to her. She had the good sense to purchase the seat beside her, so that she wouldn't have to deal with an annoying businessmen, or anyone else for that matter. Just to ensure that she wouldn't be disturbed, she placed the airline issued headphones into her ears, but didn't bother to plug them into the audio system.

The ruse didn't work. Madison had to wave off the nosy flight attendant, who had so much greasepaint on her face that she looked like she had just finished an extensive run on the Great White Way. Looking at her made Madison nauseous. Madison held a cold compress to her head, and closed her eyes tightly. As her thoughts raged from shock to dismay, Madison wished that she had brought Ashley along for moral support. And to hold her barf bag.

Despite the grim circumstances surrounding her trip, Madison was quite upbeat as she embarked on her trip to California. Graham beat her hair, and her nails were flawless. Within two days, her personal shopper at Saks found her a gorgeous, steel gray and black linen Yves St. Laurent suit, with matching shoes. It was subdued, but fly, and she had similarly appropriate travel garb. After a confident, head-turning stroll through the Red Carpet Club at National Airport in her $350 Ferragamo pumps, she was feeling quite prepared to deal with the seeing Justin as he lay in state.

The flight to California was pleasant, and uneventful. The late summer skies were clear and bright, and as Madison relaxed in her seat, her thoughts ruminated on what lay ahead. How would she really respond at Justin's funeral? Could she hold herself together? Should she seek out his mother? She wanted to see Justin's son, Ian. And part of her really wanted to see what Justin's ex-wife looked like. Yes, she knew that she was being catty, but even as she grieved, she still had to be real with her feelings. And she wanted to know the type of woman her man had actually married. In the interim, she'd sip her Perrier Jouët Ashley had special ordered for her, and contemplate her next steps.

While the flight was turbulence free, and the landing smooth, Madison's world crashed and burned as soon as she arrived at Justin's service. Suddenly, the grieving girlfriend was more akin to being a survivor from a shipwreck; a long way from home, with no resources, dazed, confused, and virtually clueless as to how to endure. There was no shelter in sight, and storm clouds loomed overhead.

It never occurred to her that the life Justin had described to her had been pure fiction. When Madison arrived at the church, fashionably late of course, she clutched the obsequies as she took a seat on one of the rear pews. The funeral director had just closed the casket, and the minister was about to start the eulogy, when Madison opened the program, and nearly shrieked from shock. The matronly woman sitting beside her tried to comfort her, but Madison was inconsolable. The depth of her despair was glaring at her, right there in black and white. There was a *Mrs. Hunter,* not an *ex*-Mrs. Hunter; and no son Ian, but *three* young sons.

Madison choked back tears, and scanned the pews until her eyes landed on the front row. There she saw a small, unassuming looking, light brown-skinned woman, wearing all black. She had a nice grade of sandy brown hair, which was tightly pulled back into a bun. The woman was sobbing uncontrollably, as she held one child, and the other two clung to her from each side.

Madison's tears evaporated rapidly as she noticed how beautiful the children were. They were the spitting image of their father. They looked just like little cherubs, with their bronze complexions, and thick, dark, curly hair. Justin's children were absolutely gorgeous. They were almost stair steps, with the oldest probably no more than six, and the youngest, maybe two.

It broke Madison's heart to know that her lover had deceived her. And that she had repeatedly slept with another woman's husband. It made her sick to her core. With her head swirling, she was barely able to stumble out of the church before she collapsed in the back of her rented limousine, and vomited in the ice bucket.

When she awoke, Madison was in a private room in the emergency wing of Van Nuys Hospital. She was hooked up to a monitor, and a IV dripped in her arm. She immediately searched for a phone, and whe she spotted one setting on a rolling table that was across the room, she tried to get up, but felt woozy. She pressed the nurse call button, and demanded to speak to a doctor. While she waited to speak with the attending physician, many thoughts trailed through her mind. Madison couldn't understand why she was feeling so ill. She had never dealt with grief of this magnitude before, and perhaps it was her body's virginal reaction to the stress.

The doctor agreed with Madison that she was under too much stress, and it was adversely affecting her health. Her blood pressure was elevated, and her blood sugar was dangerously low. It was not a good combination, so he wanted to keep her at the hospital until her vital signs improved and stabilized. And the doctor advised her to take a few days before flying. At first Madison was relieved that she wasn't seriously ill, but when she heard the doctor's complete diagnosis, she faded to black again. She was eight weeks pregnant.

For the first time since his admittance, the entire family gathered around Connie's hospital bed. He had briefly regained consciousness, and Sylvia had summoned the whole family to his side.

Harry, Joey, and Christian all arrived within the hour, and Madison showed up shortly afterward. Joey noticed that his sister was extremely quiet, and when he asked her how she was doing, she was uncommonly reserved. He figured that she was still a little perturbed with Connie, and was having a hard time putting on a good front. They were both jockeying for the spot furthest from Connie's bed, each trying to do it on the sly, under Sylvia's hawkish eye. Joey finally stepped forward, so Madison could take a seat in the corner of the hospital room.

Connie was unable to speak, but responded by blinking his eyes. The doctor's were still very concerned about the bullet, which was lodged within two millimeters of his spine. They were working under the assumption that Connie had suffered nerve damage, and that he might be temporarily paralyzed. The physicians wouldn't move or speak on it until they were able to diagnose the extent of the damage.

"I'm prayerful that your brother will fully recover," Sylvia said softly, as she placed her hand over Connie's and caressed it. "And the doctors don't think that the bullet caused enough damage to require that he wear one of those awful colostomy bags." Sylvia shuddered with disgust, but then she broke out in a wide smile. "Oh, my God. Hejust squeezed my hand," Sylvia said, as Connie's sleepy eyes flashed, and his pupils were dull and milky.

Joey wondered if his mother would survive if her precious eldest child had died. Although she always claimed to love her children equally, it was an unstated, virtually unchallenged fact that Connie was her favorite.

As Sylvia continued fawning over Connie, wiping his forehead, and rubbing Vaseline on his lips, Joey's thoughts replayed what Kelly had said about his brother. This was all Connie's fault. Despite feeling badly that he was now bedridden, it was hard to feel entirely sorry for him. Connie was a selfish, amoral person, who generally went through life unscathed. He was a survivor at any cost. He would land on his feet even if it meant landing on top of someone else. He did whatever he wanted to do, without thought or regard for any life other than his own. When Joey thought about Beverly, Stewart and the countless other lives he had devastated, Connie's near vegetative state seemed like his just due.

Christian was rather subdued, looking a little starched in his conservative midnight blue Perry Ellis suit, while their father stood close to their mother's chair. When the doctor returned to discuss Connie's prognosis, Joey checked out mentally. His mind was on how to get the drop on his uncle. He quietly excused himself from the room, and went out into the visitor's lounge.

He was so lost in thought that he didn't notice that Christian was right on his heels, until he bumped into him when Joey stopped abruptly.

"I'm sorry about that, Joey," Christian said. "But, I wanted to speak with you for a moment."

Joey was immediately confused. He didn't dislike or even distrust Christian, he really had no feelings one way or the other. Except that Chris needed to chill the hell out. His constant uptight state reminded Joey of someone who needed more fiber in their diet. The bottom line was, he and Christian didn't have a lot of common interests, so they never had a whole lot to talk about. But, Joey forced himself to converse with him. "What's up, Chris?"

Christian gestured for Joey to sit, and the two sat down together on an orange vinyl three-seater. "This whole thing with Connie has me thinking," Christian said. "A lot has been happening in my life lately. Kim and I have been having a number of issues, and I've been quite unsure of how I want to live my life. When Connie got shot, it brought a lot of things into perspective. Life is truly too short to concentrate on trivial things. We all need to be about the business at hand."

Christian wasn't hardly lying. After forcing himself through a series of painful self-reflection, Christian had reached some bitter conclusions. He was self-absorbed, and had always thought of only himself. His selfishness had been the justification for skimming money from his own family because he didn't feel like he was getting his fair share. Not to mention he had to quell Kim's constant needling for more cash. His conscious had gone unchecked until the past month, when he met and had an extramarital affair with his assistant, an older woman named Jessica. She was worldly and compassionate, and had opened up his heart, his mind and his life in ways he'd never felt before. But, she was a kind, decent woman, and when her estranged husband was diagnosed with prostate cancer, she left an unsuspecting Christian to be by her ex-husband's side.

Jessica's introduction into, presence in, and departure from his life had really propelled his ordinarily mundane life into a tailspin. Christian had a wretched relationship with Kim, and he really wanted to leave her and say goodbye to the loveless prison he called his marriage. But, then he had to think about their children. Where he normally excelled at most things, he hadn't been a great parent, and it was one of the things Christian had recently vowed to do. To become a better father and to be a more productive member of his family. And when Connie's reckless behavior compromised the family in untold ways, Christian had to also consider how his actions had punctured the family's security.

He had always been so arrogant when it came to comparing himself to his siblings, and he always faulted them for any thing that went awry. But now, he was culpable, and it didn't set very well. Suddenly, Christian had realized that his life was far more complicated than he had ever given it credit for being. His glass house was being pelted with stones, and he had to confront his eternal denial of being human like everyone else. He had to be responsible for his actions, and more importantly, he had to do something about it.

Christian had thought about confiding in Joey about his larcenous ways, especially since Joey was on the hot seat and could probably sympathize. But, then Christian had a second thought. Connie had been suspicious of him and his handling of the family's financials, that's why Connie had tried to lure him into being a co-conspirator in the unsanctioned deal. And when Christian didn't bite, he knew that he had made a serious enemy with Connie. Now, he had some difficult decisions to make. His choices were bad and worse.

But maybe Connie wouldn't survive, and then Christian's secret would be taken to the grave with him. Christian scolded himself for having such a selfish thought, but it was a possibility. Or he could feign ignorance for now, and keep his fingers crossed and hope that if Connie survived and started spilling his guts, Christian could claim that Connie was delusional. Or Christian could level with Joey, and curry his favor, and forge an alliance that might shield him from any backlash should Connie survive. But, the most immediate course of action was for Christian to rectify his financial indiscretions, and make them disappear before either his father or Joey figured it out. And, now was the perfect time, with Connie out of the loop, and possibly forever impaired. Whichever path he chose to walk, Christian knew he was entering a live minefield, and that he'd have to step extra carefully.

Joey stared at his younger brother, and tried to figure out where he was going with all of this. But, he kept quiet, and let Christian continue blathering.

"I feel bad, because I knew Connie was up to no good, and I didn't say anything. But, I was going through my own issues at the time, so I really didn't give it too much thought. But, I didn't give him the money. At least, not for the deal."

Christian cleared his throat, and Joey wondered why Christian was clearing his conscience. They weren't Catholic, and this was no confessional. Plus, Joey certainly didn't stand in any position to judge anyone, not even his selfish younger brother. He and Christian didn't have the type of relationship that would even make sharing deep-seated secrets a consideration.

"Well, what *did* you help him with?"

"I knew about the limos he acquired to set up Jury and Dante's termination. But, let me clarify. I only discovered that after the fact."

"Did you speak to Father about this?" Joey asked. He himself was still smarting from Harry's reaming out a few days ago, but at least he had been man enough to take it. "You might want to own up to it. A-S-

A-P. He's thinking about calling for an audit, so you may want to save him the time and the trouble."

"I'll talk to him about it, but I'm sure he probably won't believe me. I know that I haven't been as good of a son or brother as I could be, but I know that I can be a better person. I've done some things that I'm not very proud of, and I want to make amends about everything."

Joey shared the same sentiments, but stayed mum. One Cavanaugh exposing his soul was more than enough. Especially since that didn't occur very often.

"Let your conscience be your guide, Christian. If you've done some things that can be rectified, then that's what you need to do. Stand up and do the right thing. Before it's too late."

Christian nodded. "I agree, and I plan on doing that. I just think that now that Connie's out of imminent harm, we ought to let bygones be bygones, and try to coexist like brothers. Like a real family. Especially—"

"Especially now that Edgar and Vincent are on the scene, threatening to cause even more damage," Joey said, completing Christian's sentence. "They're holed up in the Grand Hyatt, probably scheming on how they can take us down. Or take over the family."

"Precisely," Christian said. "And, I think that it might be in our best interest to try to get Conrad on board with us too. When he's cognizant. We need to be on one accord, for once in our lives."

"Good luck," Joey said, thinking that the last time Connie had seen him was when Joey was staring down a gun barrel at him. But, it wasn't like he wasn't defending himself by reciprocating Connie's lethal actions.

"Perhaps you're right, Christian. We do need to stick together, and I'm sure that we present a united front and bring it to Connie, hopefully, he'll join us. It's going to take all that we have to keep this family together, because our relative worms from the Big Apple are probably here to do us in. But, I'm on it. I'm not about to let that happen."

Christian leaned closer, and cut his eyes at his brother. "You really think so, huh? Well, if you know something, do tell."

Joey gave Christian the abridged version of his plans to delve into Edgy's background, and he was surprised when the normally reserved Christian volunteered his participation.

"Count me in, Joey. Whatever I can do to help you, I'm in."

Joey and Christian were still conducting their meeting of the minds in the lounge, when the rest of the family trailed out of Connie's room.

"Conrad's sleeping now, so I'm going to take your mother home to get some rest," Harry said, as he wrapped one arm around Sylvia's shoulder, and held Madison's hand with the other. "Come on, my beautiful *signora*. My beautiful lady."

"But, I'll be back tomorrow. Bright and early," Sylvia said, and gave her sons a somber look. "And I expect you to stay close to your brother during his recuperation, young men. That should go without saying."

Joey and Christian mumbled a sincere reply, while Madison still remained quiet.

Sylvia turned her attention toward Joey. "So, has everything been taken care of at Conrad's? Did you do what I asked you to?"

"Yes, M'Dear. Ashley's employee is at Connie's, and is committed to being there until further notice," Joey said. He had meant to tell his mother before she asked, but it had slipped his mind.

"Well, that's one less thing to worry about, I guess. I'm sure your brother will be very pleased," Sylvia said, and turned on her heels without even thanking Joey for his effort.

The family walked out to the parking garage, where the Cavanaughs' driver waited in their stately black Fleetwood Cadillac. Joey had offered to take Madison home, but she declined. She had arranged to catch a ride with their parents.

The chrome wheels sparkled as the spotless Caddie slowly made its way out of downtown Baltimore. Sylvia's spirits were high, and she was chatting about getting on with her life, now that Connie was out of danger.

"I can't wait to get started planning my, I mean 'our' holiday soiree," she said, and patted Harry on the knee. "In lieu of everything that's happened so far this year, I think that I'm going to do something totally different. Something fresh. Maybe a masquerade ball or something unique. What do you think, Madison? That'll be a nice departure from our usual. A distinct change is probably what we all need."

Sylvia was referring to the Cavanaugh Annual Holiday Extravaganza that they hosted during the Christmas season. Normally, Madison, her Aunt Penny, and her mother planned the party down to the most minute detail. But at this moment, it was totally lost on Madison, who had more important things on her mind.

Madison took a deep breath, and raised the privacy window. "That all sounds lovely, but— M'Dear. Father. I have something important to tell you."

Sylvia prattled about the upcoming party, until Madison, who couldn't take it anymore, finally interrupted her.

"Mother," Madison said, her voice cracking.

"Yes, Dear," Sylvia said, and turned toward her daughter. Harry leaned forward, and looked at Madison too.

"This is very difficult to say, but I have to. Something very important is going on in my life, and I want you to know about it."

Harry and Sylvia exchanged glances without turning their heads, and then turned their attention back to Madison. *"Accende, il tesoro,"* Harry said. "Go on, baby."

Madison steadied her nerves. "I'm, um, well. There's no easy way to say this, so, I'll just say it." She took a deep breath. "I'm pregnant," Madison said in a voice so strong, that she kind of startled herself. She wasn't sure what their reaction was going to be, but she had to tell them.

"*What?*" Sylvia shrieked, and collapsed in the plush seat with a dramatic huff. "Have you taken leave of your senses? Pregnant? I wasn't even aware that you were engaging in sexual activity." Harry turned his head toward the window.

Madison bit her lower lip. "That's not important right now, M'Dear. What is, is that I'm carrying a child. And that's not something that happens everyday. It's not something I planned, and I tried to be careful."

Sylvia walloped Harry on the knee and huffed. "Harrison, did you hear what your child just said? Did you?" She grabbed Madison by the chin. "Who's the father?" Sylvia paused, and then rolled her eyes. "Oh, good Lord, don't even say it." Sylvia clucked her teeth. "My God, how much more of this can I take? Father God, just take me now."

Madison calmly removed her mother's hand from her face. "This isn't about you, M'Dear. This is about me, and my child."

"Your child? You say that like you plan on keeping it," Sylvia said, and clutched Harry's knee until his pants rustled. "Harry? Harry? Oh, help me, Jesus." Sylvia fanned herself with her free hand.

Since she had been informed of her pregnancy, Madison had never considered not having her baby. And, her mother's reaction didn't surprise her. But, Madison was surprised by her own calm and rational demeanor. Perhaps all of the years of being primed in the Cavanaugh couth had paid off.

"I'm not asking for your help, M'Dear. Nor was I expecting that you'd welcome this news with open arms and throw a baby shower for me. I just wanted to let you know what was going on in my life."

"I'm flabbergasted, Madison. How can you even *consider* bringing this shame on yourself and on our family? How can you ever expect to get married with another man's child?" Sylvia shook her head. "An illegitimate child? Puh-leeze. Haven't we endured enough already?" Sylvia asked, her voice pleading and shrill.

Madison gripped her armrest, and waited until the heat passed from her face. "It's funny how you accepted Connie's two illegitimate children, M'Dear. But, that's okay. I'll be fine. Me and my child will be just fine."

"Well, I certainly hope that you know what you're getting yourself into, Missy. Because you'll get no help from us, do you hear me? Not one bit."

There was an uneasy silence in the car, until Harry finally reached across his wife's lap, grabbed his daughter's hand and spoke. "That's a little harsh, Sylvia. And Madison is correct. If you've found some way to accept Conrad's children out of wedlock, well, then we will accept Madison's child also. This may not be an ideal situation, but you are our child, and we will love you regardless." Harry drew his daughter's hand to his lips and gently kissed it. "I want you to always know that your family is here for you. There's nothing more important than knowing that, do you understand, my darling?"

Chapter 7

Christian palmed his chin as he leaned on the arm of his chair. Seated behind his office desk, his mind refused to focus on anything, which made him extremely uncomfortable. His personal life was in shambles, and for the first time, he didn't have an obvious or logical solution.

He was the master of perfectionism and order, yet he had seen his talents and gifts get caught under the boulder of lies that threatened to reduce his life to rubble. His family, the cornerstone of his world, was in utter chaos. And Christian, normally the first one to assign blame, was now one of the ones to be blamed.

With the advent of Connie surviving, the drug deal gone sour was going to come back to implicate both he and Christian. Christian's conversation with Joey hadn't gone too well, with Joey not offering to side up with him. Christian normally thrived being in an autonomous state, but now he just felt vulnerable.

Then there was the threat of the audit his father called for looming over his head. Sooner or later, Christian knew that his father would figure out where the funds Connie bankrolled his illicit activity came from. And although Christian wasn't directly liable, he had knowledge of Connie's intentions, and could have tried to stop him. He didn't and Christian knew that his time was running out before everyone knew what he did. His carefully constructed house of cards was about to come crashing down, and he was the joker sitting on top of the deck.

Then there were the financial improprieties Christian had taken over the years, and that was bound to catch up with him too. He could almost hear the sound of the clock ticking, indicating that his time was up. Christian drummed his thick fingers on his desk, and sighed. Perhaps the best thing to do would be to confess, but the most logical thing would be to cover it up. Since his father was threatening an audit, Christian proactively and painstakingly went over the financial records, to ensure that his misdeeds would go undetected. He decided to take some of his ill-gotten gains and spread them across the family's stock holdings and investments. He felt a little better, but he still felt like a swindler because he couldn't return all of the money he had pilfered. He needed it to exist. His nest was thoroughly feathered, but he had a big falcon sitting atop of it. His wife Kim. And her talons were sharp and deadly.

Kim. Christian almost shuddered. Their marriage was such a sham, and just a few weeks ago, he was finally ready to leave her for Jessica. But that didn't work out, and Christian was devastated, but he knew that he didn't want to stay with Kim. But, then his five-year-old daughter Paige tugged on the brittle strings of his hardened heart, and he gave a second thought to staying for his children's sake. It had only been a few weeks, but Christian was beginning to feel that staying in his loveless marriage was a major mistake.

Kim was just unbearable as a wife, but she was a good mother. A much better mother than he ever was a father, and he regretted admitting that. But for the past few weeks, he had mad ardent strides toward making a deeper emotional connection with his children, and he could see an improvement in their relationship. But he and Kim still struggled.

Though he tried, it was apparent that Kim really didn't know him, nor did she probably ever really love him. Christian assumed that Kim realized that he could provide a lifestyle for her she could probably never acquire on her own. Christian sighed. "What am I going to do?"

He was committed to his children, including his sons Christian II and Morgan. But, he had to figure out how he could be a more integral part of their lives without saddling himself with the crushing weight of Kim's baggage. It was a difficult call. She had threatened to take him to the cleaners if he divorced her. Maybe they could just separate. Maybe not.

Christian had fallen back into his sullen old habits, feeling like he was merely existing instead of thriving and living like he was when Jessica was in his life. It was Saturday, and he was in his office at the family's corporate headquarters. Despite Connie being in the hospital, Christian had gotten up early, worked out in the gym, and taken refuge behind his desk. He checked his ever-present electronic organizer for a run down of his activities and appointments. Deftly pressing the buttons, a reminder popped up that Morgan had a soccer game later that afternoon, and Christian was going to take him.

With his office door open, Christian's eyes drifted over to Jessica's former desk in the outer office. It was the desk where they had shared many moments, laughing and talking. She had brought so much into this life. She strengthened him. She made him feel loved, and softened his hardened heart. She made him be a better man. Now, he didn't even know where she was. Or if she'd ever come back. Those warm feelings Jessica had unearthed had been quickly replaced with cold, empty ones. Feelings that he had spent too many years with before, and longed to banish them forever from his life.

Christian crested his fingertips, and closed his eyes. He could smell her perfume. The way she felt when he held her. He recalled the sweet, forbidden love they had made all over his office. She had even inspired him to play his cello again. And he hadn't touched it since she left.

He got up, and then walked over to the closet in his office and removed his prized instrument from its case. He removed the bow, and strummed out a few melodic chords. Suddenly, he felt alive, like Jessica was with him again, but his pleasurable thoughts were shattered as Kim's piercing voice infiltrated his musical interlude.

"Christian?"

Christian dropped the bow, and opened his eyes. He sighed when he saw Kim standing in the doorway to his office, holding a wicker basket that had a loaf of French bread sticking out of it.

"Kim? What are you doing here?"

"Well, you left in such a rush this morning, and when you mentioned that there was some urgent family business to take care of, I was concerned. And then when I didn't hear from you all day, I got really concerned."

Christian slitted his eyes. He had mentioned to her that Connie was hospitalized, but he hadn't told her anything else. Now she was pretending to care, and Christian wasn't buying it. "Well, Kim. I wasn't aware that I had to check in with you on a regular basis."

Kim forced a smile. "Now Christian. You don't have to check in, but you should be considerate. When you hurriedly left the house, and said that there was s a problem with the family, well, it's not absurd to think that I'd be a little worried. And then I called your parent's house, and Geneveive said that they were at the hospital. So, I didn't know what to think. But, I figured that you'd be here, if you weren't with your family." She patted the picnic basket. "I thought it might be nice to come down and bring you something to eat."

Christian eyed his wife with even greater suspicion. She was wearing a sharp, form-fitted, sage linen pants suit, with no blouse. Her cleavage was ample and a thick Gucci-link gold chain hung around her neck. Her consideration drew Christian's suspicions. He thought that she'd probably try to poison him, and he made a mental note to make sure Kim ate first.

Kim really didn't have a kind or gracious bone in her body, but she displayed great warmth with and lioness-like protection over their children. It was the one thing that Christian admired about her. But when it came to him, Christian might as well had been an ATM. Kim withdrew and withdrew, but never, ever, deposited anything.

"That was nice of you to think of me," Christian said, and held his instrument. "But, I'm not really hungry."

Kim crossed the room and laid the basket down on the sofa. "I think you should try it, Chris. It's some of your favorites. I had Millie put together a nice Italian sub, with lots of proscuitto ham and smoked turkey. And even some Gouda cheese." She turned around, with a slight smile, and held a white wrapped foot long.

Christian wondered what Kim could have slipped inside the sandwich. Cold cuts would be difficult to tamper with, unless they were rancid. Maybe it was poisoned mustard or mayonnaise.

Kim wasn't one to take no for an answer, so Christian carefully placed his cello back in the case, and contemplated his next move.

"Why are you putting that away? I'd like to hear you play. It's been so long since I've even seen you with your cello, and it reminds me of when we were in school and you were in the orchestra." Kim's eyes flashed. "Why don't you bring it home so you and the children can play together. You know Morgan is becoming quite adept on the violin, and Christian is quite the little Andre Watts."

Kim's statements were enough to push Christian over the brink. She was using every tool in her little bag of tricks to manipulate him, and Christian wasn't trying to hear it. He knew that Kim was a masterful game player, but even he wasn't about to let her play with him like he was a cat's ball of yarn.

"Look, Kim. What's going on? Why are you acting like you care about me or my playing the cello? You're giving me entirely too much."

Kim handed him the sandwich, and smiled. "I'm just trying to be a part of your life, Christian. And involve you more in this lovely family we created. I think that's something that I haven't placed a lot of effort in before. Making you feel that you are wanted and needed."

Before Christian could respond, Kim kept talking. "I'm tired of living in the past, Christian. How can we ever have a future, if we keep reliving the past?"

Christian stared at his wife. "Well, what you said does have some validity, Kim. But I have to ask you something. Why now?"

"Maybe it took for me to almost lose you to realize how much you mean to me. And to our family."

Christian twisted his mouth. "Please, Kim. You're killing me with this new found 'family' initiative you've taken. Hmmph. Just last week you were threatening to divorce me. And maybe that's not such a bad idea."

Kim continued fishing in the basket and pulled out a small plastic container. "And I have potato salad," she said, patently ignoring him.

"Damn the potato salad, Kim," Christian said, and then snatched the container from her hands. "Did you hear what I said? Our marriage is a farce, and has been for years, and you're in here offering me potato salad like that's going to make it okay."

Kim grabbed the salad from Christian and flung it onto Christian's imported Persian rug, spilling it's bright yellow contents. "Is that what you want, Christian? For me to come in here and show my ass? Well, here it is." Kim rolled her eyes. "See, what you made me do? I'm trying not to go there with you. I'm trying to save my, I mean our marriage."

Christian grabbed a tissue from his desk aand scooped up the salad. "Look at what you did," he said and shook his head. "I swear, sometimes you really lack home training." He disposed of the spilled goods and reached into his pocket and removed a linen handkerchief. He then opened his mini-refrigerator and grabbed a bottle of seltzer water. He moistened the hankie and deftly went about working on the stain. "How the hell can we save what we never had? We never had a marriage. We simply had an arrangement. A contract. A very costly one. Face it, those vows we took meant nothing."

"Meant nothing to who? You? I was serious as a heart attack when we got married, Christian. Were you?"

Christian's focus on cleaning the rug infuriated Kim. "Well, were you playing with me, Christian? I told you, I was serious about being with you. I wasn't playing a game."

Scrubbing at the stain, Christian turned his head upward and glared at his wife. "Oh you weren't? Well, what were you doing then? Certainly not loving me. Maybe you were just serious about becoming a Cavanaugh. Damn, I wish you'd met Connie before you met me. You two would've had the perfect union. Two cold, heartless, bloodsuckers together."

Kim took her open hand and right checked Christian across his square chin. "Shut up, Christian. Don't say such trifling shit like that. I didn't marry your brother. I married you."

Christian grabbed her wrist and swung it downward. "Don't hit me, Kim. Don't you ever put your hands on me again. I was raised not to hit a woman, but you're about to be the exception to that rule."

"What do you want from me? Huh? I'm swallowing my pride and I'm willing to forgive you for your little tryst with that old bag. Don't forget, I could clean your ass out for adultery." Kim slammed the basket down on the floor.

Christian glanced at his wristwatch and smirked. "Well, that's a record. I figured that you'd mention divorcing me in about twenty minutes. And you did it in fifteen and a half. Bravo."

He stepped past her, and perched himself on the edge of his desk. "Now, why don't you get out of here, with your little basket of goodies and bad tidings. Be gone," he said, and waved her away.

Kim's jaw dropped. "How dare you. You don't dismiss like I'm the hired help."

"For all intents and purposes, you are. You might as well be a well-paid surrogate. Because you damn sure aren't and have never been a real wife to me."

Kim glared at him. "Like you've been a real husband or a real father to us. You have a lot of damned nerve. What about our children? Do you think that's fair that their father is trying to leave their family because some old tired trick has turned him out?"

Christian balled up his fists and placed his knuckles down on his desk. "Listen to me. You better stop referring to Jessica in this manner. She has more class in her baby toe then you have in your whole body."

She pointed a painted finger in the air and twisted it around. "Don't compare me to that tramp. I'm a wife and a mother, not a piece on the side. *Please.* Get real, Christian. Leave it to you to get sprung by a damned piece of old ass. You can't even have an affair the right way. You failed lesson number one on how to creep." Kim pointed her painted index finger in the air. "You're supposed to screw the piece on the side and keep her there. On the side. Away from you're damned family."

Christian looked her up and down. "So, is that how you do it? Well then, why don't you show me some of your tricks, Kim? I'm sure you have a million of them. Especially, since you haven't slept with me for months now. I'm sure you keep the other guys in check. And on the side where, according to your infinite wisdom, that's where they're supposed to be."

"That was on you, Christian. You don't have a speck of dirt on me, brother man. Check this out. I don't sleep around. You left me high and dry, acting like you didn't want none of this anymore. So, I said forget you. I know how to do me." Kim twisted her neck and rolled her eyes at him.

"That's because every time I turned around, you were pregnant. What made you think that's what I wanted?"

Kim dropped her arms by her sides. "What?"

"You heard me."

"Are you saying that you don't want our children?" Her voice elevated and quivered, and her eyes stretched.

"I didn't say that. But, it would have been nice if you had at least discussed it with me. You popped those kids out without a moment's rest, Kim. *One-two-three.* And trust, it wasn't a reach to think that you'd put another one on me to make sure I didn't go anywhere. Or, if I did, that I'd be sure to leave my wallet and checkbook with you."

"Is that what you really think? Why didn't you ever tell me that's how you felt?"

"Why should I? Didn't you have enough sense to realize that pushing out kids one after another wasn't right? That's not how you make a marriage work, Mrs. Cavanaugh. We barely had time to deal with 'us' before we were dealing with children. I never wanted our marriage to be like that."

Kim's large eyes filled with tears, and she turned her head. "That's just so messed up, Christian. I never knew that's how you felt. I never knew."

Christian watched his wife as she walked to the sofa and plopped down. Part of him thought that she was gaming him, but there was something sincere and slightly vulnerable about her.

Perhaps Kim really didn't know. Communication was never one of their strong suits, and he had never told her that he wasn't ready for three little ones in four years. Kim came from a broken home, and had a number of siblings. Perhaps she thought that was what she was supposed to do. Get the man and make the babies. He wanted to reach out to her, but was afraid that she'd lash out at him.

"You really didn't know, Kim?"

The tears fell freely from her eyes as she lunged toward him. Pummeling him with all of her might, she landed blow after blow on Christian's tightened chest.

Christian grabbed both of her wrists and gripped them until her heavy gold bracelets were mashed into her skin. "Stop it. I told you not to hit me again, dammit."

Angry tears fell from Kim's eyes, and her lips quivered. She snatched her arms from his grasp. "Why can't you just act right? You've never acted right, Christian. You're so damned distance and unapproachable. I could never reach you. You never even tried to make our marriage work. Never." Kim's chest heaved, and she glared at Christian.

"I guess that makes two us," Christian said.

"You make me sick! I swear, I won't let you ruin our family. I won't," she said.

"Fuck you, Kim."

Kim grabbed Christian by the collar. "Why don't you then, since you're so big and bad now."

"What?"

"I wish you would," Kim said, sounding almost needy and chaste.

Christian yanked his wife toward him and pressed his lips against hers, locking his eyes with hers. Kim's face registered surprise, but she met him with matched force and ferocity.

"Don't play with me, woman," Christian growled at his wife with a gruffness he had never displayed.

With one swift motion, paperclips, the abacus and every other item from Christian's desk went sailing to the floor as Kim leapt onto Christian's abdomen, and wrapped her legs around him. "Come on, baby. Do me, daddy."

For the first time in months, Mr. and Mrs. Christian Cavanaugh invoked on a mission to make wild, passionate sex. Christian's pent up frustration and rage was matched by Kim's unbridled sexual prowess. She yanked his suspenders down, and grabbed at his crotch. The normally sedate and sanguine Christian unleashed his beast as he pulled Kim's slacks off, and she stepped out of her panties.

"That's right, give it to me, daddy," she said, and pushed his head back.

"I'm going to give it to you alright," Christian said, breathing heavily and ravishing her neckline. Just as Kim unhooked his belt, the telephone rang. Acting out of character, Christian ignored it and focused on his wife. Until his cell phone rang. And kept ringing.

"That might be important, Kim. I better get it," Christian said, while Kim continued relieving him of his trousers.

"Get some of this lovin' first," she said, running her ornately painted nails through his hair, and thrusting her face inside his silk boxers.

Joey shoved his cordless phone into the pocket of his silk robe after unsuccessfully trying to reach Christian. He didn't even bother to leave him a message prompting Christian to talk to their father. Joey figured that he'd wait until they were face to face, where his suggestion would have a greater impact.

He stepped into his master bathroom, and hung his robe on the hook on the back of the door, and left the door slightly ajar. He caught a glimpse of himself in the mirror and smiled. But the cheeriness quickly dissipated. He was in pretty good shape for someone who hadn't hit the gym lately, but then he was disappointed when he realized that he'd have to find another gym to join. The one he frequented was just a meet market, and Joey wasn't about to temp fate by being around a pack of sweaty, ready and available men. Moreover, he might run into Kelly there, and he definitely wasn't ready for that encounter.

The wraparound shower was on full blast, and Joey carefully stuck his foot in the stall, and slowly worked his way in until he was fully immersed. The water was so hot, it made his skin tingle and redden, and the steam filled the bathroom with dense air. Joey could barely breathe as he took his thick, soapy washcloth and scrubbed his body, and felt the water beat against his taut muscles.

He submerged himself, and let the water cascade over his face and fill his nostrils. He held his breath and thought about the events of last night. After downing a few beers, Joey had fallen asleep in front of the television, where he dozed until his cell phone rang at one a.m., from the unidentified caller. When he answered it, the caller again said nothing.

These phone calls had surpassed annoying. Who was it? Was it Kelly playing silly games? Or was it Lauren? Surely she wouldn't stoop to such childishness. He tried to dismiss it and shut off his phone after deciding to change his number the next day. Since he was wide awake, Joey got up from his resting place, slipped on some jeans, tee shirt, and a baseball cap, and walked over to Constitution Avenue, where he hailed a cab to one of the underground dance clubs. That would take his mind off of things.

Within moments of entering the darkened club, he met some hot body, and had taken him over to one of his usual hotels in Alexandria, where they had mind-numbing sex until dawn. His body was satiated during those torrid moments, but now, he felt empty, dirty and disappointed. How had his life descended into an unfulfilling series of desperate one-night stands and loneliness?

Since his foray with Lauren, Joey had shied away from any more convenient relationships with women, and had instead, thrust himself into the anonymity of meeting strange men in darkened clubs and bars, and taking them to obscure motels for illicit sex. That had happened before in his past, but since meeting Kelly, Joey was determined not to get caught up again. He'd never allow any other stranger to infiltrate his wall of secrecy, and make himself into an unwelcome guest in his life. Joey would keep it on the low, until he figured out why he was so damned confused about his life.

But, what happened with Lauren really tormented him. Initially, she was just a beard; something nice to hang on his arm, but somehow she became more. Much more. Lauren, unlike all of the other ladies Joey had gotten involved with, had a depth of character and personality that struck a chord in him. He wasn't able to cut her loose like he had easily done the others.

He really cared for her, and they had shared many special moments. She was beautiful, strong, sensitive, and had a brilliant mind. She embodied many of the attributes any man would want in a woman.

They saw each other for almost a year, but they never had a stated commitment. Their relationship was relaxed and fun, and one of the best ones Joey had ever experienced. He had even introduced Lauren to his mother and sister, which was a truly rare occurrence. She had progressed far beyond where any of her female predecessors had, and that was almost a miracle in and of itself. But, despite that breakthrough, Joey continued to keep Lauren on the fringes of his duplicitous life. And she seemed okay with that.

But, there was something strong between them. He missed Lauren and despite all of her deceitfulness and contrition, he had to admit that her actions only mirrored his. But, she had proven to be very considerate of his feelings, and hadn't revealed any of his secrets. Especially that he was Connie's shooter. Or about any other incriminating thing she might have discovered during her months of undercover surveillance of his life.

Joey lowered his head, and the warm water streamed down his neck, clinging to his eyelashes. He wiped his eyes and stared at the copper colored walls of his Italian marble tiled bathroom. What was he going to do?

And, on the other side of the fence was Kelly. He had helped Joey out so much during the time leading up to the showdown on the docks, and although the had met under less than favorable circumstances, he and Joey had shared some very special moments together too.

Initially, Joey didn't trust Kelly. Partially because they had met after a torrid one night stand, and Kelly was a cop. They were different, almost opposites, but Kelly had proven to be more than just a nameless lay. And Joey had come to like him as a person, and they had developed a strange psychological partnership. Kelly instinctively knew how to appeal to Joey's inner being, and satisfied him physically and challenged him emotionally. This was foreign territory for him, because he had never allowed a man into his life in that capacity. Especially not one he had slept with.

So, on one hand, he had trustworthy Kelly, who was a upright brother who shared his sexual peccadilloes. Then, there was Lauren. A good woman, but on the wrong side of the family's culture. The law and the Cavanaughs never mixed. Joey sighed. Life just couldn't be easy.

He continued his shower, and scrubbed himself until his skin was almost sore. He needed to cleanse, to purge. To rid himself of the filthy thoughts about his last wanton sexual indulgence. He made a tough, and hopefully not rash, decision. He was going to steer clear of dealing with anyone else until he figured whom he was going to deal with. Male or female. Kelly or Lauren. But, he also decided that he needed to face Lauren, at least to set his mind at ease about his muddled feelings. He had to find out if the feelings between them were real, and if he was even capable of feeling. And, then he'd have to address whatever it was he had with Kelly. Especially since there was a greater probability that he'd run into him sooner than later. And he wanted to make sure he'd be ready to deal with him.

Chapter 8

"That was an absolutely lovely meal, Penny," Sylvia said as she and her sister-in-law retired to the spacious glass-enclosed Florida room at Penny and Jolly's home, while Harry and Jolly indulged in cognac in the den. Sipping her sherry, Sylvia said, "Thank you so much for inviting us. I can't tell you how much I really appreciate it. It was such a welcome change from all of this strife."

They had dined on oven-fried tilapia, with crisp seasonal vegetables and robust roasted potatoes. It was a real treat, for Penny was an excellent cook and hostess, and unlike Sylvia, she rarely allowed her maid to prepare a meal. Sylvia didn't even mind when Harry heaped Penny's famous homemade bleu cheese dressing onto his baby spinach salad. Sylvia was just elated to be out and temporarily escape the hideous issues that consumed her and her family as of late.

"You're quite welcome, dear," Penny said, and nipped on her vodka tonic. "You've been spending so much time at the hospital, and with everything else that's going on, I thought it would be nice to have you and Harry over. And, it's the least we could do for your hosting us in Bermuda. We had a wonderful time."

"Pish-posh, Penny. That was nothing. You know I always enjoy you and my brother's company. After all, you are my dearest friend." Sylvia stroked Penny's hand. "But, I can't say that this hasn't been an extremely stressful time in my life. Sometimes I don't know if I'll be able to persevere."

Penny nodded. She had stood with Sylvia during some difficult moments, but this one topped the list.

"I can't imagine what you've been going through, Syl. With Conrad injured, and now Edgar coming back under these circumstances, it must be hard on you. But, I know you. You'll pull through just fine."

"But for the grace of God, I'll make it. As long as the Lord gives me strength, I'll get by. I'm determined to get through this. I just don't know what's been more troubling to me. The fact that my child was nearly killed, or that his uncle had a hand in it. Either way, the whole situation has made sleeping a real hardship for me."

Again, Penny nodded. "It doesn't seem like Edgar would want to bring any harm to Connie since he's so much like him, wouldn't you say?"

Sylvia raised an eyebrow. She didn't want to alienate Penny, but she didn't like what Penny was intimating. "I hadn't really thought about that, Penny. What are trying to insinuate?"

Penny cleared her throat. "I'm not insinuating anything, Syl. I meant that you and Edgar were so close, once upon a time, that you'd think he wouldn't want to hurt your child. You two used to do *so* much together, and he was always such a gentleman. I just wonder what might've gone wrong with him."

Sylvia sighed. Penny was right. She and Edgar were close, and despite his hot headedness and ill temper, he always treated her with the utmost regard. Whenever Harry was unavailable or uninterested, Edgar gladly squired Sylvia around town. He was fun and generous, and Sylvia had enjoyed his company. That was until Edgar took up with Marjorie Blake, and took complete and total leave of his senses. But, Edgar had always been one of Sylvia's staunchest supporters, and she couldn't imagine that he would endanger the life of her oldest child like he had.

"I know, Penny." Sylvia fanned herself with her hand. "It hurts me to my heart. But, many suns have set since Edgar and I were close, and I guess he just doesn't embrace the principles of family like we do." Sylvia shook her head.

"Is he still good looking?"

Sylvia nodded. "He's still a handsome man, what hasn't been wrought with evil. But, I mean, he looks the same. Just older and more distingushed, but it's almost like he's a complete stranger. I've only seen him once since he's been here, and I don't know anything about him. I wasn't even aware that he had children. And who did he have them with. I don't know if he's married, or if he has any other children. Legitimate or otherwise." Sylvia sighed, and shifted in her seat.

"I have to admit that part of me is curious. And then again, I guess I really don't want to know about Edgar and what he's been doing all of these years. I mean it hurt me to my heart when he left, but it was his own doing. And he didn't have to leave. But, that's who Edgar is. Never one to listen or to be patient. I guess with regard to that, he and Connie do have a lot in common."

Sylvia's mouth twisted and she sighed. "I wish I could blink my eyes and make all of this go away, but I can't. Nor can I forgive him for what he did to my child. It would be a lot easier to put Edgar out of my mind if I knew he had slithered his way back to New York, but even that's not going to happen any time soon."

"What do you mean?"

"Edgar and his son Vincent are going to stay here for a while. Perhaps, indefinitely."

"You've got to be kidding, right? Harry's okay with that?"

"Well, actually, Grand stepped in and okayed it."

"What? I need to put this drink down because I'm hearing things," Penny said, but didn't relinquish her toddy.

"You heard me. Can you believe it? Of all times. Grand just had to have a moment of clarity when Edgar shows up. And he's quite insistent about it. He says he wants all of us to put the past behind us and become one big loving family." Sylvia fluttered her lashes. "I really can't see that happening, especially with my son gravely injured like he is."

"This is just tragic," Penny added. "Simply tragic."

Sylvia continued sipping. "And then, as if that's not enough to crumble the Rock of Gibraltar, there's my darling Madison."

"What about Madison? Oh, don't tell me something's wrong with my beautiful niece, Syl. I don't think I can take hearing anything like that."

Sylvia sighed and sipped. She knew that she would have to eventually tell Penny about Madison's pregnancy, and now was as a good time as any. She finally told Penny, and glossed over some of the less savory facts like Justin's true identity and his involvement in the family tragedy.

Penny's mouth dropped, and she stood to freshen her drink. "Sylvia. You must be devastated. How could Madison allow herself to get caught like that? She wasn't using protection?"

"Using protection? I didn't even know she was out here cavorting with these young men. I just don't know anything anymore. I feel like I've failed in some way with her. And not like I'm an advocate of abortion, but she is so determined to keep this child, and won't consider any other alternative."

"I had such high hopes for my little princess. She could've had any suitor deserving of a young lady of her stature. But what does she do? She goes and lays down with some old—" Sylvia stopped short, and groaned.

"Some old what, Syl? What about the father?" Penny asked. "What does he have to say for himself?"

"Not much. He's dead. So, marriage isn't even an option."

Penny shook her head. "Well, I'm flabbergasted. I can't imagine Madison trying to raise a child on her own. What on earth is she going to do?"

"I don't know. But, she's not thinking clearly. I thought that I'd shake a little sense into her when I told her that she shouldn't expect any help from me or her father. But, she acted like she didn't care."

"It's probably her hormones raging, Syl. Maybe she'll come around and—"

"And do what? Bring more shame on this family? It's not like she can put the child up for adoption. It will be a Cavanaugh, after all. Well, part Cavanaugh."

"Oh, Sylvia, I know. I was just thinking that maybe she'd decide to— oh, I don't know." Penny placed a finger to her lips. "Please don't look at it as Madison bringing shame on to the family. I'm sure she didn't do it intentionally. Accidents do happen."

"Accidents, huh? Hmph. I don't know what's on these young women's minds today. Whether their actions are intentional or unintentional, they are just not exercising good judgment. Or even thinking about how their actions impact their own family. It's just pure selfishness. And it's inexcusable."

Penny filled Sylvia's cordial glass, and refreshed her own drink. She sat down beside Sylvia, and searched her face. "My goodness, Sylvia. I know Madison's predicament is upsetting, but something else has got you this riled up. What else is going on?"

Sylvia collapsed back on the sofa, and flung her free hand outward. "As if I haven't had enough to contend with, would you believe that I haven't even heard from that daughter-in-law of mine?"

"Who, Kim? I know you don't expect to hear much from her, do you?"

Sylvia curled her lips. "No, not her. I'm talking about Beverly."

"Whaat?"

"You heard me. I haven't heard a word. Not a peep. She hasn't called home once or even tried to reach me. And I don't even know how to reach her. I'm not sure if she even knows that her husband is here clinging to life. Or, if she knows, she obviously doesn't care."

"Oh no, Sylvia. You mean to tell me that you haven't heard from Beverly?" Penny asked. "I don't believe it. That's not like her at all. Where on earth could she be?"

"Where on earth could he be?" Harry asked. "It's not like Stewart to just disappear and not be accounted for. And how could he allow Connie to just go off on his own like this without telling you? Jolly, there are far too many unanswered questions for me. *Lontano troppo.* Far too many."

Jolly removed two aromatic Cubans from his oak humidor, and passed one to Harry. "I agree, Harry. But, you know that Stewart and Connie were tight. Perhaps too tight. And although Stewart was part of my team, his loyalties were clearly with Connie." Jolly sighed, his massive chest and belly rising and falling. "I have my men trying to find out what really happened, but no one seems to have a clue. And, with Stevie and Ellis dead, we may have to wait until Connie comes back around to get to the truth. I'm sure no one else would know. Or, if they do, they're not saying."

Harry stroked his chin, lit his cigar and then passed the lighter to Jolly. "I'd venture to say that they're not saying. I think that you need to apply some pointed pressure, Jolly, and let your folks know that even though they might've been working under Connie's direction, I still run this family. And there are no damned secrets from me."

Jolly puffed on his cigar, and settled in on the sofa beside Harry. "I agree. But, you know how reckless these youths are. The only thing we know for sure is that Connie arranged the hits on Jury and Dante to eliminate some of the competition, and that Stewart was in on that. After that, things get kind of sketchy."

Harry savored his smoke. "Yes, things are quite sketchy. And, on top of that, Beverly also seems to be missing."

Jolly raised his eyebrows. "You don't think—"

"I don't know what to think, Jolly. I wasn't here, and given everything else that's happened, nothing would surprise me."

"Hmph. The timing seems about right. But, it could be either they've run off together, or your son found out about them, and put a permanent end to their affair," Jolly said.

"No, Jolly. You don't think—"

"To coin your phrase, I wasn't here, and given everything else that's happened—"

"Nothing would surprise you," Harry said.

"Exactly. But, you know who might know? Joey."

Harry rubbed his forehead. "You're right. I get the feeling that he knows a lot more about what happened than what he's saying. But, *scoprirò*. I will find out."

"Well, Harry. You can't blame the boy if he does know something. Just look at where he's sitting— with Connie involved in all of these backdoor activities, if Joey did find out, he's compromised anyway you slice it.

"He doesn't stand to walk away clean. But, you have to give him credit. He hasn't rolled on his brother yet, and he's the one that's here facing the heat."

"I know, that's commendable. He now has an allegiance to his brother that once again is superceding what's best for this family. And not only him, there's Christian, too. Connie had to have gotten that money he used for his little drug deal from somewhere. I know he didn't have any tucked under his mattress. Hell, he spends money like an addict goes through needles. I'm going to call for an audit, since no one wants to come forward with the truth."

Harry sighed. "I swear, I just can't figure these boys out. I've got one that has shown no regard for anything, another who's so closed mouthed, I don't know what's going on with him. I want to believe him, but I just wonder if he's telling the truth. For instance, Joey wants me to believe that he was down on those docks by himself. Hmmph. That doesn't even sound plausible. And then he manages to get away from a federal agent? I just don't think so.

"And then there's Christian, who can't seem to comprehend anything that doesn't have a dollar sign attached to it. I really wonder about their allegiances to this family," Harry said. "*Faccio realmente.* I really do."

Jolly shrugged. "I tried to warn you about this, remember? I think Joey has a good heart and good intentions, but his execution can be a little flawed. And Christian, well, he's driven by the almighty dollar, and that'll probably be his downfall. And Connie, well, you know how he is. Too many things."

Harry stared at the tip of his burning stogie, like it held some magical answer. Finally, he responded to Jolly's statement. "I know. I didn't like pitting brother against brother," he said. "But, I thought, well, I hoped that they'd rise above the circumstances. I guess they didn't." Harry sighed, and finished his cognac. "I'm terribly disappointed by their failure and lack of better judgment.

"And then there's Edgar. I can't do a damned thing about him without disavowing my father's word. I have to live with the fact that he's partially responsible for my son's injuries, and for once again, having a key hand in trying to destroy our family. But, the only thing I can do is just continue to watch him. I want someone on him and his son 24-7. Everything he does, I want to know before he does it, okay?"

Jolly nodded and puffed on his cigar. "You know I'm looking out for you, Harry. Just like always."

Harry shook his brother in law's hand. "You don't know how much that means to me, Jolly. I need to know that more now than ever." They both stood and Harry grabbed Jolly's massive shoulders. "We're not blood, but you've been more of a brother to me than my own," Harry said, and the two old friends smiled and clasped hands.

"Well, Harry. Look on the bright side. At least you have one in your fold that hasn't let you down. My little princess Madison. That's got to make you feel a little better."

Harry smiled and shook his head. "My dear little Madison. *Il mio darling la mia piccola ragazza.* You're right. I didn't mention anything about her. Well, let me tell you about my darling little girl, beginning with her poor choice of men."

Harry quickly related Madison's fate to Jolly, who took the update with minimal reaction.

"So, you're going to be a grandpapa and I'm going to be a grand uncle, huh?" Jolly smiled, but it quickly faded. "Well, I'm sure my sister's not too pleased."

"*Per dire il minimo.* To say the least, Jolly."

"Well, how's she doing? Is she and the baby doing okay?"

They discussed Madison's condition for a few moments, and afterwards, Jolly confirmed Harry's thoughts. "Well, it's going to take

Sylvia a while to get over it, but I'm sure she will. She can't help but to love our little bambino."

"I know she'll come around," Harry said. "She always does. But, anyway, I guess we'd better go join the ladies before they come looking for us, and Sylvia gets on me for indulging in this cigar and taste of cognac. *That* she hasn't quite come around about yet either."

Though Beatty was no longer employed by his family's business, he readily assisted Joey in locating Lauren. Beatty was a great resource, and though it cost him a quick grand, Beatty provided Lauren's reach information before the end of the day. He was excited at the prospect of getting some clarity and closure.

Lauren had been reassigned to desk duty in a field office in Charlotte, North Carolina. The reassignment was punishment for her involvement in the ill-fated Cavanaugh investigation, and courtesy of Robeson's directive. With his lean legs pumping the pedals of his stationary bike, Joey toyed with the piece of paper with Lauren's office, home and cell phone numbers on it. After revving the bike up to over 10 mph for ten minutes, Joey decided to take a jog down to the corner store on Maryland Avenue and get a Gatorade. And safely call Lauren from the pay phone.

As he was leaving, Joey checked his mail, which was accumulating in the locked box outside of his front door. He lifted the lid, and fished out the stack of letters and envelopes crammed inside the mailbox. As he thumbed through the contents, a small, white envelope slipped from the pile. It was the same kind that had fallen out of his newspapers the other day. Joey stepped back inside, and searched his desk for the other envelope. Was the newspaper deliveryman getting forgetful or what and trying to double bill him?

Joey ripped open the first envelope, and a playing card fell to the floor. Upon closer inspection, he noticed that it was a tarot card. The Queen of Swords. What the hell?

Joey carefully opened the second one, and pulled another card out. This one was the Queen of Pentacles.

What the hell was going on? Joey dropped his mail onto the desk and stared at the colorful cards. Who would slip something like this in his mail? And what did it mean? Was someone trying to call him a queen or something? Naw, Joey thought. He knew absolutely nothing about tarot cards, but immediately felt that the cards had some significance. The only person who might know would be Grand's caretaker, who was from the islands. Joey made a mental note to ask Trudy about it when he had a moment.

But then again, maybe Joey was just overreacting. He didn't want to be paranoid about every little thing that occurred in his life. It could be some innovative new business opening in the area, and this was their way of clever advertising. Who knew? It was a possibility, but Joey wasn't too sure. With all of the continued anonymous phone calls, something about these cards made him a little concerned. He had to find out whoever was behind this, and Joey was determined not to stop until he did. And he'd first start with Lauren.

After downing a quart of the tasteless thirst quencher, a sweat-suited Joey paced in front of the small variety store. It was mid afternoon, and as the traffic and pedestrians hurriedly filled the street, Joey contemplated whether or not to make the call. Was it the right thing to do? How would she respond? Then again, was he fully prepared to deal with her, whether it was a positive or negative response?

Lauren was sharp, and her wit could be extremely caustic. But, Joey was prepared to give as good as she gave. He guessed. He really wouldn't know until he heard her voice. So, armed with a pocketful of change, Joey dialed the switchboard of the Roanoke Branch of the FBI, and asked for Lauren Murray. He caught himself and then asked for Lauren Malloy. As the operator placed his call, Joey's heart thumped through his sweaty wife-beater, and he hung up. How stupid could he be? Her phone line was probably recorded, so he decided to try her on her cell phone instead.

After a few rings, she answered. "Agent Malloy speaking."

"Lauren? This is Joey."

Joey's words were met with an uneasy silence. "Joey?" Lauren's voice wavered, and she dropped her tone.

"Yeah, it's me. We need to talk."

There was complete silence. "I never thought that I'd hear from you again."

"I never thought that I'd speak to you again, but I need to talk to you. And not over the phone."

They agreed to meet in Richmond later that evening, in the lobby of the Marriott. Joey hurried home and changed into a pair of black jeans and beige ultra suede shirt, and slipped out of town.

On the drive down, Joey called Trudy about the mysterious tarot cards, just in case there was some imminent danger lurking in his near future. Though he tried to downplay his interest, when Trudy asked where he had gotten them and he responded, she immediately picked up on his concern.

"Oh, so someone left them for you in your postals, eh? Well, if you've come across the Queens, there no harm wit' the ladies of the swords or pentacles," she said, in her thick native accent. "It could mean that someone thinks that you're an honest soul, who's trustworthy an' bighearted. Ain't a ting wrong wit' that, luv."

"Are you sure, Trudy? I mean, I don't want to think that something bad's going to happen."

Trudy chuckled, and began speaking in stacatto. "Fiddle-dee-dee. You Americans always tink that the cards always means somethin' evil. 'Taint always the case. Sometimes they used to show you good, if you have good to be shown in you. You been a good boy, hasn't you, son?"

"Yes, ma'am. I try," Joey said with a laugh of relief. He thanked her for her insight, and hung up, feeling worlds better about the meeting that loomed ahead. And since the anonymous phone calls had stopped, he probably really didn't have anything to be alarmed about. Hopefully.

He drove the remaining hour and a half in silence, with only his thoughts of Lauren as company. He wasn't sure how he was going to feel when he saw her, especially that his distrust level was so high.

He made sure that he arrived at the hotel at seven, an hour before they were scheduled to meet. He didn't trust her at all, and had planned how he would ensure that they were on a level playing field.

When Lauren arrived, he could barely maintain eye contact with her. When he did, he noticed that she looked marvelous, though, with her hair freshly cut, and a stunning, close fitting, vibrantly colored sarong top with full, flowing pants. Her face appeared leaner, but her eyes danced when she saw Joey.

"Hello, Joey," she said, and tentatively extended her hand. Her arms were sculpted and toned, and he was immediately turned on.

"Hey." Joey was purposely curt in his greeting. "I think we should go over to the Hyatt. I don't like the vibe here." What he was really thinking is that there was no way he was going to be set up in a location Agent Malloy could have someone watching him. She'd never have the game in her favor again.

"Why?" Lauren asked, and then she acknowledged his trepidation. "Okay, Joey. Whatever you say."

They took a short cab ride over to the other hotel, riding in silence. Joey paid the fare and followed Lauren into the building, covertly checking to see if they were being shadowed. Once they were in, he hugged her, feeling her up and down.

"Why are you doing that?" Lauren asked.

"I want to make sure you're not wired," Joey said, with a smirk. His smirk faded when she returned the gesture.

"I guess I better check you out, too." She expertly frisked him.

Joey suppressed his rising anger, and led her to the piano bar, where they sat next to each other at a small cocktail table.

Under the flickering light of the table's candle, Joey caught an even better look at Lauren. She was beautiful, her earthy brown skin glowing in the soft illumination. She reached for his hand, and he pulled away.

"Let's not go there, Lauren. That's not why I agreed to see you," Joey said. "I don't think we need to even think about that now."

"I'm sorry, Joey. I'm just glad to see you." She smiled slightly. "I'm so sorry about everything."

"It was your job, right? You were just doing your job."

Lauren sighed, and shook her head. "It was my job, Joey, but you know it was more than that. I really caught serious feelings for you."

Joey sucked his teeth, over the escalating sound of the rotund pianist playing Roy Ayers's "*Searching.*" He leaned toward her, until he was close enough to inhale her perfume. "You expect me to believe that? The last time I saw you, you were slapping some cuffs on me, ready to haul my happy ass off to jail. I don't recall any hint of remorse in your actions, or you trying to slip me the key."

Lauren hung her head, and then looked up at Joey with her huge, doe-like eyes. "I had to do my job. I had no idea that things were going to go down like they did. I didn't know."

"You didn't know what?"

"That you and your family were really working with the agency to take down Agent Brian Hunter. I wasn't aware of that until after the fact. And, then, it was too late."

"Too late for what?"

"To apologize. Well, maybe too late isn't accurate. I had an assignment to do, and I did it.

"I violated one of the first rules of working undercover. I broke protocol when I actually developed real feelings for you. But, I had to do what I was tasked to do. And I did it."

"So, your feelings allowed you to lay with me and spy on me? It didn't bother you in the least because you had all intents and purposes of arresting me? That makes me feel a lot better. You did a real good job, baby."

"No, Joey. That's not what I meant. I was just following orders. But, evidently, they withheld information regarding the Hunter Investiagion because they didn't want everyone to know what was really going on, so they could flush out some of Agent Hunter's allies." Lauren went on to reiterate what Robeson had already told them about how she had gotten Joey as an assignment after Connie was photographed with the known drug felon.

"It all happened so fast, Joey. It was part of this major crackdown that the Feds were calling for in the 'War on Drugs' and in the wake of Moses's death. You can call it guilt by association, but that's why they targeted you and your brother." Lauren's eyes flashed. "Speaking of your brother, how is he?"

"He'll live. But I really don't want to talk about him right now. I'm more concerned about what really happened between us."

Lauren sighed. "You don't know how many times I wanted to tell you how torn I was about investigating you, but there wasn't anything I could do without compromising my position or your safety."

"I think you could've told me while you were laying in my bed, Lauren." Joey waved to the waiter, ordered a Remy Martin and coke, and then offhandedly asked Lauren if she'd like something. She ordered a Singapore Sling, and her voice quivered.

Joey sensed her vulnerability, and decided to get as much out of her as possible. "So, tell me, Lauren. Have you been trying to call me?"

Lauren furrowed her brows, and then shook her head no. "I thought about it, and picked up the phone several times, but I couldn't bring myself to complete the call. Why do you ask?"

Joey searched her face for a trace of deceptiveness, but found none. "No reason. I, uh, I guess I just wondered that if you felt so much for me, why you didn't try to call."

Lauren just shrugged, and before she could respond, Joey switched subjects. Since he hadn't gotten the answer he was looking for, there was no need in opening up another area of his life that would draw Lauren's suspicions. "So, what else did you find out about me while you were spying on me?" Joey asked. He almost regretted asking the question, but he needed to know if she knew anything about his sexual proclivities.

Lauren firmly shook her head. "I found out that you were a decent guy. That was enough for me. And I'm really sorry, Joey. I can't apologize enough. But, I *was* doing my job. And you should respect that."

Joey folded his arms, relieved at Lauren's professed ignorance, but then he wondered how good she was at her job if she didn't know anything. He decided to drop it, and focus on her duplicity. "Respect? Now, that's different. What makes you think that I could ever respect you for what you did? I actually feel kind of used. I'm sure your employers didn't approve of you having sex with me on a regular basis."

Lauren lowered her voice, and fiddled with her empty glass. She slowly looked into Joey's eyes. "When you're undercover, you have to do what you have to do to appear credible."

"Well, bravo, Lauren. Bravo. You went above and beyond the call of duty in an exemplary manner."

The waiter returned with their drinks, and Joey shooed him away. "Joey, I didn't come here to be insulted. I've apologized, and that's all I can do. But, I'm not going to let you humiliate me until you feel better."

Joey stared at her, and felt flush. That was one of the things he liked about her. She had guts. "I'm not trying to humiliate you. I just wanted to know if you were just acting or doing your job, because I've never had this happen to me before. And I don't want it to happen again."

Lauren sipped her drink, and returned Joey's gaze. "I wasn't acting, Joey. I told you. I really have feelings for you."

"Is that why you didn't tell your superiors that I shot my brother that night?"

"It was a judgment call, Joey. I know Connie's actions and conduct are questionable, but I guess I was trying to look at the bigger picture at that moment."

"What do you mean?"

"A lot of the things that happened don't quite make sense to me, but I'm dealing with it. Like your brother's involvement, even though it's my understanding that he was working with the agency." Lauren shrugged, and stared deeply into Joey's eyes. "It doesn't really matter, Joey. I saw what happened and it was an accident from where I was standing. I wasn't about to point the finger at you." She paused and reached for Joey's hand. "That was the least that I could do for you."

This time, Joey didn't recoil. He grabbed Lauren's hand, and held it tightly. "I appreciate it. But, I was prepared to deal with the consequences." Joey was lying, but he hoped that Lauren bought it.

"I'm sure you were prepared to deal with it, Joey. You're that type of man. But, it was unintentional, and there was no point in implicating you. I figured that you'd have enough to deal with, especially with your family."

"Thanks, Lauren. I guess I owe you."

"You don't owe me anything. If anything, I owe you. You could've gotten hurt. And that would've been horrible. I don't think I could've lived with myself if something had happened to you."

She looked at Joey with a reticent expression. "I know you didn't want to talk about it earlier, but I'm concerned about you and your family. So, how is your brother doing?"

Joey repeated his earlier statement, but Lauren persisted. "His injury has to be hard on you and your family." She gave Joey a half smile. "I know you two have a kind of difficult relationship."

"Yeah, we have. But I've had to put all of that aside. You know how it is. You can't be petty when someone's facing a life or death situation. But, he's out of the woods now, and basically getting back to being the same old Connie. And I'd expect nothing less."

She paused. "Really? He's not causing you any problems, is he? Because that night on the docks you both seemed to be at odds about something."

"No, it wasn't anything like that. But, things'll be okay. Trust me, Connie'll be fine. And so will I. Both of us are tough like that."

Lauren sighed. "I hope so. I feel bad about what happened, and I wish things could be different. But, they're not, and we, I mean I, have to deal with it."

Joey wiped his mouth and placed his glass to his lips. He drank slowly, hoping to extinguish the fire that raged in between his legs. "You're right, Lauren. We have to deal with this. Because, I've been thinking about you a lot. And I was hoping that I'd get to see you again, and I'd either be so mad or numb that I wouldn't feel anything. But—"

"But what?"

"I can't lie. Looking at you is really affecting me."

"Really?" Lauren's eyes flashed. "Me too. So, uh, what are we going to do about it?"

Joey poured his drink down his throat, and grabbed Lauren by the hand. "Come on," he said, and pulled her toward the registration desk. "Let's see if they have any rooms available."

Joey readily produced his Amex Black Card to secure one of the last rooms available, which was a suite on the 17th floor. On the elevator ride up, the two played a fierce game of contact, groping and feeling on each other, and breaking apart as other passengers entered and exited the glass enclosed elevator. By the time they reached their room, they were partially disrobed, panting and overheated.

They fell over the back of the sofa, where the lovers continued their frantic pace. But, then Lauren pushed away from him, and placed her hands on his bare chest.

"Stop, Joey."

"What?" Joey could barely speak. His arousal was overwhelming, and he was ready for the breaking up stuff, wrecking the house kind of sex they shared. He hoped she wasn't going to pull some old "I'm brand new" bullshit on him now.

"I don't want you like this," she said, and forced herself from under his weight. She walked across the room, and stared out the window at the James River.

"What are you talking about, Lauren? What's wrong with how we do our thing?" He was getting agitated, but was trying not to show it. He was horny as hell, and didn't feel like dealing with Lauren's sudden stream of consciousness. Or, was this her payback?

"Give me a minute, will you?" Lauren asked, and then walked into the bedroom.

Joey sat on the sofa, and fumed in silence. After a long while, Lauren emerged from the room, and touched him on the shoulder. He started to speak, but she placed a finger over his lips and whispered, *"Shhhh."*

She led him into the bedroom, where she had lit several tea light candle. She guided him to the bed, and sat down next to him.

She lightly kissed his lips, and gazed at him, her face soft and alluring. "Joey, I've thought about us, and although I don't know what our being together tonight will mean tomorrow, I want to be with you. But not like we were. I want to make love to you. Not have sex. Not fuck. I want to feel you. Connect with you. I don't want any other stimulation or provocation. Just you and me. Together. Or does that frighten you too much?"

Joey was speechless, and could only mumble. The manner in which his heart was beating before had subsided, but now it was replaced by a more subtle feeling. It was anxiety, but Lauren grabbed his hands and kissed them too.

"Here— let me show you."

That night, Joey and Lauren made love. It wasn't a race, or a cardiovascular workout or a test of endurance, but a soft, gentle, caring and sharing. Lauren massaged every part of Joey's body, licking and tasting and feeling him, until he felt that his soul was exposed and naked. She forced him to relax, to surrender his mind and not only his body, and to take the time to feel and emote. It was an experience Joey couldn't ever remember having, and by the time the sun rose, he was more exhausted, but more satisfied, than he had ever been. With any other man or woman.

Chapter 9

Connie's condition improved to the point where his breathing tube was removed and he uttered his first words in weeks. They were practically indistinguishable, but Sylvia heard and deciphered them. She was the only one present at the time, but she quickly summoned the rest of the Cavanaugh clan to Connie's side.

Much to her dismay, everyone was too busy to drop everything and run to the hospital like her. She had to question her children's priorities, or lack thereof. Christian was attending an all-day business symposium for the D.C. Chamber of Commerce, and Joey and Harry promised to come over later. Sylvia, still hell bent on not speaking to Madison, had instructed Joey to contact her. As she manned her station by her son's bed, Sylvia wondered what on earth was happening to her family.

Madison, pregnant. It was enough to turn Sylvia's walnut brown colored hair a blinding gray. Conrad, bedridden and possibly paralyzed. That alone was enough to almost make her question her faith. Harry, Joey, and Christian: all too busy to be concerned about Connie. And Beverly. Nowhere to be found. And the crushing blow was Edgar and his criminal-minded element being on the scene, probably only to sully the good Cavanaugh name Sylvia had worked so very hard to cultivate over the years. It was almost enough to drive her to drink.

But, there were some things to look forward to. Now that Connie was on the mend, Sylvia had planned her first social outing since returning to D.C. There was an exhibit of Jacob Lawrence's work at the Corcoran Gallery of Art that evening, and she and Penny were on the exclusive guest list.

Labor Day had come and gone, and for the past few days, she and Penny had actually been making some headway in planning the holiday soiree and charity ball. Although this pleased Sylvia, it bothered her that she and Madison stll weren't on speaking terms. And when Penny mentioned Madison, Sylvia couldn't even bring herself to further discuss her daughter's condition with her closest friend. She had hoped that Madison would come to her senses and make her little problem go away before anyone else became aware of it. But, Madison was stubborn, and so was Sylvia. So the impasse continued.

Planning this function had always been a special feat for Sylvia and her daughter, and now Madison had cheated her out of this small pleasure. Would the madness ever cease? How much more was Sylvia expected to bear?

Syl could have enlisted Christian's wife Kim, but she would probably be more trouble than she was worth. She was a control freak, who didn't take direction well. And with her sour disposition and propensity to nit pick, Kim would put too much churn on the planning process. So, Sylvia and Penny would manage just fine.

The masquerade theme was an ambitious endeavor, especially since they were now into September. There were a number of critical things left to do, namely, contract musicians and florists; have the decorations custom made; find a gown; have her coveted jewel, *Il Rosso* cleaned and polished, and yes, book a caterer. None of those elements presented much of a challenge, except the last one. She and Penny would just rebook the jazz quartet and florist from last year; she'd have her personal buyer at Bloomingdale's send her some dress suggestions, and she'd get Joey to take the jewel to the jeweler. Even though most of the best caterers were already booked for that date, Sylvia was undaunted. The Cavanaugh name virtually guaranteed that she would have any of area's five-star caterers clamoring for her business, and ringing her phone at her beck and call.

Throughout the day, Connie's condition improved, and by late afternoon, when Joey and his father finally showed up, Connie was propped up in the bed, and actually attempting to move his arms and legs.

"It's a miracle," Sylvia whispered to them when they arrived. She was seated at her post, caressing Connie's face. "Doesn't he look so much better? My dear, sweet Conrad. I was so very concerned about you."

"Heyy," Connie said, his voice raspy and strained.

"And he's getting back to his old self," Sylvia said. "The first thing he wanted was for me to put that chain back on." She pointed to Connie's neck, and Joey's eyes fixated on the heavy gold chain, with Stewart's ring on it. The sight of it made Joey both angry and ill.

But anger was only one of the emotions Joey was dealing with. His thoughts were scattered in a thousand different directions. Barely a day had passed since his torrid tryst with Lauren, and he hadn't even had time to digest what had happened between them before his mother had summoned him to Connie's bedside. And then, just as he was leaving Connie's house to go to the hospital, Ashley had phoned to report that there had been an incident at Connie's house. Caligula and Diablo, his precious canines, were found dead, and Ashley wasn' sure what had happened to them.

Dead? Joey immediately thought of how Connie had trained those huge black beasts to be as intimidating and ferocious as possible, and now, like their master, they had been rendered helpless. It was sad, because they were only creatures, but they were menaces that no one could really handle except Connie. After a few contemplative moments, Joey told Ashley to see if the vet could determine what might've caused their deaths, and have them cremated and retain the ashes. Connie would be devastated to know that his dogs were gone, but he probably would like to do something with their remains. Joey sighed. This was just another issue that he truly didn't want to be bothered with.

And now that he was at the hospital, Joey didn't know what to say. He stared at his older brother, who in his weakened state was almost pitiful. Joey tried to be supportive, but his mind wrestled with the circumstances that Connie had brought to bear on his family. And he then wondered just how much Connie remembered about his shooting.

"Son," Harry said, and grabbed Connie's hand. "*Figlio*, I knew you'd pull through. You have too much Cavanaugh blood coursing through those veins not to."

"And don't forget my Russell, too," Sylvia said, with a coo.

They huddled around Connie, conveying comfort and a strong bond that made Sylvia positively glow. "Where's Madison?" she asked, and Harry responded that she wasn't feeling well. Sylvia rolled her eyes, and started gathering her belongings.

"Well, gentlemen. I have an event to get prepared for this evening, and so I hope that you'll be able to stay and spend some time with Conrad. And, Joseph, I want you to take some time out of your busy schedule to take *Il Rosso* to the jeweler for me. The sooner, the better."

Joey's thoughts were interrupted, and he absentmindedly nodded, and when he thought about what his mother had just said, he wondered why he was always saddled with something to do. Especially running this specific errand. Then it occurred to him that his mother was preparing for the annual event. "Certainly, M'Dear. I'll get to it this week."

Harry caught his wife's eye. "I'll ride back with you, Syl. I know that you've been down here all day, so I don't know if you've heard, but Simon Blake has resurfaced. And I should get back on that side of town as quickly as possible and see if Howard is back, or if Royce is aware of anything."

Harry went on to say how one of Jolly's men on the D.C. police force had reported that Simon had reappeared down by the Virginia shoreline, after being nursed back to health by some fishing family. Simon was sequestered at Walter Reed Army Medical Center, under heavy guard.

"So, Simon's reemerged from the dead. Well, doesn't that just beat all? Well, you can tell me all about it on the way home, Harry," Sylvia said, and she continued rustling her items.

Connie's eye widened, and he gestured for his cup of water. Joey held the cup, and Connie slowly sipped through a flexible straw. He made loud slurpy noises, like he was having a hard time pressing his lips together.

Sylvia leaned over and kissed Connie on the forehead. "Feel better, sweetheart. M'Dear will see you some time tomorrow."

Joey walked his parents to the elevator, and told them about what had happened to Connie's pets.

"Well, for heaven's sake, do not mention that to your brother," Sylvia said. "That would cause a tremendous setback for him, so we have to make sure he's strong enough before we tell him."

Joey sighed. Did she think he was an idiot or what? "Of course not, M'Dear. I won't mention it."

"Of course he won't, Syl," his father said as he held the elevator door open for his wife. "I know Joey knows how to keep his mouth shut when necessary."

"Ain't that some wild shit," Connie said, as soon as his parents left. "That old mother fucker's alive."

Joey was surprised that Connie could speak, more or less, cuss, so well. It figured that Connie was laying it on thick for his mother's sake.

Joey took a seat on the other side of Connie's bed, and shook his head. "Welcome back, Connie," Joey said.

"Thanks, Joe," Connie said, and tilted his head like he was afraid it was going to fall off his neck. "Guess I'll live to die another day, huh?" Connie moistened his dry lips, and then said quietly, "So, um, where's my old lady? Where's Beverly?"

Joey stared at Connie, and suddenly had an urge to wring his wiry neck. The pity that plucked at Joey's conscious was fleeting, but there was a sense of sadness and emptiness in Connie's eyes that made Joey think twice. "I really don't know, Connie. But, she's not here, and I don't know if she'll ever come back."

Connie sighed heavily, and his eyes misted over. "I know I've done some fucked up things in my life, and things haven't been right between us, but I swear that if I ever get my ass out of this bed, things are going to change. I swear. I'm gonna come correct."

Joey tried to keep a straight face, and believe his brother. But it was difficult, especially after everything that Connie had done. And although Joey felt some remorse for Connie, there was no way he was going to let him get away with murder. Literally. There was something telling in Joey's voice when he spoke to Connie. "Well, what about Stewart? I haven't seen or heard from him either. Or, should we even expect to, Connie? Isn't that his ring you're wearing?" Joey wanted to take that chain and twist it around Connie's neck until he passed out.

Connie's face drained of its color. "Yeah, it is, Joey. He gave it to me. But Stew's gone, man. He wanted out, so I gave him an out. And I know he's not coming back, either." Connie's voice was a mere whisper, and he touched Stewart's ring. "I know that I'm responsible for that shit too."

Joey shook his head, and turned away. Again, he had to battle the feeling of wanting to choke Connie until his eyes bulged out. "I'm sure you are, Connie. And you'll have to deal with that on your own. But, I've got some things to deal with, too. And some shit I'm responsible for. Like what happened the night you got shot—"

Connie raised a weakened hand. "Let's just squash all of that, huh? I don't remember everything, but I'm thinking that what went down was really foul. For real. And it shouldn't have happened, but what's done is done." Connie paused, and appeared to try to adjust his energy level. "So, how are my boys doing?"

Joey nodded. He couldn't believe that Connie actually sounded contrite and semi-sane, but was hoping that he wouldn't start in with the questions so soon. "Who?" Joey asked.

"Caligula and Diablo."

"Oh, I thought you were talking about Stevie and Ellis, Connie," Joey responded, sidestepping the subject without having to lie.

Connie flinched. "Yeah, um, them too. How are they doing?"

"They're dead, Connie. Things have changed a lot since the shootout at the harbor. Justin and your boys Stevie and Ellis got killed, and Uncle Edgy and Vincent were only slightly injured. Go figure. And guess what— now they're staying in D.C. indefinitely." Joey quickly recapped the highlights from the council, and waited for his brother's response.

Connie said nothing, but stared at Joey with a blank expression on his face. Finally he spoke. "Edgy and Vincent. Those bastards. How'd they get off the hook? How'd that shit happen? How could Father trust Uncle Edgy again?" Connie paused. "I guess I got a lotta nerve asking that question, huh?"

Joey felt like Connie was trying to be sincere, and not trying to run his regular game. And Joey hoped that Connie had momentarily forgotten about his dogs. To ensure that Connie would have something else to think about, Joey decided to tell him about he and Christian's surreptitious plans to get the goods on Edgy.

After Joey provided the details, Connie remained uncharacteristically quiet again. His eyes were shut, and Joey thought that he had drifted off to sleep. Connie eventually yawned, and then opened his eyes. He looked drowsy. "That kind of changes things, doesn't it?"

"Considerably, Connie. Considerably. And if all of us don't come together on this— I'm talking about you, me and Christian, then there's no telling what's going to happen to any of us."

Connie slowly cupped his hands behind his neck, and closed his eyes again. "I need to get some sleep now, Joey. I've got a lot to think about, and I need to get well with a quickness. Like yesterday. I tell you what— get Christian, and you two come over Friday afternoon, no, make that Friday evening. And we'll make sure that it's after M'Dear leaves. That'll give me a couple of days to regroup and mull this shit over. And when you come, be sure to bring me a backgammon board, too. It'll help me get my juices flowing. My brothers, we've got some serious shit to take care of."

Madison slowly ambled across the Key Bridge, while the traffic whizzed by her at a frantic pace. She had gotten Joey's message that Connie was conscious, but Madison felt nothing but bitterness and indifference toward him. Because of Connie, her child's father was dead, and she didn't know if she'd ever be able to forgive her brother. She didn't know if she'd ever be able to forgive herself for allowing herself to fall into such an abysmal state of being.

What had started off as some harmless window-shopping at Georgetown Park Mall, had turned into an aimless stroll in the city. For Madison not to shop was tantamount to an alcoholic passing by a bar. With every step, she questioned her very existence. She had stepped out on faith, and on the strength that her exceptional upbringing would prepare her for the difficult road ahead. Choosing to be an unwed mother.

How she got pregnant was troubling enough. She had a diaphragm, and occasionally, Justin even wore a rubber. She always considered herself cautious when it came to her sexual activities. Either he was exceptionally potent, or they had the timing and blessing of the fertility gods. Whichever it was, she was definitely with child, and with a belly that was about to start protruding.

She even briefly wondered about the sex of her baby. Would it be a boy or a girl? Would he or she look like Justin or her? Then she just thought that it really didn't matter. She only wanted, and needed, a healthy baby.

Her pending motherhood hadn't made her a complete emotional wreck. She hadn't lost touch with reality to the point that she was surprised by her mother's reaction. But, she was pleased to know that her father would stand beside her, despite her mother's high-handedness. Of the two people in the world Madison Cavanaugh thought she could always count on, one had disappointed her beyond compare. One was Joey, but she hadn't told him about her condition yet, and the one who had shaken the foundation of her world was Ashley.

Before Madison's trip to California, Ashley had joined Madison for a long overdue manicure and pedicure. Evidently, Ashley really liked the special treatment, and even managed to get in to see Madison's treasured hairstylist, Graham. In less than a week, Ashley's whole demeanor had changed. Madison called her when she returned from California, and Ashley was upbeat and really feeling herself. She was ready to get out and hang, and if Madison hadn't been in her present condition, she would've been ready to roll too. But, she needed her friend's unconditional support, and Ashley shocked her with her response.

"Madison, you've got to be kidding. How could you be pregnant?" Ashley's voice was elevated four octaves, for she was trying to speak over the loud music playing in the background of her office. She made it sound like Madison was incapable of giving birth or something.

"Ashley, I just need to talk to you right now. Can't you come over?"

"Girl, I wish I could, but I've got a date tonight, and I've got to get myself together. You know how it is, I'm sure. But, for real, you can't be serious about keeping this baby, are you Madison? You've got too much to live for to be tied down with a little crumb snatcher. And you don't have a man, either? Girl, please. Stop tripping. I'll try to catch up with you tomorrow, 'kay?"

Before Madison could say anything, the phone went dead. Ashley had hung up. The absolute nerve of her. After all they had been through, this is the best Ashley had for her. Madison was both furious and devastated. Had the entire world order completely flipped upside down?

The winds howled like lonesome wolves in the wild, and the darkening sky threatened to unleash a deluge on her at any moment. Madison ignored nature's warnings, and continued her aimless stroll until she reached the end of the bridge, and stood near a small division between the iron span and the sidewalk. She could see the water rippling below her, and wondered how something so dangerous could go unchecked. A mere step or an accidental stumble would send anyone tumbling into the raging river. What an awful thought.

She wasn't thinking about ending it all, but she had never felt so afraid or alone as she did at that very moment. Even though she was now responsible for another life, it dawned on her that she had never really been responsible for her own. And that was a pretty sad commentary for someone who was twenty-four years old. One who had traveled the world, shopped in the most expensive haberdasheries, and to whom money was no object. But she had also never worked an honest day in her life. Suddenly, she didn't feel so proud of herself.

Suddenly, she felt the urge to talk. Besides Ashley, Madison sometimes talked to Beverly, but Madison figured she still was out of town. Instead, Madison clicked on her cell phone and called Joey. Though she had been avoiding him, she was saddened when his phone went straight to voicemail, but she forced herself to leave a brief message. "I need to talk to you, Joey. I'm pregnant, and I really need your help. Please call me."

After she clicked the phone off, Madison regretted leaving the message. Through all of this, she had forgotten that Joey might be hurting too. After all, he had been involved with that chick Lauren, and could probably empathize with her. But, then again, maybe not. Joey was very private, and never really talked about his feelings. Maybe now he would. But, if Joey turned his back on her, she'd really have no one to turn to. Perhaps it would've been better if she had just left things unsaid.

Something compelled her to dial Kim, Christian's wife. She didn't know why, but she did it anyway. Kim picked up on the second ring.

"Hey Kim," Madison said, her voice barely audible.

"Madison? What's up, girl?"

Madison heard water running in the background. "Did I catch you at a bad time?"

Kim giggled. "No, uh. Not really, Madison. I'm just filling the hot tub for me and Chris. Hold on for a minute." Kim placed her hand over the receiver, and Madison heard her speaking, but her voice was muffled.

Madison sighed, and when Kim returned, Madison tried to brighten the tone of her voice. "I didn't mean to interrupt, Kim. I'm glad to hear that you and Chris are getting along."

"Gettin' along and gettin' it on, girl," Kim said with a cackle. "You okay? Is it alright if I catch up with you tomorrow?"

"That's fine, Kim. You two have fun," Madison said, and clicked off her phone. The world was truly turning inside out now that Christian and Kim were relating to each other.

Evening was beginning to fall, and the wind was picking up. Rain was threatening, and Madison felt precipitation in the air. Dressed in a bright orange polo shirt, white Nikes and a white jogging suit, Madison stood by the gap at the bridge's end and let the wind from the passing cars and the threatening storm rock her body.

The cool air wrapped around her body, and seduced her with each rising gust. The sprinkles of rain increased to tiny drops, and lightning began illuminating the sky. Rumbles of thunder beat on the horizon, and Madison became mesmerized with nature's rhythms. Her bright white Nikes gripped the edge of the broken walkway, and it was like the environment was beckoning her. If she could just spread her arms, like the wings of a bird, perhaps the air would just carry her and her troubles away.

She pressed her palms open by her side, and wiggled her fingers. All she had to do was just raise her arms, and let nature do its thing. Slowly, her limbs raised, and she felt the force of the wind underneath her.

Leaning forward, Madison closed her eyes, the rain covering her face and making the edge slipperier. With a deep breath, she thought, "This could be so easy," and she let her muscles relax, and her body and mind melted into a swift freefall.

Chapter 10

"*Harrison! Wake up. Oh, dear God, wake up, Harry!*" Sylvia exclaimed, as she shook her napping husband. "Something terrible's happened!"

Harry had fallen asleep on the sofa in the family room, with the large screen TV on, and his reading glasses cocked to one side of his face. A newspaper was spread across his lap, with the headline, "AMNESIAC MAYOR BLAKE REAPPEARS."

"Wha-what? What is it, Syl? Are you okay? You sound like you're having a conniption." Harry said, with a loud yawn. He adjusted his glasses, blinked and then squinted at his wife, and then at his watch. "Is it morning? What time is it?"

"Time for you to get up, Harry," Sylvia said, as she waved her hands in the air. "Something terrible has happened."

Harry's eyes bucked. He was wide awake now. "*Che?* What happened? Is it one of the children?"

"No, well, yes, it is. Well, sort of. It's that damned criminal nephew of yours. Vincent. I was at the Corcoran tonight, and ran into him. He barely parted his lips, but I made him speak. And guess who he was squiring? Just guess."

Harry exhaled, and rubbed his eyes. "I acquiesce, dear. Who was it?"

"Tiffany. Tiffany Blake. Tiffany Blake Baxter," Sylvia said, with a huff. "I just don't believe this is happening. I told you having Edgar and his son here was only going to bring more trouble and more infamy on our family."

"Well, why do you say that, Syl? Tiffany's happily married, isn't she? Why do you think something's amiss?"

Sylvia narrowed her eyes and then whispered, even though they were alone. "Well, you know I'm not one to gossip, but rumor has it that Tiffany and Alex's marriage is on the rocks. And it has been ever since

Simon disappeared." She raised her brows. "So, it stands to reason that Vincent might be trying to wiggle his way into her life. The miscreant."

Harry rubbed his temples. "Are you sure, Sylvia?" Harry asked, and blinked his eyes. "Are you certain that they were together, like as in on a date? Or is your imagination and your disdain for Edgar getting the best of you?"

Sylvia grunted, and then raised her voice. "Hmph. Yes, I'm sure. And they appeared quite cozy. *Too* cozy. I swear, Penny almost had to carry me out of there when I saw them together." She paused and fanned herself. "Do you know what this means? That boy could be dating his own sister. Oh, perish the thought."

This was another episode of the program called "Sylvia Cavanaugh's Ultimate Nightmares." The secret of Tiffany's paternity had lain dormant for over twenty years, and now, within a matter of a few weeks of Edgar's unwelcome reappearance, it had reared its ugly head with a vengeance. Just when she thought things had reached their absolute worse, suddenly, things got even more horrific.

Harry reached for his wife, and pulled her down beside him. "Now, try to calm down, dear. We don't know for sure if Edgar is Tiffany's father. It's never been proven. And we have no proof now."

"Proof, smoof," Sylvia said. "The scandal that could be associated with the rumor *alone* is enough to wreak havoc on us. Oh, dear, we have to put an end to this, right now. You need to talk to Edgar immediately, and if he refuses to do anything, then we'll have to take matters into our own hands."

"What do you mean by that?"

"I mean that now that Simon is back, and although he has this purported memory loss, I'm sure he knows who that child's father is."

"I doubt if he'll welcome you at the hospital, Syl. Even if you come extending an olive branch or bearing a fruit basket," Harry said, with another loud yawn. "I don't think that flowers will go far with him either."

"Well, if he doesn't want to talk, there's always Marjorie's sister Giselle. I'm sure she wouldn't want to see something as immoral as this become fodder for those clucking hens in her bridge club. I swear, I think I'm just going to have a stroke, at this very moment," Sylvia said, and fanned herself with Harry's paper. "This is really accelerating my personal summers, you know."

"Sylvia, please. Don't get yourself all riled up about this. It's late, and there's absolutely nothing that you or I can do about it right now,"

Harry said. "I suggest you just try to relax, and perhaps we can come up with something more sage in the morning."

Sylvia's lip poked out in a mock pout. "Will you promise to talk to Edgar tomorrow? First thing in the morning?"

"First thing," Harry said, and leaned over and kissed his wife on the cheek. "Now, he said, drawing her close to him. "Why don't we spend a little time speaking the language of love with each other. It's been quite a long time, my darling." Harry nuzzled his face into her neck.

"Oh, Harry. You always know the right thing to say," Sylvia said, with a throaty laugh.

"And when to say it," Harry said, with an amorous growl. "*E quando dirlo.*"

Early the next morning, Harry called Edgy at the Grand Hyatt, and invited him over to discuss some family business. That afternoon, while Sylvia was safely away, visiting Connie, Edgar joined Harry in his parlor. While Harry's security guards manned their posts outside the door, the two brothers faced each other. They were seated facing each other in two African carved wooden chairs that surrounded an authentic Madagascan ivory chess set, and Harry made strained small talk. Edgar, ever cagey, played along for a while. Finally, Harry broached the real subject of the impromptu meeting. When Harry told Edgar about who Vincent was dating, Edgy seemed extremely nonchalant.

"Why are you telling me this?" Edgar said, as he puffed on a long, thick, Monte Cristo cigar, and the swirls of smoke wafted into the air. "I'm beyond picking out dates for my son. Or is that another family tradition I've fallen short on?"

Harry, still battling the desire to smoke versus his health issues, stuck an unlit cigar in his mouth. "This does have something to do with family tradition, but not in that manner, brother. Look, let's stop playing games here. We all know that you had an affair with Marjorie, and that you could possibly be that girl's father. Don't make it seem so inconceivable that you could be Tiffany's *padre*."

Edgar, spiffily outfitted in an ecru gabardine outfit and tan alligator shoes, crossed his legs, and revealed his textured silk socks. He placed his matching Panama hat on his knee, and then laughed heartily.

"You always have to play big brother, don't you, Harry?" Edgar glanced around the room and gestured with his hand. "Some things, like you and this grandiose house of yours, *appena non mai cambiare.* They just don't ever change."

Harry gritted his teeth. "Look, Edgar. This is no joke. No *scherzo* at all. I know you don't care about a lot of things, but you know that this isn't going to reflect well on our family. Even the slightest hint of that you might be her father isn't good. You should have enough decency to know that, and put an end to the rumors once and for all."

Edgy puffed on his stogie and shrugged. "Rumors? Harry, I'm surprised at you. I never knew that you were a gossip monger." Edgy licked his lips. "Well, I don't kiss and tell, brother. You ought to know that. You want me to be a gentleman when it's in your best interest, and then a cad when it is too. *Esso i pavimenti giusti me.* Your inconsistency just floors me."

Harry sat motionless, and internalized his desire to shoot his brother right between the eyes. What made him think that Edgar would be above board about anything? His years in New York had only made him more callous and smug.

"Edgar, this isn't about you. There are other lives involved. Namely, if Tiffany is your daughter, your *figlia*, do you really want her unwittingly getting involved with your own son? I mean, think about it, man. That's sick. That's not going to benefit anyone, especially that young lady. Who just might be my niece. *Mia nipote.*"

Edgy picked up his hat and stood. Again, he glanced around the room, and pointed the brim of his fedora at the many portraits and pictures that were hanging on the wall.

"Nice collection, Harry. You've got all of your family here, from when they were little, until now. Very handsome group, I might add. But, I see one extension of your family is missing. *Mine.*" Edgy turned around and glared at Harry. "Funny you should worry about if Marjorie's daughter is really my child." Edgy shook his head.

"After all of these years, the thought must not have ever crossed your mind before. Not until I showed up. And even now that I'm standing in your face, have you even bothered to ask me anything about my family? My wife? My children? Not at all. Well, FYI, in addition to Vincent, I have two daughters, *due figlie*, Samantha and Angelia. That's right. I have a family also. But, that's never really mattered to you. It's all about you and what you think is right. Well, you know what, I don't care. And I'm not going to respond to your questions or supposition.

This is one stipulation you're not going to stick on me. I don't care if you ever find out who that girl's father is. One thing's for sure, you'll never find out from me. Never. *Mai.*"

"Why would I have ever expected you to do the right thing, Edgar? But, you know what? It doesn't really matter to me, because it's really not my issue. Now that Simon's back, I'm sure that he'll check you on that one. And he'll get the answer I'm sure he's been wanting for years now. Especially if he finds out your son is squiring around his daughter."

Edgy interrupted him. "So what? I heard Simon Blake had '*reappeared,*'" Edgy said. "Maybe I should go pay old boy a visit. For old time's sake," he said with a smirk.

Harry ignored Edgy's sarcastic remark. "Although they say Simon has amnesia, I'm sure that once he finds out about his daughter and your son, things are going to get a little heated. And I'm sure that heat is going to be directed your way. So, maybe that'll make you take things a little more seriously, huh?"

Edgar grunted, and placed his stylish dob on his head. "Don't worry, Harry. Simon and I have a real old score to settle, and it didn't start with Tiffany, nor will it end with her. But rest assured, I'm not backing down from him in any form or fashion. I'm not the least bit concerned about Simon Blake. Never was, and never will be. I'm more than ready to deal with him. More than. *Più di.*"

Sylvia was livid when she phoned Harry from the car. She was leaving the hospital when he told her that Edgar wouldn't disclose anything about Tiffany's paternity.

"That figures," she said. "I'll just have to chart another course of action. There has to be another way."

"What are you going to do, Syl? Go ask Simon?" Harry asked. "Or go dress up in a candy stripper's uniform and have him submit to a blood test?" There was dead silence on the phone.

"That's a thought, but I'm going to talk to Giselle first," Sylvia said. "In fact I'm going to call her now. I'll talk to you later, darling."

Sylvia clicked on call waiting, and dialed directory assistance. After the operator provided the number, Sylvia dialed Giselle Newton's home.

Their conversation was brusque and less than hospitable. When Sylvia brought up the subject of getting together for a social call, Giselle hesitated, and then graciously asked why. When Sylvia casually mentioned to her that Edgar was back in town, Giselle's voice turned to ice. Sylvia tried her best to finesse Giselle, but she didn't entertain Sylvia's roundabout interrogative methods. When Sylvia finally broke down and said that she wanted to know more about Marjorie and Edgar's relationship and her concerns about it, Giselle promptly shut her down.

"I don't want to discuss my sister or her business with you, Sylvia Cavanaugh," Giselle said. "I suggest that you find other methods to direct your time and energy, rather than digging in my sister's past. Good day."

Sylvia was surprised, but not shocked. Giselle was an uptight old maid, who still reveled in the past. She had to come up with some way to find out whether Tiffany was Edgar's daughter. She snapped her fingers. She'd talk to Jolly about it, because he had formal medical training and always kept up on the latest in science and medicine. Her brother wouldn't think that she was crazy, and he'd do anything to help her, if he could.

Just as Sylvia had hoped, Jolly came through. It was such a relief when he said that there was some new technology that was out, called D.N.A. testing that could prove the paternity of a child. He could get some people on it, and since Simon was in the hospital, they could easily get their hands on a sample of his blood. Getting a sample from Edgar and Tiffany would be a little more challenging. Blood was the preferred body fluid, but saliva or a hair with the follicle attached could also be used. When Jolly heard the desperation in Sylvia's voice, he agreed to help her, but let her know that it would be a time consuming process, and even then, it might not be 100% accurate.

But, it was more than Sylvia had at the moment. And, suddenly, she didn't feel like the older sister, but the needy kid sister. "Please, Jolly. Please see what you can find out, as soon as possible. I don't know how long I can bare not knowing."

Madison awakened in the back of an empty, dank police squad car that smelled of stale beer and day old body odor. She wondered how many filthy vagrants and drunks had sat where she was, and she wanted to heave. She was wet and shivering, and wrapped in a blanket. Evidently, she had blacked out, because the last thing she remembered was being on the bridge, and then being overtaken with a desire to be free like the wind.

Rain peppered the roof of the car, and streamed down the smudgy windows. Madison peered out and panicked. She didn't recognize where she was, but she was jarred back into reality when the front door snatched opened, and a policeman stuck his head in. "Oh, I'm sorry. I didn't mean to startle you," he said with a toothy smile that illuminated the darkness. "I'm glad to see you awoke, Miss. How are you feeling?"

Madison recoiled, and retreated to the farthest corner of the car. "I'm, I'm okay," she said. "What am I doing here? I'm no criminal."

"Well, at the moment, I was waiting for you to wake up. And while I was waiting, I brought you a cup of tea," he said, and shoved a stiff paper cup with a Lipton tea bag label sticking out of it toward her. Madison was immediately repulsed. Common tea. But, she took it, grateful for the warmth the cup placed in her chilly, damp hands.

She thought about her baby, and became instantly queasy. Neither she or her child needed to be in this germ-filled environment one moment longer. "I need to go. Right now," she said.

The officer held a cup of coffee, and slid into the front seat of the car, and then quietly closed the door. "I understand. But, I wanted to make sure that you were okay first. You didn't have any I.D. on you, and I didn't want to take you to the hospital, so I thought I'd wait until you woke up." He took the lid off of his cup, and steam billowed out. "I didn't smell any alcohol on you, but I need to know if you've taken any drugs today."

"What? No way. Not in my con—" She cut herself off. "I don't do drugs," Madison said. "And did you mention hospital? Why would you take me there?"

The officer appeared a little embarrassed, like he was the one that had gotten saved from jumping off a bridge. He blew on his drink, and then took a small sip.

"I didn't know if you needed to go to the hospital because of the little incident back on the bridge. Remember? You, uh, you were about to jump off, and I caught you. I assumed that maybe you weren't feeling too well about something, and maybe you needed to talk to someone about it."

Madison turned toward the window. How dare he imply that she was trying to jump. "I wasn't trying to jump. I merely slipped. And, I don't have anything that I need to talk to anyone about."

The officer sighed. "If you say so, Miss. All I know is that you were standing on the edge, and you were about to jump, I mean fall. And in my book—"

"It doesn't matter what's in your book. I'm telling you, I wasn't trying to kill myself. It was raining, and a little slippery out there, that's all. I wasn't paying close attention to what I was doing." She faced her accuser. "You don't know me. I have too much to live for to even consider any nonsense like that."

Smiling, he slurped his coffee, and grunted about it being too hot. "Well, I'm glad to hear that. Now, if you'll tell me who you are and where I can take you, I can go and punch out from work."

Madison scratched her head, and contemplated whether or not she wanted to tell him her real name. If he wasn't trustworthy, then the Cavanaugh name would be hung out to dry again. "My name is Ashley, Ashley Vickers, and you can take me to my car, if you don't mind."

"Nice to meet you, Ms. Vickers," the officer said, and then reached down in the car's console, and handed her a card. "My name is Officer Brown. Kelly Brown."

Chapter 11

"*Get out of here, you trollop!*" Sylvia clutched her chest, and she screeched when she swung open the door to Connie's hospital room. Jade, Connie's lover, quickly removed her head from under the sheets, while Connie rested the back of his head in his palms, with a glazed, satiated expression on his face.

"Oh, Mrs. Cavanaugh," Jade said, and wiped her mouth, with a sheepish look. "I'm so very sorry."

"Sorry you got caught, you whore-ish tramp," Sylvia said, and slit her eyes at Jade. "Trash!"

"Now, now, M'Dear," Connie said, with a slick grin. "Um, Jade was just trying to, you know, make me feel a little better."

Sylvia planted a hand on her hip, and flicked her other thumb over her shoulder. "I suggest you get out of here, young lady. You brazen hussy," she said under her breath. She eyed Jade with contempt as she quickly collected her belongings, with an embarrassed smirk. Once she had gotten her goods, she leaned over to give Connie a sloppy kiss, but he turned his head and laughed.

He tossed a small bottle of hospital issued mouthwash at her. "Here, take this. You need to use this before you go out in proper society."

Jade glared at him, and was barely able to suppress her amusement. "Whatever. I'll see you soon, baby," Jade said, and sauntered by Sylvia wearing a skintight copper cat suit.

"Aw-ight," Connie said, and turned toward his mother.

"Have you no shame, girl?" Sylvia snarled. "My child is barely off the critical list, and you're in here trying to give him a setback. He's in no condition for your shenanigans, Jade. I mean, have you no shame?"

Jade remained silent as she exited through the open doorway, and Connie snickered. "M'Dear. Why do you have to give Jade such a hard time? You know she just loves me in her special way."

Sylvia shook, and made sure that the door was shut behind her, with Jade on the other side. "I don't believe you, Conrad Constantine

Cavanaugh. How can you have this woman, this sluttish hussy, in here administering, well, conducting herself in such a lewd manner. I'm shocked and appalled."

Connie scratched his head, and adjusted his gown. "Well, you can't blame me for wanting to feel better."

"I can blame you. You're a married man, for God's sake. Speaking of which, where is your wife? Do you have any idea where she is? Perish the thought that she would've walked in here and seen such a display."

Connie closed his eyes and grimaced like he was in pain. "I, uh, I don't know where Beverly is, M'Dear. I wish she was here. I really need her, you know. I don't know if I'll be able to recover completely without her."

Sylvia started to perch herself on the edge of Connie's bed, but thought better. She didn't know what else had transpired before she interrupted Jade and her illicit therapy. Instead she pulled up a chair, and sat down. "Your wife should be here with you. I can't believe you don't know where Beverly is. Joey says that she went on vacation, but doesn't know where she went or whom she traveled with. Do you know who she went with?"

"I don't know," Connie said, and held his forehead with his eyes pressed tight. "Maybe she just wanted to get away for a while."

"Hmph."

Connie didn't respond, so Sylvia stood and started circling the bed. "Well, Beverly's absence is certain to draw concern, son. And not only from me." Her heels clicked on the tiled floor. "From what I can understand, your friend Stewart is missing also." Sylvia paused and stroked the top of Connie's hand. "I didn't want to say anything, but you don't suppose—"

Connie's eyes flashed open, and he snatched his hand away from his mother's grasp. "Don't even say anything like that, M'Dear. Don't even think it. Beverly's not with Stewart. No way. I know she'd never do anything like that to me. Never."

Sylvia continued stroking his head. "I hear what you're saying dear, but you might as well consider the possibility. No decent woman disappears and doesn't even bother to contact home. I would've never thought Beverly to be so completely irresponsible. But, I've been fooled worse by better, I guess."

Connie rolled his eyes. "I don't want to talk about this anymore, M'Dear."

Sylvia was like a dog on a bone. "I'm just saying, Conrad. I don't want you getting your hopes up just so they'll be dashed. When Beverly does return, if I were you, I wouldn't have her. I just wouldn't."

"I told you I don't want to talk about it." Connie's voice raised, as did his heart rate. His monitors lit up, and beeped, sounding the alarms.

"Conrad, don't upset yourself."

"You're upsetting me, M'Dear," Connie said and clutched his abdomen.

The nurse's voice chimed in on the intercom. "Are you okay, Mr. Cavanaugh?"

Connie groaned. "No, I'm not. I need something for the pain."

"I'll be right in," the nurse said.

"M'Dear, I gotta rest."

"I'll stay here until you go to sleep."

"Naw, that's not necessary. I'll be alright. Plus, the nurse may need to bathe me. And I don't need you here for that."

"There, there, Conrad, dear." Sylvia leaned over and kissed his forehead. "You're going to be fine. And it's okay. I'm sure you're right about everything. Please don't be upset. I just want your wife to be here where she's supposed to be, doing what she's supposed to be doing—taking care of you."

Once Sylvia calmed Connie down, she did stay with him until he was sedated and sleeping comfortably. Assured that he was down for the evening, Sylvia returned home, where she reported to Harry and Joey that Connie's recovery was just shy of a miracle. Despite the bullet's location, he was regaining some use of his legs. With every awestruck word, Sylvia's chest poked further and further out.

It was around ten in the morning, and Joey was enthusiastic and encouraged after finally getting a good night's sleep, thanks to the last changing of his cell phone number. It had been a few days since the bothersome late night phone calls, but Joey went forward with the number change to ensure that the pesky calls wouldn't continue. As time progressed, issues continually cropped up, and there weren't many things that he had control over, but his cell phone was one.

Joey had just swung by his parent's house to pick up *Il Rosso*. He had bumped into his father, who was on his way out to play a round of golf with Jolly, and he had given Joey yet another task to complete. Howard hadn't returned from his vacation, and now Royce was MIA.

To track down the now illusive Royce, who was proving to be as wiley as his predecessor Howard.

Always the good and faithful servant, Joey didn't balk, but added this to his litany of things to do. But, perhaps it was a good thing. It kept him busy and occupied, and helped him to delay dealing with his personal life, while handling the more immediate matters. Joey already had too much on his mind, like responding to Madison's shocking phone message. He was already struggling with how to communicate with her about Justin, and now he couldn't believe that she was pregnant too. He could hear it in her voice that she was standing on the verge of losing it, but Joey knew that he had to handle her extra gently. Then he wondered if his parents knew about Madison's condition. Maybe that was why his mother seemed additionally forlorn and testy. Joey knew that Madison was probably really going out of her mind, so he didn't just want to call her, he wanted to see her. But, he decided to wait until he had a block of time to commit to his baby sister. He had failed her once before, but he wasn't about to do it again.

He could visit with Madison today, so he called his mother to beg off taking care of *Il Rosso* for a few more days, but she was insistent that he take the jewel today, even though it wouldn't be worn for another few months. Tenacity was truly his mother's forte, and no wasn't a word that she even tried to comprehend on a regular basis.

As Joey sat at the conference table in the library, his mother went about retrieving the sacred gem from the vault. Sylvia swung open the portrait of Grand and his wife Pia, and it revealed one of the hidden family safes.

Sylvia carefully turned the combination lock, and then gently pulled the metal handle until the steel door slowly creaked opened. She rummaged around in the safe for a few moments, and then ceremoniously removed a long, flat walnut colored box. Closing the vault door, Sylvia carefully replaced the picture, and gingerly laid the box onto the conference room table.

Sylvia's eyes twinkled, and she stroked the box like it had feelings and could respond. "Oh, Joseph. I'm sure that you and your brothers and sisters just don't realize how very sacred this gem is to our family," Sylvia said, and then kept caressing the container. "Without this, our family would never be where we are today."

Joey listened, and tried to appear interested, but he had heard this speech every year, for the last ten years. At first he felt honored by the responsibility, but lately, he could really not be so bothered. Sylvia related the story of how his grandmother Pia had taken the heirloom from her Italian Family, and she and Grand had used it as the financial cornerstone of their family. Even though Sylvia's story had a different nuance from the one Grand had told him years ago, there was something in her words that triggered his thoughts.

"M'Dear," Joey said. "Why did you and Father select me to be the one to take *Il Rosso* to the jewelers? It's an awful lot of responsibility, and I'm just wondering why you two chose me."

Sylvia smiled, and carefully opened the box, and its satin lining shimmered. "Because, son, you are one of my most responsible children. And you don't mind going into the U Street area, since Jules has refused to move to a better location."

Jules was one of the most renowned jewelers in the area. He had a hand crafted, custom shop in his Shaw home, that he never even advertised or put a shingle out. Although he had worked on and created pieces for Black celebrities and socialites, he refused to leave his neighborhood. As the area evolved from a Renaissance status to its current urban blight, his stance to stay was honorable, but risky. But the Cavanaughs never had any problems.

Sylvia smiled. "You know, what I said was partially true, you know," Sylvia said, and removed a satin satchel from the base of the box. "Actually, originally, your Uncle Edgy would take it for me. And then, well, when he left, Jolly took it to Jules for a while. But, naturally, Harry and I wanted one of our own to carry on the tradition. As you all will, as the next generation of Cavanaughs grow up."

Uncle Edgy, Joey thought. It was beginning to come together. If the jewel only left its safe haven once a year, under Edgy's control, it stood to reason that Edgy would've taken advantage of his position as the sole transporter. Somehow, it just seemed odd that his mother had never mentioned that before, but then Joey assumed it crossed her mind because Edgy was back. But then Joey had a sinking feeling about what Edgy might have done to the jewel. Joey couldn't wait to get his hands on the family jewel to see if it had his Grandfather's inscription on it. But, he couldn't be too overzealous and make his mother suspicious.

Sylvia lifted the flawless jewel from the satchel, and raised it to the light. The vivid asterisms in the giant stone were offset by a platinum and diamond crusted pendant holder and chain, and was absolutely breathtaking. "Isn't it lovely?" Sylvia fawned.

"It's gorgeous," Joey said, as he stood and extended his hand. His palms were itching to get that stone. "Now, I don't mean to rush you, but I need to get going, M'Dear. Is Jules expecting me today?"

Sylvia re-straightened the portrait, until it was perfectly aligned. "I left a message for him yesterday. Have no fear, Jules will always be prepared for the Cavanaughs. Always."

Joey was also supposed to meet Kelly to pick up the cash from the defunct drug deal, but he decided to drop the jewel off first. He didn't relish the thought of carrying it around any longer than he had to, and if things went without a glitch, he'd have time to still meet Kelly and then spend some time with Madison.

As Joey drove down 16th Street, the thought of Edgy having unchecked access to *Il Rosso* was wearing on him. By the time Joey reached U Street, his curiosity was killing him.

Parked in front of a hydrant, Joey grabbed the jewel, and practically sprinted to Jules's house. He rang the buzzer and the jeweler's son, Anton, opened the door.

"Where's your father?" Joey said, as he pushed by Anton.

"He's, uh, a little incapacitated right now," Anton said. "Is there something I can do for you?"

"Who's doing his work for him now?" Joey asked, and he looked around the cramped little store, and Anton responded that he was.

"I need for you to take this piece apart for me," Joey said, and brought the box up from his side.

Anton stepped backward. "Isn't this your family's stone?" Anton frowned. "I don't know about that, Joey. That's not normally part of the cleaning process, and I don't want to be responsible for doing that."

"Just take it apart. Right now," Joey said, and thrust the box at the unsuspecting jeweler.

It was just as he figured. When Anton removed the stone, Joey grabbed an ocular or jeweler's eye, and scanned the pendant holder. His heart dropped to his feet. There was no inscription. There was no inscription of "For Our Family, P&C," as Grand had only told him about. The jewel, as it was, was a fake.

Joey's blood pressure rose, and his heart beat like a pair of conga drums. "I need to talk to your father. Where the hell is he?" Joey demanded, and grabbed Anton by the collar, knocking several boxes, chains and miscellaneous items on the crowded floor.

Joey bogarted into Connie's hospital room, where Connie was sitting upright in his bed, talking on the telephone, and brutalizing Christian in a game of acey-deucey.

When he saw the frantic Joey, Connie motioned for him to sit down. Christian heaved a sigh of relief, and abdicated the game. "I quit," he said, and stretched.

"Now that my crew's a little thin, I'm working with Uncle Jolly to line up some more folks," Connie said as he hung up the phone. "What's up with you, Joe? Come on in and take Chris's seat. I just got finished spanking his ass in a game of ace-deuce."

"A childish game," Christian said, and stood, glancing out Connie's window. He had an annoyed expression on his face, like he'd prefer to be anywhere but there.

Joey took the walnut box and flung it onto Connie's bed, and Christian jumped like it was a reptile.

"What are you doing? Isn't that *Il Rosso*? Have you gone completely mad? That jewel is worth over a million dollars." Christian glanced at Joey, and then back at the case, like he was afraid to touch it.

"You're right, *Il Rosso* is probably worth more than that. However, that," Joey said, and then pointed to the piece of box, "isn't the real deal. It's not *Il Rosso*."

Connie gingerly picked up the package with his two index fingers. "So, what's up, Joe? What are you saying?"

"Well, M'Dear asked me to take the gem to Jules, to have it polished and checked. Well, I just came from there, and guess what? Old man Jules is on his deathbed, barely able to speak. The only thing that I could get out of him was that years ago, he made a copy of the stone, and that he gave the original to somebody. But he went out before I could find out who he made the replicate for," Joey said.

"Went out? Like, what? He kicked the bucket?" Connie asked.

Joey shook his head. "Like he's slipped into some kind of coma or something. Hell, he could be dead for all I know. I tried shaking him, but he wouldn't wake up."

"This is completely preposterous," Christian said, while Connie remained quiet. "How could he do something like that to us?"

"Don't be so damned simple, Christian. He did it for the cash. What else could it be? You know money'll make anybody sell their souls. You ought to know, Mr. Finance Man." Connie smirked at Christian, then opened the case, and pulled the necklace out of the box.

"So, this is just a nice piece of glass, huh? Well, whoever Jules rolled on us for had to be somebody mighty damned well connected to get Jules to risk life and limb for. Somebody with a whole lotta juice."

"That's what I was thinking," Joey said. "Just this morning, M'Dear told me that years ago, Uncle Edgy used to take *Il Rosso* to Jules. And so—"

"And so, it figures that slick son of a bitch got it copied, and he has the original," Connie said, barely able to mask his admiration. "That bastard has had it all these years."

"I've exhausted all of the possibilities that I can think of, and Edgar is the only one that would've had motive and opportunity to do something dirty like this," Joey said.

"I don't know," Connie said. "It sounds like something's missing. Like, something's not adding up. I say the old man is still holding out, and just giving us the okey doke."

"They're doing a death watch, Connie. What did you want me to do? Choke it out of him?"

"Nothing, Joey. If he hangs around and makes it, I'll take care of him. But in the meantime, we need to act on what we know and get in Edgy's ass."

Christian finally joined in. "I agree. This all makes sense if Edgy did copy it. He would've been that vindictive," Christian said. "However, the only thing I don't understand is why would he have the stone copied? What would he need it for, other than spite?"

Joey wanted to just smack Christian's glasses off of his face. For someone that had so much intellect, he had little or no common sense. "Because, it might explain how he got his stake in New York, Christian. Think about it. He could've given *Il Rosso* back to the old family, you know Grandmother Pia's family, or either he used it as collateral to get his business up and running there. Father said that when Uncle Edgy left here, he didn't have much money," Joey said.

The three brothers fell silent, each mulling their individual thoughts. Finally, Christian spoke. "Well, then we have to tell Father."

Joey shook his head. "Tell him what? We don't have any real evidence. No proof. All we know is that we have a fake stone, that'll give our mother a stroke if she finds out about it. Until we know for sure what happened to it, we can't say anything."

"I say we torture his ass until he spills his guts," Connie said.

"Father would never condone that," Joey said, and cut his eye at Connie. "And we're not going to do anything to piss him off any further."

Connie cleared his throat, and twirled the chain around his finger. "So, you know what this means. We've got to find out what went down in New York. But, we just can't go rolling up there unprepared. We have to have cash and carry, you know what I mean?"

"No, I don't know what you mean, Conrad," Christian said. "Will you please stop speaking in such vernacular so I can comprehend what you're saying? Speak English, for God's sake."

Connie rolled his eyes, and mimicked Christian with a nasally voice. "You need to go strapped, with some heat, some guns, and some heavy backup. Lots of it. Because, if the old family has the jewel, they aren't just going to let it go like that. Now, maybe you can try to negotiate or something, but, you need some leverage. We need to let these bammas know that they can't carry us. You know what I mean?"

"No, I don't," Christian said.

"We gotta let them know that we aren't suckers, and we aren't gonna be played with. You got that?"

"I hear you. But, I don't think that bringing a bunch of muscle is going to solve anything," Joey said. "We should try to negotiate, but we're going to need some cash."

"And plenty of it," Connie said. "At least a million."

"A million dollars? Where are we supposed to get that from, Connie?" Christian asked, and his face became flush and tight.

"Shake your piggybank, bro. Or look underneath your mattress. I'm sure you're sitting on a stash somewhere," Connie said, and shot Christian a '*don't fuck with me*' look.

"That's completely illogical, Conrad," Christian said.

"Whatever. That damned Justin screwed up all of my ends, and I don't think I'll ever see them again. So, we gotta come up with something."

Joey thought about the quarter million Connie was referring to, and that Kelly now had. Joey had to get it from him immediately. "I think I can come up with some. We'll make it happen."

Connie placed the faux jewel back in the case. "Now, there's not much I can do with you right now, since I'm laid up in this joint. So it looks like you two are going to have to handle our business. I'm getting stronger everyday, but I doubt that I'll be able to make the trip with you. You two'll have to go for it," Connie said, and stared at his brothers.

"But, right now, we can sit here and figure out what we need to do. And what we need to do soon."

Christian immediately backpedaled, and fumbled with his Orville Redenbacher tie. "I, uh, I don't think that's such a good idea. I mean, I'm no street thug. I don't even know how to hold a gun. I'm not going to put myself in the position of getting killed. I have a family. There's no way I'm doing that. No way."

"Be quiet, Christian. Nobody's saying that you have to do all of that. You try that, and you'll get us all killed. Naw, you're going there to negotiate. Finesse the situation. You can do that, can't you? We'll make sure you have protection," Connie said. Joey saw the murky shades of his gangster brother re-emerging. He was wondering how long it was going to be before the old Connie showed up. And here he was. Live and in living color.

"We'll work it out, Christian. No one's going to take any unnecessary risks," Joey said. "No one."

The brothers spent the evening plotting their course of action. As they devised plans for the who's, the where's and the how's, Connie's mind was functioning in parallel order. Something just didn't feel or sound right to him. In fact, something wasn't right. And he was going to find out just what the hell was really going on.

Chapter 12

After a few days of self-imposed exiled, Madison gathered up enough strength to finally rise from her bed. She had taken refuge there after her quite embarassing momentary lapse in judgment, and first brush with the law. Her bedroom was a chaotic mess, but she didn't feel like having her maid come over to clean. So, she decided to straighten up herself, something she had never done.

She picked up the wrinkled warm up suit she had worn, and rifled through the pockets. She happened upon Officer Brown's card, and immediately had a sinking feeling. After a few moments of reliving waking up in the back of his squad car, somehow, she felt like calling him. She felt like he wouldn't judge her, and he had given her such a pleasant feeling. He had been so kind and considerate when he helped her, that she felt a little guilty about giving a false name. Not that she cared about using Ashley's name, that ingrate, but perhaps because she was feeling a little better, or a little less embarrassed about the situation.

She caught Kelly on his cell phone, and he sounded genuinely happy to hear from her. When Madison mentioned that she wanted to take him out to dinner as a kind of thank you, he hesitated and seemed surprised, but then agreed to go. Madison suggested that they go to Crisfield's on Georgia Avenue, a popular little seafood restaurant, that didn't have a dress code, but had exceptional food.

In her bedroom, she stood naked in front of her wall length mirror, and held her abdomen. She wanted to see if her stomach was protruding, but it still appeared normal to her. She wrapped her arms around her shoulders, and tilted her head. Suddenly, she glanced up and saw a massive palm print on the mirror. Then, she recalled the last time she faced this mirror,steamed up and smudged, with another set of warm arms wrapped around her.

Justin had made passionate love to her, and watched her every motion. She felt more than naked, being nude and observed. She felt raw and vulnerable. Open. Wide open. Their sweaty bodies glistened in the moonlight, as he held her, and leaned her forward, and she wrapped her leg around his thigh. As he gently entered her from behind, he held her with one strong arm, and pressed the other against the mirror. They were like poetry in motion; she consumed with him, and he with her. With every thrust, she felt a tingly combination of friction and intensity that brought tears of joy to her eyes.

Was this child conceived in love, or was this baby just a pawn in some sick game? The tears returned at this moment, and threatened to run down her cheeks. She needed to release, to cry, to feel, and to grieve. To cry for the past that was gone. And to cry for the future she was so uncertain of.

Madison's tears had dried sufficiently by the time seven o'clock rolled around, and when she was supposed to meet Kelly. She was her normally fashionably late self, and when she arrived at the restaurant, Kelly was waiting patiently for her in one of the vinyl booths.

"Hello, Ashley," Kelly said, and stood as Madison took her seat.

"Officer Brown—" Madison began, but then he stopped her.

"Please, call me Kelly," he said, and fanned his napkin out into his lap. He smiled broadly, and Madison noticed that he had really nice teeth. He was a truly good looking brother; tall, well built, and clean cut. He had an earnest quality about him, and beautiful, almond shaped eyes. Madison wondered how she missed all that, but then it occurred to her that she must've really been out of it when they met.

"I'm kind of ashamed to tell you this, but my name isn't Ashley. It's um—"

Before Madison could continue, the waiter came over and interrupted her. He wanted to take their beverage order.

"Would you like a drink, Madame X?" Kelly said, with slight amusement in his voice. His lips parted in a warm smile, and revealed a set of even, white teeth.

Madison wanted something, but then she thought about her health. Alcohol was definitely out, and she would probably have to cut out caffeine and everything else that tasted good. Then, she realized that she really needed to see an obstetrician, and get some clear direction on how to stay well during her pregnancy.

"I'll have a lemonade, please. Fresh squeezed," she said, and Kelly ordered a bottle of Heineken.

"So, you were saying," he said, and nudged her arm with his strong index finger.

"I wanted to apologize, because my name isn't Ashley. I didn't tell you what my real name was because I was really embarrassed, and well, I guess I was just ashamed."

"I could only imagine what you must've thought of me, and about what almost happened. But, I didn't want you to think that I was being shady or anything like that. I just felt a little cheap."

"I didn't think that. I just figured that you were going through something. And that you didn't want to talk about it or deal with it."

"I am, I mean, I was. I've had a number of personal issues over the past few weeks, and I guess I just wasn't thinking too clearly," Madison said.

"I see, is it something that you want to talk about now?" he asked.

Madison paused, but then the words just spilled from her lips. "I just suffered a personal loss, and then I found out that I'm going to have a baby." Madison didn't know why she was pouring her heart out to this near perfect stranger, but, perhaps it was just easier to talk to a stranger.

Kelly's eyes brightened. "A baby, huh? Well, congratulations. You and your husband must be very happy about that."

"Not quite," Madison said, and shook her head. She flashed her naked left hand. "I'm not married. And, unfortunately, my child's father was the person that I recently lost." Madison felt a tinge of emotion in her voice, and inhaled deeply. Again, she paused. "But, nevertheless, I wanted you to know how much I appreciated your care and consideration during my momentary lapse, and how you helped me out. Really, I can't thank you enough."

Kelly accepted the compliment with a bashful nod. Their conversation progressed into the evening, and they chatted about a number of things, from relationships, to work, to families. Kelly didn't have a lot to share about his life, and Madison didn't go into a lot of specifics, but she found him endearing and easy to talk to. He was strong, yet sensitive, confident and a good listener.

After a bowl of Crisfield's famous clam chowder, Madison found herself picking at her fried seafood platter, while Kelly devoured his.

"Hey, uh, Madame X. It just dawned on me that you still haven't told me your name," he said, and bit into a colossal sea scallop.

Madison parted her lips, and revealed a bright smile. "My name is—"

"Madison! What are you doing here?" Joey nearly yelled as he crossed the bar area to where Madison and Kelly were seated.

He couldn't believe his eyes. What in the hell were those two doing having dinner? Was this some type of psychological twilight zone he'd stepped into?

After Joey had left the hospital, he had decided to swing by Crisfield's and grab a bite to eat. The busy atmosphere would be a good place for Joey just to blend in and not be noticed, plus their food was the bomb. The chowder and a po' boy sandwiches were to die for, and he nearly did. When he sat down, and got ready to chomp into his sandwich, he saw Madison and Kelly sitting in one of the booths, and his heart double-clutched.

Joey tried not to stare at Kelly too hard, and he adjusted his face before he got too close to them. What third dimension had he stepped into?

"Joey," Madison said, and extended her cheek for him to kiss. "I'd like for you to meet my friend Kelly. Kelly Brown."

Joey pecked his sister's face, and Kelly grabbed Joey's hand and shook it firmly. "Nice to meet you, Joey."

Joey barely cracked a painful smile. As he stared into Kelly's face, he knew that his eyes spoke volumes. Namely, what the hell are you doing here with my sister?

"What brings you here?" Madison asked, and slid over to make room for her brother, who remained standing.

Joey tried to train his eyes on Madison, but couldn't help forcing his peripheral vision to get a glimpse of Kelly. "I just left Connie's, and figured that I'd grab something to eat. I got your message, and I was hoping to catch up with you later, Maddie."

"Yeah, uh, I guess that might have something to do with that little message I left for you the other day," Madison said. "Oh, well. We can still do that. Kelly and I were just finishing up." Madison slid toward the end of the booth and then stood. "Joey, why don't you stay here and keep Kelly company, until I get back from the bathroom." She turned to her dinner guest. "I'll be right back, Kelly. Okay?"

Both Kelly and Joey watched Madison as she walked to the ladies' room. When she was safely out of sight and hearing distance, Joey lit into Kelly, and demanded to know what was going on. And for how long had it been going on.

"Nothin's going on. And, I didn't even know that Madison was your sister."

"Negro please. How can you say that?" Joey said through gnashed teeth. "You saw her at my house, that day when you saw Justin or Brian, or whatever his name is, remember?"

Kelly shrugged. "I didn't really see her. I heard her voice, but I only saw Brian," Kelly said, and picked a shrimp off of Madison's plate.

"Well, you saw her picture hanging in my house. You can't deny that."

Kelly shrugged. "Your sister's a beautiful woman, but I swear I don't remember her or what she looked like. I guess I don't retain that kind of information when it comes to females. Or did you forget that so soon?"

"Well, how'd you hook up with her? What's that all about? Are you back into women now, or is she just a little something to do?" Joey leaned over the table, narrowed his eyes at Kelly, and lowered his voice. "Does she know about you?"

Kelly cleared his throat, and drank the last sip of his second beer. "We just accidentally met a few days ago. She's a nice lady, and she invited me to grab something to eat. That's all. A man's gotta eat."

"Yeah, right. I think that shit's quite convenient. I thought I was supposed to be meeting with you later to pick up the cash, and you're sitting over here wining and dining with my damned sister. You want me to believe this is all a coincidence? What's up with that, Kelly?"

"Nothing's up, like I said. And you can still pick up the cash. Later, after my date's over."

Date? A surge of heat rushed through Joey's body. He had a lot of nerve feeling whatever he was feeling, given the fact that he and Lauren were just together a few days ago. But, they had agreed to take things a day at a time, and they had no promises or delusions. In fact, he hadn't even spoken with her since that night in Richmond. Now, facing Kelly, Joey wasn't sure if he was jealous, exhausted or just plain angry at the fact that Kelly knew Madison and didn't tell him. But, whatever it was, he wasn't happy about the feeling.

* * *

Her pending motherhood forced Madison to put a number of things into their proper perspective. With her mother staging her silent protest, Madison didn't have any close friends that she could talk to about her pregnancy, and the only other person who could possibly relate was her sister in law, Kim.

She and Kim weren't that close, since they traveled in different circles. Kim was all into her motherhood and family thing, while Madison could barely stand to be around children. She loved her nieces and nephews, but she was far too busy to be wrapped up in child rearing. When Kim was able to get some solo time, she and Madison hung out, and their personalities meshed. Kim was raw and abrasive, and Madison liked her candor. They always had each other's backs when the chips were down, and Madison knew that she could count on Kim for some sisterly, albeit guttural, advice.

After leaving lunch with Kelly, Madison called Kim, who was apologetic for not being available when Madison had contacted her before. Madison booked some time with her for later on that evening, suggesting an impromptu girls night out. Madison was thinking of catching a movie at the Cinema and Drafthouse, but Kim wanted them to go see some male strippers. Madison wasn't the least surprised that the sex-deprived Kim would want to go there.

Once she had confirmed her evening plans with an amenable Kim, Madison was going to call Connie, but then she decided to dash over to Baltimore to see him instead. She was finally ready to confront him about his involvement in her lover's death. And she wanted to see his face when she let him have it.

After battling the stop and go traffic on the B-W Parkway, Madison was more than fired up when she arrived at the hospital. Her mood slightly diffused when she saw Connie, clean shaven and picking at a cup of Jello, and looking like an innocent little boy.

"Hey Madison. What's up, baby sis?" Connie was propped up on a few pillows, and he smiled when Madison entered his room. The TV was on blast as scantily clad hoochies with vicious bodies danced across the screen in the latest music videos. He peeked around Madison, like he was expecting something.

"Did M'Dear send me something to eat? She was supposed to have Geneva send me something decent to grub on, 'cause this hospital food is 'bout to kill me."

At first unable to speak, Madison shook her head no, and Connie just shrugged. "Oh well, maybe she'll bring it later. Hey, can you bring me a VCR? And some flicks. You know the kind I like. Something kinda freaky, you know?"

Madison's face was like stone when she found her voice. "That's not why I'm here, Connie. I'm not your little errand girl, and I'm not on your beck and call. I'm not going to do anything for you."

"Well, damn. I'm sorry I asked you to do me a favor. Well, ain't no thing. I'm sure I can get one of my boys to do it. So, what's the matter with you, baby girl? Why is your mood so foul? You PMS-ing or what? You need some Mydol or something? I'm sure they got something around here to help you out. This is a hospital, you know."

Madison placed her hands on her hips. "No, I'm not PMS-ing."

"Okay, Madison. You seem a little bent about something. And I recall that the last time I saw you, you were a little quiet too. What's up? Is somebody messin' with you? You know I'll handle that if that's the case. So, come here and give your big brother a hug and tell me what's up."

"Later," Madison snapped. She grabbed the remote, clicked the TV off, and tossed the remote onto the foot of Connie's bed, which was just out of his reach. "Look. We need to talk."

Connie sighed and crossed his arms. "About what?"

Madison hovered over Connie and grabbed the bed railing for support. "Don't act like you don't know why I'm here. It's because of Justin, and what happened when he was with you."

"Oh."

"Oh? Is that all you have to say?"

"Well, you could back up off of me. You know I don't like folks all up in my personal space like this." Connie reached for the remote, but Madison smacked it onto the floor.

"Connie, how could you do that to me? How could you endanger Justin's life by getting him all caught up in your schemes like that? You knew he and I were involved. It seems like you would've had more consideration for me."

"Consideration for you? What about some consideration for me? Do you know where you're at? Well, if you don't know, you're at the hospital. Where I'm trying to recuperate. Damn, I need rest. I don't need this bullshit, Madison."

"I don't care about what you need, Connie. I know I didn't need to be betrayed by you. And I don't care if you don't feel like dealing with it. You will, today. Now, I want some answers about Justin."

Connie sucked his teeth. "Oh, so that's why your back is all up like it is. Well, I'm sorry, Madison. But, don't blame me. I knew something was wrong with that brother. I told you, he was too damned girly-looking for me."

"For you? Here we go again. Don't you get it? It wasn't about you. If you had any doubts or suspicions, you should've come to me. It's your fault he's dead. And yes, I do blame you. And I don't think that I'll ever forgive you for it."

"Forgive me? Ahh, hell naw, Madison. You're not gonna put that shit on me. Your boy was a fuckin' double agent, and he couldn't be trusted. By you or anyone else. So, no, I'm not taking the heat for that one, baby girl. No way. He would've gotten iced sooner or later by his own deeds— not by anything I did."

Madison balled up her fist and slugged Connie in the shoulder. "You're so damned heartless. I can't believe that you don't have any more sympathy for me than this."

Connie rubbed his shoulder. "Sympathy for you? Who's laying up in here all shot up? Me. Barely livin'. It still hurts to even draw a breath. If anything, it's Pretty Boy's fault I'm here. That mother fucker. If he wasn't dead, I swear, I'd kill him."

"You make me sick, Connie. You're logic is so twisted. You're so damned ignorant and cruel, and you never want to take responsibility for the things you do. Nothing you do is ever your fault. It's always someone elses."

"I'll never take responsibility for something I didn't do. Believe that."

"You act like a child. A spoiled, rotten, selfish child."

"Yeah, well, whatever. I know I'm not a child. I'm a grown ass man, and I still have bullets in me that'll always remind me of what I've been through. And I know another thing. You need to grow the hell up, girl. That nigga didn't care nothin' about you. Wake up. I know game when I see it, and that's what he was about. Game. Big time game. Tryin' to get all that he could get from whoever he could get it from. Namely you. You were just a mark, so get over it."

Madison shook her head, her eyes filling with tears. "I guess you'd know, wouldn't you, Connie?"

Connie groaned as he leaned over the side of the bed, and struggled until he finally reached the remote. He fell back in the bed, grunting and moaning, and turned on the TV. "Trust me, Madison. Save your tears. You'll thank me later for getting his bitch ass out of your life, before he could've done anymore harm to you than just rockin' your world." Connie sniffed. "And, I'm sure he wasn't all that anyway."

Madison's voice quieted, and she sat down on the chair next to Connie's bed. "He was all that."

"Whatever. Trust me. You'll thank me one day."

"I'll never thank you for killing the love of my life, and neither will my child."

Connie whirled around and glared at Madison. "Your child? Say what? Madison, you're pregnant?"

A single tear rolled down Madison's cheek. "Yes, I am, and thanks to you, my child will never know his father."

Connie clicked the television off, and reached for his sister, but she jerked away from him. "Damn, Madison. I'm sorry. I didn't know. So, I guess this means you're going to keep it, huh?"

Madison nodded yes, and Connie's face softened. "Well, I'm really sorry. Every child should know his father, and I'm sorry that yours won't. But, I'll be here for you, Madison. Square business. Even though I do a lot of messed up stuff, I won't let you down. I promise," he said.

She wanted to believe her brother, but nothing in Connie's past had shown that his words would be more than just that. Words. He tried to reassure her for the next hour or so that they talked, but Madison knew that the megalomaniac's commitment would wane as soon as a new piece of ass or another challenge presented itself. She could never rely on him for anything, but at least for the moment, his words were encouraging. The reality was that even though Connie would never allow anyone to purposely hurt Madison, he wasn't going out of his way to ensure that she and her child's life would be any better. He was far too selfish for that.

Later that evening, as she stuffed ten and twenty dollar bills into the G-strings of the heavily hung male dancers, Madison tried to ease into the subject of her pregnancy, by making small talk with Kim until the right moment presented itself.

Kim was enamoured with the well-endowed dancers, and glossed over the updates of her life, including life with Christian and children.

Madison was relieved that Kim's attention was kind of detached, and that the waiters were attentive and kept the table flush with drinks. Kim's ears finally perked up when Madison mentioned that she had seen Connie earlier that day.

"Oh yeah. I've been meaning to visit my dear brother-in-law, but I haven't quite been able to fit it into my schedule. I guess I'll have to send him a plant or a basket of fruit." Kim smirked. "So, how is Connie doing?"

"He's doing okay. He's still Connie. And if you want to send him something, he'd probably appreciate a home cooked meal more than a plant," Madison said.

"You've got to be kidding. I don't even hardly cook myself. I know you don't think that I'd cook anything for his ass. Hmph." Kim crossed her arms. "*Pu-leeze.* I'm sure that Beverly hasn't been derelict in her wifely duties. I'm sure she's set up a kitchen and has all of the creature comforts of home up in his hospital room."

Madison shook her head. "No, not really, Kim. Beverly isn't here."

"What do you mean?"

"Beverly's not here. From what I can understand, she's been on vacation since before Connie got shot."

"On vacation? Get outta here." Kim whooped and sipped her cocktail. "You mean to tell me that Beverly hasn't been waiting on her darling hubby hand and foot?"

"Not at all."

"Well, where is she? I'm sure you all called her, and she's on the first thing smoking, right?"

"No. We don't even know where she is. So, we haven't been able to reach her. So, she doesn't know about Connie and we don't know when she's coming back."

"Well, I'll be goddamned. Old Connie must be pissed about not having his little doormat chained to his bedside, dumping his bedpan." Kim snickered and raised her glass. "Well, good for Beverly. She makes me ill the way she jumps every time Connie snaps his fingers. She couldn't have taken a better time to get away. Who knows, maybe she won't come back. And I wouldn't blame her one bit. I know Connie's your brother, but he ain't right and has never been right. So, you know what they say. What goes around comes back around. And Connie's getting his while he's laid out flat on his back. Karma's a motherfucker, isn't it, Madison?"

"Yeah, karma is a bitch, Kim," Madison said, her voice a near whisper. "And I'm just wondering what I did to deserve what I'm dealing with."

"What's that?"

Kim took the news of Madison's pregnancy better than Madison had anticipated. Madison hadn't gone into too much detail about Justin, because she figured that Christian had already spilled that info. Anything to make himself look better. Even to Kim.

Kim was sympathetic regarding Justin's death, but was concerned that now he had no way of paying child support.

"Girl, I'm sorry that your man's gone, but you need to make a claim on his estate. Whether he's dead or not, that's still his child. And he needs to be responsible for it." Kim was lean and dark, and had a propensity to wear hazel colored contact lenses. And as the strobe lights caught the light tint in her eyes, Kim reminded Madison of a sleek black panther. Gorgeous, but deadly.

Madison shook her head and drank her ginger ale. "I don't care about that, Kim. I'll take more than ample care of my child. I just can't get over the fact that he's gone."

Kim popped her fingers and drank her Mai Tai. "Well, everything happens for a reason. Allow yourself to grieve, but remember, you're carrying a little one now. Allow yourself have to be physically and emotionally healthy for him or her." Kim smiled. "So, how far into your pregnancy are you?"

"About two months."

"Oh, you're still in the early stages, baby. But, you do have to take care of yourself. Anything you expose your child to during these days is going to stay with them, trust me. That's why I kept it cute while I was pregnant. I didn't want my children being exposed to anything that might affect their lives. Speaking of which—" Kim sniffed the air, and turned her head toward a woman who was smoking, and standing close to their table.

Kim took her index finger and jabbed the woman in the shoulder. "Umm, excuse me, Miss. But would you mind moving away from our table. My sister here is pregnant, and the last thing she needs to do is inhale your second hand smoke." She finished her statement with a scowl.

The woman shot Kim a disgusted look, but she stepped off. Madison admired Kim's brashness. "That's why I wanted to talk to you, Kim. I'm going to need your help. I have a million questions about what to do, and how to do it."

"No problem, Madison. I'm here for you. And the first thing that I'd advise you to do is get a man."

"What?"

"Go get yourself a man, girl. For real, I'm telling you, pregnant sex is the best. You'll either want it all the time or none at all. But, believe me, it's so damned juicy when you do do it. And you know dudes love hitting it from the back." Kim leaned over and smacked and rubbed her bottom. "Smack it up, flip it, rub it down."

"Oh, no!" Madison cackled. "Kim, you are crazy," she said with a much needed laugh.

"I know, but I'm really serious though. I'm glad that I could make you laugh, 'cause I'm sure you need to. You gotta keep your stress down too." Kim patted Madison on her knee. "I'm your girl, sis. Anything I can do to help you through, I got it. And, I'm sure that Ashley's got your back too."

"Girl, that's a whole other story," Madison said, and rolled her eyes. "Ashley's gotten all 'brand new' on me, and doesn't have time. Can you believe that?"

"What? After the way you dragged her lame ass around behind you all of these years? Well, later for that tired heifer. So what if she's trying to show her ass? She'll always be a late bitch. Once a frump, always a frump." Kim sipped her drink and popped her lips. "Well, I know that must be disheartening, having your girl stab you up in the back like that, especially when you need her most. And I'm sure Sylvia wasn't too pleased with the news."

"Not at all. She's practically excommunicated me from the family. And she hasn't spoken to me since I told her."

"Well, you're a grown ass woman. And, although you won't have your man around to help you out, you're not alone. And, I'm sure that your mother will come around eventually. Hell, she accepted all of Connie's little bastards, didn't she? Oops, I didn't mean it like your child is going to be a bastard, Madison. I just meant—"

Madison waved away Kim's concerns. "Don't apologize, Kim. I'm not worried about that. People are going to say whatever they want to say. But, for the first time in my life, I'm really not worried about me.

I'm thinking about my baby. I just want to make sure that my child is healthy and loved. That's all."

Kim raised her glass, and clinked it against Madison's. "Well, all right then, dammit. If I hadn't seen and heard you say it, I would've never believed it. That's the way it should be. You have to do what you have to do for you and your little one. Trust me, 'I' becomes 'we' real quick." She winked at Madison. "Whoever said that you can't change." Kim's eyelashes fluttered. "And, speaking of change. You'll never guess who seems to be having a change of heart."

"Who?"

"My husband. Can you believe it? Old boy has been really coming around lately. He's more involved with the children, and he's even been taking care of my needs too."

"Really?" Madison recalled that Kim had intimated that she and Christian were getting along, so she tried not to appear astonished, but she was kind of sickened at the thought. Kim and Christian's relationship had been so benign for so long, that it was difficult to even think about them doing the wild thing.

Kim must have read Madison's mind. "I'm amazed too. I hate to say it, but that old lady he got caught up with must've really turned him out. She put something on 'em and showed him a thing or two. For real." Kim snickered and readjusted herself in her chair. "Remind me to thank her, if I ever see her again."

"Will that be before or after you scratch her eyes out?" Madison asked, and tried not to laugh.

"During," Kim said, with a wicked chuckle.

Chapter 13

Joey's eyes popped open, and he couldn't believe where he was. He had never gone over, and certainly never stayed at another man's house before, and as daylight crept under the window shade, the previous evening was just an ugly blur.

Satisfied that Madison and Kelly parted company at the restaurant, Joey followed her home and they talked. About Justin. About Lauren. About her pregnancy. And Kelly. Although she was vague about how she had met him, she assured Joey that it was a matter of happenstance, and that dinner was their first time going out. She seemed optimistic that she'd see him again, and Joey tried to persuade Madison not to get hung up on him. His argument was that she was just vulnerable, and probably not finished grieving. He even threw in the raging hormones she was probably experiencing with her pregnancy, and so Joey promised her that he'd do everything he could to support her, in his role as brother, uncle and surrogate father. He even offered to go to Lamaze classes with her.

Joey wondered if he was overdoing it, either out of true concern for Madison or was he really worried about her getting more involved with Kelly, and the fact that he had conflicted feelings. Whatever it was, as soon as Madison seemed calm enough, Joey headed over to Kelly's. To pick up the money and to set his ass straight.

"Don't play with my sister, man," Joey said as he stormed into Kelly's apartment.

"I told you it's nothing like that," Kelly said. He picked up the black duffel bag, and shoved it in Joey's chest. "Now, this is what you came here for, so take it and get the hell out."

Joey snatched the bag and hurled it to the floor. He pointed his finger in Kelly's face. "I'm telling you, don't play with her, man. If you're doing this to get back at me, well, then that's some sick shit. You can't have me, so you're going to try to do my sister? I don't think so."

"Don't give yourself so much credit, Joey," Kelly said, and closed his apartment door. "And get your finger out of my face. Right now." Kelly glared at Joey. "What's up? Are you jealous or something?"

Joey grunted. "No, I'm not. Now, don't give yourself too much credit. I just don't want you messing around with my sister. If you want a woman, then fine. There are plenty of man-hungry females out there that you can fuck around with. Do what you want to do, just don't do it with my damned sister. She's been through too much to get hooked up with a gay man now. That just might send her completely over the edge."

Kelly shook his head, and picked up Joey's bag. "You don't have to worry about me, Joey. I told you, I'm not the one who's damned confused. You oughta check yourself."

"Tell me, since you're so good at doling out advice, did you ever get with your girl, the good agent and clue her in about your double life? Or did she find out on her own and threaten you and your family?"

Joey and Lauren had discussed many things during their conciliatory meeting in Richmond, but nothing to that degree. Plus, Joey knew that Kelly was just being catty. "That's none of your business, Kelly. And don't ask me anything about Lauren. She wasn't and still isn't any of your concern."

"You're so concerned about what you want to be concerned about, aren't you Joey? Anything and anyone outside of your area of concern gets nothing from you, right? Well, you know what? That's mighty hypocritical of you. I just suggest that you take the advice you seem to have no problem dishing out."

"Don't worry about it, Kelly. I'm handling mine. You handle yours. Excluding my damn sister."

Kelly grunted. "Get, real. I'm not trying to get back at you through your sister. You're a trip. You don't want me, but you can't handle the thought of me even having a meal with someone else. Now, are you going to take this and leave or what?" Kelly again shoved the bag into Joey's chest.

"Are you going to see my sister again?"

"What's it to you? I don't answer to you or anyone. I'm free to see whoever I want to see, remember? Like you said, what you do doesn't have anything to do with me, and this doesn't have anything to do with you."

Joey stepped so close to Kelly that he could feel his warm breath on his face. He dropped the bag again.

"It has everything to do with me. Are you going to see her or what?" Joey's chest heaved, and he balled up his fists.

"Don't try to buck up in my face, Joey, because you'll get more than just your feelings hurt. Now, I said that it's none of your damn business. So, just take that bag and get the hell up outta—"

Before Kelly could finish, Joey did something he had never done before. He kissed him. Deeply. Their tongues met with a vengeful force that nearly knocked them both down.

They clawed at each other's clothes, grabbing, tugging and tossing them until both were naked and breathing fire. Like two muscular gladiators or muddy Grecian wrestlers, they didn't make love, they had wild, passionate, no holds barred sex.

They consumed each other in unimaginable ways. Until this moment, Joey had always been a top, but over the course of the night, he was a bottom, a side, an over, an under. It didn't matter. He was releasing a beast that had been wounded and trapped for too long. And Kelly met his passion with even more vigor.

Their sweaty bodies slapped and stroked until they both nearly passed out from the soaring energy level. When it was over, they were spent, and collapsed in a tangled heap on Kelly's double bed.

Kelly was snoring softly, with his arm draped around Joey's neck. Suddenly, Joey felt stifled, almost to the point of being smothered. He was choking. What had he done?

He slipped out of bed, and fumbled his way to the bathroom where he needed to relieve himself. As he urinated, he wanted to puke, but there was nothing there to bring up. He relived the torrid moments from last evening, and wanted to slap himself. Why the hell had he done that?

He took a quick shower, and slipped on his day old clothes, and quietly cracked the bathroom door. Kelly and his manhood were up, literally, and he was sitting on the edge of the bed.

"What's the rush, Joey? Why'd you get dressed? You were in and out of the shower before I could even join you."

Joey scratched his head and plotted his escape. "I've got to go, Kelly. I've got a lot of shit to do today."

Kelly reached for Joey, but he just ignored him. "This shouldn't have happened, Kelly. We shouldn't have got down like that." Joey said, and sidestepped Kelly's reach.

Kelly stood before Joey, proudly displaying his magnificent nakedness. "Come on, Joey. Why are you saying that? I thought you had moved past all of that. You know where I stand. I want to be here for you. I want to be with you."

Joey took a deep breath, and marched out into Kelly's living room. "I told you, Kelly. That's not going to happen. And I wished you'd stop calling me and leaving stuff at my house."

"What are you talking about? I haven't called you that often," Kelly said. "And I certainly didn't leave anything at your house. That must be some other nigga you've been messin' around with."

"Whatever Kelly. I know you've been trying to reach out to me, and, I'm sorry I haven't been able to return your feelings. I wished that things hadn't gone down the way they did last night. I guess I missed you, and I needed you in some way." Joey scooped up the precious duffel bag, and headed toward the door.

"So, that's how you play me. You don't want me to play with your sister, but you want to come over here and play with me like I'm some damned toy.

"I'm not seeing your sister, man. I told you, I really dig you, Joey, but damn, you're a selfish son of a bitch."

"Selfish? How can I be selfish? I stayed with you last night. I did shit with you I've never done before. Can't you see that I'm just messed up about all of this, and can't deal with it?"

"Yeah, I can really tell, Joey. You come over here to fuck with my head, and then you just roll out like nothing happened. I didn't ask to see you, you came on your own. And now you want to play games with me. But, you know what? I'm tired of you and your simple-assed games. Take your money and get your sorry ass out of my life, Joey Cavanaugh. Don't ever contact me again, you got that? Ever."

Joey had barely found refuge in his Range Rover from his altercation with Kelly when his phone rang with back-to-back calls.

The first call was from Ashley. Joey was surprised to hear from her, and even more surprised by the conversation.

"Hey Joey. It's me, Ashley."

At first, Joey barely recognized her. Ashley had a very distinct voice, kind of Valley Girl witha nasally twist, but today, she sounded quite, well, normal. And kind of sultry. It made him pause, but then he managed to return the saluation.

"Well, I was calling for a couple of reasons. Business and pleasure. But, we'll do business first."

She said that the vet had autopsied Connie's dogs, and they had both suffered heart attacks. Although they were relatively young, they both had enlarged hearts, and it was possible that they died of natural causes. It was unusual, but there was no evidence to point to foul play. Joey made a mental note to further investigate the medical history of those dogs before he told his mother, in case Connie later posed the question.

"Hmmm. Well, did the vet say that this was common with Presas?"

"He said that it could be hereditary, but we'd have to check their bloodlines."

"Is there anything that they could've been given to make it appear that they had a heart attack?"

"I'm not sure, Joey."

"Well, will you have the vet run the most extensive series of tests to eliminate that possibility, okay? I'd appreciate it. And since this is such a sensitive issue, let's keep it to ourselves until we have the final word from the vet, okay?"

"I understand completely. And you have my word that I'll only discuss this with you." Ashley paused. "So, that was all of the business I had to discuss. The next thing I wanted to talk to you about is of a personal nature."

Joey had a bad feeling. Ashley certainly knew about Madison's condition, so he figured that she was about to heap a mound of guilt on him about his sister. "What is it, Ashley?"

"I know that you and your family are going through a whole lot these days, and I wanted to let you know that I'm here for you." Her voice was buoyant and playful, and Joey wondered if he was really speaking to Ashley Vickers and not some phone sex operator.

"I, uh, I know, Ashley. And we really appreciate it. You've been such a great help in assisting us with the management of Connie's residence."

"Thank you, Joey, but I'm really talking about you. If you need someone to talk to, or if you need a home cooked meal, just call me. Or if you want to get your mind off of things and go and hang out one evening, I'm available. I mean, I'm not trying to date you while you're handling this crisis, but I just wanted you to know that I've always thought of you in a special way."

"Uh, thanks, Ashley." Before Joey could worm his way out of this uncomfortable situation, his Uncle Jolly beeped in. "Um, Ashley? I appreciate the offer, but I'll have to take a raincheck for now. This is my uncle, and I've been waiting for his call."

Grateful that he was able to pull the family card on Ashley, Joey switched over to his uncle's call before having to say something that he might later regret. Jolly summoned him to a rendezvous point near the Cavanaugh's concrete plant in Southwest, and abruptly hung up the phone. Joey's head ached. Ashley? Trying to mack him? What else could possibly happen today?

Lauren and Kelly. Lauren or Kelly. Both. Neither. At the same time. Separate and distinct. Joey felt like a heel. Like he had betrayed Lauren by sleeping with Kelly. Joey's thoughts rambled around in his mind as he could barely recall how to get to the concrete plant. He drove aimlessly; slightly paranoid about what his uncle was calling him on the carpet about and wondering if his undercover life had been exposed.

Joey felt like he was maneuvering around a live minefield. Any question or incident only added to his mania. Joey knew he couldn't continue handling his business like this, but what was he going to do? With all of his family issues, there was little or no time to address his own. But he didn't need for last night to occur. How could he have done that? His life felt like jumbled mess, with no correction in sight.

The sun beamed brightly in the early morning sky, and Joey slipped on a pair of tortoise sunshades, and focused on his drive. Uncle Jolly was leaning against his mirror-finished Jag, and smoking a thick cigar when Joey arrived. His Range Rover created a swirl of gritty dust as he sped across the gravely parking lot, and Jolly's driver, immediately hopped out of the car and began wiping it down.

"Hello, Uncle," Joey said as he approached his rotund elder.

"Joey," Uncle Jolly said, and embraced his namesake. Dressed in a beige argyle sweater and baggy trousers, Uncle Jolly looked more like he should have been swinging a golf club as opposed to meeting Joey in a dusty parking lot.

"I'm sure you're wondering why I called you. I haven't really had a chance to speak to you, and I think now's a good time to see how you are really doing. Especially with everything that's been going on in our family and what not."

Joey tried to read his uncle's face, but Uncle Jolly was known for his ultra cool demeanor. He had been a player in the game for a long time, and he wasn't about to get got by the likes of a young buck like Joey.

Jolly continued. "I want to let you know that I'm here for you if you need to talk about anything. I tried to talk to Connie before all of this happened, but it got me nowhere. I was hoping that you'd be less obstinate than he was. I'm hoping I'll do better with you."

Joey was glad that he had his shades to hide behind, because his uncle always had a way of piercing his mettle. "I'm okay, Unc. And once things settle down within the family, we'll *all* be much better."

"I'm sure. But, settling down can be a little tough, especially since there are still so many bumps in the road. You see, some things that still don't quite make much sense to me, and they should, now more than ever before. We're treading on dangerous ground these days, especially with Edgy and his family being here. But, it's a little difficult for me to do my job these days. I'm working with a skeleton crew because my whole department has been dismantled. Either I've had to fire folks, or either they've died, or either they're missing. You know what I mean."

Joey feigned ignorance. "I really don't."

"I want you to tell me what happened to Stewart. And if you know where Beverly is."

Joey sighed. Again with the questions, but Joey flatly denied any knowledge about Beverly, but conceded a little about Stewart. "Stewart, well, Connie's the only one that can tell you where he is."

"Is he dead?" Jolly asked, and blew a thick puff of smoke.

Joey met his uncle's question with silence, and Uncle Jolly waved a meaty hand in the air. "Secrets. All of these relative secrets. You and your brothers seem to be determined to continue perpetuating all of the most devastating characteristics of this family." Jolly shook his head. "Pity you didn't inherit the more productive traits like honesty, respect and loyalty."

Jolly's words hurt, but Joey remained silent, and kept his eyes locked on his uncle. Finally, Jolly spoke.

"Very well, Joseph. I'm just going to leave it at that. I tried to debrief Conrad, but he claimed that he didn't know anything about Stewart's whereabouts either. And with Stewart missing, and Ellis and Stevie killed, there isn't anyone around that knows the deal but you two. And I know Connie isn't going to say anything that might incriminate himself, and you have selective memory. So be it.

"But, let me tell you one thing. If you are sitting on any information that may potentially cause your family any more harm or trouble, then you need to disclose it now. Or forever hold your tongue. You understand what I'm saying?"

Joey nodded, but remained silent. "Did anything happen between you and that female agent that we need to know about, Joseph?"

Joey's mind flashed. Did Jolly know something? Joey took a calculated risk and played dumb. If his uncle knew something, he'd have to tell it. Joey wasn't offering up anything.

"No sir. Nothing but some great sex and some even greater deception. That's it."

Jolly shoved a thick finger in the air. "Okay, Joey. But, my gut's telling me otherwise. I get the feeling that there's a lot more to this story than what's being told. And you know what they say. What's done in the dark comes out in the light."

Joey sighed, convinced that his uncle's fishing expedition had netted him zilch. "What do you mean?" Joey asked, content that he had dodged the bullet.

"I understand that Howard's car has been located. Some divers ran across it down off of Hains Point."

"Divers? Really? Well, was Howard in there?"

"No, he wasn't. But, it looks like pretty suspicious. My inside sources say that they are treating his disappearance as a possible homicide or suicide. But, his ragtop was ripped open, so who's to say what really happened to old Howard."

"Interesting," Joey said. "But, I thought that Royce was supposed to be watching Howard. What does he have to say about that?"

"That was Royce's job. However, the last thing that Royce said, and this was a few weeks ago, was that Howard had gone to the gym and was going to meet with one of the Cavanaugh brothers. Was that you?" Uncle Jolly raised an eyebrow at Joey.

"No, it wasn't me."

"I figured as much. Well, then that only leaves Connie. And I'm sure that you don't know anything about that either, do you?"

Joey nodded. "I really don't, Uncle Jolly."

Uncle Jolly dropped his cigar on the ground, and gingerly stamped it out. "Well, I'll say it once more. If you know something—"

"I know," Joey said, and then completed his uncle's sentence.

Jolly went on to say that Royce was difficult to catch up with, and that he was concerned that something might have happened to him.

Although Joey wasn't aware that Royce was MIA, he wondered if Connie had terminated him too. His uncle was showing visible signs of worry, and so Joey decided to throw him a bone.

"Father had asked that I locate Royce, but with everything that's going on, it slipped my mind."

Jolly scratched his head. "Don't worry, we'll find him. Let's just hope he's breathing when we do catch up with him. And if he isn't, it's going to be one more mystery we're going to have to solve. Before it comes back to destroy us."

"I know. I don't know how many more disappearances and reappearances we can handle. Simon, Howard, and Royce. And having Uncle Edgar and Vincent around makes the waters even muddier."

"True, true. But, that's a delicate situation there, son. Even though things are a little out of sorts at the moment, you can't do anything to breech your grandfather's edict. But, you and your brothers need to come together, and try to honor what your father has done for you all of these years."

"I agree, Uncle Jolly. And you have my word. We're all trying to get ourselves together, Connie, Christian and myself. We can't change what's happened in the past, but we're trying to do our best to make sure we don't get messed up by anything Uncle Edgy might have planned. It's Father's edict that we don't do anything to usurp the truce Grand enacted, but we've decided that we won't stand by and let Uncle Edgy further destroy our family."

Jolly squinted at Joey. "What are you saying? You're not trying to defy your father, are you? Because if you are, you know I'm not with that. And after all that's happened, I'll be the first one to run all of you in to your father, like that." Jolly snapped his fingers.

"No. But, I get the feeling that Uncle Edgy's here to bring more harm upon us. We have to do something to protect our family."Joey stepped toward his uncle, and told him about Connie's dogs untimely death."

"Sounds suspicious, Joey. Are you trying to say that Edgy and his son had something to do with it?"

"Let's just say that I have a feeling, Unc. But, I'm going to have expert confirmation before I make any accusations."

"That's wise. I like to hear you speaking with some forethought, before acting irrationally."

"Thanks, Uncle Jolly. But, as I said, I really think that Uncle Edgy is up to no good. And I don't want us to get caught flat footed with him. We have too much to lose, but, like you said, I don't want to step out of line. So, we're going to need your help."

"Joey, you know I'm here for you. But, you're toeing the line on this one. Are you sure you can do this without making a bigger mess?"

"I'm sure," Joey said, with an even glance.

"Well, then I'm here for you. What do you need for me to do?"

Chapter 14

The life of the Cavanaughs had become like one gigantic, multi-layered, super complex jigsaw puzzle. There were thousands of tiny, intricate pieces, and none seemed to fit together. And the ones that did fit didn't complete any recognizable image.

The only relief Joey clung to was the fact that the annoying calls had ceased, and there were no more unsolicited cards appearing at his doorstep. Beyond that, Joey was completely engrossed with handling his family's slippery business dealings. One of the most difficult and pressing tasks was locating Royce. One of Jolly's men was tasked with tracking him down, and in a few days, he reported that Royce had been located. His decomposed body had been found, rotting in Howard's house. An autopsy was underway, but initial reports indicated that he had likely died from blunt force trauma to the head, and was dead for more than two weeks. The police had put an APB out for Howard, who despite his car being found, was still missing. He was considered a "person of interest," especially since the crime occurred at his house. Joey knew Royce's murder and Howard's disappearance were somehow pieces in their massive puzzle, but he just couldn't figure out how they were connected.

But, there were more immediate concerns to address. Before breaking the news about Connie's dogs to his mother, Joey had received a voicemail from Ashley, where she said that the vet was going to have to send the dogs blood and tissue samples out to a lab for evaluation. This could take a few weeks, so Joey had to give his mother the report that Connie's dogs had been found dead. Naturally, she was dissatisfied with the information, and Joey knew that her hysterical reaction was only a precursor to what was in store for them when Connie found out. But, that battle would have to wait until later.

Joey also put his transgression with Kelly on the back burner, and hoped that he'd stay away from Madison. Joey had to focus on what was most detrimental to him and his family. *Il Rosso.* Over the next few weeks, Joey and his brothers had labored over every detail of the plan, and whittled them down to the most finite detail. While Jules' life hung in the balance, and Connie was getting well enough to leave the hospital, Jolly's investigation team had confirmed that Edgar had indeed contacted the Sallones when he fled to New York years ago.

That was all that they needed to know. Armed with that information, Jolly's team identified the New York connections, Connie corralled the muscle, and Joey and Christian came up with the cash. They worked and reworked the plan, until it was etched in everyone's minds. Joey made it a point to run the whole plan by Uncle Jolly before finalizing it.

Through the efforts of many covert conversations, Joey had negotiated and secured a secret meeting with one of the top Sallone family members, Alberto, who was better known as Al. The Sallones were Joey's grandmother's relatives, and were the original owners of *Il Rosso.* When Joey mentioned that he was the Cavanaugh emissary and had business pertaining to the disposition of the stone, Al was immediately intrigued, and agreed to meet Joey at the Tavern on the Green Restaurant, in Central Park.

The plan went off without one glitch. Joey, a jittery Christian, and six of their security men staked out the Tavern, and awaited Al's arrival. In this renowned public venue, the Cavanaughs and ten armed Sallones met, and discussed business. Carefully selecting his words, Joey spun the tale about the prized jewel, and about how it had been missing from his family's possession, while Christian fidgeted with the cash laden valise.

This tidbit gave Al great pleasure to know that Grand's family now knew that they had been stripped of the stone. When he produced it from his breast pocket, Joey marveled at its brilliance, and asked to see it. Al, feeling a might generous and a bit condescending, slid the jewel across the table to Joey.

Before Joey could get his jeweler's eye out, Christian was about to offer him $500k for it. Joey kicked him under the table, and Christian almost jumped out of his chair.

Joey blinked and squinted through the magnifying eye. It had only taken a quick glace at the stone. It too, was a fake.

While Joey and Christian journeyed to New York, Connie quietly collected his belongings, hung Stewart's ring around his neck, and then checked himself out of the hospital. It was against the advice of his doctors, but a determined Connie was no match for some jive ass physicians. He had business to tend to, and with the help of two of his new crewmembers, Connie left Baltimore and paid an unexpected visit to Anton and the sickly Jules.

It was sometime that same evening when Connie's boys kicked in the door to Jules' home, and immediately made their presence known. As a cane-dependent Connie hobbled into the shop, Anton shook in his stance.

Anton sweated profusely as Connie leaned against the wall. "You know, Anton. I don't appreciate having to leave my comfy hospital bed to come over here and find out what's really going on," Connie said, and flicked a few boxes of jeweler's tools onto the floor with the top of his cane.

"What do you mean, Con-Conrad?" Anton asked, and eyeballed Connie and the hulking figures that anchored his sides.

"Just what I said. Now, my brother told me what you and your father had to say about our family jewel. That little song and dance. Well, let's just say that Joey's a little more diplomatic than I am." Connie took his cane, and flipped over a small display cabinet. "Don't try to carry me, fool. I don't go for the okey-doke, you know what I mean?

"See, in my book, if what your father said is correct, then, he did a pretty awful thing. But, he must've had a good ass reason for doing so, because he had to have known that he was putting his life straight up on the line by double-crossing my father."

Connie's cell phone rang, and it was Joey calling with the news that the New York stone was fake too. He said that he thought that Edgar must still have the original. Connie hung the phone up with a different thought, and then turned his attention toward Anton.

"It's funny how things happen, 'Twon. Now, I know that your father claims that he made a copy for someone, someone who he just can't seem to recall right now. Or, is it that he can't maintain consciousness long enough to cough up the info. But, that's beside the point. See, I believe that if he was ballsy enough to make a copy, then he probably made two. You feel me? Where I'm from, when someone double-crosses you, there are no rules. You know the old saying, 'there's no honor amongst thieves.' Well, let's just say that I doubt that your father has any honor with anyone except himself. Now, I want to know where the real stone is."

Connie lit a cigarette and puffed. It was his first one in a very long time, and the tar and nicotine felt good filling his lungs. He picked up a small can of acetone from a nearby shelf, and flipped the top open, and turned the can upside down. The liquid poured out, and created a small puddle in the floor. Connie flicked an ash from his cigarette onto it, and a bright yellow fire erupted.

"Now, I'm thinkin' that you might know a little somethin' somethin' about all of this, especially since you're the heir apparent around here. So, should I go talk to your father, or would you like to? Either way, I'm not leaving here until I have the truth, the whole truth, and nothing but the fuckin' truth. God help you."

It took a few moments of applied selective pressuring to coerce the semi-conscious Jules and the nervous Anton to admit that Jules had indeed made two copies of the stone, one for Edgar, and gasp, one for Simon. Yet, they somehow managed to keep the real stone.

Greed was Jules's initial motivation, but Connie wanted no explanation. Thinking that the truth would set them free, Anton retrieved the stone from a steel floor safe, and begged Connie for his life. Connie, carefully holding the cornerstone of his family's heritage, and possibly his guarantee to take over leadership of his family, stared at the jittery Anton and the bedridden Jules and laughed. Connie took one of the jewelry sanders and held a piece of glass to it. It pulverized it in a matter of minutes, creating a small heap on the wooden counter.

"I tell you what, gents. I'm going to go. But, because I was raised right, and before you die, I want to give you an opportunity to request your last meal. You can have whatever you'd like."

Jules and Anton looked at each other, their faces panic-stricken and confused.

"Wait a minute." Connie snapped his fingers. "It must be the drugs that have me trippin'. What I meant is that my men here will see to it that you get what ever you want to eat from the Georgia Mile." Connie picked up a handful of the glass chards, and let them slip through his fingers. "Oww," he said. "These joints are sharp as hell. Cut you up for sure. Look." Connie held up a finger. "I'm bleeding."

Connie turned to his boys. "Hell, I'm even going to join you. We'll sit right here together, and I'll make sure that you have several healthy portions of this very tasty glass to accompany your meal."

Connie pulled out a gun from his waistband, and pointed it at his victims. "And you're going to enjoy every morsel. Until your insides are shredded like a school girl's hair ribbons. *Bon a petit.*"

The Jules' collective last meal was quite a feat for Connie, and he relished the sight of the blood spurting from every orifice as they both died in agonizing pain. It only took a few hours, but the creative carnage made Connie positively gleeful.

It had been a few days since his return to the frontline, and Connie was happy as hell to be back in the cut. He missed his smoking, drinking, carousing and screwing. And not necessarily in that order. He had to get his edge back, and getting back to the homestead was the first step.

When he arrived at home, there was some old crone in the living room, dusting the artifacts. Connie quickly sent her home. He was sure that it was someone his mother had hired, but it didn't matter. He wanted his privacy, and if he needed someone to straighten up for him, then he'd deal with that at a later date.

With an overstuffed dime bag of weed under one arm, Connie collected his mail from the foyer desk, and made his way down to his basement haven. Happily seated in front of his enormous fish tank, Connie watched his piranhas, The Addams Family, swim as he rolled and smoked blunt after blunt, until he was in a weed-induced stupor. The room was filled with thick, choking smoke, and Connie rifled through his mail until he found the latest issue of *Hustler Magazine*. With a little assistance from his rag, his evening was only bound to get better.

As he settled in for his moment of self-gratification, Connie unzipped his trousers, and flipped open the magazine, and a small, blank envelope fell into his lap. Angered by the minor infraction, Connie tossed the magazine aside and ripped open the mail, and yanked out its contents. It was a tarot card.

"What the fuck?" Connie snarled, and looked around the room like there was someone there. It was an ornately decorated card, with the Five of Pentacles written on the bottom. Connie scratched his chin, and sniffed. "Man, I know this ain't real," he said to his smoked filled room. "I ain't never seen no shit like this before."

He thought for a moment, and then picked up the shredded remains of the envelope and stared at it closely, hoping that it would reveal some clue, but it didn't. So, Connie tore the cards and the envelope into tiny pieces, and placed them in the marble ashtray on the coffee table. After he fired up another joint, he took the match and lit the bits of paper, and watched them flame up.

"That's right, burn, baby, burn," he said with a paranoid laugh. "I fear no man, and I sure don't fear some fuckin' card. He picked up the magazine, and went about the business of relieving his frustration, until it dawned on him that he hadn't checked on his other pets.

His snakes and spiders appeared to be okay, but when he walked outside into the cold afternoon air and whistled, he was surprised that his dogs didn't respond. He was astonished to see that the dog run was empty. He immediately ran back into his basement and called his mother.

Though his mother had pitched a fit when she found out that he had checked out of the hospital, when Connie asked her about his pets, she became suddenly mute.

"Where are they, M'Dear? Did you board them or something? Who's been taking care of them?"

His mother sighed. "Conrad, dear. Try to be calm. I didn't want you to find out until you were strong enough to deal with it."

"Deal with what?" Connie asked, and when his mother told him what had happened to his pets, he cursed her a blue streak. After he had ranted and raved for a solid ten minutes, he slammed the phone down in her ear. How could she do something like that to him? How could she let his pets die and not even bother to tell him?

She called back several times, but Connie didn't bother to answer. He had no regrets about cussing his mother out. He didn't care. His precious animals were dead, and it was someone's fault. And even though he wasn't madly in love with his dogs, they were his. And, if it got his mother off of his back for leaving the hospital, well, then she could take a few curse words. Hell, he was back in his castle, and his mother would just get over it. Just like she did everything else.

He went back in the rec room, and flopped down on the sofa, where he resumed watching his Addams Family. He picked up the slim black remote for his Bose stereo, and cranked up Naughty by Nature's "*You Down Wit' OPP*," and Connie rapped along with Treach. Connie was in his zone. But, then he thought about how he had killed Stewart within inches of where he sat. He fondled Stewart's ring that he now wore around his neck and shrugged. He finished his joint, inhaling deeply and holding the smoke until his lungs felt like they were going to burst. Instead, his conscience did.

"Man, it's rough dealing with shit around here without you, Stew. And I'm sorry things had to go down like they did between us. You was like my brother, man. But I can tell you one thing, bro. I don't know who might be fuckin' with my head, but you know I'm not goin' out like that. You know I'm holdin' things down."

From the dark corner of the basement, a lithe, female in a skin-tight, form-fitted black jumpsuit studied Connie with calculated accuracy and disgust at how he had spoken to his mother. She wore gloves and cloth covers over her feet, and her movements were flawlessly executed. She was silent and nimble, and took breaths so shallow, that her ample chest barely moved. She drew a long, thick gun from her side, a .357 Magnum with a heavy silencer attached. She leaned forward, just beyond the shadows, and aimed the gun at her target.

Connie sipped his Remy Martin, and then pulled the real *Il Rosso* from the false bottom of his precious backgammon board, and held it in the light. "Yes, I'm back in the game," he said, and then laughed aloud.

The intruder quietly released the safety from the gun, and took aim. As her finger gripped the trigger, the phone suddenly rang.

"Yo, what's up, Jade baby?" Connie asked, as he fondled the gem. "Yeah, you can come on through. Daddy needs a little T.L.C."

He idly chatted for a few moments, making sure that Jade had specific directions for their planned evening together. "And bring some whipped cream. I feel like I need a little topping to go with my dessert tonight."

Connie laughed, and then took a small, clear waterproof pouch, and dropped the gem in it. The hitwoman/intruder pulled the gun back, and gazed at her intended victim, with a strange expression on her face. Connie sealed it too, and then put that pouch inside another pouch and then sealed it. He took a handful of black clay, and molded it around the pouch, forming a small boulder.

"Alright, I'll see you in a few. Later," Connie said, and hung up the phone. He grabbed his fake rock and cane, and then hobbled around to the back of the tank. He ambled up the ladder, and tossed the stone into the aquarium. He and the catsuited shooter watched the makeshift rock as it floated downward, and landed on the bottom amongst the other multi-colored rocks of various sizes.

"Yeah, you'll be safe there, *Il Rosso*. You'll be good to go until I need you." Connie dusted his hands and admired his handiwork. "Now that you're safely tucked away, Daddy's gonna get ready for a little coochie. It's been too damned long, and I'm about ready to bang a bitch until she's on a goddamned cane, too," he said with a raucous, hateful laugh.

Connie and Jade's reunion was just as intense as he had bet. Even though he suspected her of screwing around, Connie knew that when they got together, there would be some rough and hot sex going on. Just like he liked it.

He had many rules, but the main one was that no one came to the bat cave. None of his lays, pieces, baby mamas or girlfriends. And it didn't have anything to do with Beverly being at home. If he really wanted any of them to come over, he would not have thought twice about it. But, his home was his castle; and the one place he could lay his head and be at peace. That went without saying. And even though Jade was the mother of his son Seth, Connie didn't like all of the drama she manifested. It was cool chilling at the love nest he'd purchased for her, but his home was strictly off limits.

Not that they liked it, but Connie managed all of his women with the understanding that he saw them on his terms, and his alone. And if he allowed Jade to come over, he certainly didn't want to give her the impression that she had it like that, and that she'd have free reign at his home. Or that this was going to be a regular occurrence.

Maybe it was because he hadn't completely recovered, or maybe he was feeling a little lonely, but he was looking forward to seeing Jade and his son.

Jade came alone, leaving little Seth in the care of her mother. Decked out in a scorching hot outfit of fishnets, thongs, four-inch stilettos and nothing else, Jade stepped into Connie's house like she was on a mission.

"We have some unfinished business," she said. "The last time we were together, Mother didn't get hers. And that's a real problem. I gots to get mine, Daddy," she said, and then promptly went to work, making Connie glad that he hadn't gotten her off when he was in the hospital.

He was going to play that "I'm still recovering" card, so he could just lay back and get served, but Jade pushed him to his physical limits. They started clawing at each other in the foyer, and wound up in the forbidden zone of Connie's bedroom. It was something tantalizingly naughty about the escapade, and it made them both even hornier. Cane or not, Jade straddled him and rode like she was in a rodeo. She was a screaming cowgirl trying to stay on top of a wild stallion. She taunted and teased him, sexed and flexed him, until he needed a hit of oxygen. But, he'd never tell her that she'd worked him over to that degree.

After a few hours of high energy sex, Connie found himself flat on his back again, only this time, Jade was on top of him, and they were both heaving and panting like mating animals in the wild.

"You alright?" Jade asked, her voice hoarse and low.

"Yeah," Connie replied. "You know I can handle mines." She was pressing into his slightly tender abdomen, but again, he'd never let her know that he was even remotely still in pain. "Yo, I need a cigarette."

He tried to push her off by reaching for the pack of Newports that was on the nightstand, but Jade held tight. "I'll get them," she said, and grabbed the pack and a lighter. She pulled two from the pack, and placed both in her mouth, and the lit them. She inhaled deeply, and blew the smoke off to the side. She took one and placed it between Connie's lips. "Here."

The pain in Connie's stomach made him wince, but he took the cigarette and drew on it. He lowered his voice so the pain wouldn't seep through. "Let me up, girl. I gotta go drain the dragon." Jade sucked her teeth when he shoved her aside and scurried into the adjoining bathroom, where he promptly relieved himself in the urinal.

Jade lay on her stomach, with her rotund ass boosted in the air, and looked around the room. Flicking her ashes in the ashtray on the nightstand, she puffed on her cigarette, and started grunting and muttering under her breath.

"Umph."

"What'd you say?" Connie yelled, as he shook himself off and flushed. He didn't even bother to wash his hands, and he headed back into the bedroom, his manhood flopping in the air.

Jade repeated herself, and then added, "So, this is your bedroom. The master's suite." Every word was laden with sarcasm.

"Oh, here you go," Connie said, and fell back into the bed. "Don't start no shit, Jade."

"I ain't startin' nothin'. So, is that your wedding picture?" Jade pointed to a picture hanging on the bedroom wall. One that clearly showed Beverly dressed in a wedding gown, feeding a tuxedoed Connie a piece of white wedding cake.

"Naw, that's a figment of your damned imagination." Connie puffed and blew smoke.

"Whatever, negro." Jade kept looking around the room. "I must say, I would've thought your 'wife' would've had better taste. This joint looks like some old white woman's bedroom."

Connie gnashed his teeth, and climbed underneath the covers. "Whatever, Jade. I told you before, don't talk about my wife."

"I'll talk about her all I want. Where is she, anyway? Locked in the closet? Chained up in the basement with the rest of your pets?"

"None of your damned business. Now, quit poppin' your lips, you got that?"

"Listen, Connie. I'm about tired of playin' this bullshit game with you. Now, I don't know what's goin' on with you and your little wife, but I ain't going for being your 'piece of ass on the side' shit no more. Either you start actin' like you wanna be with me, or I'm gonna start treatin' you like you treat me."

"What's that supposed to mean? You tryin' to threaten me or somethin'?"

"I'm not threatenin' you, Connie. I'm just sayin' that we got something really special, and you treat it and me like shit. And I'm tired of it."

Connie quickly weighed his options. He wasn't completely back on his game, so the thought of not having easy access to Jade was distressing. But, he couldn't cave that quickly. He didn't want her to think that he'd gotten soft.

"Tired of what, Jade? Having me take care of you?"

"Take care of me? Connie, that line is so damned tired. As long as I have little Mr. Seth Cavanaugh, you're going to do that. Royally. But in terms of getting this pussy, trust me, you ain't the only one around here that would love to get this on the regular."

Connie shook his head, and stamped out his cigarette in the ashtray. "Whatever, Jade. I'll always take care of my son, but you? Huh. Broads like you are a dime a dozen. So, go on then, and get whoever. Whenever. I don't give a fuck." He turned his back to her. "Now, raise up outta here. I need to get some sleep."

Jade tried to bore a hole through his back, but Connie was unresponsive. "You don't mean that."

"Like hell I don't. Get to steppin'. And lock the door behind you on your way out."

"I hate you."

"Bye, bitch."

Jade folded her arms, and stamped her cigarette out in the ashtray. She took her foot and kicked Connie in his narrow ass. "Why can't you act right, Connie?"

Connie smiled beneath the comforter, but when he spoke, he maintained the edge in his voice. "What you mean?"

"Why can't you just take me out every once and a while? I'm sayin', is that asking too much?"

Connie had won, but he had to keep Jade on the defensive. He just grunted.

Jade slipped her hand under the covers, and gently grabbed Connie's manhood. She leaned over and placed her lips on it, and gave him a little kiss. "Come on, Daddy. I'll give it to you just like you like it, if you promise to take me to the Miki Howard, Keith Sweat, and En Vogue concert next month."

Connie smiled, and rolled over, and grabbed the back of her head. "You do me right, I might even let you meet Keith Sweat." Jade squealed as Connie shoved her mouth down on his hardening Johnson.

Chapter 15

Graham, Madison's hairstylist, had been running late, and his shampoo girl had washed and conditioned her hair, and had seated her under the humming bonnet-style hair dryer. It was Saturday, and the salon was exceptionally crowded, but Madison hadn't lost her composure when she arrived and Graham wasn't there.

While the heated air swirled around her head, Madison hid the copy of *American Baby* inside of the latest *Essence*, and scanned the contents. The baby articles were now fascinating, and she laughed to herself, thinking that a few months ago, she would've never been bothered with topics such as breast milk versus bottle feedings and how cotton diapers were making a comeback with the yuppies and buppies. Madison never had any interest in babies or parenting. Now, it seemed to consume all of her thoughts and energy.

She was thinking of baby names and Amniocentesis. How would she find a decent nanny? How would she get rid of, God forbid, stretch marks or cellulite? Who could she hire to convert her second bedroom into a nursery? Which private school would she send her child to? What fashion designers created haute couture for the little ones? It was a lot to consider. Especially since she was alone and had no one to really talk about things with.

But, Joey had come through as he said he would, helping her out whenever she needed it. She appreciated his support, even though he still seemed a little too preoccupied with her dating Kelly. But, Madison dismissed that as brotherly concern. Joey seemed really determined to fill that void in her life, and had put off completing his kitchen to help her get the nursery constructed. He was supportive of her, and always offered a kind ear to listen to her and a gentle hug when she needed it.

Which was a lot more than Madison could say about her best "friend" Ashley.

Ashley completely played Madison off. When she bothered to call, her whole conversations revolved around herself. Ashley, who had avoided the gym like it was a visit to the dentist, was now even working out, attending aerobics classes while Madison felt like a helium filled blimp. Ashley went on and on about how lovely her social life was now. Who she was dating. Where they were going. What was going on in the D.C. nightlife. All the things Madison used to commit to memory. Now, she just found herself sitting on the sidelines, watching. Suddenly, she was the four-eyed girl at the party with the big zit who no one was asking to dance. It was if she and Ashley had switched positions in the food chain, and Madison was resenting the fact that Ashley was so callous and shallow. It was a bittersweet feeling, for Ashley was so much like she used to be, not too long ago.

Madison thanked God that her nausea had subsided, and that she wasn't having any outrageous cravings. She wasn't too temperamental, and her hormones hadn't ratcheted her emotions to an out of control level. Madison was quite proud that she remained buoyed and centered on her new found priorities. And she had found quite a good friend in Kelly. He was considerate and kind, and always seemed to pop up when she really needed to either talk to him or see him. She liked his nonjudgmental nature, and although she was enjoying getting to know him in a friendship capacity, she still wondered why he hadn't tried to put a move on her.

It was probably because she was pregnant, but it wasn't like she was showing. Kelly was always respectful, and even when they spent time together, he never tried anything with her. Nothing. He hadn't even kissed her. And it was beginning to bother her, because Madison found him quite attractive. And her hormones were raging, with no outlet in sight. She scanned the magazine's table of contents to see if there were any articles on having sex during pregnancy that confirmed Kim's lascivious recommendation.

A flush, winded Graham suddenly snatched up the lid of the dryer hood. "Come on, Miss Girl. I know you're probably about to blow a gasket because I wasn't here on time." He pulled Madison up from her seat, and her magazines scattered to the floor, with the fat, rosy-cheeked baby on the cover of American Baby grinning back at them.

"What's *this*?" Graham nearly screeched, and the rest of the patrons and stylists stopped what they were doing to see what the ruckus was about.

Madison scrambled to pick up her periodicals, and nearly dropped her Fendi bag in the process. "It's nothing, Graham," she said, and grabbed up the magazines.

"It's true! I can't believe it. You're going to have a baby!" Graham said, and embraced Madison, who tore away from his grasp.

The eyes of almost every stunned client and operator were latched onto Madison and Graham, and then a low murmur from the crowd could be heard. Madison grabbed Graham's arm, and lead him to his booth, ignoring the stares and whispers of the gawkers. Gawkers who at one time or another were just waiting for the poor little rich girl to get embarrassed like this.

"What are you talking about?" Madison asked, as she tried to keep her voice low, and spoke through pressed lips.

"Girl, Ashley told me you were pregnant. She's a gossiping heifer that can't hold water. You know she comes here all the time now. Baby, she was a wreck up from the neck up, but girlfriend is really feeling herself now. You know I hooked her tired ass up, and now she thinks she is too fly."

Madison was floored. How could Ashley put her business in the streets like that? She collected herself, the Cavanaugh pride dictated that she get herself together immediately. "Well, Graham, I, uh, had no idea that Ashley would've said something like that." Her voice cracked and she fought back tears. Though she wasn't even showing, she felt like her stomach was dragging the ground.

Graham seemed genuinely remorseful that he had let that slip, and looked around the shop at all of the lookie-loos. "Don't you all have something better to do? Like mind your own damn business? Or how 'bout, you get some damn business to mind?" Graham screamed, and waved his hot curlers around. He grabbed Madison by the shoulders, and forced her down in his chair. He placed his hands on the arms of the chair, and looked into Madison's eyes. "Aren't you excited? Come on now, you know you're gonna have you a little diva. Or a little handsome prince. I can see it now."

Madison swallowed hard and fluttered her lashes. "I'm, um. It's not that I'm not, Graham. I, uh," Madison choked, barely able to control her emotions.

Graham read her face like a book. He placd his fist over his mouth. "Oh, I'm so sorry, sweetie. I guess I put my pump in my mouth, didn't I? Well, I thought that you'd be happy about it. But, I take it, you aren't."

Tears burned in her eyes, and her face was hot and flushed. Madison pushed Graham's hands off of the chair, stood up and removed her vinyl cape. Madison could barely speak; the shame and rage of being a public spectacle had muted her voice. "I've got to go, Graham," she said, and stepped toward the front door, but Graham caught her by the arm.

"I'm sorry, Madison. I really am. And, and, if you're not happy, and if that low down nigger's not going to do the right thing by you, then," he said, and he slid his hand down her arm and clutched Madison's hand to his chest, "I'll marry you." Graham's eyes widened, and his face creased with an earnest expression. "I'll make a great husband, and you know that we'd both be fierce. We'd work this city like its never been worked before, Miss Thang."

Madison couldn't help but laugh, and while she tried to wipe them away, the tears fell freely from her lids. Though she had just been publicly humiliated, the preposterousness of Graham's proposal was simply comedic. He had always engaged in sexually connotative banter with her, and probably had a little crush on her, but Graham's tri-sexual lifestyle was beyond Madison's scope. She laughed so hard and uncontrollably, that even Graham fell victim to her laughter.

"Thanks, Graham. I appreciate the offer," she said, and kissed him on the cheek. "And who knows, I may just take you up on it one day."

"*Nonno*, I just don't know what to do," Joey said to his grandfather, as Grand stared at him with vacant, watery eyes.

When he and Christian returned from their unsuccessful trip to New York, Joey was at his wit's end. Nothing was going well, and there wasn't much he could do about it. One thing he could do was to make good of the front money they had taken to New York. He instructed Christian to reallocate the money into the Cavanaugh heirs college fund. A fund that would now include Madison's child. But, he didn't mention that to Christian. Christian was gleeful enough to think that his children would be the most immediate beneficiaries.

Once Joey sent Christian on his way, he decided to visit his grandfather. He wished that he had taken the time to see Grand before going to New York, but perhaps it was best. There was no way that Joey would tell Grand that Edgy had stolen *Il Rosso* years ago. It would absolutely kill him. In fact, Joey had to refrain from talking about anything regarding the shootout on the docks, Connie or Edgy. Joey could never disrespect the truce. So, instead, after swearing Grand to secrecy, Joey talked to him about the other matters vexing his soul. The duplicity in his personal life. And he was reminded of that when Trudy showed him in, and asked him if he had received any more cards.

"No, Trudy. I haven't. But, if I do, I'll be sure to let you know."

"Not a problem, Joseph. I'm sure that you probably won't. At least nothing you need to be concerned with. But if you do, there are a few things to look out for, like the obvious."

Joey blinked, not knowing how to respond to Trudy's cryptic message. "What do you mean?"

"I mean that if you receive a card that isn't explicit in its description or name, you probably don't have anything to worry about. The cards to worry with— you'll know," she said. "But for now, visit with your Grandpapa. He has been awaiting your arrival."

As Joey watched the mystical Trudy stroll down the hallway, he still wondered if he really understood what she meant. But, she had again reassured him that the cards he had received were not menacing. She just didn't elaborate on their real meaning. It could be another thing to just worry his soul, but Joey didn't have the time or the energy for it, so he went on with his plans, and joined Grand in his study.

"Of course you have my confidence, my child. My word, or my *la mia parola*, is all that I have left," Grand said, and motioned for Joey to sit.

"But, Grand. I'm torn. I really care for both of the, uh, my love interests, but one is a law enforcement officer. And I know that the family would never approve of that."

Grand shrugged. "*Nessuno rispetto per l'uomo o il titolo.*"

Joey scanned his brain. Though he spoke fluent Italian, he didn't understand what he meant.

Grand noticed Joey's perplexed look, and restated what he had just said. "I said, 'Love has no respect of man or title.' If it did, your grandmother and I would've never gotten together."

"Love? Yeah, um, I'm not saying that I'm in love, Grand. What you and grandmother had was a little different than what I'm going through."

"Not really. Love is love."

"I'm not sure if I love either one of them. I know I care deeply for them, but love? I don't know." Joey frowned. The thought made his stomach churn.

"Sounds like you need to find out what you really feel. And for whom. That's what really matters. Like, which one do you share your secrets with?"

Joey looked at the ceiling. That night in Richmond, he and Lauren had talked about a lot of things like her family, her real background, and their shared interests, but nothing of any secretive nature. Joey fixed his gaze onto his grandfather. "I don't share my secrets with either one."

"Good answer," Grand said with a sly smile. "But, if you did, which one would it be?"

"Probably the police officer. I guess." Kelly was already aware of his darkest secret. They didn't get any darker than that.

"Who accepts you for the person you are, and not who you are?" Grand asked.

"They both do," Joey said, the words falling out of his mouth without hesitation.

"Don't trifle with me, boy. Now, who do you make the best love with?" Grand asked.

Joey's ears turned red, and he replied with the same response as before.

Grand whistled. "Well, I guess you do love both, huh? You have a predicament most men would envy, son. Worse case, you can marry the one that will give you a respectable marriage, *matrimonio*. And, maybe the other can be your mistress. Your *padrona*." Grand laughed, and Joey couldn't resist joining in. "That would be ideal, wouldn't it?"

Grand grinned, and winked. "Aww, yes. That's how it was done in the olden days. A man could have the best of both worlds. Your great grandfather did it, that sly old dog. But, not me. Your grandmother was just enough for me. *Più di abbastanza*. More than enough."

Joey shook his head, and chuckled at his grandfather's moment of lucidity. He knew that he couldn't keep Kelly and Lauren in limbo much longer, but he wasn't ready to have either one walk out of his life.

And it appeared that Lauren, with her powerful female intuition, had made a decision not to gingerly walk out of Joey's life. She called him while he was still chatting with Grand, and invited him up to Coolfont, a resort in Berkeley Springs, West Virginia, for the evening. Joey was completely caught off guard. When Joey protested that he had no clothes, Lauren told him not to worry. She'd take care of things.

During the two-hour drive up I-270, Joey's libido and conscience took off the gloves and did bare-knuckled battle. He was so drawn to Lauren and the nurturing care she gave him. He wanted to do the right thing by her, but there was something about her that just made him weak. And when Joey had suggested that they take things slow, Lauren had applied no pressure. She'd call from time to time, with pleasant conversation and some occasional phone sex. She'd send a thoughtful card or e-mail, and always let him know that she cared, but wasn't consumed or controlling. She was assured, but not demanding or needy. Her ability to respect his space made him want her in his life more, but he had to be cool. At least until he figured out what role Lauren would really play in his life on an ongoing and consistent basis.

But then part of him thought that she was the one that was sending him the tarot cards, and placing the anonymous phone calls. It was the part of him that wanted to never trust anyone, especially someone that had been in the position to hurt him before. But the bitter truth was that if it wasn't Lauren, then it had to be Kelly. And once again, he really didn't want to think that either one of them was capable of acting like that.

When he arrived at the spa, Lauren had left instructions for Joey to meet her at the hot spring. She was already immersed in the steaming hot Roman Bath, and beckoned for Joey to strip and join her.

After a few fiery welcome kisses, Lauren maneuvered herself over to a wall, and drew Joey into her. He lay in her arms while Lauren gently cupped her hands and poured the water over his sculpted chest. She caressed his abdomen and arms, while brushing her lips on his neck. In their private sanctuary, there was only the low hum of the pool in the background, as the steam painted wet trails on their faces and on the marble walls. Though their conversation was minimal, their bodies spoke volumes.

Joey noticed how taut Lauren appeared, more so than before. She was always in great physical shape, but now her body was much more defined.

"Damn, girl. What's up? Your body feels different," he said, and stroked her inner thigh. "It's tight as hell."

"Oh, so you noticed, huh?" Lauren said, and Joey could sense that she was smiling. "A sister's been working out a bit more lately."

Joey chuckled. “You always did that, baby. You must’ve changed something in your routine.”

Lauren licked his ear. “I’ve been taking a martial arts course. I figured that you’d appreciate it.”

Joey turned over and embraced Lauren, placing her legs around his abdomen. “Of course,” he said with a kiss. “I appreciate a lot about you.”

Lauren placed her arms on his shoulders, and played in his damp, curly hair. “Like what?”

Joey coughed, and responded with another kiss. “Like this.”

“That’s nice, baby, but I don’t want that to be the only thing that you appreciate about me. I want you to get to know me. I think if you do, you’d really, really appreciate me.”

A sinking feeling swept over Joey. Lauren wasn’t the type to be so sentimental, but perhaps he had forgotten how the opposite sex really operated. They were emotionally based creatures that eventually always wanted to nest. Despite the temperature of the water, Joey’s feet suddenly went cold.

“I, uh, um. I thought we had agreed, Lauren. No pressure, right?”

“There’s no pressure, Joey. But, don’t think that there’s anything wrong with me wanting you to get to know me better. I want to get to know you better too.”

Joey’s back bristled. “I thought you knew me pretty well. After all, I was the target of your undercover investigation, wasn’t I?”

Lauren bit her lip and sniffed. “I thought that we were going to put that behind us.”

Joey felt a little guilty, but realized that he would always be able to weasel out of any situation with Lauren as long as being reminded of her former position struck a nerve. He had to throw it in her face. “It’s just going to take a little time before I feel like I can really trust you, Lauren. That’s all. And I don’t like getting cards that have unclear meanings.”

She appeared confused, but then she sighed, and shrugged slightly. “Okay, Joey. Whatever you say. But, I want you to know that you can trust me. And that I’m always going to have your best interest in mind.”

“Thanks, Lauren. I’m sure that I will know that, one day.”

“I’m not trying to rush things, Joey. I just want you to know that I’m for real.” Lauren smiled slightly, her white teeth barely showing. “I would do just about anything for you.”

There was an inflection in Lauren's voice that made Joey pause. "What do you mean?"

"Nothing, really. I downplayed it before, but I did take a lot of heat about what went down on the docks during the shoot out. But, I would never implicate you. Never."

Joey relaxed his embrace on Lauren, and searched her face. "You said that before."

"But, evidently the severity of that situation didn't register with you. You might have appreciated my actions, but somehow you didn't really appreciate me."

"What do you mean?"

"I mean that I did what I did because I care for you. And perhaps I didn't make that clear enough for you when we were in Richmond."

Joey rubbed his eyes. "I see."

Lauren cupped his chin, and slowly looked into Joey's eyes. "I don't think that you do. All I want to do is help you. I want to break down these twenty-foot walls you have built around you and let you know that I'm not here to hurt you. I look in your eyes and see what you don't want me to see. That you're not perfect, like you're human like the rest of us. And that's okay."

He tried to turn his head, but Lauren's grip was firm. "Why won't you let me in? I know that a part of you wants to."

Joey's head throbbed. The passion he had been consumed with was being leveled by another more powerful emotion. Raw feelings. Feelings that he and Lauren and Kelly were now jagged points on a very dangerous triangle, and he was the one feeling the crushing weight of his deception from both ends. He could see that Lauren was caught up, and it was quite disconcerting.

"It's too complicated, Lauren. Really, it is."

"When you care for someone, nothing is too complicated." She brushed her fingers across his cheek. "Is it your family? Is everything okay?"

Though his relationship with Kelly clawed at his soul, he couldn't bring himself to tell Lauren. Not now. Maybe, not ever. So, Joey reached for the excuse life preserver, and secured it around his waist. "Yeah, uh, my family has a little to do with it. Connie's pretty much recuperated, and—"

Lauren's voice steeled. "And what? Now that he's better, he's not trying to cause problems for you and your family, is he?"

"No, not really. He's just trying to get better, I guess. But, let's just say that my uncle's return has opened up a lot of old family rifts. And, unfortunately, I have to try to make it all better for everyone."

Lauren sighed and shook her head. "Well, is there something I can help you do?"

The balance between truth and untruth was teetering, but Joey's conscious was relieved. Now was not the time to involve Lauren, or even delve more deeply into their fractious involvement.

"There is something you can do. You can help me enjoy today, and promise that you'll be here for me tomorrow."

She touched her lips to his and said, "I'll be there tomorrow, and the next day, and the next. I promise."

Chapter 16

As a peace offering to her son, Sylvia had two championship Presa Canarios puppies flown in from Roxbury, Vermont, for Connie. When she called him to see if they had arrived, he was cool with her, but she knew that he was pleased. It had been a bothersome few days of having Connie upset and not speaking to her, but she knew that he would come around soon.

Now that she was on the right path with Connie again, Sylvia was also trés pleased with the progress of her party planning, and everything else in her world was coming together in perfect order. If things went as planned, she'd have the problematic issue of Tiffany's paternity put to bed, very soon. And that was important. She did not want rumors to get out that the Cavanaughs were now into inbreeding. That just wouldn't do. So, needless to say, when Jolly reported that his men had gotten the DNA samples from Simon and Edgar, Sylvia craftily devised a plan to get Tiffany's.

Sylvia had invited Tiffany over on the ruse that she wanted to discuss using Tiffany's fledgling event planning services for the annual gala. After their customary greeting, a business-suited Tiffany launched into her sales spiel. Sylvia tried to maintain focus and attention, but she was consumed with getting Tiffany's DNA. When Tiffany initially declined Sylvia's offer of a beverage, Sylvia was stymied. She had planned to get some saliva from Tiffany's glass. She had to think of something else. A distressed Sylvia sat on pins and hypodermic needles, trying to conjure up another method to get Tiffany's sample. While Tiffany went through her presentation, the thought struck Sylvia like a flash of lightening.

"I hate to interrupt you, Tiffany, dear. But, who styled your hair?" Sylvia swooped down on top of Tiffany's head, and immediately began running her fingers through it.

Tiffany fought back a frown, and responded with the name of her stylist, while Sylvia kept playing in her fresh hairdo.

"It is simply lovely, dear," Sylvia said. "I must get his information from you. I do believe that Madison's looking for a new stylist, and I'd love to recommend yours."

Suddenly, Sylvia gasped. "Oh dear. I seem to have caught my ring in your hair. Hold on for one moment, darling. I don't want to snatch any of your lovely locks out."

Tiffany froze in her seat as Sylvia purposely wound two strands of Tiffany's hair on her finger and gently pulled. "I think I have it," Sylvia said, triumphant that both had strands and the follicles attached. She carefully slipped them into her pocket.

Tiffany winced, but kept a straight face. She rubbed the spot in the top of her head where Sylvia had just yanked.

"Oh, okay, Mrs. Cavanaugh," she said. "Well, that certainly smarts." She rubbed her head. "I'm glad you didn't catch any more on your ring. I didn't realize it was so sizeable."

"I do apologize," Sylvia said, and took her seat across from the watery-eyed Tiffany. Sylvia, feeling a bit sorry for Tiffany, tossed her a bone and agreed to use some of her staff for the soiree, which seemed to make Tiffany forget all about her missing hair.

But Sylvia, wanting to make sure she had every stone unturned, decided to hedge her bet. When Tiffany was ready to leave, she asked to use the bathroom. Sylvia waited until Tiffany had gone into the powder room, and then she frantically told her not to flush. Sylvia lied and said that she had forgotten that there was a problem with the commode.

When Tiffany left, Sylvia stood guard at the bathroom door, until Jolly's chemist came and confiscated Tiffany's urine and the two strands of hair. Yes, Sylvia was quite disgusted that she had to resort to such levels, but they were justified. After all, this was a small price to pay compared to the public humiliation her family would face if it was determined that the Cavanaughs were inter-dating. This was yet another Cavanaugh secret she'd take to her grave.

It was approaching the end of November, and despite a few snafus, Sylvia's party plans were on track, and getting down to the wire. Since she was still managing a number of family oriented issues, she thought it would be best to downplay Thanksgiving until things were better for all of her family.

Connie was still healing, and until he was better, Sylvia was thankful for his progress, but didn't feel comfortable enough to have her customary huge Thanksgiving dinner.

Normally, the Cavanaugh's holiday season was kicked off with a massive Thanksgiving celebration, continued through December where they held several charitable events such as working in food banks and shelters, and it culminated with the holiday extravaganza. But, because things were still a bit out of synch, Sylvia had decided to gather her family, with the exception of Edgar and Vincent, and reserve a large private room at 1789, one of Washington's premier restaurants.

The food was sumptuous, but the tone at dinner was subdued. Joey brought Grand, who was dapper in his black Christian Dior suit, and fairly cognizant throughout the evening. Christian's family was in full attendance. Madison showed up late, and then excused herself early. Sylvia could barely bring her eyes to focus on her daughter, and when she did, she thanked God that Madison wasn't showing yet. She wasn't quite ready to face those inquiries, especially from that bossy Kim.

A weakened Connie arrived, still using his cane, but walking much better and appearing stronger. Even though he was still cool toward her, Sylvia was ecstatic by his presence, and made sure he sat next to her. Still noticeably absent was Beverly. Sylvia didn't even bother to ask about her, and she just resigned herself to the fact that she didn't even care if Beverly ever came back. But, if and when she ever did return, Sylvia would make her wish that she didn't.

Throughout the meal, the conversations were forced and a little less then festive. No one seemed to really enjoy themselves besides the children. Despite Sylvia's best efforts, dinner wasn't a stellar occasion, but she had confidence that her family would pull themselves together before their year end gala.

The gala. Sylvia's thoughts drifted back to her party. The idea of a masquerade ball was simply genius. Sylvia and Penny had contacted the best costume designers from L.A. and New York to create custom masks for each of the family members. This was a six-week process, but Sylvia was assured that no one would have masks comparable to theirs. And not that some of her guests wouldn't try to upstage her. But, that was nearly impossible, since they never had anything to compare to her outfits, and no jewelry ever matched the illustrious *Il Rosso.*

A carefully selected assemble of celebrities, socialites, businessmen and political figures, Sylvia's guest list was truly a who's who. With Penny's assistance, she reviewed her guest list, and approved the final cut. The gala usually benefited one of the charities, and rotated annually. This year, the beneficiary would be the Cavanaugh Foundation, and this year, the proceeds would go to the trauma unit at Johns Hopkins, where the doctors had worked so diligently to save Connie's life.

Sylvia limited the list to one hundred guests, which meant that there would be at least two hundred people in her residence. As good etiquette dictated, she needed to mail the gold leaf encrusted invitations at least one month prior to the event, and she was dangerously close to breaching that deadline. Though the major tasks were nearly complete, between now and show time, she had a lot to do to ensure that her estate was up to par.

Madison ditched Thanksgiving dinner early so that she could go home and have dinner with Kelly. He had been working the graveyard shift, and other shoddy schedules for the past month, and wasn't the least bit surprised that he had been given the God-awful task of working on the holiday. She really felt sorry for him, and offered to have dinner with him. And though she had never asked, that's when she knew that he wasn't married or had anyone special in his life. If he did, he wouldn't have been available. Or so she assumed.

She had originally planned on taking him a dinner from 1789, but then thought again. He'd probably appreciate a home cooked meal for a change. Except, for one glaring factor: she couldn't cook.

Earlier in the week, she went to Walden Books and picked up the *"Joy of Cooking,"* while ruminating on picking up the *"Joy of Sex"* also. After perusing the menu suggestions and recipes in the one thousand plus page book, Madison concluded that there was no way she was going to be able to cook a decent meal. Not short of having Julia Child give her private tutoring sessions. Madison had panicked, and tried to roast a turkey, and have some mashed potatoes and gravy. However, she hadn't allowed enough time to cook the turkey, and she had a difficult time with the Idaho potatoes. Then, there was no gravy. Despite the step-by-step instructions, Madison just couldn't make the drippings from the turkey become the consistency of gravy. It ended up greasy, lumpy and tasteless.

By the time Kelly arrived at her home, both Madison and her kitchen were wrecked. It was like a scene from a classic episode of *"I Love Lucy."*

"It's okay, Madison," Kelly said, as he sat across from her at her ivory dining room table, and peered curiously at the tragic meal, beautifully set on Madison's elegant place setting.

"No, it's not," she said, and realized that she was getting teary eyed. "I just wanted to make you a home cooked meal. I should've known better, but I wanted to try. See, I've never had to cook before."

"Really? Well, you know that you're going to have to learn. And you need to eat well, too. You're not just eating for yourself."

A glum Madison tried not to completely fall apart. "I know, and I wanted it to be special."

"It is special, Madison. And I appreciate it. But, you know me. I'm simple. We can order a pizza and watch the game, no problem," Kelly said with a smile. "And next time, I'll help you out. I bet you didn't know it, but I can burn a little."

Madison's heart warmed. Kelly was so kind, and so real. She was so overwrought with her feelings that she reached over and kissed him, and he nearly jumped.

"I'm sorry, Kelly. I didn't mean to startle you," she said. Now Madison had really done it. She had messed up the meal, and now she was messing up things between them. The circuit was blown. She had reached maximum emotional overload.

"It's okay, Madison. I just didn't see it coming. There's no need to apologize."

Madison bit her lower lip. "But you jumped. And no man has ever done that before. I don't understand. After all of this time, you haven't tried to even kiss me or hold my hand. I bet you think that I'm repulsive, and have alot of nerve coming on to you, with my pregnant self," she said, and stifled the snivel in her voice. "You probably think that I'm a freak or something."

Kelly stood and reached for Madison. "Not at all, Madison. You're beautiful. Fine as hell. And any brother would be glad to be with you. But, I'm sorry. I know it probably hasn't been fair to you, and I guess I've been kind of selfish of your feelings. It's not that I don't find you attractive, but I, uh, I just haven't been with a woman in years. I wasn't even thinking about you like that. If anything, I don't want you to think that I'm a freak."

Madison sniffled. "Why? Are you celibate or something?"

"No, Madison. I don't deal with women. I'm, um. Well, there's no easy way to say this, but, I'm gay."

Kelly told a shocked Madison all about his past. His failed marriage, and how he had first gotten involved with men. And how now, he was trying to get over a relationship with a brother that couldn't deal with who he was. Madison was astonished. She had no idea that Kelly was gay.

Graham was the closest thing to a gay man that she had ever spent time with, and as flamboyant as he was, he never admitted to being gay. And Kelly had. And by no means did he fit the stereotypic image that Madison had in her mind. How could she not be able to tell? But, then she should've known. No man had spent more than an hour with her, before trying to crawl in her panties. No one but Justin, and that turned out to be a big head game.

Seated beside Kelly on the sofa, Madison didn't know how to feel. Kelly hadn't lied, but he hadn't been forthcoming either. But, he didn't owe her anything, and hadn't tried anything. But, the more he talked about it, the more she realized that was who he was. And, when he asked her if it would change their friendship, Madison was even more surprised by her response. Could she change him? Would she even bother to try? She only knew that he had been a friend to her, during some of her darkest times, and that was all that mattered.

"It doesn't matter what you are, Kelly. All I care about is that you're my friend."

"Well, I'd like to continue being your friend. I just felt bad about keeping that from you. Friendship is supposed to be based on honesty, and it bothered me that I hadn't really told you about me."

Madison smiled, and brushed the top of Kelly's hand. "I understand. I mean, I know it can't be easy. But, it's not like you lead me on or anything like that."

"I wouldn't do that, Madison. You're far too beautiful a woman for me not to think so, but right now, I'm just a little tripped out about this whole gay thing," Kelly said.

"I can imagine," she said. "I have to admit, I'm kind of curious about it too."

"What are you curious about? I mean, I don't know if I have all the answers, but I'll try to be as honest as I can be."

Madison sighed, and crossed her hands in her lap. "Well, I don't want to be too personal, but I would've never guessed that you were into men. Look at you. You're too, well, I'd think that you were too 'manly' for that."

Kelly laughed. "Well, Ms. Cavanaugh, you'd be surprised at the number of 'manly' men out here that are into men. The sad part about it is that they're so confused, they keep beautiful sisters like you in the dark, while dating and even being married to you, and not being honest about it."

Madison gasped. "You've got to be kidding. No way, Kelly. You mean to say that there are men like you, married and everything, messing around with other guys?"

Kelly nodded, and his face softened. "I can understand being torn like that, but honesty's the best policy. And I wanted to be honest with you. Not to say that you were thinking about me in a 'dating' kind of way. No way."

Madison elbowed him and laughed. "Of course not. Why on earth would I ever want to date a handsome, emotionally stable, and kind man?"

After their soul-baring conversation, the newly cemented friends stayed in, agreed to toss the meal, and ordered Chinese food to be delivered. Kelly turned on the television, and watched a football game. When Madison's doorbell rang, she answered it, and it was Joey. He was standing there grinning, and holding two boxes of food.

"Joey," Madison said, as she grabbed one of the boxes. "Come on in. What's all of this?"

"I saw your delivery guy in the elevator. I paid him, but I had brought you something from the restaurant. I figured that you'd be hungry by now. I'll give this take out to the homeless shelter when I leave."

Joey's smile dropped when he saw Kelly lounging in front of Madison's television.

"What the hell is he doing here?" Joey said, and clinched his fist.

"Oh, come on in Joey, and stop being so protective. Kelly? You remember my brother Joey." Madison grabbed the other box and mumbled something about being starved. She went into her kitchen, and turned on her stereo.

The two men threw daggers at each other, and didn't say a word, while Madison rattled around in the kitchen. "I left because I was supposed to be cooking dinner for Kelly, but, as you can see, that didn't work out too well," Madison called out from the kitchen.

"How quaint," Joey said. He mouthed the words to Kelly, "I told you to stay away from my sister."

"Fuck you," Kelly said.

"What was that?" Madison said, and poked her head out of the kitchen.

"He was talking to the TV, Madison," Joey said, and finally broke his gaze and looked at his sister. "Just that stupid game."

"Yeah, it really is a stupid game, isn't it?" Kelly asked Joey.

Madison looked at them and shrugged. She turned on her heels and headed back into the kitchen. Joey was about to run and punch Kelly dead in the back of his head, when Kelly's pager went off.

Kelly glanced at the number and groaned. "I knew this was gonna happen, Madison. They told me if someone didn't show up, then I might get stuck with a double tonight. And here I go." Kelly stood up and stretched. "I guess I'll have to take a rain check."

"What a shame," Joey said, unable to suppress a vicious grin.

Madison bagged up the Chinese food and handed it to Kelly. "Any time, Kelly. Any time. You have an open invitation," Madison said, and pecked him on the cheek.

Joey didn't even bother to say goodbye to Kelly, but sat on the sofa where Kelly had just vacated. It was still warm from his body. When Madison returned from walking Kelly to the door, she plucked Joey on his ear.

"What's wrong with you? What's going on? I understand your brotherly concern, but this is getting way beyond that. Why are you giving Kelly such a hard time?"

Chapter 17

Connie was really feeling it. The world had taken on a whole new perspective since his self-directed release from the hospital. He was enjoying training his new puppies, Idi Amin and Papa Doc, and they were growing like weeds. Even at this early stage, it was evident that their temperaments were as vicious as their predecessors. Things were finally settling down for Connie.

Dressed in his traditional black, and sporting a leather Kangol turned to the back, Connie was ready to step out on the town. It was early evening, and though there was a chill in the late October air, Connie didn't care. The world was his as he looked out the open sunroof of his brand new black-on-black BMW 735iL. With his recently promoted right hand man Eli behind the wheel, and Ace, one of the neophytes in the crew riding in the back, Connie was safe and secure, being trailed by three other strapped crew members in their smoked out black Jeep Grand Cherokee.

With Brand Nubians record *"Slow Down"* cranking on the stereo, Connie fired up another joint and blew the smoke through the open roof, all while singing along with the song.

"Slow dowwnnn," he sang, off key and even louder than the 300-watt sound system. "Look at that fuckin' sky, Eli," Connie said, and pointed his cane through the roof. "I swear, them clouds look just like somethin' from out of a movie." The weed was clearly talking to Connie, inducing all types of images and visions.

"Come on, hit this, 'Li. It's 'bout good as hell." Though Eli had insisted that he didn't smoke weed, Connie was determined to get him indoctrinated. Connie was not used to many people declining his rare offers, so he passed the joint to Eli, who took a short puff.

"Can I get a little bit of that, Connie?" Ace asked, his voice anxious and accommodating. Ace was young and hungry, and like an oversized puppy, who was always clumsily trying to please his master. Ace had a tendency to ramble on, and while Connie liked his enthusiasm, he could be a little annoying. But, he'd learn, and Connie could tell that he was going to make a great foot soldier one day.

"Go on, get down," Connie said, his voice cajoling and pointed. "And make sure you pass it back to Eli so he can get his too." Content that Eli was going to fall into line, Connie relaxed, and was getting back to his old self. Everything was looking up. The night would be perfect, except that his best buddy wasn't there. Connie didn't live with many regrets, but Stewart was one. And not having Beverly around bothered him too. He was amazed that she had the balls to actually leave him.

While Ace chattered on, Connie smoked and let his thoughts drift. Despite his bravado, deep down, he really felt bad that Stevie and Ellis had gotten killed in the line of duty, but hell, that was part of the job. He was sorry that he wasn't able to attend their funerals, but that was life.

But Stewart had been his dog. His partner in crime, his back. He did miss Stewart, but he'd never admit it though. And he did wonder where his wife had gone. He never expected Beverly to have the nerve to leave him, and he was kind of impressed that she had actually left. Especially after what he did to her. It wasn't like he really wanted to kill her, but he had to let her know that she was his property. And only his. And to find out that Stewart had been doing her was more than Connie could bear. That was disrespect to the nth degree, and he wasn't having that. No, he just wasn't having that.

Heavy thoughts were bringing down his high, and he wasn't about to let that happen. He had much too much to be up about. His health was improving, and he hadn't lost his touch with the ladies. He and Jade had been rocking and rolling for days now, and his endurance was only getting stronger.

Now, he was ready to deal with his family. While he had newfound respect for Joey, he hadn't forgotten that he had shot him on the docks. But, he'd let that slide for the moment. Admittedly, they were even on the exchange of gunfire, but Connie didn't have a forgiving heart. It was just easier to let Joey think that things were righteous between them, but Connie would never concede anything to his younger brother. Never.

And Connie still had Christian in his crosshairs. Connie had suspected that Christian had been pilfering money from the family, and he had basically confirmed it when Connie was planning his big drug deal. Though he didn't mention it when he and his brothers were figuring out how to handle Edgy, Connie knew that was where Christian got the ends from. But, that was okay too. Putting Christian in his place was definitely on Connie's to-do list, just a lower priority. He would never pose a significant threat because he was just a spineless, whining wonder.

Higher on his list of priorities was revenge. Connie was about to get even with his uncle and cousin. He didn't care about any truce. Connie was hell bent on getting even with Edgy, and though he mouthed camaraderie with his brothers, this was always a solo venture for him in his mind. He was the one with *Il Rosso*, and he was going to take full credit for it. And, despite his own personal treachery and deception, he knew that by rescuing the family jewel, his father would feel compelled to name him as his successor. It was part of the natural order. And once the natural order had been restored, Connie would focus on finding and reclaiming his wife. No one had ever left him, and he wasn't about to have Beverly be the first. He would see her dead before he allowed that to happen.

"Man, my buzz is comin' down," Connie said, shifting his thoughts from the uncomfortable world of personal issues back to the here and now. "Let's swing by the Georgia Mile. I ain't been there since I been sprung, and I sure could use some of that good grub right about now."

It began to drizzle, and Eli suggested that they close the sunroof. As he powered it shut, and turned on the wiper blades, something dragged across the windshield.

"What's this?" Ace asked, and pointed toward the windshield. He stuck his head between the front seats, like a happy-go-lucky kid. "Something's on the windshield, man."

Connie tried to focus in on the object, and as Eli drove, Connie opened his window, and stuck his arm out, until he was able to snatch the paper from the arcing blades.

When he grabbed it, he realized that it was a blank white envelope. The same kind that he had gotten in his mail a few weeks ago.

Connie raised his window. "Eli. Where the fuck did you have my car? And how'd this shit get on here?" Connie demanded, as he held the envelope, but didn't attempt to open it.

"What? I didn't see that, Connie. I don't even know what it is."

Connie tore open the envelope, and produced a tarot card. This one was the Five of Swords. "Damn, another damned five."

"What you mean, Connie? What's another five?" Ace asked, and turned from Connie to Eli, and back again.

Connie igged the young buck. "Yo, either one of y'all know what this shit means? Eli? Some of your peoples are from Louisiana, right? They know about this bullshit, right?"

Connie stuck the card in front of Eli's face as he drove, and Eli darted his head around it so he could keep his eyes on the road. "Damn, Connie. I don't know too much about that shit. Hold up for a minute."

"Maybe I can help. One of my honeys is Jamaican," Ace offered, and reached for the card, but Connie forced it into Eli's hand.

"Slow down, nephew. Eli's got this," Connie said, and Ace grunted and clung to the headrests.

Eli pulled the car over to a no parking zone, and studied the card. He picked up his cell phone, and placed a call to his mother, whom he asked if she knew the meaning behind the cards. After a few moments, Eli hung up the phone, and his face was grim.

"Yo, she said that the Five of Swords is like, well, dishonor or something. Discord. Like, not on the up and up."

"Damn, that sounds shady," Ace said.

Connie grunted. "Shut the hell up, Ace. Shady? That's some bullshit. Everybody knows I'm on the up and up. Damn, I meant to have you ask your mother about another five. The Five of Pentacles."

"She mentioned that too. I think she said that had something to do with ill health or being sick or something. Why, did you get one of them too?"

Connie rolled his eyes. "Yeah, somebody's trying to clown my ass, and I don't like it. Not at all. I'm not into this hoo-doo, voo-doo shit, but you know what, I'm not sweatin' it. Whoever it is can leave all the cards they want, and even send Avon calling if they want to. I got something for their asses. Now, let's go. I'm hungry as a mug."

"Me too," Ace said, and rubbed his belly.

It was like old home week. Connie directed Eli to park right in front of the restaurant, straddling a fire hydrant and Metro Bus zone. Connie tossed a twenty to one of the vagrants to watch his car. It was his customary practice, and it felt good to be back in the zone.

A cane dependent Connie strolled into his favorite spot with his crew covering his back. It was noisy and crowded, full of warm, familiar faces. Connie took great care in minimizing the pronunciation of his limp; he wasn't about to let these common folks think that he was crippled.

After issuing a few greetings, Connie peered over toward his favorite table, the last booth in the back, and noticed that it was occupied. That presented no major problem. The staff knew to clear out whoever was seated there by placing their tab on Connie. It was always a surefire way of him getting his way.

"What's up, baby doll?" Connie cooed to his favorite waitress, Doreen, as she swung by, expertly handling a tray overflowing with piping hot food.

"Hey sugar," she said as she blew him a kiss. "I'll be right with you."

Connie nodded and leaned on his walking stick. "Yeah, it's good to be back in this joint," he said to no one in particular, but Ace readily chimed in.

After a few moments, Doreen returned, and gave Connie a big hug. "Welcome back, stranger. I was wondering when I'd see you again."

Connie completed Doreen's hug with a playful pinch on her rotund behind. "You know I was comin' back to see you, girl. Now, what's up with my seat?" Connie pointed his cane in the direction of his table.

Doreen cleared her throat. "I, uh, don't think those guys are gonna move, Connie. I already told them you'd pick up their tab, but they just laughed."

"They laughed, huh?" Connie gave Doreen a kiss on the cheek, and motioned for his boys. "Put my order in, baby. And bring some 'to-go' boxes for our guests. I'm going to have a little chat with them, and I'm sure that they'll be leaving soon."

With smoke coming out of his ears, Connie and his crew maneuvered through the crowd, until they reached the last booth. And when he saw the occupants, Connie realized why they hadn't moved.

"Yo, gents. What's up?" Vincent said, as he and three of his boys sat crammed in the tiny booth with plates of half-eaten food strewn over it.

Connie's guys immediately reached for their pieces, as did Vincent's boys, but Connie shook his head. "This isn't the time or place, boys."

"Don't worry, Connie. We got your back," Ace said.

Vincent glared at Connie's underling. "This definitely isn't the time or place. Fellas, I'd like for you to meet my cousin, Conrad."

The grunts kept their eyes riveted on their counterparts, and didn't respond.

"How gracious," Connie said. "And this is my Cousin Vincent."

Vincent wiped his nose, and smiled. "I was wondering who was trying to move me out. I should've known it was you." Vincent continued eating. "I didn't know you were out of the hospital. Welcome back," he said, the smile fading from his face.

Connie took his cane and tapped the bottom of the wooden table. "Would you mind? This is my spot, and I'm not about to be carried by you or anyone else up in this joint."

"Carried? Is that some kinda country slang?" Vincent asked, with an exaggerated expression. "I was just kidding. I meant no disrespect."

"None taken. As a matter of respect, cousin. The booth you're sittin' in is mine. It's just that when I'm not here, I'm gracious enough to allow others to sit here. Understand?" Connie gritted on Vincent.

Vincent matched Connie's grit, and then finally motioned to his boys. "Hey y'all. Why don't you go grab a smoke while I chat with my cousin here."

Connie signaled for his folks to clear out too, and when their protection left, the cousins sat face to face for the first time since the dockside shootout.

"Strange meeting you here, huh Connie?" Vincent said, staring at Connie like he wished he would drop dead.

"Strange? Yeah, right. Especially since the last time I saw you, you were tryin' to cancel my ass."

"Ah, yes, cancel as in terminate," Vincent said. "Speaking of termination, my sincere condolences on the death of your pets. What a shame. I understand that they were outstanding specimen."

Connie fought the urge to flip the table over and beat Vincent into termination. Instead he intensely absorbed his cousin's words. "Thanks for your sympathy. That'll be one more thing I have to properly thank your ass for later."

Vincent shook his head. "Whatever, Connie. But, I can't take credit for it. Let's just say, I *heard* about it."

Their conversation was interrupted when Doreen arrived with Connie's food, and cleared out the discarded plates. She also handed Vincent a big, raw white potato, and when she caught Connie's eye, she scurried off.

Connie was still fuming about Vincent's innuendo to the point that he'd lost his appetite for the succulent food. Vincent chuckled, and then removed a knife from his pants pocket, and began expertly carving the vegetable. He cracked another smile. "Come on now, Cuz. That was *so* long ago. And like our grandfather said, all that's been forgiven, right? A truce is a truce, according to him."

Connie leaned against the table and honed in on his cousin, who was still whittling away at the spud. "You don't strike me as someone that would give a damn about what Grand said. Or anybody else for that matter. Except for your pappy. Now, he seems to have you under his manicured thumb."

Vincent stopped carving and folded his arms across his massive chest, and looked Connie up and down. "You better get something straight, cousin. I have respect for my father, but I ain't no little flunky. And he knows that. But, let me put it to you this way. I would've never tried to play my father like you tried to play yours. But that's probably the difference between us. I got a little more going on upstairs," he said, pointing to his temple. "Than you evidently do." He gritted on Connie, and went back to his sculpting. Within moments, he had crafted an accurate replica of the Washington Monument.

Connie picked at his food, and stared at his cousin's work of art. "Well, I see you got some skills, Vincent. That'll serve you well when you go to the joint, huh? You can whittle up a gun and use it to bust outta there, just like in the movies. Or did they use a bar of soap?" Connie shrugged, and continued eating.

Vincent shook his head. "Very funny, Connie. Did you have such a keen sense of humor before you got that metal up in you? Or is this a side effect?" Vincent laid the statue down on the table, and played with it. "Maybe that bullet in your back will improve some of your other senses too. Like your hearing. And then maybe you won't wind up getting' played like you did on the docks. Because you didn't know when to listen. Or who to listen to."

Connie, exercising unprecedented constraint, fought the urge to toss his plate into Vincent's face. "You might be right. I guess I'm just wondering why I'm sitting here listening to you now."

"What's that supposed to mean?"

"It means that we have some unfinished business, Vincent. Namely, I don't usually let niggas, family or otherwise, try to kill me, and then act like it never happened. I don't play that."

Vincent shrugged. "We can finish it right now, if you want, partner. I ain't above blowin' this spot up with you in it. That's how we do in the big city. We don't talk about it— we are about it."

Connie had been itching for a showdown with Vincent, but this wasn't the time. Or the place. So, he calmly picked up his fork, and began eating his macaroni and cheese and fried pork chops. "In due time, Vincent. In due time. I thought your father would've taught you better than that. We Cavanaughs don't participate in such public acts."

Vincent smirked. "My father? Right. He doesn't give a damn about what *you* Cavanaughs do."

"Is that right?" Connie asked. "So, I guess he's not interested in upholding his father's wishes either, huh?"

Vincent's jaw dropped, and he scratched his chin. "I didn't say all of that. All I'm sayin' is that my father has his own way of doing things, and until he finishes his agenda, nothin's gonna stop him. It never has. And that's not about to change."

Connie sensed that Vincent was backpedaling for a reason, and it had something to do with Edgy. "Not about to change? I think not. If your father plans on staying in this town, he knows he's got to answer to Grand. And to my father."

Vincent laughed, his thick chest heaving. "Whatever, Connie," he said, and plunged his monument into Connie's macaroni and cheese.

Connie plucked Vincent's model from his food, and bit it in half. Chewing on the raw potato, Connie slowly responded. "Yeah, I got your whatever, Vincent. You better recognize that my father has the juice here, not yours. And if old unc can't deal with that, then he, and you, need to get to steppin'. Like he did before."

While Vincent and Connie were verbally sparring at the Georgia Mile, Edgar was preparing to finish some long overdue business himself. Part of his plans included meeting with none other than Simon Blake himself, at Simon's behest.

At his suite at the Grand Hyatt, Edgar paced on the balcony. Not that he was nervous about seeing Simon after all of these years; it was just that he had planned on initiating the contact. But Simon had beaten him to the punch, and it irked him. The hotel's general manager had called to ask if it would be okay to show Edgar's suite to a guest. And when Edgar requested the guest's name, he was stunned to discover that it was Simon Blake.

Puffing on his cigar, Edgar steeled his composure. He always prided himself on being the best strategist and executioner in the family, and it bothered him that Simon had gotten the jump on him. Simon topped Edgar's list of unfinished business, and it had always been his intention to make Simon pay for killing the love of Edgar's life. And Edgar didn't care that over twenty years had passed since Simon had disposed of Marjorie. Payback was a debt that was eternally owed; with no expiration date.

It would be too easy to toss Simon's grimy ass over the balcony, so Edgar had to think of another way of eliminating him. Plus, Edgar knew that Simon was coming prepared, and that meeting Edgar on his turf was part of Simon's scheme.

"No, tonight I'll listen. And Simon will say something. Something I can use to rid myself of him later," Edgar said, as he puffed his cigar in the still oppressive afternoon air.

And Edgar was on point. Simon's visit was to discuss the fact that Tiffany and Vincent were dating, and that he wanted Edgar to put a stop to it. The question of Tiffany's lineage had risen again, and Edgar coolly watched as he saw how distressed Simon was by it. Or, was he disturbed that he might lose another one of his women to a Cavanaugh? Either way, when Edgar declined to intervene, Edgar knew he had Simon right where he was most vulnerable. Challenging the fact that Simon might not be Tiffany's father.

"Tiffany *is* my daughter, Edgar. I didn't buy it then, and ain't buying it now," Simon said, his eyes reddened but his voice remained controlled. Too controlled.

Edgar smirked. "Well, I say you don't know that for a fact, Simon. And if you did believe that Tiffany's your daughter, why are you here? *Perché lei sono qui?*"

"Enough with that Italian bullshit speak, Edgar. I'm neither scared nor impressed by it.

"I'm here because I don't want my daughter taking up with the likes of you. She's a decent young woman with a fine husband and family. But I know that probably makes him just that more interested in her. Like father like son." Simon paused, and stared at Edgar. "I guess. But, don't let me get ahead of myself. That would be true if he really *is* your son. Who knows, you may be around here claiming someone else's child— again."

Edgar puffed on his cigar, and thought about extinguishing it in the center of Simon's forehead. "Now, now, Simon. Trust me, I know Vincent is mine. Just like—"

"Just like what? You know Tiffany is yours? Negro please. If you did, you are an incredibly sick bastard. You'd actually want your daughter dating your son? Even you shouldn't be so low down."

"Low? Well, you ought to know. How much lower can you get than murdering your wife because she rejected you? You couldn't stand that me, a much better man, had beaten you. And I was going to take your wife. Trust me, Simon. I think you've sunk to depths I could never reach. Not even on my worst day."

"And if Tiffany and Vincent's dating bothers you so much, then to me it's worth it. To know that you are so concerned makes me just that much more unconcerned. But, I also know that you get a little irrational when things are out of your control, so I'm telling you— neither one of them better be harmed. I don't want any ill-timed accidents or fatalities occurring around them, you got that?"

Simon leaned forward, his eyes never leaving Edgar's face. "Is that a threat? You know, I don't do threats very well."

"Consider it a promise, Simon. Consider it a promise. C*onsiderarlo una promessa*."

Simon stood, and inhaled deeply. "Promises are often broken, Edgar. But for now, I'm done with all of the yak-yak. I'll let my actions speak for me. But, I promise you, it's not over. We will put this issue to rest— once and for all."

"I'm looking forward to it, Simon. *Sto osservando in avanti ad esso*."

Chapter 18

The coveted invitations had been mailed, and RSVPs were coming in by the droves. For as much help as Penny was, being a great substitute, Sylvia sorely missed Madison's assistance, and the little nuances they shared. Like catching up on the gossip, and speculating on who was going to wear what and bring whomever. She just missed her daughter, and she nearly told her that morning when she bumped into Madison as she was coming in the front door of the family manse.

"M'Dear," Madison said, her voice dry and terse. She was so cold, Sylvia could almost hear the sound of ice cracking.

"Madison," Sylvia said. She was on her way to meet Penny, and was surprised to see Madison. Sylvia hadn't spoken to her child in weeks, and she tried to indiscreetly look her up and down to see how her pregnancy was progressing. Madison's face was a little fuller, and even though she was wearing a wool coat, Sylvia could see a slight protrusion in her waist.

Madison's hair was parted and braided in two long plaits that stuck out from under her wool Burberry hat that matched her overcoat. She looks like a child, Sylvia thought.

"I hope you don't mind, but I had spoken to father yesterday, and he said that I could borrow some family photos."

"Photographs? For what? I certainly hope that you don't plan on disrupting things and getting it all out of place around here. You know that I'm in the process of preparing the house for the gala."

Madison shrugged. "I won't disrupt anything. I'm just going to pick up a few pictures, make some copies, and then I'll return them this afternoon— if that's okay with you."

"Photographs of whom? What do you need them for?" Sylvia's eyebrow arched. She was truly concerned. Madison was a Cavanaugh, with a notorious Cavanaugh temper. That factor, coupled with Madison's bubbling cauldron of pregnancy emotions, gave Sylvia pause. She envisioned Madison taking scissors to her precious photographs, and gouging their eyes out or drawing moustaches on them just for spite. And then Sylvia was additionally worried that because Justin was Creole, he might've taught Madison some other evil things, like make voodoo dolls of her or something crazy like that.

Madison studied her mother's face, and must have read her mind. "I want to make a border for the nursery. So, instead of ducks and bunnies, I thought that I'd do something creative like put all of our baby pictures up." She pursed her lips. "Plus, it may be the only way my child gets to see *some* of you," Madison said, and then sucked her teeth, as she headed toward the parlor.

Sylvia felt ashamed and a bit foolish. Her daughter had more resolve than she had given her credit for. Madison was a creative girl, and had always been. She always loved to draw, and spent countless hours reshaping her Colorforms, and modifying outfits for her dolls. She even staged full-blown fashion shows before she was ten. As the pigtailed woman blew past her, Sylvia saw the pigtailed little girl who she had watched grow and evolve into this beautiful young woman. Sylvia felt a pang of guilt over how she had been treating her only daughter. And what she was missing by being so obstinate over Madison's decision to have a child out of wedlock. She knew it was something that she would've never considered, and Sylvia secretly envied Madison's tenacity.

"I miss you, Madison," Sylvia said, but couldn't bring herself to turn around. She stood with her back toward her child.

Madison halted in her tracks. "Excuse me? What did you say, M'Dear?"

"I said, 'I miss you,'" Sylvia said, and finally forced herself to turn around. She held her arms open. "And I'm sorry for the harsh way that I've treated you." Sylvia paused. "I love you. And although I don't agree with what you're doing, you do have a right to do it." Sylvia's eyes filled with water, and she walked over to her child, and drew her into her arms. "My little girl is a grown woman now, and I have to start seeing you as such."

Madison closed her lips, and tears welled in her eyes also. "Really, M'Dear? Really?"

"Really, darling. Now, tell me all about how you're doing. How are you feeling? You know you have to watch out for swelling. We Russells are especially susceptible to that. Especially around your ankles. Child, your ankles will look like tree trunks if you don't keep them elevated. And tell me how you've been doing. And don't forget a thing."

A crisp, heavy snow had blanketed the city, and made for an arctic white, sedate Christmas holiday. But, as it melted and the city got back to it's normal state of business, anybody that was somebody was preparing themselves for the event of the season. The New Year's Eve gala at the Cavanaugh Estate.

Sylvia was finally breathing a little easier. Things were finally getting back to perfect order at the Cavanaugh mansion. She had reconciled her ill feelings for the still missing Beverly, and she was determined not to even think about her until Beverly came crawling back. And then she'd give her a piece of her mind. Sylvia was too elated that Connie had gotten over his ill feelings towards her, and that Madison was back in the fold. She had taken up temporary residence in her old room just to make sure that she was available and on hand to help with the arrangements at any given moment. With Madison so close to command central, Sylvia felt confident that every detail was accounted for, and that a lovely time was going to be had by one and all.

The custom masks Sylvia procured arrived a few days earlier, and she made it a point to ensure that each of her children received theirs by having her driver personally deliver each one. She had tried to take into account her children's personalities, and had masks crafted that were representative of their individuality.

She and Harry were wearing red and gold accessories, and Harry's mask was solid black, with red and gold accents. Sylvia's was a handheld mask, with vibrant ruby red feathers to match *Il Rosso*.

Connie's mask was seductive, with a devilish flair. Christian's was shaped like an old English barristers, and Joey's had a Romanesque, athletic flair. Madison's was by far the most imaginative, with it's silver and gold feathers, which resembled plumes from a colorful peacock. Sylvia congratulated herself on her uncanny ability to characterize her children. And she looked forward to greater love and family closeness in 1993.

"Yes, my dears. Despite the traumatic year we've endured, the new year will be simply wonderful," Sylvia said as she stood at the top of her winding stairwell, and gazed down at the expansive marble foyer. She envisioned the revelers that would fill her home in just a few weeks, and smiled. "Yes, I'll be glad to see this year come to an end. And erase these awful memories from all of our minds. I just can't imagine another year like this one. I just can't imagine."

Though he had sidestepped Madison's questions about Kelly on Thanksgiving, Joey knew that his time was running out. He felt cornered and guilty, now that the slightly showing Madison had sequestered him to put together baby furniture on this blustery December afternoon. Every time she opened her mouth, Joey expected her to mention something about Kelly.

As she busied herself with the finishing touches on her ingenious border in her newly converted nursery, Joey sweated the details of assembling the huge white crib.

"Now, tell me again. Why didn't you just have the furniture store put this together?" Joey asked, as he sat Indian style, mulling over the complex instructions.

Madison held up photographs and colorful renderings she had petitioned an artist to complete. She was carefully arranging the pictures along the wall with temporary tape, so that her interior decorator could permanently affix them later.

"Because, I didn't want some old smelly men in here fumbling around with my child's bed. Plus, you said you could do it."

Joey was about to say something, when his cell phone rang. From the caller ID screen, the name anonymous was visible, and Joey clicked on the phone and said hello.

The caller didn't respond, but Joey could hear someone breathing. "Hello? Will you say something please?" Joey almost yelled, and Madison looked at him with a curious expression.

"What's wrong?" she asked.

"Nothing," Joey said, and then held the phone for a few moments, until he finally hung it up. He hadn't gotten a call in weeks, and now it was just irritating. Again, he had to wonder who was playing on his phone. And on his nerves.

"Someone's been calling, but not saying anything. Even after I got my phone number changed. But, anyway, it's no big deal."

"Good," Madison said. "Because I don't want anything to happen that's going to give you an excuse for not finishing my crib today."

Joey rattled the papers. Normally, he was quite adept at constructing things, but Madison was making him a little nervous. But, at least he was doing it, and she hadn't summoned Kelly for the job, which would have really pissed Joey off.

Kelly hadn't called him since their tryst, and based on the way they had nearly come to blows on turkey day, Joey figured that he wouldn't even hear from Kelly. But, he wanted to know if Kelly was still spending time with Madison, but he didn't want to bring it up. Joey figured that Madison would, and within moments she did.

"I can do it. It's just that it's a little complex, Madison," Joey said. "Plus, it would help if you offered me something to drink. Damn woman, don't you have any manners?" he laughed.

Madison waved her hand, and stared at the walls. "You have a lot of demands for someone who hasn't really done any work yet. But, I'll get it." She turned and walked out the door. She returned a few minutes later with two bottles of water and tossed one at him. "Here. I swear, good help is hard to find," she said with a laugh. "I guess I better ask Kelly to put the bassinet together. Especially since I only have a few more months before the baby arrives. And I don't want to overwhelm you."

Joey's smile quickly faded. "I'll do it." His voice was gruff and humorless.

Madison opened her water and took a big swig. "What is the matter with you, Joey? I know you have this big brother thing going on, but you're a little much when it comes to Kelly."

Joey fixed his eyes on the instructions, and drank his water. "I mean, I don't get a good vibe from him, Madison. What are his intentions? What does he want from you? Why is he so desperate that he has to spend time with a—"

Madison picked up a roll of tape. "With a what? A pregnant woman? Does that make him desperate because he's spending time with me?" Madison narrowed her eyes and heaved the tape at him. "You've got a lot of nerve, Joey. I always thought better of you, but I see you're no better than most doggish, narrow minded, sex-hungry men. You figure that if you can't get in some woman's panties, then there's no need to even be around her. You're a trip."

Joey dodged the roll, and focused on his sister. "That's not what I meant. I meant that I just don't trust him. And I'm wondering why you seem to. You don't really even know him, do you?"

"Because I do," Madison said, her voice high-pitched and shrill. "Because Kelly has proven to be nothing but honest and real to me. And plus, he doesn't want me. He's—"

Joey's jaw dropped. Kelly never told him that he had told Madison about his lifestyle. "He's what? What is he?"

Madison shook her head and went back to her border. "He's my friend. That's all. And you should be glad he is."

Joey wondered why Madison didn't spill the beans. She had a protective air when it came to Kelly, and even that bothered Joey. What in the hell was really going on?

If Kelly had told Madison about his lifestyle, then why was he still hanging around her? Just trying to stay connected to him, Joey reasoned. But why did their friendship annoy him so?

Madison did need a friend, and if Kelly could be one, without trying to do her, then it should be okay. But, for some reason, the thought of them being friends wasn't a relief. Maybe it was because Joey knew that he and Kelly could never openly be friends or otherwise.

"What's up with you and him, anyway? I mean, I don't understand why you find it necessary to keep this dude around. Don't you know that you're too vulnerable? You probably haven't even gotten over Justin yet, and—"

"And what? I know I still haven't gotten over Justin. Damn, I'm carrying his child. I probably will never get over him, but I have to deal with it. But, what about you? What are you dealing with? What about Lauren? Were you really into her? Have you checked your feelings or gotten over her yet? Oh, but, that's right. You're Joey. You don't get your feelings caught up with anyone. You shouldn't be questioning me, Joey. You need to get your shit together. When are you going to allow Ms. Right to come into your life? And stay?"

"This isn't about me, Madison. Yeah, Lauren and I might've been involved, but not to the degree you and Justin were. I'm just concerned about you and your vulnerability. You certainly don't need to allow any other strangers in your world that might cause you pain. Especially not a cop."

Madison squinted at Joey. "How did you know he was a police officer? I never told you that."

Joey's mind scrambled, and he scanned his brain to try to recall if Madison had ever mentioned that. Evidently, she hadn't. "I, uh, I saw his squad car outside that day I left. And your doorman confirmed it."

Madison sucked her teeth. "That nosey old cuss. The nerve of him telling my business. I should have him fired."

"Don't do that," Joey quickly said.

"Hmph. Well, I'll be sure to give him a piece of my mind when I see him."

Joey sighed with relief. "Don't do that. He's just looking out for you. Like I asked him to." Joey hated to lie, but there was no legitimate explanation he could muster.

"And who appointed you my keeper?"

"It was a self-appointment," Joey said, and stood holding the roll of tape. "And I plan on looking out for you and my little niece or nephew for a lifetime." He walked over to his sister and gave her a big hug, which at first she tried to wiggle out from, but Joey wouldn't let her go.

"Well, me and my little one welcome you in our lives, Joey. But don't go overboard. I am allowed to have other men in my life, and I like Kelly. And he likes me. So, get over it. He's going to be around. Plus, he's going to take me to the holiday soiree."

Madison's words singed Joey's ears. When she told him about Kelly coming to the party, Joey didn't give it any energy, but immediately started thinking about who he could bring. He had planned on going solo, but now he would never appear without a pretty prop on his arm. And that would be Lauren.

As soon as he escaped Madison's servitude, Joey placed a call to Lauren. He left an alluring voicemail on her cell phone, and figured that she'd leap at the opportunity to go out with him to a public event.

As he waited for the valet to retrieve his Range Rover, Joey felt good. He had diffused a near disaster, and with Lauren by his side, he'd be ready for anything that came his way that night.

"Yes, Mr. Kelly. You can show up all you want. But, I've got something for you and I hope you can handle it."

Though she was relatively happy about attending the traditional Christmas gathering at her parents' home, Madison was ecstatic about having spent Christmas Eve with Kelly. Now that their friendship was more defined, she felt so comfortable being with him, and even he seemed more at ease.

The night before, Kelly had taken off work early, and picked Madison up from her home. They drove out to an old farm in Waldorf, Maryland, where they picked out a huge Blue Spruce tree and wreath. Tree shopping was an event that Madison had never shared with anyone before, and she found it so enjoyable, despite the bitter cold and needle pricks.

Kelly had deposited the tree in Madison's house, and left her with strict instructions to be ready, and dressed warmly, for a Christmas Eve to remember.

And it was a night to remember. Kelly surprised Madison by literally taking her out on the town. They did all of the touristy things like going to look at the Christmas Tree down on the Mall, and driving by the National Cathedral. They even rode through neighborhoods, snapping pictures of the ornately decorated houses, joining carolers and playfully searching for any signs of Santa Claus. They dined at Ruth's Chris Steak House on Connecticut Avenue, and then picked up tree ornaments at Neiman Marcus in Mazza Gallerie. They completed the evening by trimming the tree at Madison's, with a pine-coned filled inferno blazing in the fireplace. While sipping hot chocolate and eating mounds of imported and domestic candy, they debated about which house was the best decorated. It was an argument that neither one of them won.

Sitting Indian style in the middle of her living room, Madison had to admit that spending the evening with Kelly had been the most clean fun she'd had in a long time. But, when Kelly wanted her to pop some popcorn to string on the tree, Madison had drawn the line there. She was enjoying herself, it was true, but even she didn't want her tree to be too tacky. They compromised by stringing it along the mantle.

"Thank you, Kelly," she said, and nibbled on a miniature Nestle's Krackle. She tried not to laugh as Kelly struggled with the tangled lights.

"Thanks for what?" he asked, with a string of flickering lights wrapped around his neck, and a candy cane stuck in his mouth.

"Thanks for being here."

Kelly managed to attach the lights on the tree, and stepped back, admiring his work. "You're welcome. Thanks for having me here."

With the Jackson Five singing, "Have Yourself a Merry Little Christmas," Madison and Kelly were deep in the bubbly holiday spirit.

"You're welcome."

Kelly's eyes trailed from the tree to Madison's face. "I really should thank you again, Madison."

"For what?"

"For making the holiday special for me. And for your friendship." He sighed and knelt down on the floor near her. "You know, when I told you about my lifestyle, I just knew that you were going to kick me to the curb. And when you didn't, I was real surprised."

Madison shrugged. "Well, I guess I appreciate your honesty. Unfortunately, I think that I've lived a life where either it's been difficult for people to be honest with me, or either they just were dishonest people. I don't know. But, I've had a lot of time to reflect, and whatever way it was, isn't the way that I want it to be going forward. I need honesty, and I'm glad that you feel that you can be honest with me."

Kelly smiled. "Well, it wasn't easy. You're the only person I've ever told."

"Really? Not even your family?"

"Nope."

"Well, it's not that you wear your sexuality on your sleeve."

"I know, but for some reason, I wanted to tell you. And I like that you accept me for who I am. Despite—"

"Despite who you sleep with? Well, I must admit, I am kind of curious. I mean, we spend an awful lot of time together, so whoever he is, you must not be together too often."

Kelly sighed. "Aww, see, I was waiting for you to ask me something about that. Let's just say that I'm not really dating anyone special at the moment. I was dealing with someone that I really dug, but things just didn't work out. I know you can understand. You know better than I do that a good man is hard to find."

They both laughed, and Madison caressed her belly. "Well, I have a reason why I won't be attracting any 'good' men anytime soon. Hell, I had a hard enough time meeting a decent man *before* I became pregnant. And, I can't say that I'd be all that interested in sleeping with a man at the moment, although I will say, my hormones are screaming otherwise."

Kelly smiled. "Don't worry, Madison. A good man will come along. One that will love you and that beautiful baby you're carrying. And probably when you least expect it. And in the meantime, you can focus on being healthy and strong for yourself and for little baby Gucci."

"Gucci?"

Kelly stood, and hung a few more lights on the tree. "You know you're gonna have that kid in designer diapers. You might as well name him or her after one of your favorite designers."

"Very funny. I didn't know you were a comedian."

"Now you know all of my secrets, Ms. Cavanaugh."

Madison smiled, and passed him an ornament. "Yeah, so you say. But, I've just learned another one of your secrets. You are quite the tree trimmer, Mr. Brown. Just look at your handiwork. The tree is simply lovely," she said, and the lights shimmered in her eyes.

"Yes, it does," he said, and hung the silver bell on a limb. "And so do you. So, let's go make some more treats." He reached for her hand, and helped her to her feet.

"More treats? Like what? I've already eaten enough sugar to rot my teeth and my baby's teeth out."

Kelly laughed, and gave Madison a warm hug. "Well, that's not too good of a thing, now is it? Maybe we can make some nachos instead. With cheese. Cheese is healthy, right? Right?"

They spent the rest of the night, eating cheesy nachos, with loads of salsa and jalapenos. Watching "*It's a Wonderful Life*," Madison dozed off on Kelly's shoulder, thinking that hers was truly a wonderful life too.

True to his word, Connie squired Jade to the concert, which happened to fall on Christmas Eve. Going to a show was a major event in DC, and everyone wore their best holiday attire. In a sea of furs and jewels, Connie and Jade stood out in their matching coyote coats and hats. As they entered their box seats at Constitution Hall with Eli and Ace as their bodyguards, Connie felt his mojo coming back strong. He and Jade were moving and grooving to the soft melodies of Miki Howard's *"Come Share My Love,"* and *"Baby, Be Mine,"* and Jade was preparing herself for Keith Sweat performance. That was until an usher delivered a single red rose to her, with a small card attached.

"Oooh," Jade said, and whisked the flower from his hands. "This is so thoughtful of you, baby." Jade kissed Connie's face and started opening the card.

Connie's face dropped, and he snatched the card from her hands. "I didn't send you this corny, played-out shit," he said, and ripped the card open. It read: "Next time, let a real man take you out."

Connie's blood boiled, and he crumpled the card up in his hand, and tossed it to Eli. "Get rid of this crap. And go get that usher and find out sent this shit. *Now!*" Eli nodded and headed out of the box.

"What'd it say?" Jade asked, and Connie ignored her, and crushed the flower until the petals fell to the floor.

"Don't you worry about it." Connie scanned through the darkened crowd, but his search was futile. Ten minutes later, Eli returned, unable to find the usher. Connie fumed all during Keith Sweat's set, until the lights went up during intermission, and he spotted Vincent smirking at him from his box seats across the hall. He was accompanied by two of this crew, and some anorexic looking model type, with flowing tresses and too much beat on her face. Vincent winked at Connie, and it infuriated him. Connie couldn't wait to confront his cousin, so he motioned for his boys to join him as he hobbled to his feet.

"Where are you going?" Jade asked. "To get me backstage to see Keith Sweat? You didn't forget, did you?"

"Naw, you can scratch that. I got some business to handle."

"Business? It better not be some little skank you're trying to holla at. And don't be too long, either. And bring me a Courvoisier and coke when you come back."

Connie ignored Jade's request and quickly maneuvered his way down the staircase and toward Vincent's seat.

"Yo, boss. What's up?" A clueless Eli asked, with Ace behind him.

"That damned Vincent is over there, staring me down. I know he sent that damned weak ass flower to my girl, and I'm not havin' it. I will not have this clown frontin' at all of my spots, disrespectin' me. Fuck that. I don't want to look up and constantly see his fucked up grill every time I'm out and about. He'd better recognize. I've already warned his ass. This is my town, goddammit, and he's about to catch a beat down."

"We got your back," Ace said, and stepped ahead of Connie, clearing a path through the throngs of concert-goers.

Before Connie could reach Vincent's box, they ran into each other in the vestibule. With both sets of bodyguards by their respective sides, Connie and Vincent's meeting looked like the showdown at O.K. Corral.

"Your girl like the flower?" Vincent asked, with a sneer.

"So you like roses, huh? I'll be sure to have some sent to your funeral, you punk assed bitch. I warned you before, now I'm gonna have to show you. Don't try to carry me, Vincent. I'll fuck you up."

Vincent chuckled. "Come on, Connie. You know you can't handle old girl. Especially in your condition. Plus, I'd be doing you a favor, 'cause don't you have a wife? Hmmph. Where's she at tonight? Home tending to the little bastards while you two fun and frolic?"

Connie's jaws slacked, and his boys reached for their pieces. "Very funny, Vincent. But, I told you, I'm not playin' with you. Now, you're going places you ain't gonna be able to come back from. You won't disrespect me, or my lady. You got that?"

"I got it all right. And I can give it to you right now." Vincent flipped open his jacket and revealed the leather handle of a switchblade that was tucked under his belt.

"We got this, boss," Ace said, and stepped in front of Connie.

"Oh, that's a great trick you taught your pet ape, cousin. I meant to tell you that I'm quite impressed that he speaks so well." Vincent laughed with his cronies for a few moments, and then he abruptly stopped. "Now, you just need to teach him how to shut the hell up."

"Don't worry about him, Vincent. I got somethin' to teach you first. And it's called a D.C. ass whupping."

"Oh, word?"

"Word is bond. Bring it on, mother fucker," Connie said, and swung his cane and whacked his cousin on the side of his neck.

The crowd parted as their bodyguards jumped in, and a few good blows were landed before the security guards arrived and broke up the fracas. They were about to toss them all out, until one of them recognized Connie, and Connie assured him that the beef was squashed, and that they would go their separate ways. The security guards disbursed the crowd, but Connie made sure Vincent got a message before they parted company.

"It's not over, Vincent. Not by a long shot."

"Any time, any place," a tussled Vincent said, and slowly walked away.

Connie gathered his cane and his boys, whose suits were a bit disheveled and Ace's jacket was ripped. Connie was more angry than anything else. "This is about to get real interesting," Connie said, as tucked in his shirt tale and limped back toward his box.

"Yeah, I can see that. But, we can handle things," Eli cosigned, as he straighten out his clothes. They took a few steps through the crowd, when he suddenly stopped.

"Yo, Connie. What about Jade's drink? Ace, go get it, while we go back to our seats. And try to fix that jacket so it's not so noticeable."

Ace nodded, and Connie and Eli maneuvered their way back to the box. EnVogue had already taken the stage when they arrived, but that didn't stop Jade from looking for her drink. Connie settled down in his seat and told her to chill until Ace brought it back.

Connie was too busy sulking about Vincent and couldn't even enjoy the provocatively dressed songstresses of EnVogue. They had sang a number of songs including *"Free Your Mind"* and *"My Loving,"* before Eli nudged Connie and whispered that Ace hadn't returned.

"Maybe the line was long or something," Connie snapped.

"Maybe," Eli said, and then the sound of stumbling could be heard in the staircase leading up to the box.

"What the—" Connie said, as he, Eli and Jade spun around to see Ace falling through the drapes, clutching his mouth. A single red rose was stuck in his breast pocket, along with his bloody, severed tongue.

Chapter 19

Sylvia was immensely grateful for a quiet, uneventful Christmas, yet a little antsy about New Year's Eve sudden arrival. It was approaching six p.m. on the magnificent day, and the excitement was building. The event was scheduled to begin at nine, but Sylvia was working out some of her last minute jitters. There was a whole host of activities planned, including a simulated ball drop at midnight from the upper level of the winding stairwell. While going through the final preparations, Sylvia had Madison recheck the guest list while Penny made sure that all of the hired help was present and accounted for.

Jolly's security people were on site and in position. Tiffany's employees were on time and ready for duty. A staff person was stationed in the service area to work with Christian to accept and tabulate the donations. A bonded coat check person was prepared to monitor the numerous furs. There was more than sufficient wait staff and servers. Valet parking attendants were going through their routines, and Sylvia checked the final headcount. The number of personnel required to pull off this event had grown exponentially since last year, but, Sylvia was undaunted.

The success or failure of this event didn't hinge on the ice sculptures or the band. It was all about the guest list. And, as Sylvia's make up was being applied by her private artist, Madison combed through the list. She was less than pleased to see that Ashley and a guest were invited. When Madison explained to Sylvia how she felt, they both acknowledged that there was no acceptable way to un-invite Ashley at this late hour. But, Madison did have the consolation of knowing that her outfit would be the talk of the ball.

Despite the confidence Sylvia exuded externally, internally, she was fretful. Because of the snow storm, the results from Tiffany's DNA test hadn't arrived, and Jolly had spent all week trying to track the package. But, at least she didn't have to worry about Tiffany and Vincent coming together to the party. Tiffany had RSVP'd for she and her husband. And, Sylvia had the added satisfaction of not inviting Tiffany's Aunt Giselle. She'd teach that woman a thing or two about common courtesy. And for not responding to her in the correct manner.

Connie and Joey were coming solo, but Sylvia had ensured that there would be a bevy of beautiful young ladies to garner their attention. Madison invited a date, and although she said he was just a friend, Sylvia silently vowed not to be judgmental. She was extremely concerned about Madison's choice in men, and anxious to meet this mystery man.

Yet, there were a few folks on the list that Sylvia wasn't overly anxious to see. The first was Simon Blake. Out of respect for his former position, Sylvia had invited him, but she had hoped that he'd decline. She was nearly devastated when he RSVP'd that he was coming. With a guest, nonetheless.

The others Sylvia hadn't wanted to invite were Edgar and Vincent. But, she had to, just for appearance's sake. Then she thanked God for the masks. At least she wouldn't have to see their deceitful faces all night, and she wouldn't have to even acknowledge their presence, if she chose not to. This party was going to make all if the ill-natured events that had occurred over the course of the last few months seem trite and insignificant. As she lovingly placed *Il Rosso* around her neck, Sylvia knew that she hadn't lost her touch. And, she was ready to let the world bear incredible witness to it.

Though the weather outside was threatening snow, it didn't deter the exclusive invitees from coming to the festivities. The party was a rousing success, with partygoers treated to every sensory pleasure. Their ears were filled with wonderful music, their palates teased with great food, their intellect stimulated with superb company, and their eyes pleasured with colorful masquerade regalia. It was just as Sylvia had envisioned.

While the soothing sounds of the jazz combo played in the background, bright flashes from the photographer's camera were fired so rapidly; it was almost like a strobe light was on. The photo bug captured every heady moment and Sylvia was elated to see the enormous turnout and jubilant atmosphere. Gorgeous people in their designer duds, styled and profiled, while others made animated gestures as they laughed and smiled, and engaged in jovial conversation and witty repartee. Whatever the partygoers' disposition, servants attended to their every whim or need. This would certainly go down in the annals of society as one of the best events she had ever hosted. Even the presence of the masked Vincent and Edgy couldn't interfere with Sylvia's enjoyment or sense of accomplishment.

A dapper, Armani tuxedo clad Joey was grateful to wear a mask, especially since he wound up coming stag. Lauren had returned his call, and though she seemed thrilled by the invitation, she had already accepted another one. She did say that she would try to drop by sometime that night, but Joey said it wasn't necessary. He didn't need the gratuitous gesture.

He also didn't want to deal with his jealousy over Lauren having other plans. He realized that he had no right to be miffed, and while he admired the fact that she wasn't hanging by the phone waiting for him, he was annoyed that she was busy. So, perhaps it was for the best. While he enjoyed her company, he didn't want to feel like he was using her as a beard or a crutch to support him when he had to face Kelly. But, Joey sucked it up. He was safe behind his mask, and he intended to stay there for the duration of the evening, while he dealt with his family and personal issues.

That was until Kelly showed up with Madison swinging on his arm, and steam streamed from Joey's ears. Joey watched as Madison introduced Kelly to their parents, and when they came in his direction, Joey barely spoke. He resigned himself to the fact that he'd deal with Kelly at a later time and place. At the moment, Joey had greater concerns to address.

Ashley had finally called back, and told Joey that the results from the animal's testing had indicated that they had been poisoned with chocolate, which accelerated their blood pressure and caused the heart attacks. Ashley's disclosure only fueled Joey's theory that Edgar and Vincent had been the culprits behind their poisoning.

After she shared the results with Joey, Ashley tried to weasel an invitation to the gala from him, but he shut her down. After she failed in her effort to be Joey's date, shades of the former Ashley re-emerged, and she meekly ended the call. He wasn't mean, but Ashley's feelings were the least of Joey's concerns.

He and his brothers had agreed to wait until after the gala to tell Harry about Edgy's ultimate betrayal with *Il Rosso*, especially since they now had proof. They all agreed that there was no reason to ruin Sylvia's party.

There wasn't any reason until Simon and his date showed up, and his date was wearing a necklace that looked eerily similar to *Il Rosso*. Sylvia was the first to spot it, and she immediately grabbed Kim, and sought out Tiffany.

"I've got to find out who that hussy is with that charlatan Simon. Wearing that fake piece of costume jewelry at my affair. I can't believe that he had the audacity to bring her in here with that cheap knockoff. The nerve of him," Sylvia said. "You'd think that amnesia would've made him forget how tacky he can be."

"Don't worry, M'Dear. We'll find out who she is," Kim said, the Cabrini-Green rushing out of her. "There's Tiffany over there," she said, and pointed the base of her champagne flute in Simon's daughter's direction.

Sylvia and Kim made a bee-line for Tiffany, and cut her off before she could disappear into the crowd. Sylvia could barely contain herself as she asked Tiffany who her father's date was.

"She's his executive assistant, Mrs. Cavanaugh," Tiffany said in a distracted tone. Her eyes were searching the room like she was looking for someone, but Sylvia was not about to be denied.

Stepping into Tiffany's line of sight, Sylvia grabbed her arm. "I see. She seems perfectly charming, but we've never met. Tiffany, darling— would you mind making an introduction?"

Tiffany's eyes rolled under her mask. "Sure, Mrs. Cavanaugh." And then Tiffany kicked back into work mode. "Are my people working out well?"

Sylvia slipped her arm into Tiffany's, and guided her toward Simon's guest. "Splendid, dear. Absolutely splendid," Sylvia said, even though she had no clue. She had one motive in mind, and that was getting to the bottom of Simon's little ploy.

As Tiffany made a brief introduction, and with Kim hovering over her shoulder, Sylvia's eyes were drawn to the neck of Simon's date.

"Jessica, I'd like to introduce you to our host. This is Mrs. Sylvia Cavanaugh and her daughter-in-law Kimberly Cavanaugh. Sylvia and Kim, this is Jessica Bates."

The ladies shook hands, while Tiffany's attentions were obviously elsewhere. "Well, if you will excuse me, I'd like to go and check on my workers," Tiffany said, and scurried off.

Kim almost gnawed through her mask when she realized who Jessica was. "Oh, so you're Jessica. Isn't it nice to finally meet you. If you'll wait right here for a moment, I'd like to introduce you to someone," Kim said, and practically raced off on her three and a half inch pumps.

Sylvia wondered why Kim was vacating her post, but she was mesmerized by Jessica's necklace, and barely heard Jessica speak.

"It's nice to meet you, Sylvia. And what a wonderful party you're having," Jessica said. "I'm so honored to be here."

"Uh, yes. Thank you, dear. I love your outfit," Sylvia said, but her pupils never left Jessica's neck. "And that's a lovely piece of jewelry you're wearing."

"Oh, thank you, but it's not mine. Simon let me wear it tonight. He said that it would really compliment my gown."

"Really," Sylvia said. But before she could say anything else, Kim had returned, with a hesitant Christian in tow. Kim brazenly interrupted them.

"Christian, I'd like for you to meet Simon's date. I believe you know her. This is Jessica. Jessica Barnes."

Both Jessica and Christian's faces dropped, and Sylvia honed in on the change in atmosphere immediately.

"You two know each other?" Sylvia asked, with one eyebrow raised.

Christian stammered and stuttered like Porky Pig. "Yes, um, M'Dear. Jessica worked me, um, I mean worked for me a few months ago." He shoved his mask up over his forehead, and stared at Jessica.

"I'll say," Kim said. She folded her arms across her chest and gloated. "It's a small world, after all, now isn't it?

Simon returned and swept Jessica away, right before Kim was about to rip her to shreds. Sylvia, dissatisfied with the results from her investigation, abruptly left to find Harry and notify him of Simon's antics. So, Kim dug her claws into her husband's arm, and turned her rancor on him.

"So, that's the old broad you were doing, huh? Well, from the look on your face, I can tell that you didn't know she was back in town. I guess your shit wasn't good enough for a second round, or either she's moved on up with Simon. Oh well, Christian. You poor, poor thing," Kim said.

"Don't patronize me, Kim. That was a low blow, but right on your level. You didn't have to haul me over here and try to embarrass me like that." Christian tugged at the base of his tuxedo, and sweat trickled from under his mask. "In front of my mother, of all people."

"Please," Kim said, and flagged over a server and whisked a glass of bubbly from her tray. "You should be glad that I did it, because if she's all hooked up with Simon now, you ought to know that she never meant you any good. Hell, she was probably working for him when she was working you. It was probably in her job description."

Christian huffed. The thought of Jessica being back almost made him ill. But he wasn't about to let Kim know it. "That's preposterous, Kim. That's what you'd like to think, but it's not true."

"Oh really? I know you think Miss Jessica can do no wrong, but trust me, I know shade when I see it. And that broad is about as shady as they come. Don't you know she came waltzing up in here with a knockoff of *Il Rosso* on?

"What did you say?"

Kim flicked Christian's ear. "You heard me. She had a cheap imitation of *our* family jewel draped around her wrinkled neck."

"Our family jewel? You mean *my* family jewel."

"Don't start that shit again, Christian Cavanaugh. I have that last name too, so I can say 'our' from here to eternity."

"Whatever, Kim. I'm not about to get in a pissing match with you about that. Or anything else for that matter. But I asked you before not to speak ill about Jessica, and I'm not going to ask again."

"Now, what you said is just downright crazy. Maybe her jewelry just looked like *Il Rosso* by coincidence."

"Nothing is by coincidence, Christian," Kim said, swilling her drink. "You need to get your head out of the clouds and recognize. Because I can tell you one thing. Old girl has been around, and I don't mean just around the block. And Simon's got her doing his bidding now, so don't think it's so ridiculous. It's highly likely."

"You're wrong. Loud and wrong," Christian said.

"Whatever, Christian. You just stay away from that tramp because even though your mother doesn't know the real deal, she knows enough to know that old girl spells trouble. T-R-O-U-B-L-E, and you," she said, running her hands down her sides, "have enough to contend with right here." She downed her drink in one fluid motion and stormed away, nearly mowing Madison down in the process.

"Kim, what's the matter?" Madison asked.

"Can you believe that Ashley's aunt's here? You know who I'm talking about. Jessica. The one who was carrying on with Christian," Kim said, and swiped another glass of champagne from a passing waiter.

"You don't say. Ashley's here, huh?" Madison quickly scanned the room for her former friend Ashley. Though everyone had their masks on, Madison was able to spot Ashley because she knew that her big feet would be a tell-tale sign. And when she spotted Ashley's clodhoppers stuffed into a pair of beaded pumps, Madison headed straight for her, with Kim on her heels.

"Ashley," Madison said, as soon as she was close enough for her to hear.

"Oh, hey, Madison," Ashley said. She lowered her mask, and peered around the room. "Where's that fine brother of yours? I've been looking for him all night."

"For what? Oh, you've got to be kidding, girl. I'm not here to talk to you about that. I can't believe that you brought your philandering aunt here," Madison said. "Especially after her scandalous behavior."

A newly toned, flyly outfitted Ashley shrugged, and tossed Madison a nonchalant look. "I'm not my aunt's keeper. She's a grown woman, and free to do her own thing. And plus, I didn't bring her. She's not my date."

"Very well, Ashley. If that's how you feel. I think that you should both leave. And spare yourself any more embarrassment."

"Embarrassment? Please, Madison. I'm not the one who should be embarrassed. It should be you, Miss Pregnant and Unmarried," Ashley said, and sucked her teeth.

Kim's jaw dropped, and her head dipped to the side. "Oh no you didn't. Don't come in here trying to get loud, Ashley. Don't even go there, because I'll go right there with you. Except, I'll come back, and your frumpty dumpty ass won't."

"That's okay, Kim. I got this," Madison said, and nodded toward Ashley.

"You got nothing, Madison," Ashley spat. "Especially nothing on me. Not anymore. Those days are long gone, and never to return again."

Madison narrowed her eyes at her former friend. "Ashley, you are so petty. Why are you going around saying things about me behind my back?"

"Because, I'm sick of you, Madison. You and your *'I'm better than everybody else'* attitude. I can't stand the way you've treated me all these years, and now I'm not going to let you push me around anymore. So, if you don't like what I have to say, either don't do things so I can't talk about them, or don't listen to what I have to say. The choice is yours."

With his mask perched atop his head, Joey splashed water on his face, and stared at his reflection in the mirror. He looked great, his skin and eyes clear and even. And his tuxedo fit him like an English driving glove. With the help of the lighted candles and scented potpourri in the Cavanaugh's basement bathroom, Joey tried to ease his mind. Tonight was the night all hell was probably going to break, and he had to be steadfast in his every move. He forced thoughts of Kelly and Lauren out of his mind, and focused on the mission at hand. Taking his uncle down.

As he exited the bathroom, he bumped into none other than Kelly. Joey immediately recognized him behind his black leather mask.

"What are you doing down here?" Joey looked around to see if anyone was within earshot. He was relieved, and then a little nervous that they were alone in the massive basement.

"I'm here to use the bathroom. Evidently, the same reason you were here."

"Are you following me?"

Kelly brushed past Joey, and stood in the doorway of the bathroom. "Don't flatter yourself. I was just helping out with your security folks, and had to take a leak— if that's okay with you."

"Man, whatever," Joey said, and turned away. He heard Kelly close the bathroom door, and before he locked it, Joey did the unthinkable. He pushed it open and barged in.

"What the hell are you doing?" Kelly asked, with a confused and agitated expression on his face.

Joey gritted his teeth, yet remained silent. Finally he spoke. "I don't know."

"I think you better know, Joey. And get the hell outta here."

"I don't like you dating my sister, Kelly. And although she knows about your lifestyle, I still don't like it."

Kelly unzipped his trousers and took out his manhood. "Add that to the list of things you don't like about me." Kelly proceeded to take a leak, while Joey leaned against the bathroom vanity and tried not to look.

"You think this is easy for me?" Joey asked. "This is so damned hard, and you're making it harder. Just by being here."

"What do you want me to do— leave?" Kelly asked as he shook and then stuffed himself back into this pants. "Well, I'm not. Madison invited me, and unless she asks me to go, I'm staying. And I guess you'll have to deal with it."

Joey wanted to reach for Kelly, but something inside stopped him. "That's the problem, Kelly. I can't deal with it. I know I can't be the person you deserve, and it's killing me. It really is."

Kelly washed his hands and wiped them on an ornate hand towel that hung near the sink. "You're right, Joey. You're not the person I deserve, and you probably never were. You might be a decent person, but you hide behind too much shit. And I'm not talking about who you get down with. I'm talking about you. You can't be real with anyone, but that's probably because you can't be real with your damn self. At least Madison is real. She knows she's not perfect, and she's happy being who she is. And not who everyone wants her to be."

He grabbed the doorknob and flung it open, but Joey shoved his foot at the bottom to prevent Kelly from opening it all the way. "Remove your foot, Joey. I'm walking outta here and leaving the door open. Remember, you're the one that insists on living his life under a mask and behind a closed door. Not me." Kelly marched out of the bathroom, leaving an unmasked and astonished Joey in his wake.

"Are you okay?" Kelly asked as he handed Madison a glass of punch. He had filled a glass from one of the sparkling fountains, and had noticed Madison from across the room, where she appeared to be being accosted by some masked woman.

"I'm alright," she said, her jaws tight. She wore a mortified expression.

"Who was that? And why was that woman giving you a hard time? Is there something that I can do?"

Madison sniffled, and tried not to sob in her drink. "That was an old friend. And she was letting me have it because, I guess I haven't been a really nice person for most of my life. And now it's my payback for it."

Kelly grabbed Madison's shoulders, and hugged her warmly. "Come on, Madison. You're being too hard on yourself."

"No, I'm not. I was quite a bitch. A high riding bitch."

Kelly tried not to laugh, but the look on Madison's face was a bit comedic. "You're being too hard on yourself. Now, I know you'd mentioned that before, and trust me, that says a lot. I'm sure that was kind of tough for you to say."

"Not really, Kelly. Especially when it's publicly thrown in your face." Madison sighed. "I guess I really need to reevaluate my life, and figure out what I've done and how I've gone wrong."

"We all do," Kelly said.

Madison sighed. "I think that I really need to make a change in my life. A permanent one."

Kelly lifted Madison's chin and gazed deeply in her eyes. "I've been thinking about making a change in my life, too, Madison. A big one."

Sylvia was seething when she nearly knocked Joey back down the stairs as he was coming up from the basement. He asked her why she was so bothered, and she just mumbled that she had to find Harry. Immediately.

When she and Joey found Harry, he was enjoying a cigar with Jolly in the parlor. When she mentioned the necklace, it immediately grabbed Joey and Jolly's attention. Joey hadn't even thought that Simon might somehow be involved, but it was highly possible. Sylvia was about to begin a tirade, but she was interrupted when one of the catering staff knocked on the door.

"Mrs. Cavanaugh. A courier has just delivered a package for you, and it's in the butler's pantry in the kitchen," the server said.

"Oh good. That must be the test results," Sylvia said, and started off toward the kitchen with the server in tow.

After a few steps, the server turned back to Joey. "Oh, I almost forgot. Mr. Cavanaugh, a young lady was looking for you. She said she couldn't find you, but wanted me to give you this," he said, and reached into his pocket and handed Joey one of those ominous white envelopes.

"A young lady? What was she wearing?" Joey asked, and held the envelope while his parents stared at him. His mother poked him in the side, prompting him to open it, but Joey tucked it in his breast pocket.

"She was dressed in red, sir," the server said, and then Sylvia whisked him off.

Joey excused himself from his father, and found a quiet corner to open the note. He nervously opened it, and looked at the tarot card. It was the number ten, Wheel of Fortune. Although he didn't know the real meaning behind it, the card made him feel like his luck was going to change. Joey immediately smiled. "It must be Lauren," he thought. And although he was glad to know that she was behind the mystery cards, he was a little bothered that she hadn't told him. But, it hadn't caused him any harm, and he was glad that she had come. But, her timing couldn't be worse. With this jewel thing rearing it's ugly head, he'd definitely have to keep her at bay until he had completed his family business. There was no way he was going to involve her in yet another Cavanaugh illegal fiasco.

Joey rejoined his father, just as Harry was telling Jolly to gather his men, and round up Simon and that necklace.

With his adrenaline pumping, Joey checked his watch. It was eleven-fifteen. He was also expecting a special delivery before midnight, and he wanted to make sure that he didn't miss it. He was tempted to alert his father, but thought better. With Simon being thrown into the mix, Joey had to make some calculated moves to make sure, once again, that he didn't create more problems for his father.

"Well, father, you may want to bring Uncle Edgar in, too," Joey said. "There have been a few things that have happened that lead me to believe that he may have some knowledge of the stone."

Harry glared at Joey with a puzzled expression. "What are you saying, Joey? Edgar has something to do with Simon? And *Il Rosso*? Are you certain?"

"It's the stone, Father. But, I'll have to explain later. Trust me," Joey said, as he ventured back into the party, and searched for his brothers. "I won't let you down," he said under his breath.

Connie, in his black on black Halston tuxedo, leaned on his cane, and was mesmerized by the flawless beauty in the tight, fire engine red gown with matching mask. She was medium height, and had the body of an aerobics instructor. When she sauntered into the room, it was like she was commanding a runway.

But, he wasn't the only one intrigued by the enchantress. Every time he looked up, his cousin Vincent was eyeballing her too. They basically dueled with their eyes, but Connie could barely control his anger at his cousin's arrogance.

Connie was still seething about Vincent's maiming of Ace. Even though he couldn't prove it, and Ace didn't see his attackers, Connie knew that his cousin was behind it. Connie wanted revenge, but he had to exercise constraint. He had too much riding on this to mess up now, but he wouldn't rest until he got Vincent back. And he had the ultimate trick up his sleeve, that would avenge the way that his uncle and cousin had tried to play him.

There were a number of gorgeous women at the party, but this woman was absolutely exquisite. She had a confident air, and even though she hadn't said a word, her body language was speaking to Connie, and he heard her loud and clear.

And, when she danced, her moves were hypnotic. Her full hips swung, and her shoulders gyrated, and she made every man just sway in his stance. Connie was getting hard just gazing at her.

She slinked off the dance floor, nibbled hors d'oeuvres, and sipped champagne. From behind her mask, she flirted shamelessly with Connie. And then with Vincent. He and Vincent were circling her like prey, and both were determined to go in for the kill. Like two male lions, there would be a territorial fight to the death for this female enchantress.

The stage was set until both predators got sidetracked. Tiffany interrupted Vincent and managed to take him away and just as Connie was about to make his move, Joey grabbed him.

"Come on, we've got to find Christian," Joey said, and tugged on Connie's sleeve. "It's about to be on with Father, Edgy *and* Simon."

Connie yanked away from Joey's grasp. "What? Simon? What does that old bastard have to do with anything?"

"I'll tell you on the way," Joey said, and nodded for Connie to join him. Joey patted his breast pocket, hoping that the Wheel of Fortune would definitely bring him good luck.

Chapter 20

Christian scoured every room searching for Jessica, yet was careful to avoid bumping into Kim. He was slick enough to remove his easily identifiable, ornate Cavanaugh mask, and donned one of the guest masks in his covert quest.

The switch worked, for he was able to evade Kim, and sidle up to Jessica the moment Simon left her side. She was out on the terrace, standing near one of the huge heating units, embracing the still, cold night.

Christian was shaking in his designer tux, but determined to confront this woman who had broken his heart.

"Jessica," he said, struggling to keep his voice from cracking.

"Christian." Jessica removed her mask and sighed. She reached for his cheek, but he turned away. Her hand landed on her bare neck.

"Don't do that," he said. "How could you just leave me like you did?" Christian opened his hands in a questioning manner. "How could you just walk away and not even bother to call me or anything? And then you show up here, like nothing ever happened. With Simon Blake of all people."

The corners of Jessica's mouth fell. "I'm so sorry, Christian. Really, I am. I never meant to hurt you."

"Was I some sort of game to you? A toy? A plaything? A joke? Or were you paid to service me so that Simon could infiltrate our company and damage us?"

Christian's question was answered with a smack to his cheek so hard, that his plastic mask split, and threatened to cut his face. "Paid to service you? I don't know what you're talking about, Christian. And Simon has absolutely nothing to do with you and I."

"Sure. Just like you wearing that necklace. What did he do, give it to you?"

Jessica touched her neckline. "Please, Christian. He just let me wear that because it matched my gown. What on earth are you talking about, and why would you even care about what I do with Simon or whomever."

"Because, I do care. And by the way, where is your little accessory?"

"Simon has it. He said he needed it for a moment. What difference does it make?"

"I want to see what it takes to buy your services for the evening."

Jessica raised her hand to smack Christian again, but he caught her by the wrist. "Don't you dare question my integrity or say those things to me. Don't you dare," she said.

"I'll say whatever I want to say. It must be the truth for you to react so violently about it."

"You don't want to know the truth, Christian. You can't deal with it. That's why I didn't bother to tell you. It would require that you think of someone else other than yourself. I knew you wouldn't listen, and if you did, you'd never be able to comprehend it."

"You don't know what I'm capable of understanding. You didn't even have the decency to talk to me. You didn't even try."

Jessica sighed, with a pained expression on her face. "I know, Christian. But I figured that you wouldn't understand. See, I went back to my husband, despite how he had treated me. Despite the fact that we were separated and he had left me for another woman. He was sick, and he needed me. And at the time, I thought it was the right thing to do."

"Right thing to do? Was it right leaving me hanging like you did?"

"It wasn't about you, Christian. It wasn't about us. It was a moral obligation I felt."

"So damn what we had, huh?" Christian glared at her.

Jessica reached for Christian's arm, and this time he didn't withdraw. "No, it wasn't like 'damn what we had.' What we had was so very, very special, Christian. But we both knew it couldn't last. You were married, and I wasn't about to be the reason for your marriage failing."

Christian shook his head. "My marriage had failed long before I ever met you. That was no secret."

"But I've also been in your wife's shoes before, and I swore that I'd never be 'the other woman' again. I told you that."

"You were more than that, Jessica. You opened up things in me that I never knew existed. You know you were never just the other woman."

"Maybe in your heart, but in reality, that's what I was. And I could never live with myself knowing that," Jessica said with a heavy sigh. "That's why I chose to leave. But leaving you was one of the hardest things I've ever done. Seeing you again has been the second hardest thing."

Christian swallowed. Looking into his former lover's face conjured up intense memories for him. She was just as beautiful and radiant as ever, with that warm inviting nature that swept him in. "Seeing you isn't easy either. And being without you for all of these months has been like purgatory."

Jessica placed a gentle finger to his lips, and Christian inhaled her fragrance as she spoke. "We had no future, luv. And now we can't live in the past."

"What about the present? Why isn't it possible for us to be together? Why?"

Jessica had no opportunity to respond to Christian's questions, because they were interrupted by a frantic Joey, and a wobbly Connie, who was downing shots of blue agava tequila.

After briefing Christian on the imminent events, Joey and Connie lead the semi-distraught Christian into the study where the men were about to forum. On the way to the showdown, Joey reminded the doorperson that he was expecting a special guest at around eleven-thirty, and to direct him to the meeting room.

The room was filled with burly men in dark suits and shades, and a crackling fire blazed in the corner fireplace. The atmosphere was heavy, and the silence was deafening.

Finally, Simon spoke. "What's this all about?" Simon asked, and then looked at Harry with a poker face. "Say, aren't you Harrison Cavanaugh?"

"Spare me the theatrics, Simon," Harry said from the head of the table. "I want to know where you got the necklace from."

"You mean the necklace my friend was wearing? This?" Simon said, and produced the jewel from his pocket. "Let me see. I can't really recall the specifics, but I definitely got it from Edgar. He tried to purchase my wife with it."

"What?" Harry piped in.

Edgar lunged at Simon from across the table, but Jolly's men sat him back down. "Lies, you son of a bitch. *Le bugie*. Vicious lies. That's simply a bare faced lie by a bare faced liar."

"Interesting," Harry said. He took the necklace, and handed it to Joey, who with trembling hands, took a quick glimpse at it through his jeweler's eye, shook his head, and handed the jewel back to his father.

Harry laid the jewel down on the table, and motioned for Connie to pass him the lead crystal decanter. He slowly poured himself a Glenlivet. "Where are my manners. Would anyone care for one?" Before anyone could answer, Harry smashed the decanter down on the jewel, and it shattered into a million pieces.

"Well, this looks pretty worthless to me," Harry said, and then he looked at Simon. "If your story is correct, Simon, it appears that Edgy didn't think very much of your wife. Not to try to buy her with a pretty piece of glass." Harry downed his scotch, and shuddered. "Now, get this fool out of my sight, before I permanently erase he and his memory," Harry said, and signaled for one of Jolly's men to remove Simon. "Be gone. *Sia andato*."

Simon smiled broadly. "You gents really know how to throw a real nice party," he said, gestured for Jolly's men not to touch him. "I really appreciate the invitation, and Edgar, I'm sure that you'll agree that *now* our business is complete." Simon winked, and tilted his head. "Again, gentlemen— thanks for your hospitality. And I hope that you'll allow me to make a little announcement later. It is of the utmost importance."

Edgy shook his head, and shot daggers at Simon's back as he exited through the doorway. "I can't believe that you listened to Simon's garbage. He's not trying to do anything but get you to do his dirty work and kill me."

"And he may very well succeed in his quest. But now that the interloper's gone, I'm going to give you one final opportunity to tell me where the real stone is," Harry demanded. "Tell me! *Dicami!*"

"I have it," an old Italian man said, as he strolled through the library door. He was trailed by two large, thick-necked goons. He removed his mask, and fixed his hair. He revealed himself to be none other than Al Sallone.

Al shook Harry's hand, and then turned to Edgar. "Remember me, Edgar?" Al asked.

Edgar's head dropped. "Al, um, wha, what are you doing here?"

"I got wind that there might be something questionable about our decades old transaction." Al winked at Joey, and then carefully removed his jewel from his breast pocket. "Harry, this is what your brother gave me as a peace offering to our family. It was his safe entrée into New York, and guaranteed that no harm would come to him, despite the history of our families. And now, I'm not quite sure if that was such a smart thing to do." Al handed Harry the piece of jewelry. "Would you do the honors?"

Everyone in the room held their collective breaths as Harry took the decanter, and smashed it down on the jewel. Again, the second piece of well-crafted, colored glass shattered.

The normally ice cold Edgy began to melt. Beads of sweat broke out on his brow, and he shook his head. "It, uh, wasn't supposed to happen like this, Al. I swear. Jules must've cheated me. I thought it was the real one. Give me some time. I'll get to the bottom of this."

Edgy was nearly babbling, and Harry sat down and placed his hand on his chin. "Tell the truth, Edgar. *Dire la verità*. For once in your life, tell the truth, man. It may be your only chance to survive."

He loosened his tie, and opened the top button to his shirt. Edgy pulled the necklace over his head, and laid it on the table. "Okay, okay. Here it is. And, I was going to give it back to you tonight. For forgiveness." Edgy's eyes pleaded with Harry, who remained stoic.

"So, the liar and thief wants forgiveness, huh?" Al grumbled.

Joey breathed a sigh of relief. After the wild goose chases, and imposters, finally, *Il Rosso* had been found. Joey rubbed the lucky card in his pocket.

Harry stared at his brother, and exhaled. "Edgar, I can't believe you did that. How did you expect to get away with it? What made you think that any good would come from you further dishonoring your father?"

Al picked up the stone, and fondled it. He picked up the decanter, and without asking, he smashed it down. The entire room gasped as it too, shattered.

"What the hell?" Harry said. "Edgar, how could you be so stupid as to do this? How could you?" He grabbed Edgy by the collar, and shook him, lifting him from his seat. He shoved him back in his seat, with a look of disgust covering his face. "I'm through. *Sono attraverso.*"

Al Sallone wiped the dust from his fingers, and leaned over the table. "Come on, Edgar. We have a little ride to take." Al's goons ambled over and stood by Edgar's side, and lifted him out of his chair by his elbows.

Edgy was frantic. "Harry, Harry. Aren't you going to do something? Aren't you going to help me? I'm your brother, for God's sake. Please help me. *Per favore!*"

Harry stood and turned his back on his brother, and everyone else in the room followed suit.

"Don't forget about Vincent out there, too," Connie said, and pointed his cane toward the door. "Better still, I'll go help you find him."

Connie's moment had finally come. Now, he'd get payback for Vincent's trying to kill him on the docks, and for the showboating he'd done since he weaseled his way into town. Connie owed him for his antics that day at the Georgia Mile, and for what he did to Ace, and for his smugness regarding the death of his dogs. Oh yeah, it was going to be real sweet.

When Al's goons found Vincent with Tiffany, upstairs in one of the vacant rooms, Connie stayed in the hallway. It was truly coitus interruptus, and as Vincent was dragged away from Tiffany's clutches and down the rear stairwell, Connie made it a point to let him see him standing at the base of the steps.

"Yo, Vince. Hate to see you leave in such a rush, but it's not like I didn't warn you, huh?"

Vincent glared at Connie like his gaze could annihilate him. "Fuck you and your warnings, Connie."

"No, fuck you, Vincent. Your ass is gonna get everything you got comin' to you. An' some more shit."

Vincent hawk spit on the marble floor. "Listen, I told you before, I'm not scared of you." Vince's face was an amalgamation of fear and anger. "Where's my father? What's up? Are you behind all of this bogus bullshit?"

"I wish. But you not only crossed me, but you really upset some of the big boys." Connis shook his head. "When they finish with you, you're gonna wish it was only me that you had pissed off."

"Whatever, Connie. I'm not the least bit worried about you or them," Vincent said and motioned toward Al's goons, who were clamped down on his arms. "It'll take more than this to bring me or my father down."

Connie clapped, with his cane in hand. "Well, bravo, cousin. I must admit, I kind of admire your balls, man. You're staring at your mortality and still talkin' shit." Connie folded his arms. "I wonder how much talking you'll be doing when they cut *your* tongue out."

Vincent smirked. "Cut my tongue out? That only happens to idiots who talk out of turn. And that's not me. I don't talk shit. I can back up what I say, partner." Vincent gritted on Connie. "And besides, this isn't over. You and I have some unfinished business."

"Oh, now that's where you're wrong. It's over. More than over. And by the way, as homage to my pets and my boy Ace, I've asked these fine gentlemen to make sure that your last hours include a little quality time with a couple of Presas. In fact, I'll even let you serve them their meal for the evening. Your tongue. That'll be for my boy Ace."

Vincent struggled against his captors, as he tried to get his gigantic hands on Connie. "Trust me, I'll get you back, Connie. I will."

Connie took his cane and jabbed Vincent in the chest. With eyes darkened and cold, Connie dropped his jaw. "Maybe you'll get me back when I see you in hell, Vincent. But it surely won't happen on this side of the earth. Believe that. I'm taking great pleasure in knowing that in the here and now, my face'll be the last Cavanaugh face you'll ever see. And those dogs' teeth will be the last thing you'll ever feel. Believe that, cousin."

Immediately after Al had left with Edgy and Vincent in tow, Sylvia burst into the room, with a large manila envelope in her hand. "I have them, Harry. The results are right here. Harry? Where's Edgar? We'll finally put the question of Tiffany's heritage to rest."

Harry took the envelope from his wife, tossed it into the fireplace, and it and Sylvia's hopes went up in flames. "Some things are better left unsaid, dear."

Sylvia stammered. "Well, Harrison. Do you realize what you've done? Why on earth did you do that?"

Harry patted Sylvia's arm, and grimaced like he was suffering from indigestion. "Some secrets are relative to us, and some are not. Let's just say that at this point, Tiffany's lineage is no concern of ours." Harry peered at the wall clock. It was almost midnight. "Now, please excuse us, dear. We have a few more matters to tend to, and then we'll be out to join you for the countdown in just a moment."

As Harry ushered a flustered and frustrated Sylvia out of the room, Joey could tell from his father's expression and demeanor that he was troubled that he had sent his only brother to a certain grisly death. But that was just the way things were. And how things were going to be. But what disturbed Joey was the mystery of where the real *Il Rosso* actually was.

"I have it," Connie said, as he entered the room. He leaned against the wall with his cane, with a smug look plastered on his face.

"What?" Joey and Christian said in unison.

"I have it. Jules kept the real stone, after he made all of the copies he wanted. I got it out of him a few weeks ago," Connie said, and poked his chest out.

Joey and Christian glanced at each other, and they shared the same expression. They had been robbed. They had trusted Connie, and he had selfishly screwed them again. He knew all along where the real stone was, but he kept them in the dark so that he could present himself in a much better light.

Harry's face brightened. "You don't say. Well, why didn't you mention that before, son? It's a great relief to know that our stone is safe, but you could've saved us a great deal of heartache and grief."

Connie's face creased with fake concern. "I was hoping that you'd understand, Father. I just wanted to make sure that anyone who was involved with this little charade would play themselves, and they did, Father."

Harry sighed, and patted Connie on the shoulder. "Whew. Well, you can give me the details later. Right now, I'd like to see the heirloom. So, where is it? Did you bring it with you?"

"No, I didn't. But I will go and get it. Right after midnight. I've got this little honey out there that I'd like to ring in the New Year with."

Joey shot Connie the last eye daggers. Joey thought about his lucky card, and frowned. All that he had hoped that he and his brothers had achieved in their newfound brotherhood was a sham. Connie was the most selfish, egotistical man he'd ever met. With the exception of Edgy. And Joey shuddered to think about what horrors awaited him.

"That's fine, son. You have more than enough reason to celebrate. Just be sure to bring me that jewel some time tonight," Harry said. "It needs to be home where it belongs. And before your mother finds out about it. So, none of you, please don't say anything about this to her before we have *Il Rosso* securely back."

The woman in fire engine red stepped into the grand foyer behind Joey as he exited the study, but he didn't notice her. He was too engrossed with finding Connie. Joey couldn't understand why his father wasn't more upset by Connie's actions, nor could Joey believe that his father had let Connie get away with waiting until after he got his groove on before producing the stone. That might have been good enough for his father, but Joey was determined to make Connie cough up *Il Rosso* now. And Joey didn't care if it was inconvenient for Connie or not. He wanted to know why Connie had screwed him royally again. And this time, Joey wasn't about to let him get away with it.

As the glittery ball dropped, the eager partygoers counted down from twenty. Connie sidled over to the masked woman in red, and whispered in her ear, and at the stroke of midnight, he planted a wet kiss on her lips, and tongued her deeply.

"Would you like to come home with me?" he asked, and his beautiful enigma nodded yes.

They skipped out on the party, taking her darkened limo, and in the backseat, she prepared him for what awaited him. She removed his jacket and cummerbund, loosened his tie, and bit his nipples through his shirt, and ran her manicured fingers up and down his chest. She unzipped his trousers, and massaged him until he stood at full attention. She licked her lips and kissed the head of his erection, and rapidly flicked her tongue around it, until he almost came. She was forceful, yet sensual, and when she refused to let him touch her, it drove him wild. He couldn't wait to get his hands on her.

Shortly after midnight, the music was brought down, and Sylvia made her announcement, with Harry planted beside her side. "On behalf of my wonderful family, we are very pleased to announce that given your generosity, we have raised $95,000 for our charity. Please give yourselves a hand."

The audience roared with enthusiasm, and after a few moments, Simon made his way to Sylvia's ear, and then grabbed the microphone, where he proceeded to announce that his son-in-law, Alex, was going to run for mayor. The announcement took the whole room by surprise, and was met with gasps and applause.

Sylvia leaned over and whispered in Harry's ear. "Well, I never. I can't believe that this tasteless man has used my own event to try to upstage me."

Harry patted Sylvia on the arm, and tried to calm her. "I'm sure no one's taking it as such. Simon's grasping for ways to stay in the limelight, and Alex is obviously his conduit."

Harry frowned. "I forgot to tell you that Simon mentioned that he'd like some time to make an announcement. But, with all the hubbub, it slipped my mind." Harry slipped his arms around his wife's waist, and turned her toward him. "We have our own reasons to celebrate, dear. This year will truly be a new beginning, with a lot of our old fears finally quelled."

Sylvia was visibly distraught, but she kept a smile plastered on. "I sincerely hope that's true, dear. I had hoped that since Simon has amnesia, that he would forget his station in life. However, it appears that he is as dastardly as ever."

"It may be a new year, my darling, but some old things never change," Harry said, and stroked his wife's cheek. *"Alcune cose non cambiano mai."*

Chapter 21

Once they arrived at Connie's house, a semi-erect Connie tried to lead her upstairs, but his mystery lady nodded her head no, and then whispered, "May I have something to drink? My throat's a little dry, and I need for it to be very wet. *Very.*"

While Connie poured the drinks, his masked lady disappeared. She was taking an unauthorized tour of his house, but wasn't too upset by it. He kind of liked her boldness, but he couldn't let her know it. Not yet. He'd have to put her in check, to see if she could handle being manhandled. To him, she appeared to be the type that just might enjoy getting a little punishment for her insolence. Or at least give as good as she got.

Connie found her downstairs in the dimly lit basement, admiring his huge fish tank. He handed her a glass of Hennessy, and she placed the tumbler to her full lips and poured the cognac into her mouth. She pushed Connie's precious backgammon board onto the floor, and shoved him down onto his cocktail table. She then leaned over and pressed her lips on his, and let the warm liquor seep from her mouth into his. What trickled out onto his face, she seductively licked up.

While Connie leaned back on the table, his mystery lady removed four pieces of cord-like rope from her elbow length gloves. Connie licked his lips. He was really loving this bondage thing. It had been a while since he had let a woman tie him up, but this one let him know that she was a freak to the core. In between hot, wet kisses, she removed his shirt and undershirt, and then tied his arms to the thick table leg. Then she removed his trousers, and then slowly tied a leg. Before Connie knew it, he was spread eagle, wearing only black silk boxers, on the massive cocktail table, facing his fish tank. "It doesn't get any better than this," he thought.

His mystery lady slowly caressed his bare chest, but seemed intrigued by the gold rope chain hanging around his neck, with Stewart's ring on it. She seemed fascinated by it, and toyed with it before she ravaged every part of his willing body. Connie was so turned on by the combination of the woman's sensuous touch and the restraints that he almost came.

"Oooh, Daddy's a little excited, huh?" She spoke in a sultry whisper, and she flicked his ear with her tongue with every word. She slid her hand in his boxers, massaged his penis and slapped his thigh.

He wanted to slap her back. And bite her, and touch her, but he couldn't. The tantalizing foreplay was driving him insane. But, then he realized that the more he moved, the tighter the restraints got. In fact, they were beginning to cut into his skin, like tortuous Chinese slipknots.

"Damn, baby. You think you can loosen these joints a little bit?" Connie asked, but his silent seductress placed a gloved finger over his lips to shush him.

She reached under her gown and withdrew a stack of cards. Without even looking at it, she flipped the top card over and laid it on Connie's chest.

"Oh, so you're the one with the cards?" Connie grinned broadly. "Aww, shit. I guess that means you been checking me out for a while, haven't you, sweetie?"

Miss Mysterious stayed silent, and without looking at it, she picked up the card and showed it to Connie. It was the number two, the High Priestess.

"Hey, I know what that means. That's, um, that's the mystery sign, isn't it? Damn girl, I like your style. You 'bout mysterious as hell."

She barely smiled, and started kissing his chest, working her way down his abdomen, where she by passed his rock hard penis, and kept going. He begged her to suck it, but she ignored him. She licked from his inner thighs right down to his ankles, where she knelt between his legs. She laid the cards beside him, and as she caressed his knee with one hand, she took a leather pillow from a recliner with her free hand, and shoved it under his butt.

She took another card and flipped it onto Connie's chest. It was the number six, The Lovers, and it's meaning was clear.

She stood between his legs, still completely clothed, and lifted her flowing gown. Connie salivated. That was until he caught a glimpse of what was underneath her dress. It was a mammoth dildo, that had to have been at least a foot long, and about four inches around.

Connie's eyes bulged. "What the fuck?" he yelled. "Oh, hell no. You ain't fuckin' me. Fuck you. I don't swing like that, beautiful. Shit, you ought to be able to tell that. I'm all beef, baby, and I like pussy. P-U-S-S-Y."

"Well," his mystery lady whispered. "You can't fuck me because I, unfortunately, can't use my pussy." She snatched her mask off, and threw it to the floor. Connie gagged and then choked: it was his wife Beverly.

"It can't be you. What happened? You didn't look like this before."

"I've been working out. I had a lot of time on my hands while I toured the Caribbean, so I picked up some new hobbies. Like Tai Chai and tarot reading." Beverly lifted another card from the stack, and tossed it onto Connie's heaving chest. "Oh, look. It's the number sixteen. The Tower. Do you know what that means, Connie? It means this is a sudden change for you. I'm pretty good at this, huh?" She cleared her throat and then tossed another card on top of The Tower card. It was number eighteen, The Moon. "Ahhh. Look at this. Guess what? The Moon means fear. Are you afraid, Conrad?"

Connie glared at his wife. "I'll never be afraid of you."

"Well, you should be. The cards never lie." She tossed another card onto the stack, and it was the number twelve, the Hanged Man. "Um, um, um. I guess this means I'm going to have to sacrifice you."

She pulled a small, four-inch, pearl handled switchblade from her garter belt, and cut his boxers off. She took the knife and plunged it into the table, dangerously close to Connie's ear. She stuffed his shorts into his mouth, and he struggled with her, scattering the revealing cards over the basement floor as Beverly fucked him in his ass until he bled like he was on his period. Or like she bled that hideous night when he cut her clitoris off. Connie's muffled screams and blood curdling cries filled the room, and were met with Beverly's hysterical laughter.

The puppies, Idi Amin and Papa Doc began yelping from the utility room, and Beverly stopped midstroke.

"What's that?" she asked, and tilted her head toward the origin of the sound. "Don't tell me you have more dogs? Are they the same kind of beasts as before? Well, then I guess I'll have to get rid of them too."

"What do you mean? You killed Caligula and Diablo?" Connie words were barely decipherable through his wadded mouth.

"Your dogs have good taste. They really loved all of that rich Godiva chocolate I gave them. So good going in, so bad coming out."

"You are fuckin' nuts!"

"And look who made me this way," Beverly said, as she plunged into Connie's ripped rectum.

She screwed him until she was physically exhausted. She yanked the shorts from Connie's mouth, and he screamed bloody murder.

"You fuckin' bitch! *Aaarrggghh!* I'm gonna fuckin' kill you, you crazy ass whore! I should've killed your fuckin' ass a long time ago, you stupid bitch!!" Connie yelled at the top of his lungs, and hot, angry tears filled his eyes. Sweat poured down his face and chest, and the veins in his neck pulsated.

"Ahhhhhh!" Beverly mocked Connie's screaming. "Go on and scream, Connie. No one can hear you. Just like no one heard me." Beverly grabbed his balls and twisted them with all of her might. Again, she whispered seductively in his ear. "I just wanted you to get a little dose of how you made me feel." She licked his ear and frowned. "My goodness, Conrad. Is that sweat I taste?"

"Fuck you, Beverly," Connie said, through tears of pain and rage. With sweat dripping from his brow, he snarled, "I'm going to get you if it's the last thing I do. Believe that."

"You already *got* me, or do you mean that you're going to *get* me like you *got* Stewart?" Beverly caressed the ring that still hung around Connie's neck, and then snatched it off and hung it around her neck. "It'll never happen, sweetheart. And you know why? Because I've already got you." Beverly took another card from the dwindling stack and held it up to Connie's face. "Do you see this? It's number twenty. Judgement."

Beverly walked around to the back of the aquarium, and grabbed a long handled net. She climbed the stairs and plunged the net into the water.

"What the fuck are you doing?" Connie yelled, but Beverly ignored him. She fished around on the bottom of the tank until she finally caught Connie's fake rock in the net and pulled it out.

"I was here the other day, Conrad," Beverly said, as she threw the wet net onto the floor. "And I started to shoot you then. But, I waited and watched you craft this little item, and it dawned on me. You have *Il*

Rosso." Beverly laughed, and smashed the faux rock against the wall. She opened the waterproof bags, and removed the magical gem. She hung the stone around her neck, and laughed as she walked over to Connie. "And I bet your family didn't even know you had it, did they? In fact, I know they didn't." Beverly shook her head. "I guess this bad boy belongs to me now, huh, Sweetie? This is the least you can do for fucking me up the way you did. Boy, you're a greedy, evil dog, aren't you? You'll fuck anybody to get what you want, and this time it's your family." She paused and inhaled deeply. "You'll never change."

Connie struggled to get up, but the cords cut deeper into his skin with every movement. The inside layer of his skin was showing, and blood trickled onto the ropes. "Fuck you!"

Beverly yanked the knife from the table and laid it on Connie's sweaty chest. "Do you like my new toy? It's a little something I picked up while I was in the Islands," she said, with a wicked laugh.

"Now, I'm going to give you a choice, Conrad. A choice you didn't give me or Stewart. I can sit here, and cut you up, piece by piece, and feed you to your precious fish. Or you can go and dive in that tank. The choice is yours."

"You wouldn't dare, Beverly. You ain't got the heart."

"I don't need heart. I have a knife," she said, and with one swift motion, Beverly took the knife and sliced off the tip of his penis, and flicked it into the tank. Connie howled, while the Addams family fought to devour his severed family jewel.

Connie struggled to break free, yelling at Beverly. "Bitch, I'm gonna kill you! I swear, I'm gonna kill you!"

Beverly again lifted her gown, and this time removing from her thigh sheath a small .22-caliber gun. Pointing it at Connie's head, again she said, "The choice is yours, Mr. Cavanaugh. What's it gonna be?"

Connie's eyes flashed. "Damn, Beverly. When did your balls get bigger than mine?"

Beverly cocked the trigger. "When you took away my vagina."

Connie struggled to get loose, but it was a losing battle. He was tired and exhausted from being violently raped, and weak and lightheaded from his loss of blood. In a hoarse and raspy voice he agreed, "Alright, Beverly. I'm through. You win. I'm too fuckin' tired to fight you anymore."

Beverly smirked. "Well, that's good because," she said, and reached down and plucked another card. She looked at it and smiled. "Because you've drawn number thirteen. Death."

With the gun in one hand, Beverly took the knife and cut the rope from Connie's arms. "Now, don't you dare move," she said as she bent over to cut his leg restraints.

Connie grabbed his bleeding penis, and when he noticed that she was having trouble with ropes, he quickly hit her gun arm, and then grabbed her by the throat. Squeezing her neck, he said, "See, bitch. I told you I was gonna get you."

Beverly struggled, and fell to her knees. With perfect aim at his abdomen, she fired the gun. Flinching, Connie released his grip on her throat, and grabbed his stomach. "Oh shit, you shot me," he yelled, his face scrunched in pain and disbelief.

Beverly's chest heaved as she gasped for air. "I will shoot your ass every five minutes until you take a dive. You will end up in that tank, Connie. Let's just make it easy and not make me work any harder than I have to, okay? I'm already tired."

"Fuck you. You're just gonna have to shoot me, 'cause I ain't no punk and I ain't goin' out like that, you hear me?" he said in his most manly voice.

The gun went off again, and Connie crumpled over. He grabbed his right thigh, pain etched on his face. Beverly had shot him again.

He yelled. "Okay, goddammit. Okay. I give. I can't believe that you actually loved that bastard that much to put me through this bullshit."

Beverly finished taking Connie's leg restraints off, and motioned for him to stand. "This isn't just for Stewart, Connie. It's for me, him, Joey and all of those other innocent women whose lives you've fucked up. Now, go get your ass in the tank."

Connie stumbled backwards and up the steps, pleading with every stride. "Come on, Bev. It doesn't have to end like this. You know I didn't mean to hurt you, baby. I love you, girl."

"Yeah, right, Connie. Keep moving."

"Seriously. I had to do somethin'. You disrespected me. I'm a mother fuckin' man, and you betrayed me with my best friend. You was fuckin' Stewart, and I had to kill him and teach you a lesson. I just had to. I was hurt." Connie's eyes filled with tears as he pleaded with his wife. "Come on, baby. I love you."

Beverly's upper lip quivered. "Yes, Conrad, I know. I love you, too, sweetheart," she said. When they reached the top of the steps leading to the tank, she leaned over and kissed him and then blew the back of his head off. He fell into the tank, and the Addams Family attacked his wounded, thrashing body.

While Connie's arms flailed, splashing bloody water around, Beverly turned around, with an extremely satisfied grin stretched across her face. "My goodness," she said aloud, and totally unaffected by the macabre scene she had just directed. "It looks like I have some serious cleaning to do."

Though he had been looking for her for a while, Joey was unable to locate the mysterious woman in red. Perhaps the waiter had garbled the message, because Joey figured that Lauren, with her sleuthing skills, would have found him sooner. But, as usual, Joey had been so inundated with family issues, that he was too sidetracked to make a substantial effort to find her himself.

Then it happened. Someone embraced him from behind. She blew on his neck, and when he turned around, he was pleasantly surprised to see Lauren, peeking from under a feathery red mask, and outfitted in a tight red gown.

"Hey, lady," Joey said, his teeth spreading into a smile. "I've been looking for you. Where have you been?"

Lauren reached up and planted a warm kiss on his lips, and smiled. "I told you I'd be here. Don't tell me you missed me, not with all of these fine women here."

"None finer than you, baby. But seriously. I thought you had been here for a while. And that you were looking for me. I got your card."

Lauren wiped the traces of her lipstick from Joey's lips and shook her head. "No, baby. It wasn't me. It must've been another one of your little hotties trying to hunt you down."

Joey's brows furrowed, trying to think of who the other woman was. He hadn't seen anyone else who fit Lauren's description all evening. Granted, he had been busy, but it just struck him as odd. Joey looked upward, but Lauren brought his thoughts back to her by pressing her firm body against him.

"Oh well," Joey said. "Suddenly, whoever it was doesn't matter, right? You're all I'm thinking about."

They were still embracing, when Harry approached them, and tapped Joey on the shoulder. "Son? I hate to interrupt."

Joey kept Lauren embraced, and turned to face his father. "Father, this is my friend Lauren. Lauren, this is my father."

At the mention of Lauren's name, Harry's eyebrows arched, but he extended a very courteous greeting to her when they exchanged hellos.

"I hope you don't mind if I borrow my son for a moment," Harry said, and then guided Joey to a quiet corner. "I'm getting a little concerned. Conrad hasn't returned, and he hasn't called either."

An unsettling feeling swept over Joey, but he tried not to let it show. "Did you try to call him yet?"

Harry placed a hand on Joey's shoulder. "Your Uncle Jolly tried to reach him, but he didn't get an answer. So, I think that you need to go over to his house and see what's going on. With him and *Il Rosso*. And bring them both back here."

Joey glanced over at Lauren, and really didn't want to leave her. "Do you think that's really necessary, Father? I mean, he's probably just with that woman, and I'm sure he'll be back soon."

"That's not good enough, Joey. I want him back now."

Joey wondered why there wasn't anyone else capable of fetching Connie, but his father's response was typical. "I understand, Father. I'll see if I can find him."

Harry patted Joey on the cheek, with each pat becoming more forceful. "Good. *Buono*. Now, hurry along." Harry turned toward Lauren and tilted his head. "Nice meeting you, young lady." Then he turned back to Joey. "Lauren? Hmmm. That names sounds quite familiar. Well son, I guess we'll talk about your young lady later."

It bothered Joey that their reunion had been interrupted, and after uttering a half-hearted excuse about a family emergency, he promised to hook up with a disappointed Lauren later. She seemed to tell that he was floundering, but she didn't challenge him about it. She only asked if she could help, but Joey declined. He realized that she had probably gone to a great deal of trouble to be with him, and once again, Joey felt like a heel when he had to run off.

Since his car was blocked in, and the valets were busily addressing the other guests' concerns, Joey thought quickly about the first vehicle he could grab. He trotted around to the family's four-car heated garage and cranked up his Ducati motorcycle.

Though the roads were slick, Joey carefully maneuvered his way over to Connie's house. Thankfully, he had a thick Shearling coat and matching gloves to shield him from the cold, but it didn't protect his lungs as they felt like they were on the verge of freezing solid.

As he pulled into Connie's driveway, Joey spotted a long black limousine. The doors were closed, and the windows sealed, and as Joey jumped off of his bike, he was barely able to get the stand to hold it up in the slushy mix. He ran toward Connie's front door, and skidded on the icy walkway. From his peripheral vision, he saw the limo pull up beside him, and the rear window descended. Joey saw a masked woman staring at him with an eerie smile. Joey nearly jumped in his skin. He instantly felt uneasy, but he returned her vacant gaze. He looked at her red mask, and then down to her neck. His knees buckled, and he almost fell onto the snowy ground. The woman was holding Connie's cane, and around her neck was *Il Rosso.*

The woman winked at Joey, and he heard her laugh as she stuck her hand out of the window. Wrapped around her wrist was Connie's chain, the one with Stewart's ring on it. Joey's eyes fixed on her hand, and he watched her toss a playing card into the air. It landed face down onto the ground, next to Joey's feet. He took the toe of his shoe and flipped it over, and the number eleven glared up at him. Number Eleven. Justice. The woman in the car cackled as she raised the tinted window and the limousine slowly pulled off.

Joey's head throbbed, and he thoughtlessly ran after the limo. He was only able to take a few strides before he slipped onto the icy driveway. "*Who are you?!*" he yelled at the disappearing taillights, and the heat in his voice lingered in the cold air and created a frozen cloud. "Who the hell are you?" Joey asked, as his chest heaved, and frost formed on his moustache.

He forced himself up, and wiped the snow and ice from his trousers. Just who the hell was she? Joey's mind raced and he felt his fingers tingling from the cold. And then it struck him. It couldn't be. Was it? It couldn't be Beverly, Joey thought. With his heart hammering in his chest and nearly blinded by the anxious tears that burned his eyes, Joey raced toward his brother's house, crushing the Justice card into the snow.

"*Connie! Connie!*" Joey yelled as he entered the house. He was overcome with an eerie, sinking feeling. He flicked on the light switch and it barely illuminated the basement. It was evident that someone had either unscrewed the bulbs or disconnected something.

"Damn," Joey said. But there was no turning back. He took a deep breath as he approached the basement stairs, and slowly descended them. With every creak of the steps, his heart nearly stopped beating. He wished he had a weapon or something to protect him for whatever lay waiting for him.

"Connie?" Joey whispered, as he cautiously stepped onto the rec room floor. He was overcome with that same eerie feeling he felt the last time he went into Connie's basement. Except this time, it was even more daunting.

Joey flicked another light switch on, and he saw that the room was empty. The fish tank hummed as Joey peered around, and nothing seemed out of sorts. Except there was a faint aroma of bleach in the air, which seemed a little odd to him. The room did appear to be uncommonly tidy, except for a few items on the cocktail table. There were a few pieces of rope and a gigantic dildo.

There was no sign of Connie. Nothing. Joey stuck his head in the utility room, and the puppies were sleeping in their heated kennel. Still, a strange feeling engulfed him. As he walked back into the rec room, he looked down, and spotted another card lying beside the cocktail table leg. It was the death card.

Joey slowly picked up the card with trembling fingers. Something in his spirit compelled him to look toward the fish tank. His eyes slowly trailed over to aquarium, and he gasped. The water was murky, a reddish-brown color, rocks floated around. The piranhas thrashed about, with their stomachs protruding. Joey was overcome with an especially sick feeling. Suddenly, he knew exactly where Connie was.

In a few uneasy moments, Joey's feelings ran the complete gamut from feeling ill, to panicky, to totally helpless.

"I guess it's all over now, huh Connie? You're gone, *Il Rosso's* gone, and there's not a damn thing that can be done about it." Joey said, as he looked at the last tarot card that he still absently held. He shook his head. "And there's no way I can ever even explain this," he said with a sigh. "I guess it really is all over. *L'indovino è realmente sopra.*"

THE END

about the author...

"Relative Secrets" is Author Collen Dixon's fourth novel, and final entry in her "Simon Says" "quadrilogy." Collen is a native Washingtonian, and she is diligently working on her fifth novel, "Rocked Star."

An avid reader, Collen enjoys Feng Shui and tending to her bonsai trees, collecting art and automobiles. She also enjoys "viewing the world from two wheels," skiing, traveling and entertaining. A huge movie buff, she recently successfully underwent treatment for an addiction to online auctions.

She and Chadwick, her fur-faced little boy, currently reside in Mitchellville, MD. Her motto is "Always be grateful, never be satisfied."

How to Reach Collen:

www.collendixon.com
email: author@collendixon.com

acknowledgements

First giving all honor and glory to God. Thanks for loving me, in spite of me.

To my parents, Frances & Lee; and family, Linda, Portia & Brandon. Thanks for showing me more about life than I could ever imagine or create.

To Grandma Susie: You mean more to me than you'll ever know.

To my sister Lynette: With you, I know that I'll never be alone.

To Mickey & Morgan: I'm so very proud of you! Please keep up the great work.

To my favorite cousins: Mary and Yolande Brown. Thanks for always being there for me, no matter where I've been.

To Twanda: Thanks for always lending a helping hand and a compassionate ear.

To Chad and Diamond (The O'Reillys): Thanks for bringing such joy and entertainment into our lives.

To my extended family, Gary Palmer & Family, Butch & Phyllis Fisher, Tim & Mary Campbell, The McIvers, Mumfords, Browns, and Lakins.

A sincere thanks to Shirley Olden & Melony Black. Thanks for taking such great care of my best friend!

To Maggie: Thanks for being my unofficial publicist, and for getting me mentioned on the "Wendy Williams Show." You give me exceptional encouragement & support: and great M&Ms!

To Mena: You've truly restored my faith in friendship. I can never thank you enough for your shelter during my storms.

To Brenda: Thanks for always being a great big sister and even better friend.

To the Kels in my life (Kellie "Minor" Muse & Kelli "Major" Wynn). Thanks for allowing me to be part of the "PMS" trio.

To Starr: You are truly destined to create your own galaxy! I am so proud and happy to know you.

To my other moms, Dr. Sandra Newsome of Bowie State University, Ms. Pat Buck, Mrs. Ida Hutchison and Mrs. Vivian Gaunt.

To my friends: Rodney Akers, Katrina Allen, Renee Anderson, Emile Brown, Yolanda Ezzel, Mike Graham, Flora Hurley, Robb Jackson, Lisa Jeffress, Don Johnson, Eugene Lowe, Meryl McDuffie, Toney Monroe, Darrell Morgan, Vonda Munden, Ros Murphy, Greg Parrish, Cheryl Roberts, Val Robertson, Trina Savage, Mario Scribner, Doc Smith, Sandi Holly-Star, Cynthia Talmadge, Louis Thomas & Mike Walker.

To Tomika Reid: Thanks for your insight and critical analysis.

To Pat Sugick & the ladies at Affinity Hair Salon. Thanks so much for your continued support.

A special thanks to Janevie Brooks: Thanks for the great editing!

To the HBCUs, and Dr. Delores Thompson and Virginia Union University & Carla Reid and Johns Hopkins University. Thanks for making "Simon Says" required reading for your Freshman Classes.

To PG County Schools, and a special thanks to Denise Buck and Fairmont Heights Senior High; Nathan Burns and Sheila Wise and Central High School.

The Bookclubs: Thanks for embracing me so warmly. First, my DC Metro Book Clubs: Novelties Book Club (See, you're first!); Sistas in Voice, Woodmore South Chapter One Book Club, Divas Are Reading, Mahogany Literary Circle, Girlfriends Reading Circle, Sister to Sister Book Club, Nubian Knowledge, Novels and Nutriment Book Club, Almost Gold; The Indigo Book Club (NJ), The Sistah Circle, Circle of Friends (NC), Club Mimosa (PA), APOOO, RAWSISTAZ, Sistas Are Reading (NJ), Sisters Rising, AmiGals, Journey's End Literary Book Club (NC), Deep in Thought Book Club, Ebony Expressions (DE), PSSST Book Club (VA), and STAR Book Club (PA).

An extra special thanks to: Shirley Johnson & The Enoch Pratt Library System & Metropolitan United Methodist Church (B-More); Dr. Richard Cooper of WURD (Philly), Justine Love of WPGC (DC), Donna Blackwell of Baltimore Reads, and Gary Johnson of www.blackmeninamerica.com.

To my agent: Sara Camilli, and my publicist, Angie Pickett-Henderson: Thanks for helping me to be all that I can.

Again, a special thanks to my girl Zane. I'm proud to call you my inspiration and my friend.

And finally, to my true partner in crime, Dywane Birch: Thank you for making this journey so incredible.

Collen Dixon
"Bringing new definition to the literary game."

QUADRILOGY

\'qua·dril·o·gy\ kwä-dri-le-jç\ *n*, [ca. 2004]:
1 : a series of four sizzling, suspenseful thrillers by Author Collen Dixon **2** : a novel by Collen Dixon bringing new definition to the literary game.

SEE: SIMON SAYS **(2001/2003)**
BEHIND CLOSED DOORS...
IN MY FATHER'S HOUSE **(2003)**
EVERY SHUT EYE **(2004)**
RELATIVE SECRETS **(2005)**

the first in the "quadrilogy" - "Simon Says"

Simon Says is a bold, riveting tale of intrigue, suspense, political thrills and romance. It is the gritty, compelling journey of Alexander Baxter, a young man of treacherous beginnings from one of Washington, DC's most notorious ghettos. Seemingly sentenced to a life of crime, Alex is plucked from the clutches of fate by Simon Blake, who becomes his Svengali, and who also happens to be the city's charismatic mayor. A malleable Alex does exactly as Simon says and flourishes, propelling himself from his doomed surroundings into a storybook environment. Alex's life is charmed, reminiscent of Camelot, and he becomes everything he ever dreamed of being. Or does he?

Through a series of thrilling plot twists, Alex's life of self-discovery, savagery and victories is told in a gripping fashion. Every facet of his life is intricately woven as Alex learns that no good deed goes unnoticed... or unpunished. And to be careful what you ask for, you may end up getting it. And then what?

Discover the shocking conclusion for yourself. Simon Says. Life's a game...

Are ***you*** ready to play?

"Collen Dixon's 'Alex' is an everyman/sleuth-reluctant hero--an 'Easy Rawlins' for the 21st century!" - *Christopher Chambers, best-selling author of "Sympathy for the Devil" and "A Prayer for Deliverance."*

ISBN 0-9710566-4-1

and now, an excerpt from the sizzling sequel to "Simon Says"... "Every Shut Eye."

He emerged from the murky waters of the rancid river. Exhausted, spent and nearly mortally wounded, he takes a few wobbly steps on the embankment and collapses. It is nearly dawn, and he awakens to the sound of airplanes taking off and landing at National Airport. He warily checks his surroundings, attempting to gauge his whereabouts. He had to be somewhere down the Virginia shoreline, he thought. After his battle in the choppy waters, he had dead man floated downstream, far enough away from his point of near fatality to where no one would ever think to look for him.

He found a spot near the brush, and rested briefly, alternating between hawking up phlegm and applying pressure to his wounds. "So, is has what has become of me," he said out loud. He looked around, and hoped that no early morning fishermen would happen upon him."Well, if they think they've seen the last of me, they all have another thought coming," he said, supressing the pain and injuries that would've killed a lesser man.

Printed in the United States
125511LV00003B/163/A

9 780971 056602